The Construction of Shadows

Dakota Jackson

Dreamsphere Books
Winnipeg, Canada

For my brother-in-law, Brandon Hogan.

A few years back, I gave you a terrible synopsis of this book after a few too many drinks. You still told me it sounded "dope."

This one's for you. I hope it lives up.

DIVINITIES OF THE SUN

ATARU OF THE SUN
IRENE OF THE WEATHER
KAITSJA OF WILDLIFE
ABUNGU OF NATURE
AMADA OF LOVE
CHAE-WON OF CREATION
OMNI OF ORDER AND PEACE
DIVINIA OF PROPHECY

THE WINGS OF GUIDING LIVES

DIVINITIES OF THE MOON

MAHINA OF THE MOON
TAL OF STORMS
HALA OF HUNTING
PERCE OF DESTRUCTION
ZILLA OF HATE
NIRNASHA OF DEATH
EBEN OF BATTLE
VIERA OF IGNORANCE

THE REAPERS OF GUIDING SPIRITS

The Construction of Shadows

Prologue

It took hundreds of years before their tiny human bodies stopped exploding at the slightest bit of bestowed power.

It took another hundred years for humankind to truly harness the powers they were gifted by their Creators, the sixteen Divinities of the Sun and Moon—then only a couple of centuries after that to squander them entirely.

Humans are, at their core, selfish beings. Give a little and they take all. Give all and they find a way to take some more. So, it's no wonder the country of Malumvia has ended up here: divided, unchecked, and clueless.

At a Moon Temple in Division Four, a boy with a bare chest full of scars and blood-stained hands knows this better than any.

Correctional officers routinely visit places like this one in their country's lower Divisions. In small packs, they perform simple checks to ensure no enemies have returned since their last visit. It's a safety measure they've cooked up to protect themselves from a repeat of history. More specifically, it's their way of reassuring themselves that another Lunar Eclipse Massacre—the exact one that drew a line in blood between Sun and Moon mere years ago—will not happen.

This system they adhere to makes them feel safe, but it's almost too easy for the boy to put a crack in it. Learning their schedule took him no time at all, and now he only needs to wait. Four Sun-descended officers step over the threshold and into a Moon temple they have no right to be inside of, and none will leave it. Perching himself on a ledge in the rafters of the temple, his trap is set.

Years ago, this temple was clean and beautiful; engravings of their Moon Divinites bright and clear, Mahina's statue gilded. Now, after being abandoned so long, it is no more than a dilapidated building holding onto the fear of a nation. The boy angles himself to watch them come in without being noticed himself. He even allows them time to look around. One by one they step over broken floorboards, run their fingers over dusty pews, and roll their eyes at intricate engravings on the walls and the rusted statue of Mahina of the Moon at the entrance.

The boy wants fresh fear.

When a careless officer scrapes his fingernails over Mahina's statue, peeling off a layer of her arm like crusty wallpaper before flicking it to the floor, the boy finally jumps. He flies from the rafters like a bat and lands on the officer's back. With the prick of a needle in his wrist, the boy is able to draw enough blood from his body to mold a dagger between his hands. He only has to weave his hands through a few short signs to control his power, unlike other Divine descendants who need long orchestrated patterns.

The first officer only has enough time to scream before the dagger of blood pierces him through the chest. He and the dagger both explode, splattering over the boy and his next victims. The second officer barely has the time to raise his hands in surprise before blood soaks him through, too. He buckles under the weight, smacks his head on the hard ground, and goes silent.

The third officer, a tall female, wipes blood from her mouth and shouts, "Freeze!"

Holding out her hands, palms up, fingers stretched wide and slightly bent, she summons a storm. Her eyes pop with a foggy blue color as thick storm clouds materialize overhead. Instantly they spill buckets of heavy snow that pierce the walls when blown around by harsh gusts of wind.

"Who are you?" Her voice carries with the storm, another snowflake among the millions of them.

The boy simply smiles. A storm created by the blood of Irene, Sun Divinity of the Weather, is nothing against the blood coursing through his own veins.

Dragging the needle between his fingers down his bare torso, the boy opens a cut much larger than the mere pinprick from earlier. As blood spills from his body in increasingly large amounts, his hands build swords and arrows and bullets. The snow turns red as the officer is impaled on one of the swords. The storm ceases, leaving nothing more than an abnormal chill in the air, as she collapses completely.

By the time three of the four officers are dead, the boy is lightheaded from exhaustion and blood loss. Stopping to survey his work, he sucks in a breath and staunches the bleeding.

Silence rings before a garbled cough interrupts it. The final officer lies halfway between life and death a few meters away, his wrinkled hands clutching over an open gash in his abdomen. When he realizes he's been caught, his panic turns the coughing to choking.

The boy approaches him slowly, wanting to suck his fear out of the air and drink it down, taste it, savor it.

"Clinging to your life?" he asks with a sneer. "That's the problem with us Divine descendants, isn't it? *Tenacity*."

"We are—we are not... No Divinity would make you like this," the older officer cries.

"No," the boy agrees, scraping over one of his newly-closed cuts with a nail to re-open it. "The Divinites did *not* make me."

"Then you must be a demon sent from Nirnasha's Underworld!"

The man feebly attempts to knock the boy off his feet as he steps closer, but it's to no avail. His legs flail like wet noodles, doing nothing to deter the boy. Soon enough, he's hovering over the elder like a dark spirit, his eyes as crimson as the blood on his hands.

"Could be," he says easily. "When I send you there, why don't you find out for me?"

Once more he pulls blood from his own veins in order to destroy one of them. It's done in the blink of an eye.

Painted in red, the boy leaves a single mark behind. *A*

symbol of revolution, he thinks, *a historical symbol that can't be ignored no matter what they all think.*

Larger than his body, a single letter is slathered across the wall:

M

1
Meiling

Meiling Katz is a nobody. Or at least that's what everyone tells her. Ever since her parents were slaughtered over thirteen years ago in the Lunar Eclipse Massacre staged by the Miyako family—the only lineage in history to survive living with abilities passed on by the Moon Divinity Mahina herself— she's needed daily medication and weekly visits to the doctor.

As one of the unlucky sixteen percent of people in the world without Divine blood, she has a weaker constitution than most others. While the surviving Sun-descendants of the Massacre got off with no more than exercise-induced asthma or long-faded bruises, Meiling has battled a litany of unidentifiable ailments. From three years old then to nearly sixteen years old now, she's been saddled with experimental prescriptions and constant doctor's visits.

"Stay still."

Meiling tenses her shoulders as the needle pierces her neck. It comes away thick and crimson-red, leaving behind a burning sensation.

Monthly visits with Doctor Sutherland—her primary

doctor—has been the norm since the Katz family took her in as a toddler. With a myriad of pills and his Chae-Won ability, he has kept her healthy.

Doctor Sutherland pivots away from her as he drops the blood-filled needle into a safety-sealed container waiting on his steel rolling cart. In scratchy handwriting, he prints her name across the front in bold black marker.

Divine Blood Testing.

Though Meiling has already done this a thousand times before, proving time and time again she has nothing of the sort, this is a requirement for acceptance into the Zialitos Academy for Sun-Gifted Children.

Although there is no precedent for someone without Divine abilities like her being accepted into The Academy, there is no ruling against it. So long as Meiling passes the entrance exams, there is nothing anyone can do to send her away. Which is precisely what she plans to do. It's the only way she stands a chance at rising into the ranks of Malumvian lawmakers. Lawmakers who, unlike her, stand with the opportunity to actually change things in their country.

In the aftermath of the Lunar Eclipse Massacre, everything changed. Dozens of Descent Segregation Laws were put into place, restricting everything from schooling to marriage based on Divine heritage. The entire country of Malumvia grew so fearful of another tragedy, expecting every lunar eclipse to bring with it the devastation of entire city blocks and the extinction of entire Sun lineages, that even ability-less people turned into threats. Anyone not with them, they thought, had to be against them.

When Meiling was seven, her adoptive parents took her out to lunch in Division One of Malumvia, a place where laws dictate only those of Sun Descent can live. It was an overcast afternoon, with fog rolling in through the crowded streets like phantoms. While Meiling was in the middle of chewing a rice cake, the clouds shifted in the sky overhead to bury the last beam of sunlight.

At the table next to theirs, a middle-aged woman screamed. She scraped her chair back, grabbed the hand of the young boy sitting beside her, and took off down the street without paying for their half-eaten meals. Her outburst caused a domino effect of panic. Sun descendants screamed and ran for cover, eyeing the dark clouds as if they'd fall to Earth and crush them all.

"Mass paranoia," Meiling's father, Jax, said. "It's a commonly shared trauma response leftover from the Massacre."

Meiling slipped her hand into his, nodding along. At the time, she didn't entirely understand what his words meant; only that they were outsiders in a Division known for hating outsiders.

Rushing through the crowded streets toward the train to take them back home, Meiling felt eyes following her and her parents. Jax Katz was descended from a Divinity of the Moon, and although nothing in his outward appearance gave this away, the Sun Divine seemed to know it anyway.

People began to whisper. *What's he doing here? What has he done? How do we stop him? What if he's with them?*

Their voices grated in Meiling's ears, making her

release her parents' hands so she could cover them. The moment she was out of their grip, she was out of their sight, as well. Meiling was too small to hold herself steady through the jostling crowd. Soon, she was all alone beside an alleyway between two towering apartment complexes. Heart rampaging in her chest, Meiling slipped into the darkness of the alleyway to wait it out.

In the alleyway, the gloom turned to shadows so heavy Meiling's chest constricted. She broke into tears at once, apologizing out loud to the Sun Divinites for getting lost in darkness in hopes at least one of the eight would hear her and bring light again.

That's where five Zialitos patrolling officers found her.

The sunlight between their hands burnt a lash across her cheek before she even got the chance to ask for help.

"Stand down!" one of the men shouted.

It took Meiling a long time to realize they were talking to her.

"Please help me," Meiling said at last, her hands trembling. "I lost my parents."

The officers only scoffed.

"Identification Card. Now."

Identification Cards came about after the Lunar Eclipse Massacre. Mandated annually, they listed blood status and potency across all Divinities. This way, no one with Moon Descent stood a chance at slipping through the cracks into their strongholds again.

Meiling tore her card from the laminated holder she carried around everywhere and thrust it toward the closest officer. His sun-circled hands singed the little hairs on her own as he snatched it.

He stared long and hard at her image. With sleek black hair, big red eyes, and soft pale skin, Meiling knew from a young age that she carried many of the physical features of a Moon descendant without actually being one. It tended to turn eyes, but it had never gotten her cornered by a bunch of Zialitos officers before then.

Only after reading the giant lettering beneath her image about a thousand times over—*NO PRESENT DIVINE BLOOD*—did the officers agree to let her go.

Meiling snatched her card back and ran, limbs heavy, until she found her parents a few streets over. Similarly, they were batting away over-cautious patrolling officers who didn't believe their innocence.

Meiling took her parents' hands and refused to let go. She couldn't believe this was Malumvia, home to the Zialitos, the best country in the world.

The sheer probability of every last Miyako being involved in the Lunar Eclipse Massacre is little to none, so how Malumvia as a whole took to condemning every Moon-descended individual, and even those who may seem a little too suspiciously like one at the time, seemed absurd even to Meiling as a little girl. She never deemed herself as someone who could take a stand against it until that afternoon in the alleyway. After that, her resolve was set. She'd rise in the ranks of lawmakers, uncover the full truth of the massacre, and serve as a voice for those wrongly faulted in the aftermath.

Starting with attending the Zialitos Academy for Sun-Gifted Children.

The thought snaps Meiling back to the present, sitting in the sterile doctor's office, a needle of her blood gleaming crimson under the overhead fluorescents. She's on her first step to success.

With a quick flick of Doctor Sutherland's wrist, the bleeding spot on Meiling's neck seals itself shut at last. With another flick, the searing pain settles into nothingness. Meiling heaves out a breath, scratching the spot reflexively.

No matter how many times doctors use moves like that on her—strong healing abilities passed down by the Divinity of Creation, Chae-Won—it never gets any easier to adjust to. In the aftermath of pain mended by Chae-Won abilities, there is an aching emptiness. At times it makes Meiling feel as if she'd prefer to heal in the long, agonizing and naturally human way. According to Doctor Sutherland, he's never met another person who shares the same sentiment.

"Meiling Katz," Doctor Sutherland says, addressing her by her full name even though he's known her nearly forever. He peels blue latex gloves from his pale wrinkly hands. "I trust you understand the risks of attending a boarding school with an ailment such as yours."

"Yes, Doctor Sutherland."

"Especially in Malumvia's current climate," he tacks on, eyeing the morning paper sitting beside his laptop. The front story image is a large, grainy black and white of a letter M painted in what appears to be blood across the inside wall of an abandoned Mahina Temple. A number of patrolling officers were recently killed there.

"Yes, Doctor Sutherland."

Doctor Sutherland flicks his beady brown eyes over to Meiling's parents sitting silently on the other side of the glass window. The examination rooms aren't exactly private around here; they're more like viewing rooms where parents like hers can see and hear everything all while pretending the glass separator ensures privacy.

Even so, both Meiling's mother, Reena, and her father, Jax, stare back with grim expressions as if they have understood every word spoken in these bright white tiled walls anyway. Though they are clearly opposed to the answer Meiling herself has given, they make no move to do something about it.

"Well." Doctor Sutherland clears his throat with an audible click. "I simply cannot permit it without rather drastic adjustments to your medication, Miss Meiling Katz. Adjustments that may very well have undesirable consequences. Do you understand?"

"Yes." Meiling frowns. Her medication has always come with undesirable consequences: headaches, stomachaches, backaches, any sort of ache possible. But these side-effects are still preferable to the consequences of *not* taking the medication.

From across the glass, Jax frowns with her.

Reena taps her fingernails on the glass and mouths the question, "How drastic?"

Doctor Sutherland hooks a pulse oximeter over Meiling's left middle finger before moving to check his clipboard. He quietly flips through the many pages bound to it as if the answer to Reena's question is hiding somewhere along the handwritten notes he took to questions like; *within the past seven days, have you experienced any uncommon pain or discomfort* and *have you had any trouble sleeping?*

Meiling's answer to both: *no more than usual.*

It takes a long while before Doctor Sutherland sets down the clipboard, letting the pen roll off to the marble floor by his feet, and answers the question.

"Perhaps double her usual dosage would do the trick. To begin with, at the very least."

He unhooks the pulse oximeter from Meiling's finger, rolling his eyes at whatever result presents itself. Meiling, from what she's been told ever since she could understand it, is apparently a doctor's worst nightmare.

Jax stands up abruptly, the usual seafoam green of his eyes dampening with flecks of black while he stares through the glass window, unblinking, at Doctor Sutherland. His long eyelashes twitch so much they seem to send shock waves through the air.

Meiling sits up straighter in the padded white chair she's in. Jax Katz is not normally prone to using his abilities, given their origin: Viera, Moon Divinity of Ignorance. But it is clear he's trying to use them now. To do so openly in a Zialitos-managed hospital is just asking for trouble.

With immense effort, those of Viera descent are said to be able to read minds. Not in the sense they can clearly see a person's every thought and opinion, but in the way they can sense hidden intentions or lies, and feel for the general gist of a person's mindset.

The issue with Viera abilities is that they are nearly useless unless there is so much potency in one's blood they're basically courting death anyway. In Jax's case, this is the loophole that allowed him to marry Reena of Sun Divinity Irene descent despite the many laws against it.

"Dad," Meiling hisses, waving her hands around in a feeble attempt to dissolve his abilities into thin air. With many descendants, these things can actually be done due to the tangibility of their abilities. Unfortunately for Meiling, it does not work for his.

"It's quite all right, Meiling Katz," Doctor Sutherland says casually. "As your father is quite aware, I will surely not report him for such things."

As he finishes the sentence, he meets Jax's eyes with a harsh glare of his own. Black momentarily takes over the entirety of Jax's irises before seeping away again. Once they return to seafoam green, he slumps in his chair, seeming to give up on trying to read Doctor Sutherland's mind. He has a bad habit of turning to his Viera ability to sense lies when it comes to Meiling. Reena places a small hand on his shoulder to console him.

Meiling raises one eyebrow, skin buzzing with the residuals of someone else's abilities, and says, "So then double it?"

Doctor Sutherland sighs heavily. Meiling has the sound burnt into her memory from how often he does it during their visits.

"I will need a parent's signature," he says, though he is

already tapping the buttons on his computer to adjust the medication. It's happened so many times over the years Meiling has the sound of the keys to do so memorized as well.

"You'll get one," Meiling says quickly. She motions for her parents to come inside and they stand at once to join them.

Jax and Reena will sign anything if it gets Meiling into the Academy. She's hardly shut up about it since she was nine years old; everyone knows how deeply she desires this. Besides, being ability-less and orphaned by the tragedy of the century, people tend to go a little easier on her in general.

As if none of that would be enough on its own, Meiling adds, "Surely we owe you for not reporting him, anyway?"

If Doctor Sutherland were to tell anyone—literally *anyone*—about her father's brief loss of control over his Viera abilities, the last thing Meiling would need to worry about is missing out on the Academy. All three of them would be thrown in prison for life for threatening a medical professional, regardless of if it was actually a threat.

Doctor Sutherland huffs out a laugh. "Yes, you Katz owe me greatly, don't you?"

An hour later, Meiling leaves the doctor's office with a bag full of new medication and a startling *PASS* stamped in thin red lettering across her pre-Academy health screening.

2
Suraya

Suraya Zialitos is the best of the best and she knows it. Coming from the prestigious Zialitos bloodline—the only lineage in history to survive living with abilities passed on by the Sun Divinity Ataru himself—she is an elite. She has been since birth. Her future is as bright as the sunlight she can cradle between her palms.

Which is exactly why she's going to apply and get accepted to The Zialitos Academy for Sun-Gifted Children all on her own.

The admissions board is made up of mostly her older, distant relatives. As such, seeing as Suraya is an heir to the Zialitos lineage, they could take one look at her Identification Card and guarantee a seat in the top class with her name on it. But Suraya refuses such a method. For one, she's no coattail rider; she's the descendant of both Divinity of the Sun, Ataru, and his younger sister, Divinia, Divinity of Prophecy. For two, she doesn't want acceptance in name, she wants it in *power*.

Crumbling the day's morning newspaper into a tight

ball, Suraya is reminded why she is so determined by the headline crushed within her fist.

Unidentified, unrelated M-attacks. That's the genius term Una Zialitos, Head of Malumvia , has given the increasingly frequent acts of terrorism claimed by the Miyako family around the country. So far, they have stayed well within the borders of Moon-descendant-riddled Divisions Four and Five, but it's clear they're branching out farther each day.

A couple crushed to death under heavy shadows when traveling to Division Five found with matching M's painted over their cold hands? *Unidentified, unrelated M-attack.*

An entire Kagiso family's farmland razed to ashes, the dead crops and animals curved together into a giant M? *Unidentified, unrelated M-attack.*

A small elementary school exploded to pieces, taking with it the lives of a dozen children inside, the only remaining structure at all a jagged M made out of what used to be a classroom wall? *Unidentified, unrelated M-attack.*

Rage simmers underneath Suraya's skin. Who would leave an M in blood if not the Miyakos? They've done it once, they would obviously do it again. Unlike the cowards running Malumvia, Suraya is willing to take matters into her own hands before that continues to happen.

If not for her family who were nearly wiped out in the Lunar Eclipse Massacre over thirteen years ago, then for her mother who can't seem to move on from it, or even for herself for having to constantly combat the endless condolences people give her because of it.

Suraya is not a victim. She's a living legend. They'll see.

With her pre-Academy health screening out of the way, the only thing left to ace in order to guarantee her acceptance are the written and physical exams. To prepare, Suraya studies two hours a day at her bedroom desk and trains for three hours in the wide-open backyard field of her house. Her parents, as any respectable Zialitos family in Division One, earn hefty sums to cover the expenses of a well-maintained house and training grounds.

For families like Suraya's, there is a special training program called The Beams. The name is stupid and nonsensical given none of the employees are actually of *Sun* descent, but the training is no joke. At the press of a button, a variety of people with Moon descent are sent over to act as enemies for all-out sparring sessions. Suraya suspects there isn't much acting involved at all with the sorts of people they are, but that's what makes it so thrilling for her each time she wins.

"Bring it on," Suraya snaps at today's crowd, tying her long hair up into a haphazard knot over her head. The red outside and silver underside mingle as one, a perfect mix of Ataru and Divinia.

All at once a dozen of The Beams employees come racing toward Suraya where she stands across the yard. Immediately, the clean air grows clouded with the dark residuals of Moon abilities.

Suraya scowls as she sidesteps a fist of thick bronze

knives rather than fingers. The closer it gets to the physical exam, the harsher the opponents The Beams send her. Days ago she fought no one except for weak storm bringers from Storm Divinity Tal and disappointing hand-to-hand fighters from Hunting Divinity Hala. Now, it seems, they have finally deemed it worthwhile to show her what the real bulk of Moon descendants in Malumvia are like: foul and relentless.

The fist of bronze knives returns, catching Suraya on her cheek. She tumbles to the ground spitting blood. In her nearly sixteen years of life, Suraya has never had much trouble winning a fight. The Zialitos family is akin to royalty in Malumvia. Rare, powerful, and politically in command, there's hardly a person alive who wants to fight them to begin with.

Jumping to her feet with a bloody smile, Suraya calls upon her sunlight. Heat pulses through her veins as Nature Energy from within her body and ultraviolet rays from the Sun race into her control. They materialize as thick sunbeams in her palms. With one meaningful blink of her eyes, her vision snaps into focus. With Ataru's blood, it is clear, far, and wide.

Suraya beckons bronze fist forward once more. She's ready.

This time when the fist swings at her, Suraya sees it coming. Moving to block with her arm, the sunbeams curve around her skin like armor. Bronze is strong, but it can still melt. The heat of her sunlight at its strength melts the knives into a puddle in the dirt. Once those are gone,

Suraya kicks the man square in the chest to knock him down for good.

After he's down, half a dozen more follow. There's another man whose back sprouts thick leathery wings and floats overhead, and another who weaves his fingers in circles that generate pocket-sized tornadoes. Then there is a woman whose body produces so many animalistic features she appears to be a massive stag with fangs, another who snaps sparks of fire from her fingertips, and another who summons a thunderstorm overhead without missing a step in her run forward.

With the plethora of thick clouds, Suraya's sunbeams shrink from full armor to chain link wrapping around her. Rushing backward, holding the opponents at bay with rogue sparks of light, Suraya tries to tug more sunlight down to replace what's been lost. Her vision cuts through the clouds to show the Sun high in the sky, but before she can yank any of its power down, the clouds thicken and rain pours. Soaking wet and freezing cold, Suraya's sunlight dwindles further.

A mini tornado knocks her off her feet and her sunbeams scatter. Left defenseless in the dirt, Suraya holds her breath while a couple of The Beams women close in on her.

"I expected a lot more," one of them whispers to the other.

Suraya crouches, waiting. Divine abilities are drawn from Nature Energy, and Nature Energy takes patience. Heating herself from the core out, Suraya braces herself for the taunting that is sure to come. *Soon*, she thinks, *I just need to wait a few moments more.*

"Pride of the Zialitos?" the other asks mockingly, finding Suraya's eyes. "I don't see it."

Suraya grins. The existence of Divine descendants is precarious. It took nearly a millennia before anyone could live with their Creator's blood. The Zialitos, as the sole lineage to call Ataru their Creator, is even more special. As their family expands, marrying into and beginning families with those of any other Descent, the early dangers of Divine blood rise again. There's never a guarantee that a child between a Zialitos and any other will survive to be born and withstand Ataru's blood. If they do, there remains the possibility of ability dysfunction—a phenomenon in which Divine blood courses through one's veins, but the gifts meant to course with them do not. For the Zialitos, this is as much a death as a flat line.

So Suraya, the daughter of a woman with Ataru's blood and a man with Divinia's, born with the highest Blood Divinity Count in history, is a true gift from the Divine. Not only can she live with the strength of Ataru's blood, but she can control it.

From birth, Malumvia gave her a nickname: *Pride of the Zialitos*. If The Beams don't see it now, they will soon.

A pair of hands sparking flames reach out to grab Suraya. She only feels the gentle press of additional heat to her body before she sends everything in a five-meter radius flying. Rings of gathered sunlight burst out of her with a resonating buzz.

Exhaustion begins to set into her bones quickly after.

Pushing through, Suraya jumps to her feet and runs, thrashing out with smaller sunbeams indiscriminately to take out the rest. Horns are severed off the stag's head, storm clouds are zapped out of thin air, and giant hairy wings are singed down to charred chicken legs.

Suraya slows to a stop, breathing heavily. Even the strongest Moon fighters sent by The Beams have nothing on her, Pride of the Zialitos and future Head of Malumvia itself.

"Is that all you got?" she shouts, cackling. She expected a win, but this is hardly even a fight.

The dozen of them moan and groan on the ground in response. Suraya snickers as she brushes herself off and breathes. Another upside to being of Ataru descent is self-healing abilities. As the rest of them nurse black eyes and broken noses, Suraya heats herself up until the only pain she has is her own irritation.

The piercing sound of a nearby siren knocks her attention off course. Stumbling backward, she swats at the air as if the noise could be dispersed by her fists. When there's sirens, there's crime. When there's crime, there's bound to be Miyakos, or, at the very least, those related to them.

It takes all of Suraya's willpower to stay put. The anger in her veins builds and builds, burning the way her abilities used to when she was little. The Miyakos can't be out there drawing their initials in blood onto something else already, can they?

As anyone playing with dirty tricks would, The Beams catch her while her back is turned.

Collapsing to her knees in the gravel from the force of the shove to her shoulder blades, Suraya feels her skin tear open and immediately begin to bleed. With a heavy breath, she releases the sunlight from her fingertips and drops the magnification in her eyes. If it's dirty tricks they want, then it's dirty tricks they'll get. Suraya can sit here pretending to be beaten into submission until the perfect moment comes for her to strike them all down at once. *Again.*

That's exactly what the Miyakos did, after all. Over thirteen years ago, they were pretty much dormant before the Lunar Eclipse Massacre. After being threatened by the Zialitos for their constant steps out of line, most of them went into hiding. They stayed there until they came back out to slaughter ten percent of the country's Divine descendants in one fell swoop.

"Worried about the *unidentified, unrelated M-attacks,* kid?"

Suraya swings her head toward the source of the voice, fists clenched to swing. Her eyes always take a while to readjust after she's used them for long distances, so they water and blur as she zones in on the person blocking the sun. Standing like the personification of a shadow above her, there is a person she did not notice earlier when The Beams showed up. They are small and ghostly pale with pitch black hair and matching eyes. Thick eyeliner brushes out in wings like horns over their eyelids. Despite the odd appearance, nothing appears all that special about them. No visible abilities at least.

"Or are you worried they *aren't* unidentified, unrelated M-attacks?"

Suraya scowls so hard she gives herself a pulsing headache.

"Can't speak?" they ask next. Small lips curl into a smile.

Fire splits through Suraya's skull the moment she parts her lips to prove otherwise. Clutching at her scalp, a scream is torn from her throat. It feels like there are twin snakes slithering through her ears into her skull. With the sensation comes the visions.

As if a fast-forwarded movie reel, the worst moments of her life are torn to the forefront of her mind. No matter how much self-healing she performs, or how much sunlight she summons, it won't stop.

It begins with the recent M-attacks. Suraya sees a glimpse of the bloody photos plastered in the newspaper before her mother incinerates the entire thing in a fit of despair. Her pained scream echoes everywhere.

Then it's the first day of middle school when everyone drew extended family trees, but seventy-five percent of Suraya's were labeled *deceased*.

Then the week she lived out of the hospital at eight years old. Her mother was on a mandated hold for a mental breakdown. Suraya slept on stiff pull-outs each night, the glare of the Moon a constant taunt through the barred windows.

Next a cold night bundled up on the kitchen floor as a toddler, staring at her mother sobbing over the sink. The blood on her palms stained the counter where she braced herself. Handprints remained long after she released it to tug back her messy hair.

Suraya heard only one clear word out of her mother's mouth in the countless hours she sat there alone:

Miyako.

The memories melt away in a puff of murky vapor. The pain stops as suddenly as it began. As though hurling into a brick wall at one hundred kilometers an hour, she's released from that inhuman ability.

Mind manipulation, Suraya thinks bitterly. She always assumed the existence of Viera descendants strong enough to actually use such abilities was a myth to scare Sun-gifted children.

"It's not a myth," the person answers steadily.

"Get out of my head!" Suraya tries to shout, but her voice comes out scratchy.

"Have you figured out anything about who I am yet?"

"You're Viera scum," Suraya spits.

"Sure, but what else?" they respond. Sirens echo in the distance and the anger comes back full-force in Suraya's mind.

"Zilla," she snaps, understanding dawning on her suddenly, "Divinity of Hate."

The one with *emotional manipulation* abilities. They can make you feel all the worst feelings at all the worst times in all the worst ways. What a nasty combination this person has.

The descendant of Viera and Zilla snaps their fingers and says, "Ah, so perhaps there are some intelligent Sun descendants, after all."

"Watch your mouth." Suraya sits up and stars assault her vision at once. Every ability leaves its own aftershocks; it's no wonder those of the Moon are this awful.

"It's not so easy to realize some abilities overpower even yours, now is it, young Zialitos?"

"Get out," Suraya demands, even though she hasn't met her three-hour quota for training yet today.

"As you wish."

As is old tradition toward those of high power—meaning anything from a government official to a toddler in the Zialitos family—every one of The Beams bow to her before leaving. They lower their heads while their left hands make a fist and their right hands cover it in front of their chests, and then they lift their heads at the same time the fingers of their right hands raise to point toward the sky. The in-sync greeting of respect makes Suraya want to tear off all of their fingers, every last one.

After this, the entire group of them, mostly defeated, aside from the dirty manipulator, drag themselves away. They're transported away in a flash of light, popping out of existence like holograms.

Suraya sits in the dirt, hastily wiping sweat and tears from her face. What sort of fight was that? People with rotten abilities like theirs shouldn't be allowed to work for The Beams. It's unfair. It's *dangerous*. Far more dangerous than the average fight, and this is Suraya who thinks so— Suraya who seeks out a thrill in any possible scenario she can; binging horror films, jumping from cliffs, sparring with random Moon descendants on the daily.

People like that black-haired criminal shouldn't be allowed near her. They shouldn't be allowed *anywhere*.

"Suraya!"

She whirls around to see Meiling stumbling through the solid silver gate, a wrinkled paper clutched between her hands. From afar, her freckles look like stars poured across her pale cheeks, and her big pale-red eyes are larger than planets. Momentarily, the black of her hair makes Suraya jolt backward. But the bangs slapped against her forehead remind her it's only Meiling; friendly little ability-lacking Meiling.

When Meiling makes it to Suraya's side, kneeling in the dirt, her expression falters. She swipes a finger under the curve of Suraya's jaw and it comes back stained red with blood.

"Oh Divinities, Suri, what happened? Are you okay?" Somehow Meiling's eyes manage to get larger as her eyelashes flutter about.

"Nothing." Suraya brushes her off quietly. "Training."

She can't let Meiling know. If she does, Meiling will try to fix it. And if Meiling tries to fix it, who knows what will happen to her. She's not Sun-gifted. She's not gifted at all. If there are other Moon-gifted jerks who are able to catch Suraya off-guard—Suraya who is the strongest of her age, of her lineage, of probably everyone else in this whole Divinity-forsaken country—then they could *kill* someone like Meiling. It's bad enough she wants to attend the Academy. Suraya already has her hands full trying to stop that fantasy.

"Are you sure you're all right?" Meiling asks.

"Fine," Suraya says, but she sways sideways into Meiling as she says it.

Meiling quickly folds up the wrinkled paper and slips it into her pocket so both hands are free to hold Suraya upright. Suraya recognizes Doctor Sutherland's scrawl before the page is tucked away out of view. She lets herself droop into Meiling's hold with a sigh.

"Take me inside," she says, scanning the training grounds again to make sure no one is lurking in any shadows.

"Of course."

Meiling serves as a crutch as they hobble back to the house together. Suraya isn't weak enough to need this sort of assistance, but it's better to have Meiling here. At least when she's where Suraya can see her, she stands no chance of getting swallowed up by the shadows of Malumvia.

"Want some tea? I'll make the mint chai you like," Meiling says, stumbling through the doorway and plopping Suraya on a stool at the counter. "It might make you feel better."

"Make a pot; we can share it," Suraya says, staring down at the counter where a stack of newspapers is scattered. *Unidentified, unrelated M-attack. Unidentified, unrelated M-attack. Unidentified, unrelated M-attack.* One after another after another. All glaring reminders of what she needs to do and why.

The second Meiling turns her back toward the stove to begin brewing the chai, Suraya sets the entire stack of newspapers alight with brilliant sunbeams. She watches the reports of the Miyakos burn into ash and pictures the day she will be able to do the same to them all for herself.

3
Meiling

True to their bloodline, the Zialitos show up with a flash of blinding light. It cuts through the blinds and glitters across the silver trim of the bathroom mirror Meiling is staring into.

"Meiling!" her mother shouts. "Come down here. The Zialitos are here!"

"One minute!" Meiling calls back.

In the dusty reflection, Meiling's eyes are a deep red—a color so rare, even for those with Divine blood, that it's comical she's so ordinary. They taunt her as she uncaps her medicine bottle and pours out two big blue and white pills. Her newest medication: twice the size of the previous.

"Meiling, come on!"

Her mother's voice is so much closer this time. Meiling jolts in surprise. The large pills fly out of her fingers, roll in two big circles around the bowl of the sink, and disappear straight down the drain.

Meiling stares at the porcelain with a slack jaw. Her new prescription is so high Doctor Sutherland can only give her a couple weeks' worth at a time. She can't afford to lose or misuse even a single day of them.

When she was younger, she occasionally forgot to take her pills. Aside from a few fitful nights of sleep, nothing happened to her during those times. *So*, she wonders, flicking on the faucet, *what harm could there be in skipping one day more?*

The three Zialitos are in the living room by the time Meiling comes down the stairs. It's always a strange culture shock to see them here since they're Zialitos from Division One and Meiling belongs to a mere Division Three family. Division Three is the largest one of the five in the country, and it's split wildly between Sun and Moon descendants, making it rather unfavorable for people of high standing like Omar, Taru, and Suraya Zialitos.

"Are you feeling better, Suri?" Meiling asks in greeting.

Suraya meets Meiling's eyes for half a second before looking away again, her lips a tight line. She nods once. Meiling thinks of the blood under her chin the other day and wonders why Suraya tries so hard not to tell her anything.

"Hello Omar, hello Taru," she says to Suraya's parents.

"Hi sweetie, how are you?" Omar sweeps her up into a tight hug. "I think the girls are a bit nervous right now about those exams."

He motions backward to his wife and daughter. Suraya's eyes are fixated on a stain in the carpet and Taru is gnawing at her bottom lip as if to take it off. Taru has always been as prone to sudden anger and hatred as Suraya. Half the time she treats Meiling like a stranger on the street, polite but impersonal, and the other half she glares as if Meiling has murdered her whole family. Tonight is apparently the latter.

Meiling hums. "I'm fine, Omar. Excited, actually."

Suraya's eyes flicker up in surprise. Meiling smiles at her and she looks away again. Suraya's been trying to talk her out of attending the Academy for years. The closer it gets, the less kindness she has in her efforts. With the Academy exams coming tomorrow, Suraya seems downright pissed off tonight. Meiling supposes that might be due to the reason the Zialitos are here in the first place: to prematurely celebrate.

Omar Zialitos has been friends with Meiling's adoptive parents Jax and Reena Katz for as long as she can remember. That's the only reason she's had the honor of getting to grow up beside Suraya, Pride of the Zialitos herself. Taru has never seemed too fond of any of them, especially Jax with his Moon blood, but Omar is. He even encouraged Meiling to shoot for the Academy before Jax and Reena got on board with the idea. So, of course, he believes she'll get in tomorrow, right beside Suraya. Tonight's dinner is to celebrate.

"Okay everyone, come on," Jax says, motioning them into the cramped dining room. "Come sit. Let's eat."

The oval-shaped table in the dining room is barely long enough to fit six seats around. Bamboo placemats overlap one another and the arms of mismatched chairs criss-cross. Jax has to plaster himself against the wall to let

Reena by and Omar climbs straight across Taru's chair to get to his own. Meiling and Suraya meet each other's eyes from their respective spots across from one another and try not to laugh. Suraya bites down hard on her lip to stop her smile, seeming desperate to stay upset with Meiling. Knowing her, she probably thinks if she does, Meiling will eventually give up on her dream.

The table before them is filled nearly to the point of collapse with dishes. Pitchers of water and tea, juice and wine; plates of roast beef and spiral ham; pots of congee and lotus soup; pans of spiced eggplant and sticky mango rice; all topped off with the promise of shortbread and truffles lying beneath the tinfoil-wrapped dishes in the center. Meiling's father is a phenomenal, but often excessive, chef. They'll be eating for hours at this rate.

"Dig in," he tells them proudly.

Suraya snatches her chopsticks from her napkin like they're knives. Her father serves her a small portion of each dish and she stabs at them without eating much of anything. In trying to keep her attention off of Meiling, she's resorted to glaring at everyone else. Her eyes stop on Jax for so long Meiling fears for his life.

Fear for his life is quickly replaced by a flash of anger. Jax has done nothing to earn such a look. Meiling knows Suraya isn't the biggest fan of Meiling's goal to attend the Academy and join the Malumvian lawmakers, but she certainly has no right to take it out on anyone else.

"Suri, can I talk to you?" They can't avoid this conversation forever; they might as well clear it up now.

"Right now?" Reena asks.

Meiling pushes her chair back and stands. "Right now."

Suraya sighs and stands without a word. Together they retreat to the den a room over. With giant bay windows, the room is flooded in light. Perfect for a Zialitos. Suraya finds the place where the sunlight filtering in is the strongest and stands there. Meiling hovers in her shadow.

Meiling cuts right to the chase: "What's going on with you?"

A sharp laugh breaks through Suraya's tight-lipped frown.

"There's nothing going on with me. There's something going on with *you*, and there's something wrong with both our parents for pretending there isn't."

"Is this seriously about the Academy? I told you already I know what I'm doing. I've done enough research, I'm smart, and I'll have you, Suri. It will be *fine*."

"Of course, this is about the Academy," Suraya snaps, her eyes twitching. "I don't care how much research you've done, Meiling, it isn't safe for you."

Meiling softens, reaching out to hold Suraya's hand. "I'll be fine. Doctor Sutherland even gave me a pass. I meant to show you the other day."

Understanding flickers through Suraya's bright eyes. Then she begins to laugh again.

"I get you're worried about me," Meiling continues, louder than Suraya can laugh, "and I appreciate it, I really do, but I promise I'll be fine. I'm ready for this."

"You're not," Suraya says, tugging herself free. Her cheeks are pink.

The chandelier light above their heads flickers to a nearly-blinding brightness in tandem with her voice. Meiling flits her gaze to the windows to make sure no hairline cracks have appeared.

"You'll be surrounded by people stronger than you. I can't be there all the time, you know. You're gonna get yourself killed. And for what, huh? For *nothing*. You're at risk enough as is. Give it up, Meiling. *Please*."

Meiling's adrenaline spikes as if a tangible thing within her bloodstream. She can feel her heartbeat in her temples.

"Don't say that," she whispers. "You don't mean it."

"I do. You're too weak."

"I'm not weak!" Meiling knows she's raising her voice, but she can hardly hear it over the blood pounding in her ears.

"Prove it then." Suraya snaps her fingers together and a collection of sunlight materializes in the palm of her hand. She slides a meter back on the hardwood floor and raises her hand as if to strike.

Meiling has been with Suraya her whole life; she's seen her through everything, fighting everyone. But never once has Suraya raised a hand at her.

"Suri…"

"Come on then."

"Suraya, wait!"

Panic rises. Meiling's pulse jumps in her neck. The next thing she knows there is a resounding crash and the overlap of multiple ear-splitting screams coming from the dining room. Peeling her eyes open, having no clue when she squeezed them shut, Meiling sees nothing.

All around them, giant clouds of thick black smoke have settled. The bay windows that bathed them in sunlight seconds ago are suddenly buried in darkness instead. Knowing all too well who darkness like this is associated with, Meiling's head fills with static .

"Meiling?" Suraya says. A second later her hand latches around Meiling's wrist. "Get over here."

Meiling allows herself to be tugged behind Suraya. The faster she blinks, the more she can see through the darkness. Meiling knows this shouldn't be happening, yet her vision continues to clear, even as she watches Suraya flail around them, attempting to get back to the dining room. *She can't see through it like me*, Meiling realizes suddenly. Why can't she see through it like me?

Meiling jerks them both to a sudden stop. This is her chance. Even before the exams, even before the Academy itself, she can prove to everyone that abilities are not everything . While the Divinely gifted collectively do nothing, she can do *something*. Her heart races faster in her chest.

"Meiling?" Suraya asks in a gruff whisper, tugging on her wrist tighter. "What is it?"

Blinking rapidly, even more of Meiling's vision comes back. All it takes is a little extra focus. She strains her eyes until she can see everything. The wide pupils in Suraya's eyes, the hardwood floors beneath their socked feet, the chipped paint on the white door frame leading into the dining room.

Meiling quickly swaps their positions so Suraya is the one being held and Meiling is the one leading the way. Suraya sputters in protest, a tiny beam of sunlight breaking through the shadows in her hands, but she doesn't fight back any more. Her fingers do tighten around Meiling's, though.

In the dining room, glasses are spilled all over the table, a few plates are chipped, the wallpaper is peeling at the corners, and Taru's chair is on the floor, broken. She's on the floor, curled in on herself, hands clenched over her ears in protection. Taru doesn't seem aware of Omar's hands, rubbing her back. Reena stares blankly at Jax as he swings around rapidly, murmuring a word repeatedly. Meiling can't be sure, but it sounds to her like "rain."

If he's asking his wife to produce some rain with her abilities passed down from Irene, Divinity of the Weather, then she isn't doing a great job at listening.

Among the chaos, Meiling doesn't see a cause for the strife. No intruders, no enemies, no threats at all. Disappointment bleeds into Meiling's veins. Her shoulders drop and Suraya's hand squeezes tighter in hers .

The light returns so abruptly it strains all six sets of eyes. Meiling physically jerks backward, feeling fire behind her eyelids.

In silence disrupted only by heavy breathing, they each readjust to the light and look at one another in shock. Meiling notices her father's eyes are stuck on her, close to tears, and her mother looks absolutely horrified. Suraya is ashen, Taru is trembling, and Omar is suspiciously blank, as if his attention has simply tapped out for a while.

To her own credit, Meiling is shaken, but due less to fear and more to pure exhaustion and disappointment. Her eyes strain as if chlorine is stuck in her lashes and her chest aches as if something heavy is laying on top of it. She isn't afraid of the Miyakos, despite what they did to her birth parents and a ton of other people that night thirteen years ago, but she is afraid of what it means for them to be active again.

Surely if the Miyakos are out of hiding, wreaking havoc across Malumvia after all this time, they're doing it with a reason. Any reason strong enough to have them risk themselves like this is a reason she won't be able to solve alone. That puts a serious damper on her plan to make a case for some of them being innocent.

As if she's only now remembered her lifelong grudge against anything and anyone even remotely reminiscent of the Mahina-descended Miyako family, Suraya turns on her heels and storms out of the house with sunlight circling her every limb. Meiling can hear her screaming down the streets, "Come out and face me head on, you cowards!" until the increasingly familiar tune of sirens drowns it out.

Omar wraps his arm around Taru as she curls into his side.

"I think it's time we go," he murmurs as they stand from crouching on the floor. He leaves his coat hanging on the back of his chair, but he doesn't seem to notice as he ushers his unspeaking wife outside.

In the silence ringing after the Zialitos leave, Meiling feels heavy. Her skin itches and her chest aches, almost exactly the same way it feels every time her medication needs an upped dosage. Although the Doctors have never been able to give one solid name to her ailment, they've linked it to her chest cavity. Something about her heart and blood flow doesn't function properly.

Meiling thinks about the pills she dropped down the sink drain earlier. It must be a coincidence. Meiling was willing to have her medication increased if it meant earning a shot at the Academy, but she doesn't want to live on it forever. Losing her dosage for today was actually a relief. Anytime anyone sees her and hears of her sickness, they coo at her with pity. But Meiling doesn't want pity; she wants respect. No matter what Suraya says, Meiling knows she's strong. All she has to do is wait for another opportunity to prove it.

Standing with the intention of following the Zialitos outside, Jax wraps a hand around Meiling's wrist and says, "Not you. You stay inside."

Meiling sits alone while Jax and Reena rush outside into the darkness and blaring sirens. Her breathing slowly steadies and her chest relaxes. In the aftermath, she feels better than ever: Alert and energetic with none of her medication's side effects around to tire her out. She makes a silent promise then to give herself more days like this.

Only when Jax and Reena return half an hour later does Meiling learn that one block over, deep into the land of Division Three, another M has been drawn in Sun-divine blood.

4
Suraya

On the day of the Academy exams, the last thing Suraya cares about are the Academy exams.

From the dawn of Divine descendants, the Miyakos and the Zialitos have wanted each other dead. They weaken each other by sheer shared existence. And as the strongest in the Zialitos family, Suraya is a walking target for the Miyakos. Technically she always has been, but with the Miyakos in hiding ever since the Lunar Eclipse Massacre, it's never actually mattered before now.

Every ability has a distinct feeling. While they differ from Divinity to Divinity, those of the Moon tend to be heavier. Suraya is confident in this since she's put in countless hours working with The Beams.

She's certain it was the Miyako's handiwork last night at the Katz residence. Despite the dozens of officers claiming it was only a blackout, Suraya knows better. A random blackout at the same exact time another M-attack killed three people down the block? Seems unlikely.

It's no question the Miyakos are responsible. Despite going into hiding after their Lunar Eclipse Massacre failed to do anything more than wipe out thousands of people, including many of their own, everyone knows they're out there. The leader of the massacre, Kaito Miyako, has been long confirmed dead and no new leader has risen in the ranks since. But it doesn't matter, anyway. A Miyako is a Miyako. They're historically evil.

The real question is *why now?*

Suraya paces back and forth outside the banquet hall where the Academy exams are to take place, her mind running rampant. For some reason, the Academy exams are taking place in a banquet hall down the street from her house rather than at the Academy campus itself—which is technically down the street from her house, as well, just in the opposite direction.

Suraya kicks loose gravel on the ground, memories of last night playing on loop in her mind. A couple of prospective students swerve around her to go inside with furrowed brows and whispers about her sanity. Suraya curses and throws a few rays of sunlight out of her palms. They scatter out and hit the pathway where more students are arriving.

"Watch it," one of them says.

"Watch yourself," Suraya grumbles. She wipes her sweaty palms off on her pants and breathes. She needs to focus. First the exams, then the Miyakos.

Once the doorway is empty again, Suraya enters alone. A number of Academy Administrators are waiting. As Suraya is led by one of them to the ballroom for the written portion of the exam, it's clear this won't be like her thirteenth birthday party: chandeliers, oversize bay windows, and a marble tabletop full of gifts. Looking around at the bleak walls, scraped-up tile floors, and dusty rectangular windows lined along the ceiling, Suraya realizes this may very well be the storage room where people tend to stuff excess chairs. Suffice to say, the Academy isn't living up to its grandeur so far.

With a long-suffering sigh, Suraya walks to the back row of desks and takes a seat in the center. From back here, she gets a full view of every wannabe-Academy student as they file in. Though some interesting characters waltz through—like twins of the legendary Kagiso family and a few Irene descendants with clouds and rainbows over their heads—not a single one of them is a Zialitos. Meaning, of course, she has no real competition here.

As nervous chattering picks up, Suraya's calm silence is quickly shattered. Locking her eyes onto Meiling, who is currently keeping to herself in the front row with slumped shoulders and messy bangs, Suraya wonders if today will be even worse than she expected.

When thick stacks of the exam are passed down each aisle of prospective students, the chattering peters out into uneasy silence. Suraya blocks her exam between her arms, ignoring the administrator's spiel, and jumps right in.

Five minutes in Suraya finishes the first four pages out of the ten-page exam. The questions are elementary. The first few consist of simply writing out the big eight Sun Divinities and their one grouping, and all of the corresponding Moon Divinities for each. Suraya could list these alphabetically with her eyes closed and her hands tied behind her back in the middle of a life-threatening battle.

Suraya scoffs to herself. *At this rate*, she thinks, *any idiot off the street could get into the Academy, the most prestigious Divine school in the world.*

As the timer runs out, papers are swept forward by the soft wind controlled by an administrator of Irene descent. Standing front and center in the stuffy room, she shuffles pages in the air before her without lifting a single finger. Precise control of that caliber is rare and exceptional, even for a Sun-gifted individual instructing at the Academy. Suraya can't help but watch as the papers move around while the woman's short brown hair blows back lightly.

In the distance, a blisteringly loud whistle is blown. With the increase in piercing sirens around the country recently, you'd think they would have a bit more sensitivity about these things. Half the room jolts out of their chairs with abilities firing off in a split second.

"Relax," Suraya announces to the room, "it's only the cue to move on to the physical exam."

Hearing her voice, Meiling swings around to find Suraya. Her eyes are heavy and dull, lined by purple bruises. Suraya raises a brow. Meiling may not be gifted enough for a place like this, but as much as Suraya is loath to admit it, she's more than smart enough. She was top ranked in academics all throughout elementary school. Aside from a creepily impressive memory, Meiling *likes* to learn. Suraya can't imagine this measly exam knocking her down so badly.

Meiling swallows thickly and turns away, joining the

hordes of other people as they stalk out of their seats to follow the sound of the whistle. Suraya watches until she's out of sight. Only then does she slide out of her own seat and leave.

Down one hallway and around one corner, there is a makeshift gymnasium where the physical exam will take place. The room is only a tad bit larger than the backyard training field Suraya uses at home. There are no windows, which will make gathering sunlight harder, but there is plenty of open space as well as crevices to hide in or sneak attack from. The walls are entirely made of thick squishy material and the floors are flat gray rubber. The only light comes from fixtures high up on the ceiling, caged in under thick steel bars. They flicker when the far doorway slams open and Headmaster Anji strides in followed by a few dozen people in black athletic suits.

Headmaster Anji, who has led the Academy for longer than Suraya's been alive, is a short, stocky man who confidently walks in with a gilded cane, even though everyone knows he has no limp or injury requiring him one. His hairline is receding, but his beard and mustache remain lush and thick, brown hairs sculpted to perfection.

"Gather around, children."

He punctuates each word with a tap of his cane against the floor beside his shiny shoes. Students flock to him eagerly, but Suraya stays on the outskirts. She spots Meiling crushed somewhere in the middle, swaying back and forth like a limp noodle. Her hair is frizzy and her eyes are beginning to glaze over just like when she's tired or overwhelmed. Suraya shakes her head. *I tried to warn her*, she thinks, *and now she's already gotten herself into more than she bargained for.*

"Welcome to the final round of examinations for The Zialitos Academy for Sun-Gifted Children," Headmaster Anji announces, bird-eyes scanning across the prospective students like pieces of meat. His voice echoes as if he is speaking into a microphone. "It is my utmost honor to be here with you all today. As the exam proceeds, I urge you to remain calm, as all of life's best laid plans succeed only with a sound mind."

Suraya bites back a sound that could very well be a laugh and a scoff all at once. A very pale girl with long blonde hair in an obscenely high ponytail on top of her head turns around at the noise. She's much taller than Suraya, but she is all skin and bones. Even her eyes, which are annoyingly bright blue with tiny blobs of silver, appear to be too thin, almost as if her entire body is in a constant state of near-disappearance.

Suraya expects to hear some stick-in-the-mud nagging, or a simple sharp glare meaning *where's your respect*, but the girl only catches her eye and smiles. Then she turns around again as if it never happened. Suraya steps up to stand by her side.

As Headmaster Anji rambles on with incomprehensible advice and halfhearted hopes of seeing each and every student in the halls next month, though they all know the Academy holds an acceptance rate of about ten percent on a good year, Suraya finally takes note of the people who entered with him.

Roughly estimating, there looks to be about fifty of

them. They vary in size and appearance quite drastically, but every one of them is done up in tight black athletic suits and chunky sneakers. Most haven't lifted their gazes from the floor so it's hard to get a good look at their faces. Something about them strikes Suraya as familiar nonetheless. She attempts to discreetly lower herself in an attempt to see a face or two. She spots nothing more than a scarred chin and some chapped lips before being jolted back to reality.

"Now, without any further delay," Headmaster Anji booms, tapping his cane once more. Suraya straightens. "The final portion of your entrance exam."

At last, the people in black suits shift about. They raise their heads and assume positions across the entire back side of the gymnasium. Their formation is far too organized for it to be a coincidence. Murmurs rise throughout the crowd of students.

"I'm sure most of you are familiar with The Beams program?" he asks, eyes landing on Suraya who feels ice drip into her veins at the name. She wants to scan over them in search of the dark-haired person, but she can't move. She holds eye contact.

Headmaster Anji continues, "This group is their most elite team. All of Moon descent, of course. Each one of them has been assigned a numerical value; that of which has been decided upon by myself and the rest of the Admissions Board based on the potency of their blood, the power of their abilities, and the value of their wit. Your job is simple: take them out. At the end of thirty minutes, those with the most points are our passing students."

The murmurs come to a sudden halt. Jaws fall open and stay there. Suraya keeps her own firmly shut, teeth grinding from the force. Headmaster Anji's focus shifts from her to somewhere in the middle of the crowd, somewhere where Suraya is certain Meiling's tripping over her own two feet. Suraya briefly wonders if it's still possible for her to take Meiling out of here by force.

Before there is a chance for anyone to do anything other than take a few steps backward, another whistle is blown and the countdown begins.

5
Meiling

The room swirls around Meiling. Her stomach churns and her eyes refuse to focus. The floor seems to break open underneath her feet, knocking her down with it. Whether that be an effect of the abilities going haywire around the gymnasium or not, Meiling isn't sure. Everything is happening faster than she can keep up with. It's like her brain has decided to put itself on a ten second delay all of a sudden.

Shaking her head, Meiling refocuses. This is her only shot. No known Malumvian lawmakers have come from a school other than the Academy. She has to get in. Her entire future is at stake here in this gymnasium.

From the corner of the room, Meiling catches Headmaster Anji's watchful gaze. All around her, people are already fighting. Each time someone goes down, he waves his hand and points appear on the projector against the far wall. Someone in a black suit slams into that very wall, and the stats shimmer like film before resettling. Suraya's number skyrockets when the person doesn't stand back up.

Headmaster Anji raises a brow as if to say, *and what can you do?*

Meiling curses, pulling herself to her feet. She'll show him exactly what she can do. She hasn't spent her entire life studying the abilities of Divine descendants for nothing.

In spite of her swimming vision, it's clear enough where she should go and who she should go after. The matching outfits are a Divinity-send. With the Headmaster's eyes on her, reminding her that everyone is waiting to see her fail, Meiling pushes forward.

Creeping around the corner, so slowly it must be a stroke of good luck no one immediately takes her out, she approaches someone from the back. He's tall, broad-shouldered, and completely immersed in his current one-on-one with a dark-skinned boy with light pink curls, eyes, *and* clothing.

Birds are flocking around the boy, seemingly in an attempt to help him out, but they're in panic-mode. Every time they dip low enough to be of use, the broad-shouldered man opens his mouth and exhales as if attempting to breathe fire and they scatter away again. The boy scowls down at his bare arms and watches as roots attempt to take place there. They sprout and immediately wilt.

The broad-shouldered man laughs. The vibrations of it are rough and uneven. Meiling theorizes he must be of Perce descent: The Moon Divinity of Destruction. Some of them can breathe out toxic gasses much the same way. They're the antagonists of nature. That pink boy must be a descendant of both Abungu, Divinity of Nature, and Kaitsja, Divinity of Wildlife. If Meiling is guessing right, that makes him a member of the Kagiso family.

Although Meiling feels bad for the Kagiso boy stuck in his worst possible one-on-one scenario with a Perce-descended man, she's thankful it allows her to fulfill *her* plan: sneak attacks.

Knowing nearly everything there is to know about all Divine descendants, even those least documented like Perce, Meiling is under no illusion she can take this man down head-on. Her best bet is to catch him while he's off guard, distracted by someone else. It feels underhanded, as if she's stealing points, but this is the best method she could come up with given her lack of abilities.

Using every ounce of her dangerously low energy and stability, Meiling rushes him from the back. She winds up her arm and throws the hardest punch she can muster directly at his neck, hoping it'll be enough to knock him out. The Kagiso boy notices only at the last second, leaving no time for his shocked expression to give her away. The man goes down with a resounding boom. Meiling nearly falls down after him, but a large hand keeps her up.

"Thanks," the Kagiso boy tells her, his voice soft like honey. She suspects the animals love that.

"Oh, uh, yeah, of course," she replies, breathless already.

His hand on her arm is the only thing keeping her upright. The room is shuddering and so is she. Her head thunders. Her vision spots. When it comes back, she notices the man on the ground lifting his head. He's dazed as their eyes meet. With a thick, audible swallow, he lays back down and shuts his eyes. The points under her name shoot up.

"What?" she mumbles, dumbfounded. Her body moves to pitch forward and the Kagiso boy hauls her upright yet again. "Why?"

He looks between her and the man knocked out on the floor multiple times before repeating, "What?"

Meiling stumbles away, tugging herself from his grip. She shakes her head until color bursts behind her eyelids. Not only is she on the brink of collapse, but she's so tired and hazy she's imagining things. She could have sworn he was getting back up until they locked eyes.

The Kagiso boy gives her a tight-lipped smile, clearly confused but grateful for her help nonetheless, and takes off in the other direction. Leaves curl around his arms and birds swarm in circles around his body. Meiling watches in awe as he takes out another member of The Beams within thirty seconds flat. She's not sure she has another in her. Her body is practically shutting down.

The room is in chaos. Bodies are flying—both literally and figuratively—and the abnormal noises and lights feel like a club. The sunlight flashes and screeching weapons pierce into her brain and stab her throbbing eyes. She slinks back to where she'd been hiding earlier and buries her head in her hands. It blocks out some of the chaos, but not enough. Her heart slams against her ribcage like a trapped animal fighting to be free.

Time is nearing its end now. Headmaster Anji

announces the five-minute countdown, but his voice is barely audible over everything else. Meiling peers through her fingers at the state of the gymnasium around her. It looks like an honest to Divinity *war*. Students and The Beams alike are bruised and bloody, unleashing their abilities full-force with no regard for the damage it leaves behind.

Holes are torn and burnt in the walls, the rubber of the floor is somehow cracking, and the light fixtures high in the ceiling have been shattered through their protective coverings. Meiling, against her deepest desires, is terrified. This is exactly what she wishes to change in their world— this fighting between people based on their blood, on the things they can't control. It's sickening to experience it first-hand, even if it's not technically real.

"*You.*" Meiling shrinks further into herself at the sound of Suraya's angry voice. "I knew it."

But she's not looking at Meiling. It doesn't seem like she has noticed Meiling at all yet. Suraya's eyes are wide and wild, boring holes into the short, dark-haired person a few meters away in the other direction. The person looks back at her and grins. There's blood in their mouth. Suraya has a string of sunlight twirling between her fingers like a lasso. It's so thin and dull, it's obvious she's tiring. With one sharp jerk of her arm, it lashes out and trips the other person. It flickers like a weak lightbulb, but Suraya somehow keeps it alive long enough to drag them across the floor to her feet. Meiling can't make out the expression on her face, but she can make out the tears of blood curling down her chin. This alone is enough to make her nearly unrecognizable as Meiling's childhood best friend.

"Who are you working for?" Suraya asks.

The person manages to move their arm just enough to motion around the room. "The Beams obviously."

Suraya brings her foot down hard on their chest. Meiling hears a sickening crunch of bone. The person coughs out more blood.

"I know it was you," she growls, sweat falling down the column of her neck. "You followed me to the Katz's house. You made the dark cloud. So I'll ask again, who are you working for?"

Meiling pulls herself to her feet. Suraya is going too far. That person is clearly near their breaking point. Otherwise they would have fought back by now. And what's that about her house? How could this person have had anything to do with it?

"Suraya," she tries to call, but her throat is in shreds. She can hardly breath as is.

The person continues hacking, but Suraya won't let up. The string of sun somehow brightens with time. It coils tighter around the person's ankles and up their legs until their entire body is being strangled by it. A boa constrictor of sunlight.

"I don't"—they choke off and try again—"I don't know what you're talking about."

"Liar." It winds further up their neck.

"Suraya!" Meiling tries again. She stumbles forward on her feet until it's impossible not to notice her. Suraya swings on her with a fierce look. It falters at the sight of her. This single falter is enough for her sunlight to die out. The person rolls over onto their hands and knees and coughs. Suraya looks furious, ready to recapture them immediately.

"Stop it," Meiling says, putting her hands out in a placating gesture. "I think they've had enough."

Suraya smacks her hands down and it's enough to send Meiling toppling to her butt on the floor. Suraya stares at her hands as if misunderstanding her own strength. Then she squints down at Meiling.

"Stay out of this."

Suraya clutches her temples as if there's something there. There isn't, from what Meiling can tell, but granted, she can't tell much. She's not even sure which version of Suraya is the real one. Or if the dark-haired person on their feet behind her is a figment of her imagination or not. She tries to raise a finger to point them out, but her arms have officially given up movement.

The person turns their attention to her and grins a bit maniacally. Meiling stops seeing the gymnasium altogether.

Instead, she sees a suspiciously familiar woman laying face down in concrete. Someone is screaming behind her and someone else is sobbing by her side. She can't see any of them clearly. She can only see the woman laying down like the brushstrokes of an oil painting.

With a tiny, plump hand, Meiling reaches out and brushes a strand of the dark gray hair away from the woman's face. Her skin is pale and covered in freckles like

Meiling's own. Her eyes are squeezed shut and her mouth is slightly ajar. She's not breathing.

Meiling screams. Suddenly there is a sobbing boy by her side.

"Lay down with her," he whispers.

Against her will, Meiling feels herself shifting to lay down beside the bloody woman.

"There you go," the boy says, "Now play dead. I'm sorry. I'm so sorry."

Meiling screams until the vision vanishes.

All around her the gymnasium is silent and still. The timer has long since gone off and The Beams are making their way out single file. The dark-haired person backs away without taking their eyes from Meiling. Suraya is watching her, too. She can't tell what's causing the lines across her forehead. Meiling's not sure of anything other than the fact the exam is over. It's over and she's certain she failed it.

She swivels to look at the scorecard wall, but it's blank. She can't tell how badly she failed.

Beside the wall, Headmaster Anji stands smiling—if you can call the tiny curve at the corners of his mouth a smile. It rises a bit higher when Meiling forces herself to stand straight and catch his eyes. He crosses the gymnasium toward her slowly. The tapping of his cane is the only sound aside from heavy breathing. He stops by Meiling's side and extends a gloved hand to her. She takes it and is surprised to find he's strong enough to tug her up on his own.

"I expect great things from you, Meiling," he says, voice so low she's not certain she heard it right.

Then she's alone, back to swaying on her feet. Headmaster Anji meanders out of the gymnasium without another word. He leaves behind nothing but a strong scent of eucalyptus and the words ringing inside of Meiling's already overwhelmed head.

For a long while after, there is no movement. Students stand around dazed and confused, their battered bodies strung up on adrenaline. It is only when the Academy Nurses come bustling in that they seem to realize the severity of the exam. The room bursts into noise and movement; gasping, crying, groaning, stretching, crawling, limping. Blurs of color go in every direction. Meiling thinks she sees two Kagiso boys, but one is covered head-to-toe in black clothing instead of pink like she remembers. When she blinks they both disappear, already having been moved elsewhere.

Meiling stands still, gasping for breath. Aside from her, only one other person in the entire gymnasium remains motionless and alone despite their injuries: Suraya.

While chaos swirls around them, their gazes drift until they can only stare only at each other. Meiling tries to ignore the narrowing of Suraya's eyes. She knows what that means: *I told you so.*

6
Anji

"Divinia of the Prophecy, I humbly present you an offering in exchange for your infinite wisdom in which I seek."

Anji tears a golden gem from his cane and tosses it alongside a strand of his gray hair into the short flames of fire inside his hearth. The Headmaster's office provided by The Academy has grown over the years. What was once no more than a broom closet is now a one bedroom apartment complete with a bathroom, kitchen, and an oversize fireplace.

Flames burst upward and shift into a beautiful silver before relaxing into their usual orange once again. The air feels lighter and clearer, tinged with the scent of clean linen, as the flames settle.

Messengers, such as Anji and his family, have special blood, different from those borne from the Divinities. With offerings of both their own DNA and something of value, they can recruit Divinities into lower forms and communicate as they desire. Anji most often calls upon Divinia of the Prophecy whose endless knowledge has yet to steer him wrong.

She appears at once in the flames, her body a shimmering silver projection over a waterfall. The flames lick up the silky fabric of her long white dress without burning. She says nothing in greeting, she never does, but her eyes fix on Anji in anticipation. Her eyes hold every imaginable color—rainbow swirls that make it difficult to face her head on. The rest of her is a pale white; from the long straight hair to the smooth hands interlaced over her chest. Divinia is an otherworldly being Anji has loved for as long as he's lived.

"Your grace," he greets, allowing his cane to fall as he drops to kneel before her.

"Sir Anji."

Divinia has a monotone voice, one that travels through the air with no clear place of origin and no clear destination. Sometimes when she speaks, it feels like being lulled into a trance. Much to Anji's displeasure, she gives so little away in her speech. Many would say this means she lacks emotion, but he knows better. She simply cannot fall prey to emotion. Not with her gifts.

"I seek your wisdom in the future of my academy," he tells her with as strong of a voice as he can muster in the presence of her power. She appreciates directness and hates hesitance. He does what she wants.

"What of it?"

He tries to catch her gaze, but trying to make eye contact with Divinia is the same as trying to find the center of a kaleidoscope.

"Meiling Katz has passed the exams, but I fear the consequences of her acceptance."

"You wish for my divine intervention in the rejection of a singular student?"

Her voice rattles his framed accomplishments and blows away the stacks of paperwork on his desk. His skin burns from the height of the flames. He remains on his knees at her full mercy.

"I seek your wisdom in what those consequences may be, and if they may prove profitable in our future."

The corners of Divinia's thin lips quirk. She takes a moment to think, as always, before she answers. With Divine insight, her voice is even farther away. It sounds like it has been funneled through a thousand speakers before it reaches Anji's ears, clear and calm, distant and detached.

She says, "Meiling's existence holds great weight in the future of Malumvia. Her possible paths are endless, but the outcome remains the same in every one. She is a case I have not seen the likes of in centuries."

Anji lets Divinia's words wash over him and repeat endlessly through his head while he wonders whether or not that divine wisdom is one he wants to take his chances on. He believes it probably is.

"Be that as it may," Divinia continues, a sliver of emotion beginning to seep into her words. Though, what that emotion is, Anji is unsure. It's so unfamiliar in her voice he can't place it. "You cannot control the response of society to her. She may prove to be a vessel of great change, Sir Anji, but it is my responsibility to urge you to—"

The fire roaring shakes her form and drowns out the

rest of her sentence. The air instantly morphs from clean and clear to dense and dim. Debris and ash from the fire swirl in the space before him, blurring his view of the hearth. Breathing becomes a chore, the air heavy like lead in his lungs. It tastes like burnt leather. He nearly chokes on it.

"Ignorance from a lowly human I expected," a scratchy voice fills the room, "but from you, my dearest sister? It's rather counterintuitive, is it not?"

"We are not siblings," Divinia replies quickly, almost as if she's been programmed to snap back should anyone call her a sister. Then she falls silent once more.

When the smoke clears, Divinia is no longer alone in the flames. Standing by her side, body shimmering in the exact same shade of silver, is Viera, Divinity of Ignorance. Anji curses himself for seeing the resemblance, for admitting—even to himself silently—that he can see them as siblings. Viera has equally pale skin and long white hair, all sleek and perfected like Divinia's. Even his way of dress is the same: silky white cloth covering nearly every centimeter of him. The only clear distinction, aside from the feeling of their presence, are their eyes. Viera's are entirely black. Looking directly into them is like staring down a starless night sky: infinite nothing.

"Ouch," Viera says, his holographic-seeming hand moving to clutch at his chest. Divinia scowls.

Anji cannot find words. He's never summoned a Divinity of the Moon before. It's forbidden to do so without explicit permission from the government. They seem to always find things like that out, even if one is as cautious and discrete as humanly possible. And yet he knows this is Viera in the fire, and somehow it is his fault for bringing him here.

The Divinity must notice his floundering and confusion because those black eyes turn on him. Viera tilts his head, examining Anji, and a log pops by his feet, fire jumping out. Anji pulls his hands back just in time to avoid them being burnt by some of it.

"You call for advice, you receive those who can give it. Divinia and I share the same plane to reach your land. It's not difficult to know what the other is up to. Nor is it difficult to join them. Isn't that right, sis?"

Another log pops, but the fire from it shoots across from Divinia's side of the hearth to his. It only makes his grin grow wider.

"Headmaster Anji, I believe you have a question for me? Seeing as I am the Divinity of Knowledge and all?" he asks, smiling.

"*Ignorance,*" Divinia corrects. "Divinity of Ignorance."

Viera feels much harsher than Divinia, but his voice is more human. *He* feels more human. Anji carefully considers the dangers of such a trait, and then decides it is worth the risk. Messengers like him are constantly overlooked in Malumvia, made out to be like slaves to those of Sun descent, so why shouldn't he try catering to those of the Moon for a change?

"Ugh. You call out the ignorance of people *one time.* Then your intelligence doesn't even matter anymore, the new title just sticks to you like tape." Viera pulls a face. "Wait, is that right? Tape? Or is the saying—"

"*Viera*," Divinia cuts in.

He waves her off. "Fine. Whatever. Doesn't matter. This conversation involves me either way."

"It does not."

"It does too. Meiling is not of Sun descent, now is she? *You* can't even claim her. This is a much bigger issue."

"I see her future, Viera, and it is…"

In his awe, Anji misses the rest of their argument. He moves his head back and forth between them as they bicker like a couple of school children. He's never witnessed something so unbecoming of a Divinity before. It lights up a new viewpoint in his mind; one where Meiling's importance is truly impossible to ignore. Going out on a limb, he interrupts them to ask Viera the same question he originally summoned Divinia for.

Divinia falls silent and Viera chuckles. It's a deep, bone-rattling sound, but not wholly unpleasant like Anji would have expected it to be.

"People are ignorant. *You* are ignorant," he answers, though it's not exactly clear if he's saying this to Anji or Divinia, who is continuing to glower by his side. "You think you know that child now? You think with Divinia's vague wisdom, everything will work out? No. No, silly little human, it won't be that way. Divinia cannot lie, but she can certainly withhold."

Divinia's eyes flash with color. Her shimmering body sways back and forth with the flames.

"Then tell me what I can do," Anji pleads. Although history does not show it, admitting a child like Meiling to the Academy has happened before. Anji himself has let it happen before. He cannot do so again in good faith if the consequences will be the same now as they were then. "Shall I allow her in, even with her blood as it is?"

"Especially with her blood as it is," Viera confirms, his form becoming more solid and clear. "Her fate holds what you seek, Marion Anji."

Anji shivers at the sound of his full name in Viera's mouth. The flames grow within the fireplace, but the room is bitter cold. Anji licks his lips and thinks the words over. If Meiling's fate can lead him to what he desires, he does not care what catastrophe that very same fate might bring along with it. He only cares that Meiling fills her role.

"Enough Viera," Divinia cuts in once more. "Do not let him lead you astray with false promises, Sir Anji."

"Tell me," Anji begins, lacing his hands over his cane. "Is Meiling's fate a prophecy?"

"The words have come from a prophet, have they not?" Viera responds, stretching out like a cat in the sunlight across the fireplace. Divinia frowns in the corner where she is now squished.

Legend has never called Viera a prophet, though Anji supposes it only makes sense. For every Sun Divinity, there is a Moon Divinity counterpart. Their abilities, while opposing in nature, draw a fine line of similarity. Ignorance is a power all the same as knowledge.

"Thank you, your grace." Anji bows deeply. "Is there any more you can say on it? Perhaps in relation to the Miyakos and these recent M-attacks?"

"Pfft. Miyakos. M-attacks. Yes, I knew you'd hope for

a simple solution to those. Let me tell you one last thing, then: the first step to stopping these M-attacks is Meiling's acceptance to the Academy."

Anji's eyes light up. If he makes the choice to accept Meiling, and Meiling really can stop the M-attacks, he will be praised for a lifetime at the least. Being overlooked as a mere Messenger will never again plague him.

"Do not—"

Before Divinia can continue, Viera winks and pops away with a cloud of smoke, dragging her out with him. The fire turns bright red for a fraction of a second before resettling. Divinia's clean linen scent disappears immediately, leaving behind only Viera's burnt leather. Breathing in deeply, Anji finds it to be something of an acquired taste.

In the wreckage of papers strewn across his floor, he finds Meiling's applications and test scores. Accompanying her Divine Blood Tests and doctor's authorizations, she has written a formal letter of interest addressed to him personally. Smiling, Anji staples her written exam with a ninety-nine percent score—the highest of any—and stares in awe at her physical exam score, as well. Taking down that Perce descendant, one of "The Beams" best fighters, skyrocketed her ranking just enough so she scored in the top ten.

With the words of Viera in his mind, but those of Divinia on paper, Anji writes the official Academy acceptance letter for Miss Meiling Katz.

7

Suraya

Suraya has roughly one million problems and all of them can be accredited to one Meiling Katz.

Acceptance to The Academy based solely on her own strength and intelligence was supposed to be the biggest news of the year in Malumvia, and Meiling's *lack* of acceptance was supposed to be her biggest relief. Yet both of these plans have fallen to a bunch of tiny little pieces now that Meiling has secured her spot beside Suraya in the Academy's upcoming class. How is she meant to focus on studying to be the next Head of Malumvia when she has Meiling's safety to worry about?

Suraya groans as her father drives her to the dorms. Her mother was supposed to come and help her move in, or at the very least say goodbye, but she changed her mind once she heard the Katz would be there. They may be Omar's friends, but they aren't Taru's. She's terrified of Jax. She could never handle watching him move his ability-lacking kid into a dorm meant for the Zialitos elite.

The Academy campus looms at the top of the hill in the near distance as Omar turns the car onto the main road. Before they can drive any closer, the tires screech to a halt and the vehicle shakes. A loud, delayed echo of an explosion follows, the entire street quaking.

The front windshield shatters as Suraya wrangles in a raging sphere of sunlight twice the size of her own head. Unnatural disasters can only mean one thing, and Suraya will not pass up the chance to destroy them.

"Suraya Zialitos!" her father shouts, jerking up the emergency brake as the shaking ground flings them forward. "Put the sunlight away!"

Sirens. Suraya grits her teeth and holds onto the sunlight tighter. She's tired of hearing sirens.

It takes a moment for her to realize only half the noise ringing in her eardrums is actually from the sirens. The other half is from the shrill, relentless ringing of her father's cellphone.

Omar answers the call with one hand and brushes a lock of Suraya's hair behind her ear with the other. It's only half a second of contact, but it's enough: his Divinia-passed ability to draw forth happy memories floods through Suraya's brain at once. Her anger ebbs away until her ball of sunlight is half its original size. Suraya hates that aspect of Divinia's blood almost as much as she hates every aspect of Mahina's.

The ground has stilled beneath them by the time Suraya's mother shrieks through the phone, "They're back, oh Ataru, they're back. Are you alive? Omar, are you alive?"

"I'm fine, Taru," her father says gently. Even the tone of his voice works to hold Suraya's mind in a place of positivity. No matter how much she shakes around against it, her thoughts remain firmly on the memory of her first summoned sunbeam. "They aren't back. Calm down. It was only a minor earthquake."

This statement does little to appease Suraya or her mother: earthquakes can easily be created by those of Moon descent all the same. Not Miyakos, of course, but those with the blood of Tal, Moon Divinity of Storms, certainly could. Who's to say they aren't working together to begin with?

"It was not!" Taru yells. Suraya winces and leans farther away from the phone. It's not even on speaker. "It was another attack, Omar. The Mahina Temple in Division Five. They blew it to pieces. All evidence of the first M-attack, gone. It's on the news already!"

"Gone?" Suraya echoes, clenching her fists. Tiny pieces of glass from the windshield draw blood between her palms as she does.

"Gone! They haven't reported any injuries or deaths yet, thank Ataru, but it's only been a few minutes and all that evidence... Divinities, what do they *want*?"

Suraya releases her fists and lets the glass and blood drip out of her palms. The sunlight climbs her arms in protective rings.

"Bring my bags to me later."

She doesn't wait for a response from her father before throwing the door open and waltzing right out into the middle of the street. Alongside the sirens wailing in the distance, there are plenty of people wailing right here.

Suraya storms up the winding road toward the Academy and ignores every last one of them.

Suraya may not be as hysterical as her mother, but she can't help but wonder the same question: What in Nirnasha's Underworld do the Miyakos want? The evidence may be destroyed, but it was already documented elsewhere. This hasty cover-up attempt won't save them.

Nothing will save them so long as she's alive.

Suraya squeezes past parked cars and crowds of people toward the Academy campus. People are flooding out of their homes and businesses into the streets with cameras. Suraya spots a middle-aged woman sobbing and thinks again of her mother.

"What happened?" A random passerby asks her in a panic. "Why are you out here alone? Where are your parents?"

"Oh Divinities, it's a Zialitos!" says another. "Are you okay, Miss Zialitos?"

"Let us walk you, let us walk you. Ataru above, it isn't safe for you out here."

Suraya blows out a long breath. She stops, bows once quickly to the elders, and says, "I'm fine, but you're right, it isn't safe. You should get inside yourselves."

They bow back, each giving her the prayer to Ataru, and race off for the nearest building to hide inside. For the remainder of her walk up the hill, Suraya keeps her eyes on the ground and runs.

Headmaster Anji is standing guard outside the large bronze gate when she arrives.

"Miss Zialitos, for Ataru's sake, what are you doing out here alone?"

The Academy campus is set up on top of a massive hill in Division One, making the giant bronze gates and winding pathways seem otherworldly. Standing before those very gates, Anji welcomes her with the same off-putting grin he watched Meiling with during the physical exam.

"I could ask the same of you," Suraya replies, arching a brow. Anji may be the Headmaster of the Zialitos Academy for Sun-Gifted Children, but Suraya is a Zialitos herself. A mere Messenger like him could never stand above her.

His smile goes lopsided.

"There is nothing to worry about. It was merely a scare tactic," he says, jerking the latch on the gate free with his cane. "Una Zialitos announced that thus far they've found no evidence to suggest it's anything other than a nonviolent M-attack."

Suraya bites back a short laugh. Nonviolent M-attack. Una Zialitos sure knows how to name things. One day Suraya will take Head of Malumvia from her and do a much better job.

Behind the gates, the Academy campus sprawls out across the horizon. Dorm halls with high arched windows, class buildings with golden trims, jagged pathways made of cobblestone and steel, and a courtyard full of Sun-gifted students. And Meiling.

Suraya spots her by the fountain at the edge of the courtyard. She seems lost in thought, murmuring aimlessly to one of the Kagiso twins: a boy decked out in pink who's petting koi fish in the water with his bare hands. If she's heard the news about what rocked the country not ten minutes ago, she doesn't seem to care very much.

Suraya rolls her eyes so far into her head she loses sight for a full five seconds. When it comes back, there's a tall girl with a long blonde ponytail and bright blue eyes standing beside her. She's just far enough away to not get burnt by Suraya's sunlight bracelets.

"Can I help you?" Suraya asks.

"I'm Evie!" she says, her smile blinding. "Evie Shineski. I'm of Omni Descent. I can see spirits and talk to them and sense bad energy and stuff. Oh, and I can shift into a bodiless spirit state in the spirit realm, too, but not for very long. I'm not good at holding it yet."

"Great. Thanks for sharing, Eve."

"Evie," she corrects, completely unfazed. "You're a Zialitos, right? You've got the eyes."

Suraya bites down her tongue. Being known for nothing more than her family is exactly why she wanted to get into the Academy on her own. That way she could just be Suraya for once. But, of course, her bright silver-blue eyes are too much of a dead giveaway. She grunts in acknowledgment.

"I'm so glad to see you here," Evie continues. "It's super cool you took the exams. I mean, we all know you didn't have to, but you did anyway! I think that's super cool. Very respectable. Anyways, what's your name?"

Suraya regards Evie from the corner of her easily-identifiable Zialitos eyes. Evie, while so thin and pale

Suraya thought her to be in a state of near-disappearance when they first met, is full of life. So full of it, in fact, it's actually rather annoying.

Regardless, Evie here is the first person to acknowledge Suraya's personal achievements over her family name in probably her entire life, and she can't help but be pleased by it. As far as potential allies go, she isn't a bad start.

"My name's Suraya," she answers finally.

"It's nice to meet you, Suraya," Evie says, ducking her head into a bow. "Pretty crazy move-in day, isn't it?"

A chill ripples across Suraya's skin. Flicking her enhanced eyesight to life, she swirls around to search the area. In every corner there are people playing around with their abilities, showing off, but nowhere are there any of the Moon.

"Uh, Suraya?"

Suraya shushes her quietly. A chill like this can only come from Moon residuals. It's nearly the same as the one she felt at the Katz residence days ago.

Straining her eyes, Suraya focuses on seeing father. Ataru passes down a litany of abilities, namely those to manipulate the Sun, but also those to identify anyone who manipulates the Moon. Thicker skin, stronger eyes, longer stamina, self-healing bodies; it's all her Divine-given right. Her body, blood and all, is made for moments like this.

Past the bronze gates where she came, there are two paths down the hill—the windy street she walked up on, and the unpaved walking trail into the woods. Perched within the trees clustered around the trail, Suraya finds her target.

Whoever it is, they're cloaked in dark robes and an elaborate mask. The feathers on the mask are entirely black, but the beak section over their mouth and the fabric stretched over their eyes is a pale yellow. Suraya can't tell for certain because of this fabric, but it seems whoever this is, they are watching someone in this very courtyard.

Normally the Academy has a stationed patrolling officer from the Zialitos Headquarters for safety. Today, because of the Mahina Temple attack, every last officer in the country is either in or on their way to Division Five.

A perfect diversion.

"Evie," Suraya says, low and stern, not daring to move her eyes away from the person in the tree, "go get a teacher."

Evie clumsily rushes off with a nod. The person in the tree shifts, branches rustling around their body. A feather gets tugged off and floats down to the ground below. Suraya understands who they are at once.

When a sleepy-eyed teacher shows up by Suraya's side with Evie, she wastes no time.

"Down the trail on the right. Tallest tree, two branches down."

The teacher braces his big hands on his knees and squints toward the tree. Without eyes like hers, it takes him much longer to pinpoint the threat. When he finally does, he exhales what very well may be the longest sigh Suraya has ever heard in her life.

"I see." He straightens up and pats Suraya once on the shoulder. "Good catch, kid."

Suraya puffs up her chest with a self-satisfied grin. Of course, it's a good catch. She doesn't have Ataru's eyes for nothing.

Without another word, the teacher turns on his heels and walks away. His feet drag through the grass and kick up dirt.

"Oi, hold on!" Suraya reluctantly tears her gaze from the tree to jog after him. "Where are you going? You saw who that was, didn't you?"

"Who is it?" Evie chimes in, her voice high and uneven. Everyone is on edge today enough already.

"I saw who it was," the teacher confirms dryly, rubbing his temples.

"Then where are you going?" Suraya shouts.

The other students turn their way at the disruption. A number of them drift closer and form a semi-circle around the teacher who looks like his entire life is up in flames.

"For the love of Kaitsja, give me a minute," he says, holding the students off with both arms.

"That's a member of The Birds of Prey," Suraya snaps, unable to play it cool anymore. She rapidly swings her head back and forth to make sure the bird guy hasn't moved yet.

The teacher's eyes blow out wide. He hushes her, but it's too late. Everyone has heard her already.

The Birds of Prey are a gang of criminals with the blood of Eben, Moon Divinity of Battle, who scout and assassinate—mostly for the Miyako family, as history has it. They're one of the biggest threats in the country. If they're out of a decade-long hiding to watch a group of Academy First Years on their move-in day, there's something seriously wrong here. Suraya won't have some slow-moving teacher getting them killed over it.

"Moon-descended criminals," Suraya emphasizes, as if anyone should need explanation on this. "Psychopaths who dress like birds and prey on people for sport. Notorious for working with the Miyako family, who, as we all know, are quite active these days. Remember that explosion earlier?"

Slack jaws and silence answer her from the students. The teacher rubs his jaw and begins, "Miss Zialitos, please—"

"Is any of this ringing a bell to anyone?"

Evie, in a voice much quieter than earlier, breaks the tense quiet after Suraya's outburst to say, "The Birds of Prey. The name's a bit on the beak, don't you think?"

Suraya blows out a long breath. If The Birds of Prey choose to attack, she's confident she's their only chance of not dying.

8
Meiling

One second Meiling is sitting on the edge of the courtyard's fountain, watching Callum Kagiso pet koi fish and wax poetic about algae, and the next she's sprawled out in the dirt from a gust of wind made by a bunch of giant flapping wings.

Half the students go running and screaming toward the Academy entrance while the other half square up to fight. Meiling herself can't find the energy to do either. Through shaky vision darkened at the edges, the norm since she's periodically given herself medication-free days, she sees The Birds of Prey closing in.

"Get back!" someone yells.

Meiling thinks it's another one of the First Year teachers—one currently un-pecked by a monstrous aviator—but she can't be too sure. There's a tinny ringing in her ears that only Suraya's voice clearly overpowers. And although it's not hard to make out what she's shouting, Meiling isn't inclined to repeat a word of it.

Shifting into a seated position with the help of Callum's damp hands, Meiling searches the area. The

Academy courtyard is a vast open space in front of the main building. Aside from the oversize fountain full of koi fish and the mismatched pathway to the bronze gate leading out, there's nothing more than grass and the occasional flower patch. Due to this, it's startlingly easy to locate the assailants.

From what Meiling's untrustworthy eyesight can make out, there are three of these Birds of Prey people. All of their masks are made of black feathers, but each one is a different bird—an eagle, a raven, and an owl. All of them appear to have been gifted with flight from their Eben blood. Eben, the Moon Divinity of Battle, passes on what Meiling personally deems to be the strangest mix of abilities for any lineage. Many have modified bodies capable of producing nonhuman parts and weapons, some have animalistic creatures residing inside of them, some can fly and feel absurdly intimate attachments to the sky, a rare few can mimic the speech of any living being, and others simply have nothing more than quick-wit and enhanced survival instincts.

With a vast and powerful mix of abilities, it's interesting that so many of Eben's descendants end up as members of this gang working for others. Those like the Miyako family.

Meiling's gaze catches on the Raven. Unlike the others, this one has no fabric over their eyes, just tiny open holes in which the green of their irises is visible. Also different from the others, the feathers are scarce on this one. Most of the mask is a black-painted skull so intricate it's hard to believe it's not a real skeleton. The Raven stares back, pupils shifting between large and small rapidly. It feels like receiving a full body X-ray, tingly and body-freezing.

The fabric pooling around their chest opens like a gaping pit, a cluster of angry grayish-brown finches bursting from within. With a gasp, Meiling realizes they're flocking her way.

She has nowhere to run, nowhere to hide, and absolutely no one to help.

Meiling attempts to swerve out of the path of the finches, but they follow her with every maneuver. On the ground, swatting away finch after finch, Meiling realizes the Birds of Prey are not chasing anyone else.

The other two—the Eagle and the Owl—are simply creating chaos to occupy everyone else in the courtyard. The Raven is the only one hunting, and it's only hunting her.

"Why me?" she cries, covering her face from the danger of those pecking beaks. Like a million tiny needle points, they pierce her hands instead. Once they tear skin and spill blood, coating each beak thoroughly, they retreat in a gust of wind.

The phantom pain in her hands is eerily reminiscent of the thick needles Doctor Sutherland uses on her all the time. Meiling sits up sluggishly, scratching at the open marks dripping blood down her fingers.

"Why me?" she asks again, but there is no one around to answer even if they wanted to.

In a shockwave much too similar to the explosion

from the earlier M-attack, the earth tremors underneath Meiling's body.

The Birds of Prey and the students fighting them freeze at once. Their expressions show parallel images of shock and fear.

"Hey!" Meiling shouts, trying to project her voice over the sudden panic, "Hey, birdies! Yoohoo, over here!"

A dozen heads snap her way, the Birds of Prey included. The Raven remains fluttering in the air a meter or so ahead , the Eagle perches on top of the fountain, and the Owl lands on the ground twenty meters away. All of them watch her with interest.

Meiling sucks in a breath and pushes herself to her feet. She refuses to let them come in here, cause a ruckus, cut her hands open, and leave again just like that. They owe everyone some answers, and Meiling is going to prove herself right here by being the one to get them.

"Okay," she says, swirling her tongue around her mouth. It feels heavy, as if there's an anchor weighing it down inside her mouth. "Okay, listen here, Birds of Prey, we don't want to fight."

"Speak for yourself," Suraya chimes in from somewhere to her right, somewhere near the fountain. Meiling knows this because she hears a splash of water, presumably from the Owl, and the answering flash of sunlight sizzling it away into steam in the air, obviously from Suraya.

"We don't want to fight," Meiling repeats, her head buzzing. The harsh fluttering of the Raven's wings ahead is not helping her keep focus here. "We only want to know what you want. Tell us what you're here for and maybe we can settle this am–amickle—amickely—"

Meiling cuts herself short, frowning deeply. Not only is her tongue heavy, it's useless. She's slurring her words now. A distant part of her wonders if this is due in part to her skipping her medication this morning. In fact, she's skipped it most days since the first time.

The pause stretches into a terribly awkward silence until someone guesses, "Amicably?" and Meiling snaps her fingers in relief and agreement both.

"Yes! That. Amicably. *Am-ick-ah-blee*. Amicably."

"What in Ataru's name is wrong with you?" Suraya asks.

Meiling wishes she had an answer, but she has no clue what's wrong with her. Is there something wrong with her? She feels a bit drunk right now—despite never having been drunk before for comparison—but otherwise she's honestly not too bad. The heavy ache that typically lies deep in her chest—the one Doctor Sutherland tells her came from her mysterious sickness as a toddler—is lightening up at last, even without the medication.

"We're here to scout," one of the Birds answers belatedly. The voice echoes in Meiling's ears from all directions, making it impossible to tell where it truly came from.

Meiling forces her mouth open to ask a follow-up question, but thankfully someone else beats her to it with a much clearer voice.

A very tall boy with black hair tied into a half bun on top of his head comes to stand beside her. Holding her steady by the elbow, he asks the Birds of Prey a simple, but important, question:

"Scouting for who?"

Meiling blinks rapidly, hoping to snap herself out of her haze, when she notices the Birds hesitating to answer. Their heads are shaking around on their necks like loose bobbleheads. Meiling has only seen visceral reactions like that in response to questions asked by those of Divinia descent—those who can force people to speak the truth.

Her eyes light up with the quick realization: of course, this boy is of Divinia descent; this is the Academy for Sun-Gifted Children. He straightens his back, somehow getting taller, and zeroes in on the Raven. His brown eyes flare into a golden brown the longer he stares.

"Scouting for who?" he repeats, louder now.

Meiling holds her breath as his abilities flood through the air and a singular word gets ripped from the Raven's throat.

The answer: "Mikazi."

Without missing a single beat, the skinny girl with the long blonde ponytail that was following Suraya around says, "Who in the world is Mikazi?"

You took the words from my mouth, Meiling thinks. She's done more research on Malumvia and all its little facets in her near sixteen years than most people do in their entire lives, and still the name Mikazi rings no bells. Which, quite frankly, means there's little to no chance it does for anyone else. Meiling shrugs helplessly. This is not turning out the way she planned.

"Have patience," the Raven says, voice a bit rougher

now that the truth has been forcibly pulled out through it. "In due time, not a single soul, living or dead, will not know him."

Him. Meiling clings to that. It's not an answer, but it rules out what everyone else is clearly thinking: *Miyakos.*

The doors to the Academy fly open behind them with a bang. An army's worth of students equipped with the strangest display of abilities and weapons Meiling's ever seen spill out. The Birds immediately flock together into the sky and escape through the clouds. A few of her classmates, including her new friend with the pink hair, Callum Kagiso, attempt to chase after them. In the end it means nothing; they escape as easily as smoke rises.

Leading the pack racing to their aid is a fluffy guinea pig. He crawls underneath a pile of clothing strewn across the grass and immediately pops back into a human, fully clothed.

"Is anyone hurt?" he shouts out.

A chorus of *no*'s fill the air from the students. Meiling flicks her gaze down to her bloody hands, curls them into each other to hide the damage, and says absolutely nothing.

The man's shoulders droop and he lets out a deep sigh. It squeaks almost as if he's still half a guinea pig.

Meiling realizes with a start that this is her new homeroom teacher, Mr. Arredondo. She can't believe she didn't process it right away; she's read about him in the Academy archives only about a thousand times. His descent comes from both Kaitsja, Sun Divinity of Wildlife, and Chae-Won, Sun Divinity of Creation, explaining why he can so easily transform into a fluffy little animal. Any combination of Divine blood comes with its own unique, hybrid abilities. Although under those of the Moon, there's not much data to speak of. One day Meiling will track that down, too.

"We learned something about the Miyakos movement," Suraya announces, addressing not only Mr. Arredondo, but the entire crowd forming around them: other teachers, other students, Headmaster Anji, Academy Administrators, some fancily-dressed people with no clear position at all. Gasps answer her.

Meiling chances a glance at Headmaster Anji. He inclines his head at her and responds to Suraya with, "I would be delighted to hear it, Miss Zialitos."

Meiling thinks, *Yeah, me too.*

"And I will make certain I do," he adds, pivoting away from Suraya. "Meiling Katz, Arthur Ono, will the two of you come with me, please?"

Suraya's jaw drops open with a gasp in protest. Meiling looks around in bewilderment, wondering if someone saw the way the Raven targeted her and tattled to the Headmaster. Then her eyes meet the warm brown of the Divinia boy next to her and relaxation floods through her veins to drown the thought out at once.

Mind manipulation abilities with the power to take effect this quickly are a rare, and slightly unnerving, talent. Meiling can't help but freeze in place, wondering just who this boy is and how she managed to make it into the same class as him.

"Come on, we'll be all right," he says gently.

"Okay," Meiling says, genuinely believing him. She stumbles forward, her hips like rusty door hinges. Arthur catches her around the arm again to keep her upright and keeps it there as they slowly walk through the parted crowd toward Headmaster Anji.

Belatedly, she tacks on, "Thanks, Arthur."

"Call me Artie."

Aside from Suraya's muffled complaints, no one makes a sound. Headmaster Anji waits, hands interlocked over his cane, until they are directly before him. Then he smiles that strange smile of his, turns on his heels, and walks away without another word.

Meiling looks to Artie once more, just to feel another rush of relaxation, and then they move to follow.

Light pierces through the sky as a cloud passes overhead. Meiling feels a heavy weight bloom inside her chest.

9
Suraya

Ten stacks of notebooks, one laptop open to a dozen obscure files, a full desk of assorted history books, and an entire suitcase worth of newspaper clippings later, and Suraya still has nothing. Not a single lead on who Mikazi could be.

When Suraya had barreled up the steps of the dorm hall to the room with Meiling's name slapped on it earlier, she expected something of use to be hidden within her collection of research and rambling notes. Meiling *always* has something of use; she's an academic genius with a penchant for obscure information. Suraya never would have picked the lock and emptied every suitcase the Academy staff had meticulously stacked at the end of Meiling's bed if she knew there would be nothing.

Now she's stuck here on the carpeted floor of Meiling's dorm room three doors down from her own until it's safe to slip back out again. Until the footsteps of their classmates outside the door officially stop, Suraya refuses to leave this room. She slowly begins to pack back up the notebooks, embarrassed to have done this in the first place. After telling Meiling she doesn't belong here, Suraya has no right to rely on her information.

No one can know. If they do, Suraya will have no choice but to hurl the entire sun into their face.

In comparison to the dreary, mismatched outside of the Academy buildings, the inside of the First Year Dorm Hall is practically an architectural masterpiece. Long hallways, high ceilings, arched windows, stained-glass window panes. Walls the color of scorched caramel, wooden floors the color of burnt oak trees, and decorative carpets with the Zialitos insignia stitched into them—a vibrant flaming sun of gold, orange, and red.

Voices amplify in the hallway outside Meiling's door. Footsteps stampede past. Suraya holds her breath as they rush by, twisting her fingers around a thread she's tugged loose from the fiery rug. She watches shadows fall through the crack under the doorway until silence reigns again. Then she yanks the loose thread straight out of the rug and goes right back to flipping through Meiling's notes.

With renewed determination, she tears pages out of notebooks, opens folders, sifts through newspapers, and reads all the faded, messy text on each. There has to be something. Meiling has an absurd amount of information on everything under the Sun and the Moon.

Back when they were kids, Meiling used to study Suraya before she turned to old textbooks and biographies. She'd take notes on Suraya's abilities, track her growth, hypothesize ways to accelerate it, and then create shockingly effective tests to prove her ideas. The only reason Suraya mastered long distance sight was because nine-year-old Meiling set a strict regimen of using and improving it. Suraya may not want her here at the Academy, but she knows better than anyone that Meiling knows the most about it. Including who might want to attack it.

Old news headlines read about the lineages between more than one Sun Divinity and the hybrid abilities that developed because of them, the split between descendants of the Sun and the Moon and the litany of bloody disputes between them, and the displacement of those with no Divine blood at all to the outskirts of the smallest, least cared for Divisions Four and Five. On and on the newspapers go, growing older and more ridiculous every time.

Suraya groans as she flicks through each of them, wondering why it seems like Meiling has made it her life's goal to keep track of every little thing every little person has ever done in Malumvia. Every last article is covered in highlighter and handwritten notes in the margins. At first glance, they are disorganized and thoughtless. At second glance, they are organized and thoughtless.

And on third glance, Suraya understands all of it.

Meiling is tracking someone. Every article or cover image in this entire stack of newspapers has notes on the same idea. Meiling has left dates in the corners, theories in the margins, circles on blurry faces and distant figures in crowds.

Meiling is tracking someone, and she's been tracking them for years. Almost like some of those overly devoted followers of the Divinities who think they'll be able to spot them in the flesh waltzing down Main Street if they connect enough unrelated dots. But, if that's true, then why under Ataru's Sun is Meiling Katz searching for a Miyako? And worse than that, why does she have a stack of cropped photographs where it looks like he's wearing an Academy uniform?

Suraya stares at the photographs, these questions burning in her mind until her vision goes blurry and she falls asleep right there on Meiling's dorm room floor.

Suraya wakes to the sound of a door opening. A moment after fresh air rushes in from it, someone shrieks and Suraya flings upright.

"Suri?"

Suraya blinks the blurriness out of her eyes to see Meiling standing above her. Meiling's feet are precariously straddling the scattered stacks of her own belongings, and her eyes are large as they stare down at Suraya curled up on the floor with dried drool on her chin. Hovering in the open doorway behind her is Mr. Brick House, aka Arthur Ono, aka *Artie*. His head bobs back and forth between Suraya and Meiling like he's having immense trouble working through a very simple equation: the same way he's seemed since Suraya first spotted him.

"What's with the screaming?" Suraya shifts to snatch a loose newspaper clipping and hide it in her pocket. Unfortunately, the stack of photographs has fallen over and slid underneath the corner of the bed, so there's no chance Suraya can grab those inconspicuously, but she refuses to leave empty-handed, so better this than nothing. Besides, it's horribly embarrassing to be caught here to begin with; she needs a consolation prize.

"What are you doing?" Meiling asks.

Suraya clears her throat, avoiding Meiling's gaze as she hops to her feet and brushes her pants off. Her neck is hot with shame. The last thing she wanted was for Meiling to know she ransacked her belongings for information. Now she'll never stop asking questions, and Suraya can't keep her safe if she never stops asking questions.

"I believe I was napping."

There are heaps of clothing and figurines pouring out of the suitcases, lopsided piles of textbooks, and a ridiculously large amount of pill bottles mixed within it. Suraya didn't notice the bottles before Artie shouldered his way in to examine them.

Meiling scans the room slowly, taking everything in. Her eyes flash when she sees the pill bottles in Artie's hands, dull when viewing the newspapers, and flash again when she spots exactly what Suraya did not want her to: the photographs strewn beneath the corner of her bed.

"What did you—why is that—how could they—"

Suraya scowls. If Meiling can't get out a singular thought, those photographs must mean even more than she thought. First the "nonviolent M-attack" this morning, then the Birds of Prey attack moving in, and now this? Suraya is rapidly filling to the brim with reasons to hunt down the Miyakos. As if she needed more reasons.

"What?" Suraya asks.

Meiling's mouth flaps open and closed, open and closed, open and closed. Suraya knows, even before it closes for the last time, she won't say anything else. She may be overly-optimistic ninety-nine percent of the time, but she still has some sense.

"What's this?" Artie chimes in, holding up one of the many pill bottles.

Meiling darts her gaze from him, to the pills, to Suraya, to the photographs. Her breathing instantly triples, stuttered gasps filling the air.

"What are they for?" Artie goes on, utterly oblivious. He spins a bottle between his hands, bending his whole upper body to try to read the white label on it.

"Medicine," Meiling says belatedly, reaching out to yank it from his grip.

She unburies a tote bag from within the wreckage of her suitcases and begins stuffing loose pill bottles into it. As much as Suraya loathes to be in the presence of people like Artie—Divinia-descended, dim-witted, *male*—she approaches him to take one of the other three bottles he's already picked up from the floor. Meiling has taken medication her whole life, but Suraya has never seen so much of it at once.

The bottle is unopened and filled with white and blue pills. They're larger than Suraya remembers them being as kids. Meiling's name is printed across the top, and the instructions are printed below—*take two pills by mouth with a glass of water every morning and night*—but otherwise the label is blank. There is no stamp of a doctor's approval, no warnings about side effects or drug interactions, no expiration date, and not even a name to identify what it is inside.

"Meiling," Suraya begins, shaking the bottle for emphasis. "What's going on? Why do you have so much? Where are the labels?"

"I don't— " She sucks in a harsh breath that rattles in her lungs. The tote bag slips from her grip to the floor at her feet—right over the glaring sun of the Zialitos insignia. Suraya picks it up. "It's my medicine. I don't know. I've always taken it until…"

"Until what?" Suraya asks, squeezing the handles of the tote bag. Sunlight sparks in her fingertips.

Meiling tries to respond, but her words come out as mush. Her face goes as white as Evie's—whose skin reflects her ability to turn into a literal washed-out spirit.

Dear Divinities, Suraya thinks. *She's serious.* She has no idea what her medicine is aside from medicine. Twice a day she puts those things into her body and she never once stopped to wonder what they are. And now is she even taking them at all?

Artie comes up beside Suraya, wrinkles his nose at her, and asks, "Wait, who're you?"

His voice is genuine, so genuine it's like he forgot Suraya was even in the room before she started questioning Meiling. This pokes at the flickering anger in her gut like a branded metal rod. She's Suraya Zialitos, for Ataru's sake.

"None of your business. What are you even doing here?"

"I'm helping Meiling," he says.

"Are you?" Suraya asks. "'Cause it looks like she's about to pass out."

"I'm—I'm fine," Meiling says. "I just… I can't—I can't breathe."

She claws at her chest, gasping for breath. Her pupils are large and shaky. Suraya's pulse jumps in her neck with concern. It's been years since Meiling had an asthma attack.

"Meiling?" Artie darts across the mess on the floor to put his arm around her.

Meiling continues to gasp, one hand around her throat and the other reaching for Suraya. Suraya's pulse jumps again. The sunlight flickering in her fingertips soon spreads to her palms and her wrists into her arms.

Long ago when people first gained control over their Divine abilities, the system was imperfect. Even now it remains that way. Too much of an ability runs the risk of exploding someone to bits from the inside out. Suraya, with as much power as she has in her blood, toes that line every day. It seems she has one foot inching over it right now.

Suraya reaches out to take Meiling's hand. As kids, they made up their own language through hand motions together. The simplest is one squeeze for yes, which isn't much of a creation at all, but it does come in handy for moments like this.

"Did you stop taking your medication?"

One quick, tight squeeze to her fingers.

"Ataru's sake." Suraya fishes out a bottle from the tote bag, breaks the cap off, and pours out two of the giant pills. "You have to take them, Meiling. Didn't I tell you the Academy wasn't safe for you? Why purposefully make it worse?"

Meiling hangs her head in shame, her chest rising and falling rapidly. Her breaths are short and squeaky. Suraya presses the pills into her palm. Meiling takes them and pushes Artie off. She drops down onto her mattress and dry swallows both pills at once. Her skin seems to have a sheen around it buzzing like the Nature Energy of the Kagiso family.

"Meiling?" Artie asks, sitting down beside her. He grabs Suraya's water bottle off the nightstand and hands it to her. Meiling chugs down half of it in a second.

"F–fine," Meiling chokes out. "Thank—"

Before she can finish, she curls over herself and vomits. Artie reaches around to hold her hair back while Suraya stumbles away grimacing. Meiling has thrown up both pills, water, and a bit of blood.

"That's it, you need to go home and see Doctor Sutherland."

Meiling pops up to shake her head violently. She wipes spit and blood from her lips.

"We're not having this argument anymore, Meiling. I warned you, you ignored me, and now it's hurting you. Enough."

Suraya stomps forward to grab Meiling and pull her up. She'll carry her straight out of the building to the doctor if she has to. Meiling swats her away and shouts in protest. Each touch of her clammy hands against Suraya's skin is like fire.

Artie flings forward to push Suraya away, eyes flashing gold, and a tidal wave of heat rises in Suraya's chest.

With a flash like lightning, everything goes still. Suraya notices as she's falling backward to the floor that her hands are suddenly empty.

10
Meiling

Peeling her eyes open, Meiling blinks into focus. There is an ache settled deep inside her bones and a sharp headache stabbing at her temples. Surveying the space around her, she knows this must be the nurse's wing, but none of it is familiar from the many historical texts she's read about the Academy. It looks too blank and lifeless for that.

Flat on her back on a thin cot, wavy white curtains hang to either side, and nothing more than a blank brick wall stares at her from ahead. A machine whirrs and beeps distantly. An IV drip pokes out of her purple-tinged left arm. Murmuring voices filter through the air, but where they come from or who they belong to is impossible to tell.

One day at the Academy and Meiling is already waking up in the nurse's wing.

The harder Meiling squeezes her eyes shut, the easier it becomes to sit herself upright. The less the glaring overhead light hits her, the less pounding in her skull. Only when she's sitting does she register the tell-tale burn of medication in her bloodstream. Large doses always feel like fires set inside her chest at first.

So much for not taking her medication anymore.

"Is your reason truly good enough to risk the safety of this school, Headmaster?"

Meiling sucks in a breath and holds it. The thin white curtain to her left sways, revealing tiny cracks through which Meiling can see a handful of doctors and the decorative brilliance of Headmaster Anji's cane. Now fully awake, their voices are crisp and clear.

"My reason is a prophecy from the Divinities, Mrs. Rekow," comes the low voice of the Headmaster, "do you mean to undermine them?"

The nurses gasp. Meiling bites her tongue to keep from doing the same. A prophecy from the Divinities is practically unheard of. The last time anyone recorded one was well over a couple hundred years ago when Divinia foretold a revolution in Malumvia that would lead to full annihilation unless the Zialitos seized control. It was well on its way to becoming reality by the time the Zialitos took over and peace reigned once more.

"Never," the nurse tells Headmaster Anji quickly. "Though true Divine prophecies are meant to have *protocols*, are they not?"

It's written into Malumvian law that anytime Divinia passes a prophecy, it is to be done in perfect structure so as to avoid previous mistakes. The first step is a Divine meeting before the Head of Malumvia, the second is to write a clear transcription of her words on the sacred stone tablet of the Kagiso family, and the last is to host a country-wide gathering and share it. Unless Meiling's been asleep for far longer than she thinks, there's no chance all of this happened without her knowing it.

"How dare you question her grace," Headmaster Anji snaps. Meiling realizes this is not an answer.

"I only mean to say that with the Miyako family moving as they are, we must be positive the prophecy is a prophecy, exactly as you said, Headmaster. After all, mere Divine insight would never be enough to condone something like this."

Headmaster Anji chuckles lightly. The sound ricochets Meiling back in time to a few hours ago when she and Artie sat in his office to relay the Birds of Prey attack. Meiling sat stunned and silent, her head spinning far too much to answer any of his questions. Artie calmly retold the story for her. When he finished, Headmaster Anji laughed in much the same way: quiet and pleased— though for what, no one knows.

After a long pause, Headmaster Anji responds to the nurse, "Miss Meiling is our ticket out of this mess with the Miyakos." Meiling's ears begin to ring. "If I must risk some safety and skip some standard procedures to keep her here, then I will."

"And what if she learns the truth?" another doctor asks.

"So long as you keep her properly medicated, she never will."

"No," Meiling croaks, yanking sheets from her legs and tugging at the needles in her arm. The voices outside the curtain halt. "No, no, no."

The only thing worse than being the center of a

Divine prophecy—or at least what is being broadcasted as one—is being purposefully kept here, in the dark, while her life threatens others. Suraya and Artie could have died earlier, and Meiling could have been the reason.

Apparently, she still can be.

The curtain wades harshly forward and back, bringing with it a new face. A stout old woman with wrinkles around her eyes and dull orange hair curling around her sunken cheeks appears at the end of Meiling's bed. Her eyes are large as they land on Meiling, standing in her hospital gown and bleeding where the IV once was.

"Miss Katz, please sit back down," the nurse says. The fear in her voice makes Meiling feel guilty. "Please relax. You need rest."

The thick smell of antiseptic and blood twists up Meiling's nostrils. Both of these scents remind her so much of her worst, most blurry memories that she collapses backward onto the cot whether she wanted to listen or not.

The loud clanking of Headmaster Anji's cane grows more and more distant until it is only an echo.

"Suraya," she gasps, searching the nurse's expression for any hint of what happened. "Is she okay? Please tell me she's okay. Oh Divinities, and Artie. Poor Artie. Is he okay? Are they both okay?"

Contrary to popular belief, Meiling is not accustomed to the feeling of helplessness. As one of the unlucky ones in Malumvia without any Divinity to call her Creator, people expect her to be a wreck like this all the time. But the truth is, it's never gotten Meiling down and desperate before. At least not like this.

Right now, Meiling's eagerness for a response thrums like a moving part inside her body. She would do anything to hear Suraya and Artie are okay. Anything at all.

Thankfully the nurse seems to realize the gravity of the situation. Before she even opens her mouth to answer, Meiling knows the answer as clearly as if the words have already been spoken: *Yes, they're both okay.*

Relief floods through her body. It knocks the wind out of her lungs and she slouches in the bed, exhausted.

The nurse tugs her lips together and smiles tightly. With lightning speed, she reinserts the IV into Meiling's limp arm and drowns her system in more medication.

Meiling's mind goes blissfully blank as she's knocked out cold.

When Meiling wakes, Headmaster Anji is long gone. Only the lingering scent of leather and eucalyptus remains in the air. Nurses can be heard murmuring as they pass around rattling pill bottles and patient files, but a splitting headache keeps Meiling from seeing any of it clearly.

A thin rectangular window overhead lets in no sunlight, giving Meiling her only indication of how much time has passed while she laid unconscious here. She tears off the paper-tape holding the needle on her arm down and then tugs the needle itself until it pops out. She presses two fingers to stop the bleeding as she swings her legs off the mattress to stand.

The floor creaks underneath her feet and three nurses immediately fly through the curtains to meet her. Meiling recognizes none of them from the conversation earlier. Shifts must have switched already.

"What are you doing?"

"Leaving," Meiling says.

The nurses share a silent look.

"You need a new prescription," one says slowly.

"Prescribe it, then?"

Meiling can't be bothered to filter herself. Her mind is jumbled, somehow lagging and racing at the same time. At times like this, she understands Suraya's shortness better than anything.

The nurse clears her throat and nods quickly. "We will bring it to your dorm room within twenty-four hours, Miss Katz."

Meiling nods. She couldn't care less when or where they bring the new prescription of her medication; she has no intention of taking it. Whatever Headmaster Anji plans to medicate her into not knowing, she will learn. With or without help.

On the long walk alone from the nurse's wing in the M ain Academy B uilding to her room in the First Year Dorm Hall, Meiling thinks about the Divinities. Although the world brims with Divine abilities, belief in the Divinities themselves is still unsteady. What should be a place of one clear religion is actually split down the middle and tearing at the edges. So why should a prophecy, or even a Divine insight, change anything for every last one of them?

Most people seem to believe in the existence of the Divinities. Many prescribe to specific customs in an attempt to appease them because of that belief, others simply believe and that's it—as Suraya puts it: *yeah, the Divinities exist, but why should I care?*—and on the outskirts there are a very rare few who ignore the Divinities altogether. Most of those people are from other countries. Malumvia, as the country with the highest percentage of Divine descendants by population—a terrifying ninety-eight percent—is hard pressed to find people with that kind of resolve.

Meiling isn't sure what the extent of her thoughts are on the matter. She can't ignore the influence of the Divinities, but she's not so sure she can *believe* in them either. Belief is something entirely apart from acceptance. And acceptance is all she's ever had. If she put her belief, her blind trust, in these Divinities, she's afraid they'd let her down.

One day into the Academy with a "prophecy" hanging over her head and blood she no longer trusts running through her veins, the Divinities have already let Meiling down.

Despite her rocky relationship with the Divinities and her questionable faith in them, Meiling arrives at her dorm room praying to them. Before she unlatches the lock, she uses the sacred gesture to pray to Ataru—a fist with the thumb out tapped over the heart, then the forehead, then back down to the heart again. For good measure, and to settle a rising unease in her gut, she does the same thing over again with her thumb wedged between her pinky and ring finger this time—a prayer to Mahina, Divinity of the Moon. She needs all the help she can get.

Suraya's loss of control may not have hurt any of them, but that doesn't mean it left everything else unharmed. Meiling has years' worth of information in those files inside she can't imagine parting with.

The door bounces off the wall behind it as Meiling throws it open. At the same time she yelps in surprise at the sight of Suraya in her room once again, Suraya curses in defeat.

Suraya has a thin layer of white bandages wrapped around both of her arms, starting just below the elbows and ending all the way at the tips of her fingers. They're clean and loose. There is more redness to the skin circling her eyes than usual, but the irises are as clear blue and silver as ever.

"You're okay," Meiling says, because it's one thing for the nurse to tell her, and it's another to see it with her own eyes.

"Tch. Of course, I'm okay. As if that could hurt me."

"I'm glad. What are you doing here?"

"What was that earlier?"

Meiling averts her eyes from Suraya's to the gloom around them. Through the arched window, a singular sliver of moonlight slants through the shutters and falls on the Zialitos insignia carpet. As for visibility, this is all they've been granted. Realistically it's far too late in the night for otherwise, but Meiling can't help but feel snubbed by Ataru himself anyway.

Suraya crosses the room to stand before Meiling in

two long strides. The air is a thousand times warmer with Suraya close. She radiates heat instinctively. Before tonight, Meiling has never felt the need to flinch away from it as if it truly burns.

"What are you hiding from me?"

The tail end of the conversation between Headmaster Anji and the doctors pops into her mind. *Prophecy. Meiling is the key. Safety. She'll never know.* It comes and goes in broken parts. Meiling never meant to hide it; she just didn't know anything herself. She still hardly knows anything herself.

"I don't know—"

"Don't lie to me," Suraya demands.

"I'm not—"

Suraya surges forward and grips Meiling around the shoulders with searing hot hands. She seems to want to shove her backward, but can't bring herself to do it. Sharp, bright eyes search Meiling's own. Meiling presses her chilled hands over Suraya's. She flinches without pulling away. As children they used to hold hands all the time. Meiling is relieved to see it still works to smooth out the lines between Suraya's brows.

"Tell me the truth," Suraya whispers. "What do you want from a Miyako?"

The air stills. Meiling swings her gaze this way and that, searching for the photographs of her hero without a name. The place underneath the corner of her bedframe where she remembers seeing them scattered earlier is now empty. No dust, no torn shreds, nothing.

When Meiling was five years old, she found a stack of

photographs haphazardly stored within the old crates of paperwork and junk in her father's closet. It was sheer dumb luck finding him: this nameless teenager in a Zialitos Academy uniform with features so identical to the Miyako family there was no possible denying of his lineage. She doesn't know who he is, or if the cropped images she's collected are even real seeing as the Academy has no history of accepting anyone other than the Sun-descended—and now her—but they've always inspired her.

From that day at five years old, to the day she decided the Academy would have her, ability-less or not, at eight years old, to today at almost sixteen, Meiling has held that teenage boy in her heart with high regard: almost like a Divinity of her own.

"I don't want anything from him." Meiling's heart is simultaneously plummeting through her stomach and slamming against her ribcage. "I don't even know who he is. I found his pictures and he inspired me, Suri. That's all."

"Knowing everything, he still inspired you?" Suraya swallows thickly. "Why wouldn't you tell me this?"

"It wasn't about him being a Miyako, it was about him doing something no one else thought he could. I didn't mean to keep this secret from you, but you're my best friend and you don't even want me here, Suri. I needed something. I needed *someone*."

Suraya nods. Meiling scans her room once more and feels the urge to cry. Her secret hero and all the evidence he might have existed in the first place is gone. He was the only one who helped her keep faith when things got tough.

Suraya drops to kneel on the carpet. She begins to push newspapers around with the tips of her fingers as if the photographs are hiding somewhere underneath them. Meiling falls to her knees on the floor beside her, hoping this will somehow be the case.

Two full minutes pass before she acknowledges it can't be. Her heart—which is somewhere at the bottom of her stomach right about now—thumps aggressively.

"Why?" she croaks, feeling so tired and confused, and so out of her depth despite all the notes she's taken to prepare herself for the Academy. "Why are they gone?"

"He really was a Miyako," Suraya muses bitterly.

Meiling swipes underneath her eyes. "So what? If he got into the Academy then he earned his spot just like I did."

"Don't compare yourself to him," Suraya snaps, tearing a hole into a loose page with her fingernail then shoving it away with so much force a mini tornado of newspapers flies across the room.

"Suri."

Suraya stands. Her body is a rigid line. Turning to Meiling with a deep frown, she says, "You allowed your future to hinge on this? Some nameless Miyako in a fake Academy uniform?"

"It isn't fake," Meiling tries.

"I tried to warn you, Meiling, this isn't a safe place for anyone outside the Sun-descended. You'll only do harm by staying here. Especially if *that* was your motivation this whole time."

Beneath the anger and disgust of Suraya's voice, there's something fragile: *betrayal.* Meiling's heart makes its way back up to her chest where it should be just so it can patter there pathetically.

"It's not like that," Meiling says gently, reaching for Suraya's hands. Suraya jerks away, jaw clenched.

Guilt climbs in Meiling's throat. Suraya, a Zialitos, lost a large portion of her family in the Lunar Eclipse Massacre, an act of terrorism organized by the Miyakos. For Meiling to secretly idolize even one of them... She never thought of how much it might hurt Suraya.

"Wait, Suri, please—"

Suraya turns on her heels and storms out of the room. The door slams shut behind her, rattling the entire frame and half the dorm room walls with it. It will be a miracle if Meiling's new neighbors and fellow Red Class One classmates, Karina Kagiso and Vale Lochnen, aren't awoken at once.

Meiling watches the door, smoke rising from the handle, and wonders if Suraya might be right, after all: *She'll only do harm being here.*

11
Suraya

In her dreams, Suraya can't breathe. There's plenty of air; she can feel it buzzing around her, and her body is fine, too; she can feel her lungs shifting around beneath her ribs, but still she can't breathe. Every puff of air passes through her like she's made of mist. The lack of oxygen sends her into an immediate panic, body trembling, throat aflame, chest panging sharply. Even that passes through her. All panic and pain subside like a calm wave on the shore.

Suraya is aware none of this is real. She has vivid dreams sometimes, but they're always just that: dreams. She's a *lucid dreamer*, her father says. She knows when she's dreaming, and she knows it's not real, and sometimes she can even take control of them. It's only that she's never felt so trapped in a dream before. Normally they feel like an alternate reality, but this feels…

Real, for lack of any better word. Suraya isn't watching from afar, but rather dangling right in the center of it all. She's not in a fantasy world but in a real one, feeling every effect of it as clearly as she would if she was awake.

"Suraya Zialitos."

The voice vibrates through her skull and zips back out again. It isn't familiar, but it feels like it *should* be. It's loud but even, commanding but welcoming. The sound is engraved inside of her like a branding. A branding that burns as the voice says her name again, echoing closer.

"Suraya Zialitos."

Ataru. Suraya has never seen him in the flesh—and she still hasn't, she reminds herself, because this is nothing more than a dream—but she knows without a shadow of a doubt it's him. There's no one but a Divinity who could do something like this, and no Divinity but Ataru who would come to see her personally. Suraya's heart slams in her chest.

In a flicker of blinding light, he appears in front of her. His feet make a resounding thump against the ground as he lands—though on what, Suraya can't tell. To her, it seems like they are both floating, tetherless, in a world of only outstretched pale-blue skies and blinding light. Even she has trouble keeping her eyes open to see through it.

"My child." Ataru's voice is equally as warm and unpleasant as his presence itself.

Suraya opens her mouth to respond and not a single word comes out. Heat rushes in and down her throat instead. It tastes like the masala chai with manuka honey her mother used to brew every night when she couldn't sleep as a kid. Against her will, it makes her whole body relax.

"Do not speak," he says gently. "Simply think. I will hear you."

Suraya thinks, *This cannot be real,* and a soft laugh echoes from every direction in response.

"It is a pleasure, as always, to see you, my child."

Suraya wonders when Ataru has ever seen her before. She's spent her whole life loving him for the blood he's given her and hating him for making that all she is, but praying to him every sunrise either way. She used to ask for a sign, any sign, that he was listening. On the nights her mother's nightmares got worse and her father's Divinia abilities fell short, Suraya would stare into the sky and beg him to say something to prove he's a worthy Creator.

He never did.

If Ataru has heard these thoughts, he doesn't bother giving Suraya an explanation for any of it, even now.

Instead, he glides across what appears to be clouds toward her. Although he does it with grace, Suraya feels a laugh bubbling up in her throat at the sight of him. He's wearing a collared shirt with sailboats all over it, bright yellow short shorts, and strappy fabric sandals. If she didn't know any better, she would think he's just another old man headed to the beach. After years of idolizing Ataru, the Divinity of the Sun, her very Creator, he is nothing much in the appearance department.

Ataru smirks as if he knows this already. "I do not have much time."

When Ataru comes face-to-face with her, the levity melts away. For a moment, it feels like looking into a mirror. When Evie told her she had "the eyes," she thought it was stupid. Sure, the Zialitos eyes are unique, but she never thought Ataru himself had the exact same ones.

"I trust you know the constraints of my Divine Laws?"

Suraya blinks back into focus, seeing all of him at once: from the steely eyes matching hers, to the discolored skin of his face with no one skin tone taking precedence, to the thin strings of bleach blonde hair braided down to his shoulders. Ataru, Divinity of the Sun, who hardly looks different from any passerby on the east end of Division One by the water.

Yes, Suraya thinks, *I know them.*

The Divinities, like their descendants, have structure and rules to abide by. Once they each established at least one living lineage hundreds of years ago, it was no longer reasonable to interfere with their lives. Aside from communication with Messengers and the occasional prophecy, Divinities must remain safely out of reach, never to aid their own blood in mortal affairs.

"As expected, you are well-educated. Now let me ask you something, my child; can I trust you to keep this between us, should I bend those Divine Laws a bit?"

Channeling her best Meiling, Suraya quickly floods her mind with over-excited agreements so Ataru hopefully won't see the hesitation and disappointment beneath.

"Brilliant. Then I shall cut to the chase, as they say: The Miyakos at large want nothing more than destruction. *Vengeance.* They will take any means to come off the sidelines they've been pushed to. I need you to do your duty and stop them before it shatters Malumvia's entire system of governmental control. The current path is far too dangerous. So many needless deaths. I fear Divinia has lost her touch."

The dream shakes in tandem with Suraya's thoughts. *Vengeance?* What need do the Miyakos need for such a thing? They're the criminals here. *Needless deaths?* Does Ataru mean the M-attacks? Countless people have needlessly died in those, after all. But how can simply stopping them now make up for those already killed? *Divinia has lost her touch?* Divinia is the Divinity of Prophecy herself, how could she possibly lose her touch?

Besides, Suraya's Divinia blood is so thin compared to her Ataru blood that there's no reason *she* should be the one asked to solve this.

Wait a minute, Suraya wonders, *what is* this *anyway?*

"Oh?" Ataru questions, his breath like a gust of wind through her hair. "Has the Divine wisdom about your friend not been made public knowledge? How strange, indeed."

Suraya is mortified when Ataru reads her next thought, her immediate thought when hearing the word friend: *Meiling?*

"Meiling," he confirms tensely. Before she can question him further—*what Divine wisdom about Meiling?*—he continues on to say, "Never mind that. I will stand behind you so long as you end this conflict in my place. We cannot have it going on for much longer. We cannot have the future Divinia claims to have seen."

Suraya bristles. She knows the Miyakos need to be stopped, and that they need to be stopped soon, and that's exactly why she's been planning to do it herself anyway. She doesn't want to be credited for doing so only because Ataru said so now. He is her Creator in name, not in anything else. She's spent her whole life trying to prove that, even more so after he ignored her during every one of her lowest, loneliest times.

His rumbling laughter vibrates through Suraya's entire body again.

"Good… That's good. Steady on, my child."

Suraya tries to shout after him for more information, but still her mouth refuses to cooperate. Instead, her thoughts do all the work once again.

With a small, tight-lipped smile, careful not to blind her with his ridiculously bright white teeth, Ataru gives her one last thing to be annoyed about.

He says, "Oh, and Suraya, my child? Don't you ever think of those photographs again."

Suraya wakes angry, thinking immediately of those photographs if only to spite Ataru for thinking he can command her like that.

If she's going to put a stop to the Miyakos—who Ataru has all but confirmed are on a warpath of revenge against the entire country through recent nonsense: the M-attacks, the Birds of Prey, the general destruction across all Five Divisions of Malumvia—then she's going to do it her way. The Birds aren't going to trick her with their little white lie about some made-up Mikazi character, and neither Meiling nor Ataru are going to hold her back from hunting down the man in those photographs. If he's alive, Suraya will make sure she finds him.

And then she will bury him with all his photographs that give hope to girls like Meiling who have no power to protect themselves with and far too much blind faith in others.

Suraya quickly slips into her uniform. The bright letter Z stitched against her breast pocket glares under the sunlight cutting through her window shades. The Academy created them this way; flashy and completely useless. She has the fleeting thought of burning it clear off as she races down the hallways to the Red Class One classroom, but manages to resist. Barely.

The last thing Suraya wants is to find her desk front and center where eyes from every direction can gawk at her for hours on end, but, of course, that's where it is; she's Suraya Zialitos.

Sliding into the chair with a huff, Suraya curls a hand over her pant pocket. She stuffed the newspaper clipping she stole from Meiling's room yesterday there so it's ready to examine any time she gets too bored with the first day of classes rambling. It crinkles every time she shifts, loud in the otherwise tensely silent classroom.

Including her, there are only ten of them. They sit in five rows of two desks facing a short wooden podium and an old wooden chalkboard. Compared to the Academy brochures and advertisements, it's hardly glamorous.

When the teacher arrives, any last shot at glamour flies out the window. With sleepy eyes, dark jeans and a hoodie instead of an issued uniform, and footsteps heavy like horse hooves, Mr. Arredondo is not the embodiment of power an Academy student should expect to learn from.

"Morning, children," he grumbles.

"Good morning," a scattered few reply.

Mr. Arrendondo stops at the podium and looks them over as if personally offended they added the word *good* to his morning. Suraya tightens her hand around her pocket. She gets that.

"Welcome to the Zialitos Academy for Sun-Gifted Children. I'm Mr. Arredondo. I'll be your homeroom teacher."

"Hi, Mr. Arredondo!" comes Evie's peppy voice from a seat behind Suraya.

He narrows his eyes, nods once, and says, "Hello."

Another voice from around Evie pipes up to say hello to Mr. Arredondo as well. From there it's a domino effect of the class one-by-one greeting him awkwardly. Suraya lays her head against the top of her desk until it ends.

Then there's a new voice, even louder and more irritating than the rest.

"Good morning Red Class One!"

Suraya lifts her head. Decked out in golden trimmed uniforms rather than the all-white one the rest of the students wear, Suraya quickly identifies the three people in the doorway as the Academy Moguls. The Academy Moguls are the top three ranked students of the Fourth Year Classes—both in academics and Divine strength. When honored with the position, the three students are immediately nominated to join the ranking of their choosing upon graduation: Malumvian Authorities,

Malumvian Government Officials, or Academy Staff.

Scanning the sorry lot of them, Suraya's disappointment grows. Not a single Zialitos.

"My name is Tia Rekow," the dark-skinned girl in the front says. "To my left is Connah Melendez and to my right is Emerson Canmore. We're this year's Moguls and we are so happy to meet you!"

Suraya can already feel Meiling losing her mind in her assigned seat directly beside her. A Rekow, a Melendez, and a Canmore? Meiling must be going into shock. Suraya drops her head back down onto her desk to keep from turning to see the look on her face. Meiling's eyes fill with stars when she's excited. Suraya's always liked that, but she doesn't want to anymore. Meiling idolizes someone who killed half her family. She can't forgive her so easily.

Every Divinity has a family lineage known as its strongest. For those of Sun Descent, half of them belong to the Zialitos. The four that don't are the Canmores of Omni, the Rekows of Chae-Won, the Melendezes of Amada, and the Kagisos of Abungu. Which means right now, in this tiny little classroom, they have at least one of each. Even Suraya has to admit this makes things slightly more interesting than they were thirty seconds ago.

And significantly more stupid. The Miyakos are on the move, for Ataru's sake! Why put the strongest ability users in one room?

"Oh my Divinities," Evie hops out of her seat and stalks toward the front where Emerson is flickering in and out of a spirit state. Their skin is not as pale as the usual

Omni descendant, making the in-and-out much more apparent. And unsettling.

"It's you! You're a legend. Like seriously a legend. I'm Evie. I'm of Omni descent, too. But I'm no good at holding the bodiless spirit state yet. Oh Divinities, you're so cool—"

Emerson disappears into the chalkboard. The Amada-gifted red strings curling around Connah's tan arms twitch in response as if wanting to chase them down into the spirit realm and force feelings of love into their system. Suraya wouldn't put it past him: all Amada descendants are the same. She still remembers the first time she met one at four years old. His name was Elliot, he was five years old, and he had red strings as thick as his fingers. Suraya didn't get the chance to introduce herself before he struck her in the temples with them and made her blubber over how cute he was for the next fifteen minutes. He even made her kiss him on the cheek.

Suraya zapped half his red strings to ash with sunlight and then *she* got in trouble for it all. Elliot's fellow Amada-gifted parents thought the whole thing was rather cute. Suraya's hated that shade of red ever since.

"Please sit down," Mr. Arredondo says, rubbing his temples. "I need you to introduce yourselves one at a time. Due to the *unique circumstances* of this year, Una Zialitos and the Academy Administrators have deemed it necessary to introduce cross-year and class involvement. Hence the Moguls. Go on and mingle."

Emerson pops back out of the spirit realm, their arms crossed and their gaze locked onto the floor. Connah jumps nearly a meter into the air, those red strings flying in all directions. Suraya ducks, lashing out with a small ring of sunlight just in case they get too close. No way she's letting anyone of Amada descent touch her.

"I'll go first," a lanky boy with messy blonde hair and neon green glasses says. "My name is Kai Van Alst. I'm a descendant of Chae-Won so, of course, I'm a super fan of the Rekows like Tia. I'm great at healing, but not so great at creation. Although I did start getting better after transitioning last year, so I bet that'll change even more soon! Oh, and I'm colorblind, but that's not why I wear these bad boys."

He taps his own glasses. His pupils look giant behind them.

There's an awkward moment of silence. Then everything dissolves into chaos as everyone chimes in to introduce themselves alongside a bunch of fun facts no one cares about.

Suraya stays seated in silence, listening to every name and Divine status as they're shared. When she hears Meiling quietly sharing she has no Divine blood, her patience runs out.

Suraya shoves her hand into her pocket and drags out the crumpled newspaper clipping. As if to spite her, the headline across the top reads of the very first M-attack at the Mahina Temple months ago: MAHINA TEMPLE ATTACK LEAVES A DOZEN DEAD WITH NO TRACES TO FOLLOW.

The pixelated image of the scene shows the Mahina Temple with caution tape wrapped around it, dark splotches of what must be blood spilling out onto the pavement. A bunch of officers are milling around it all, examining bricks like they will somehow reveal the truth. Meanwhile, a blurry figure stands around the corner in the shade of the alleyway, completely unbothered.

Suraya enhances her vision, grateful she isn't anything like poor Kai Van Alst. The blurry figure comes into focus just enough for her to prove he is no officer. Rather than a full uniform, he's dressed in torn pants and no shirt. Blood drips down the lines of his torso.

Suraya huffs. It can't be this easy, can it? If this figure is a Miyako like she thinks he is, can he be behind everything? The M-attacks, the Birds of Prey, the photographs Meiling stockpiled, everything?

"Whatcha doing?"

Suraya nearly lights the newspaper clipping, and the entire classroom around it, up in a flare of sunlight at the sound of Evie's voice so close to her ear. She scrambles to cover the newspaper as Evie leans in closer with Kai closely behind.

"Nothing," Suraya snaps, shoving them both away with her free hand.

"Come on, we're supposed to be mingling," Evie wheedles.

"Mingle somewhere else."

"But this is for our safety," Kai chimes in. Suraya snaps her gaze to him and belatedly realizes her eyesight is still enhanced—showing her the close-up pores of his face. "I mean, Mr. Arredondo didn't need to say that to say that, right? Everyone knows…"

Suraya opens her mouth to snap at them both some more, but she bites down on her tongue at the last second. The Academy is forcing them to mingle for their safety, as if some short-lived camaraderie will matter when the Miyakos show up. But Suraya, with this new lead, has the opportunity to do much more.

Kai's Creator is Chae-Won, Divinity of Creation. Evie's Creator is Omni, Divinity of Order. Both of those could be pretty useful in resolving a conflict, couldn't they?

12
Evie

Evie's first day at The Zialitos Academy for Sun-Gifted Children is going just about how she expected it to: a late start after sleeping through her alarm clock, a new best friend (Kai Van Alst, her long lost twin), meeting her literal idol Emerson Canmore themself (who is absolutely terrified of her), and now a Zialitos dragging her down the hallway after class for Omni-knows-what.

This place rocks.

Suraya has her by the wrist, flying down corridors and ducking around corners. She hasn't said a single word since they came up behind her reading an old newspaper like some crazed grandmother. Being a Zialitos, she must know the tangled layout of the Academy building well because she never hesitates on a turn.

Kai scurries along behind them, calling out, "Hey, scary Zialitos girl, slow down!"

This doesn't help the danger Evie's life is currently in. Her wrist is uncomfortably hot from Suraya's hand around it.

Honestly though, it's pretty fun. Evie has never had to

fear for her life before. One day into the Academy and it's already happened three times: first with the explosion on the way in from the nonviolent M-attack, again with the Birds of Prey, and now with Suraya Zialitos dragging her around like a dog on a leash. *Suraya Zialitos*, the Pride of the Zialitos, the only person to live with a Divine Blood Count so high it's written in history books as the cause of death for hundreds of thousands of their ancestors. Evie feels important at her side. She'd do anything to help someone this legendary.

After roughly a thousand turns and shoves, Suraya finally comes to a skidding halt. Evie realizes only a split-second in advance and screeches to a stop behind her. She has to circle her arms wildly to keep from toppling over and knocking them both down. She highly doubts Suraya would find any humor in something like that.

"In." Suraya swings open the door to their right—a door that had to be opened with a heat-activated lock created for Zialitos only—and waves Evie forward first.

"Uh, ha, why—"

Huffing and puffing, Kai comes up beside them and says, "I'll go!" He races through the open doorway before Evie can tell him to think with his brain first.

With a sigh, Evie gives in and follows. She did tell herself she'd do anything to help Suraya.

Suraya clicks the door shut. With an appraising look at Kai, she says, "If you're gonna stay, at least lock it, Van Alst."

"Okay!" Kai pulls a small combination lock out of nowhere and hooks it around the door handle.

"Oh, come on," Evie groans. Aren't Chae-Won descendants only supposed to be capable of creating items that can help take care of others? Something to trap them in here with a very irritable Zialitos can't possibly be on that list.

Suraya pats him once on the back in approval. He grins and shrugs at Evie as if to say, *What, did you want me to tell her no?*

Evie can't argue with that sort of logic.

When the overhead lights buzz to life, it reveals a small training room. The Academy has plenty of these scattered throughout the main classrooms and gymnasiums, but most are at least three times the size of this one. This one is a glorified broom closet with reinforced walls and a sunroof at best.

For a moment, she fears Suraya will shatter the glass with some fancy sunlight and fry her like an egg.

The Divinities must be watching over her because the only thing Suraya says is, "Come sit down."

Suraya moves to the center of the floor and plops down in a crisscross position. Once she's situated with Evie and Kai on either side of her in an odd small circle, she removes the crinkled newspaper clipping from her pocket and flattens it out in the space between them. Kai practically climbs on top of it to read the faded words. It completely blocks any possible view Evie had.

"What are you doing with this?" he asks. "This is kinda old news these days."

Evie gives the back of his uniform jacket a light tug so he'll let her read it for herself. Even upside down, the bold headline of the newspaper clipping is clear: MAHINA TEMPLE ATTACK LEAVES A DOZEN DEAD WITH NO TRACES TO FOLLOW.

"The first M-attack?" Evie wonders aloud. "That was months ago now. What are you doing carrying this around?"

After everything that's happened since then, the Mahina Temple and the dozen Zialitos officers that got killed there are old news, as morbid as it sounds. And unless her body goes full spirit mode and becomes an alphabet-enthused criminal while she's sleeping, it has nothing to do with Evie anyway. Plus, Una Zialitos, the Head of Malumvia, has stated time and time again they have the situation under control. The Miyakos are trying to scare them into submission. All they have to do is not submit.

"Oh, Chae-Won, did you lose someone at the Mahina Temple attack?" Kai asks Suraya.

"Does it matter?" Suraya asks.

Evie forces out a weak laugh, sincerely hoping Suraya is kidding around. When a tiny crack forms in the window over their heads, she knows Suraya is not, in fact, kidding around. Duly noted.

Kai must take note of the very same thing because he quickly answers, "Of course not. Nope. Doesn't matter at all."

Suraya pinches the bridge of her nose hard enough to leave two white marks behind. Then she says, "You're practically a medium, aren't you, Shineski?"

"A medium? Like I can talk to spirits?"

"No, I meant your shirt size," Suraya says, throwing her hands around. "I was thinking of getting us all matching outfits."

"Oh, matching outfits sound fun," Evie muses. Kai hums in agreement. The three of them could totally be like a little club. The shirts could be neon green like Kai's glasses. Evie's never had friends close enough for that before.

"Ataru give me strength," Suraya murmurs, looking up at the Sun through the windows. "Yes, like talking to spirits, you idiots."

"Oh," Evie says, disappointed, "yeah, I can do that." It doesn't seem very cool anymore though.

"What about finding out if someone is a spirit to begin with?"

Kai picks the newspaper up with a frown. Suraya shoots him a warning glare, but otherwise leaves him be. His glasses might need a new prescription because the paper is practically against the frames and he's still squinting.

"You mean like figuring out if someone is dead?"

"Sorta."

Suraya snatches the paper back from Kai. His blue eyes have dots of yellow all around them that seem to spin like balls juggling when he blinks himself back into focus. Suraya flattens out the creases his fingers put in it. Then she sets it down on the floor between them again with an intimidating look of determination on her face. Evie works to keep herself from jumping or flying backward into the spirit realm.

"I need you to locate this guy for me." She taps a tiny blob of a person in black ink in the smallest corner of the headlining photograph. Evie hadn't realized that was a person at all until she pointed him out. "It's urgent."

"Uhm." She turns the paper to get a better look. It's a person all right, but she can't make out any defining features. She's good at talking to the dead and all, but this is impossible. To search, she at least needs a starting place: like a name or a face. "Who is he?"

"That's what I'm asking you to figure out."

Evie is glad to feel needed, and especially glad she's needed by Suraya Zialitos, but she's afraid she can't help this time. She can't scope out a darkness she knows absolutely nothing of. Gearing herself up to admit this aloud is a whole 'nother thing though.

"What's this about anyway?" Kai asks, saving the day. Man, she loves this guy already.

"None of your business, glasses."

"Kai," he corrects, fixing his glasses nervously. "We have names, you know."

Suraya groans, throwing up her hands. They light up like a flashlight is pointed directly at them. Kai and Evie both flinch away instinctively. Ataru's abilities are volatile.

"Suraya," she cuts in slowly, "If I may… Uhm, it sort of is our business? Since you dragged us here and all."

Suraya shoots daggers at Kai as if to let them all know she most definitely did not drag *him* here. Evie puts on her best smile. When in doubt, smile. Happiness is the best medicine, contrary to what Chae-Won healers might say.

Apparently, Suraya is immune to that medicine.

"Ugh, you both suck." She buries her face in her hands. In a flash the air grows muggy with heat. "Listen, I'm only gonna say this once. And I'm only saying it 'cause I hate secrets, so, it's only fair I explain myself, all right?"

"All right," they both reply.

"Ataru spoke to me in my dreams last night and—ah, nope, don't even think about interrupting me, bug eyes— he may have entrusted me with a very important task. I know what I need to do, but I'm stuck. The way to get unstuck is through this guy right here." She taps that blurry figure again. "I think he's a Miyako, and I think he's the M criminal, and maybe even this Mikazi guy, too. If my theory is right, he wants revenge on The Academy and Sun descendants because he apparently used to go here."

"What?" Kai exclaims. "A Miyako went here?"

"I told you I wasn't repeating myself," Suraya says.

"But if he's behind the M-attacks, why search the spirit realm?"

"To make sure he isn't dead yet so I can kill him for myself," Suraya says matter-of-factly. Kai sucks in a sharp breath. "And perhaps to find someone who died because of him. Either way, we get answers."

"I can work with that. I'm just warning you, though, searching for spirits isn't easy. I'll get exhausted real fast looking for someone related to him. Limited information complicates things."

"Good thing you've got yourself a healer, then." Suraya turns her gaze on Kai. His chest puffs up at once.

"Yeah!" He scooches closer and places both hands carefully over Evie's wrists. "I'll rejuvenate you like you wouldn't believe. I mean it, I'm good at this. Like this one time—"

"All right, all right, we get it," Suraya says, but it's not unkind. Evie dares to think there's a curve to the corners of her lips.

Evie laughs. This is great. She's made two friends—yeah, Suraya is her friend now whether she likes it or not—and they're already getting themselves into some serious stuff. This is the start of something huge. And they're gonna be the heroes.

She shuts her eyes because it's easier to start searching for the darkness when in the darkness yourself. With that blurry figure, a bunch of scattered, disconnected pieces about a Miyako who attended the Academy, and the ongoing M-attacks in mind, Evie plunges through a world of spirits.

The cool thing about being of Omni descent is that once you're in the zone, using your abilities, it's exactly like normal life. When Evie opens her eyes, Kai is still holding her wrists, Suraya is still watching her, and the newspaper is still on the floor between them. The biggest difference is instead of an empty broom closet of a training room, it's a spirit-filled broom closet of a training room.

What's even cooler about this ability is how she can see everything while no one else can. She's somewhere else they can't possibly reach. She knows how people feel around spirit shifters like her—their abilities are freaky, but they're impressive, too. Sometimes this leaves Evie feeling invisible herself, but right now she feels seen. More than she ever has been before. She's seen by Kai, who is mumbling encouragement under his breath and pulsing energy through his skin into hers; by Suraya, who is waiting patiently, a glint of anticipation sparking in her eyes; and by a plethora of gathered spirits, who often drift to where Omni-descended people are in the living world without fully realizing it.

"Hello Evie," one of them says.

After lots of practice, Evie has gotten so good at communicating with spirits that a few of them have become something like friends to her. Which, yes, sounds depressing out loud; *Evie has so few living friends she's resorted to speaking with the dead*, but it's totally fine! She gets on well with the spirits, and they obviously come in handy. Wrangling the more distant ones is well worth the effort. Like now, when she can motion over her good ole buddy Saoirse and dive right into obtaining her goal here.

"Saoirse! So good to see you."

She feels confident enough with Kai's healing to reach out in her bodiless spirit state and hug her dead friend. In moments like this, Evie wishes everyone knew spirits aren't freezing cold or filmy; they're warm and solid like the real people they were.

Saoirse smiles, and it's strange how the smile ripples through the air, fighting for a place to remain. Then Evie's form flickers, snapping momentarily back into her physical body, and Saoirse takes a long look around at the set up they've got going on.

She asks, "What are you doing with my cousin?"

"What?" Evie jolts, looking at Kai in an entirely new light. There's no resemblance at all. Kai is blonde and lanky whereas Saoirse has dark red hair and is super muscular. He has huge eyes and a big nose while she has sharp eyes and a button nose. Family doesn't always look alike, she knows that, but she never would have thought—

"Not him," Saoirse says, motioning her head to Suraya.

Oh. Now she can see the resemblance. It's faint, but it's there, the way it always is for her family. Those Zialitos genes are strong. Saoirse has slightly lighter skin, and fuller lips that actually *smile* sometimes, but they're related all right. Those Zialitos eyes. Evie feels like an idiot for not realizing it before now.

Nonetheless, she repeats in complete disbelief, "Your cousin?"

"Suraya, isn't she? Taru's girl?"

"Uhm." It takes a lot out of Evie to shift completely back into her physical body so she can speak to Suraya. Kai's body trembles with the effort of keeping her steady. As quickly as possible, she asks what her mother's name is. She receives back a confused, but immediate answer: "Taru."

"Yeah," she tells Saoirse when she's back in the spirit realm. "That's her."

"Wow. I haven't seen her since she was a baby. She's my second cousin technically. Taru is my first… Taru and I were rather close. For cousins in the Zialitos family, at least. Our family isn't the closest overall. We never did any of that touchy feely stuff, but Taru was always good to me. Just like an older sister. I remember the day Suraya was born. She'd never been so happy. But things weren't good in the world, you know? It was hard to maintain every relationship with Miyakos and Zialitos fighting all the time. We drifted a bit. I started doing more with the lineage and she started doing less."

Saoirse gets this faraway look in her eyes. "I died almost fourteen years ago. Have I ever told you that?"

Evie startles. It's a bit of an unspoken rule with the spirits that you don't say the d-word. They all know very well what they are, but they don't talk about it. It's taboo. So, of course, she's never been told when Saoirse died. She shakes her head as well as she can manage.

"Well, I did," Saoirse says, sighing. "Barely twenty-two years old. The Lunar Eclipse Massacre, go figure."

Evie feels her heart rate picking up, which is awful because reminders of her living body make communicating with the spirits much harder. It's like a tether dragging her back so she won't get herself killed by staying too long. She's feeling a bit like risking it right now, though. She's been friends with Saoirse for a long time and all she's ever learned is her first name and her favorite pastimes as a spirit. That can't compare with whatever she's going to say right now.

"I'm so sorry…" Evie wants to reach out to her again, so she tries. Her body fights against it.

"It's okay, Evie. You were only a baby, what could you have done?" she asks. Then she frowns sharply. Shaking herself out of it, she adds, "Besides, isn't there something you wanted to ask me?"

Yes, Evie wants to scream, *so many things*. Except the things she wants to ask aren't exactly important right now.

She's forgotten all about the point of being with the spirits in the first place until Suraya's voice breaks through the haze.

"Hey, Shineski! That's enough, you can come back now!"

Oh shoot, she hasn't gotten anywhere. Suraya will be miffed beyond repair if she comes back with absolutely nothing other than, *Hey, turns out I know your dead second cousin, Saoirse. Small world, huh?*

Evie's heart pounds so hard she feels it in her temples, but she pushes through. She thinks it might pop a blood vessel to stay here much longer, but what other choice is there? They'll solve nothing if she can't get some sort of clue from this.

"Okay, Saoirse, I'm in a bit of a rush now, but I'm looking for someone. You see that newspaper? The guy in the alleyway? I'm trying to find him. Think you can help me?"

Saoirse crouches down beside the newspaper and gives it a look-over. Kai and Suraya bristle as if noticing a change in the air, but otherwise have no clue there is a spirit beside them. After a beat of silence, Saoirse stands again. Her pupils are huge—which Evie has never seen on a Zialitos before—and her lips are twitching erratically.

"No."

Evie jolts. Kai's hands tremble around hers to keep her steady in the aftermath.

"No, you can't help, or no you don't know him?"

"No!" Saoirse's voice echoes and her form shakes. Evie

feels another tug from her body. She sees that this time it's Kai, trying to forcibly drag her back out by the wrists.

"Please, this is super important. Anything helps. Suraya has to figure this out or we're all gonna be in danger. Please—"

"Stop. You shouldn't follow this lead. He's dangerous," Saoirse cuts her off, clenching her jaw. She can't focus on any one thing. Her gaze keeps darting from Evie to some of her fellow spirits and back again. She's much quieter when she continues, "He's not who you think he is."

"So, you do know him. Who is he? He's dead? How is he dangerous if he's dead?"

"He's *not* dead, Evie. *Please*, you have to let this go."

Evie follows Saoirse's gaze to the group she keeps eyeing. Most of them are ambling about restlessly as per usual. Most of them look bored and tired. The defeated looks on their faces make it seem like they're wondering why their desire to dissolve away isn't enough for it to happen. But one of them is still as a statue, staring at a wall. Spirits aren't clouds of mist or dust, but this one makes her think twice. He looks like a swirling blob of murky water.

"Who—"

Saoirse shushes her, but it's too late. The guy turns. His eyes are a deep red—not only in the irises, but all around them as well. Intensely bloodshot, almost as if he's been crying since the very day he died. His hair looks black, or maybe it's very dark purple. His jaw drops when he spots them.

Evie feels her own do the same. She's seen him before. Not as a spirit, but somewhere else. Why has she seen him before? Why is he looking at them like that? Is he seriously coming this way? Saoirse shoves Evie so hard her bones rattle and she feels the world shift beneath her.

The ground meets her body with a harsh thump and suddenly she's back in the land of the living.

13
Suraya

"You mean to tell me you spent half an hour talking to spirits and the only thing you learned was that you befriended my dead cousin?"

"Second cousin," Evie corrects, but she winces with regret the second the words are out.

"You're lucky I don't send you to join her for eternity," Suraya gripes, but she can't afford to have a cold-blooded murder on her record so the thought isn't even fun to entertain. As with absolutely everything else as of recent, it's just disappointing.

"Wait, tell us again about this grimy spirit," Kai suggests.

Evie recounts how her encounter with Saoirse—Suraya's spirit second cousin—went down, right up to the point where she shoved Evie away from the "grimy spirit." It's the second time hearing the story, and Suraya understands a bit more now, but it still feels like vital pieces are missing. Not necessarily from Evie's memory or understanding, but from something much bigger.

"Forget about that," Suraya says, disrupting Evie and

Kai's intense sidebar about the mysterious spirit man with the red eyes and dirty form. "Saoirse said our guy isn't dead, right? Nothing else matters right now."

Turning her attention down to the blurry alleyway guy in the picture, Suraya magnifies the tiny things on paper, her Zialitos eyes working like camera lenses. This time when she examines the newspaper clipping, she can clearly see the guy's hair. It's strangely spikey. The more details she can get, the easier he'll be to hunt down.

"Yeah, she said he's alive, but..." Evie trails off, eyebrows furrowing. Suraya is fairly certain Kai doesn't realize, but he copies her and does it, too. Together they're two scrunchy-faced weirdos well on their way to snapping her last nerve.

"Spit it out."

"She said he isn't who we think he is, remember?"

"I know what I'm doing," Suraya says. "I don't need more input. You think I'm gonna believe every word you heard from a dead person? She's *dead*. Clearly her instincts didn't get her very far."

Evie pales. "The Lunar Eclipse Massacre."

Suraya shifts uncomfortably. This topic of conversation is not one she's willing to engage with. It never has been. Her entire family avoids talking about it like some blotted out ink on paper. Even Jax and Reena Katz don't indulge in any talk of it, and neither of them had stakes in it—family or friends lost, memories ruined. Suraya, on the other hand, lost many. Her grandmother was murdered, her cousins murdered, her distant aunts and uncles murdered. She doesn't want to think about how

Saoirse might be one of them. But if the alternative is losing a promising lead to her target, she's left with no choice.

Suraya's skin crawls as she asks, "What about it?"

Evie notices her discomfort and waves her hands out erratically. She knows she's crossed an invisible boundary.

"Sorry," she rushes to say. "I just mean it wasn't her fault she died because it happened during the Massacre…"

Suraya has never wished she had any life other than her own up until now. Because now summoning sunlight feels worthless and all she wants is for the ground to swallow her whole; take her far away from here. If she was someone like Evie or Emerson Canmore, she could do that. She could shift into a bodiless state and escape all of this. She could talk to Saoirse and solve this herself. But she's not. She's only Suraya Zialitos.

There are chunks of her childhood that feel like nothing but tears. Her mother cried so much Suraya didn't know she could smile until she was ten years old. She's always known it was because she lost someone, like many, in the Lunar Eclipse Massacre. It's just that it never felt productive to ask who they were. Now that she knows, she wishes it wasn't such news to her. She should've asked.

No, her mother should've told her.

Suraya swallows around the lump in her throat and forces her voice steady as she asks, "What does that have to do with trusting her about this guy?" She taps the blurry figure pictured in the old newspaper.

Evie frowns and shakes her head. *Nothing*. For a minute there, Suraya had foolishly hoped Evie brought up the cause of Saoirse's death because this nameless man is connected to it. But if he is, they have no proof, no witnesses, and Suraya is right back at square one.

"Forget any of this ever happened."

Suraya snatches the newspaper and leaves. Neither Evie nor Kai try to follow her, but she knows it's futile to try to shut them out of this now. The second they get another chance, they'll stick their noses right back in. Suraya can only hope the chance never comes.

"Based on the movements of recent M-attacks, both violent and nonviolent, a border lockdown has been declared on Division One."

On the First Year Dorm Hall common room television screen, Una Zialitos, the young Head of Malumvia, stands before a massive Zialitos insignia flag holding only one thin sheet of paper to read this news from for a country-wide press conference. For many days since Evie spoke to Saoirse in the spirit realm, the only things of substance that have happened are the continued M-attacks. Both violent and nonviolent.

One night it's a blown-up building in Division Three that kills four people and the next it's a field of apple trees burnt to ashes at the Kagiso-owned Essex Orchard in Division Four, not a single person hurt.

Either way, the letter M is left in the blood or rubble each time. Suraya tracks every location, every death count, every date and time. Two weeks of this le d her to only one conclusion—which Una Zialitos seems to have only now figured out for herself: the attacks are slowly inching closer to the strongholds of Division One.

"Tracking data shows the violent attacks began at the Mahina Temple in Division Five, and are now as close as a post office in Division Two."

As Una Zialitos rattles off the information, a bullet point list appears on the screen beside her face with dates and locations. Three months of violence condensed into one hundred centimeters of a screen. Suraya clenches her jaw, tunes out the murmurs of classmates around her, and continues to watch.

"The nonviolent attacks also began at the Mahina Temple in Division Five, however, after seven more , they have only reached the Mystic War Memorial in the middle of Division Three."

Ironic, Suraya thinks, seeing as the Mystic War is a centuries-old conflict from *before* Divinities successfully passed down their abilities.

Suraya scribbles down notes on the latest M-attacks and adds the sheet to her collection alongside the newspaper clipping of her Miyako target. She's taken to carrying it around in a folder.

"Given the circumstances, the border lockdown will be put into effect immediately." Una clears her throat, awkward as ever. "Division One will not be touched by this senseless violence. The Miyakos will be caught and apprehended…"

Suraya shakes her head in disbelief. No longer reading off the script sheet in her hands, Una Zialitos is a trembling mess.

Despite her role governing nearly every faction of the country—schools, hospitals, housing, policing, travel—the Head of Malumvia only works personally with three organizations: the Malumvian Authorities (a vast portion of which are Zialitos O fficers or recent Academy graduates turned detectives), the lower level Malumvian Government Officials (a board of representatives comprised of a pair for each Division and each Divine lineage), and the Academy Administration Board (a bunch of elder Zialitos and Headmaster Anji).

One of each stand behind Una Zialitos now, wincing at her lack of control over the broadcast.

The Authorities are either inexperienced or tenured puppets. The inexperienced do too much and the tenured never do enough. Living off a rule book written by Descent Segregation Laws, their roles are majorly made up of scouting the Divisions for anything amiss. Before the Miyakos began moving this year with the M-attacks, they never found much.

The Government Officials, the lawmakers, are so few and far between that even Suraya has never met one in the flesh. With two per Division and two per Divine lineage, there are forty-two of them total. Based on public records, all forty-two of them are Sun-descended. Over half of them come from Divinia descent alone. Meiling has been hung up on that since they were kids. She thinks she can single handedly change the inequality of representation.

Then there's the Academy Administration Board. A bunch of elder Zialitos and the Messenger- type Headmaster Anji. As the place known for grooming

Malumvia's next Authorities and Officials, the Academy is considered the most important of the three. Given that, the Board often makes choices *without* the Head of Malumvia present, if only to remain time sensitive.

In many ways, Una Zialitos is no more than a trophy on a shelf for the rest of the country to look at and pretend is in charge. Inheriting the position young and for no other reason than her Ataru blood, it's no shock. Suraya will make sure her own experience is much different.

Una Zialitos sweats as she tries to justify the border lockdown as a means to handle the M-attacks. But even the first year Academy students ambling around Suraya know a border lockdown means nothing. The brainless Authorities will stand guard at the perimeter of the Division, but what does that mean to a bunch of Miyakos? They'll surely kill their way through with another M-attack.

Suraya grabs the remote and shuts the television off. A few students groan in protest, but they hush themselves when they realize who she is. The Zialitos run this country, and Suraya is sure to run it soon with them. As the strongest lineage under Ataru's Sun, it's only natural.

Irritated, Suraya slams the remote down and leaves the common room entirely. Aside from the theater-sized common room lined with U-shaped couches and overstocked bookshelves, the ground floor of the First Year Dorm hall has a kitchen with double every appliance in sleek silver, two separate dining rooms in opposite levels of elegance, a large gym filled with treadmills, full length mirrors and a wide selection of dumbbells, and a small technology room with a dozen computers and a landline phone.

Across all of these rooms, nearly half the first years and a handful of fourth years are milling about, but still they appear empty.

Nearly f ourteen years ago, after the Lunar Eclipse Massacre wiped out families and raised anxiety levels so high even those left alive had no interest in attending, enrollment in the Zialitos Academy for Sun-Gifted Children plummeted. Before that, there were seven ranked color classes from Red to Violet and two sections—A and B—to each. Twenty or more students filled each seat. Now there are seven color classes, hardly twelve to each, and ability-less people like Meiling leading the charge in Red.

Suraya paces into the kitchen, combating all attempts at conversation on the way. Meiling and a bunch of other Red Class One students are attempting to cook a banquet-style dinner. Suraya props herself up against the doorway and watches. Meiling is an awful cook so this is bound to be entertaining.

Working on either side of Meiling are Artie Ono and Callum Kagiso. Which means Callum's twin sister Karina Kagiso is also somewhere nearby, hiding and watching over her brother in that creepily silent way she always does. Suraya would rather choke than ask for help from these three—or four—so she moves on to the next grouping of people.

Standing over the stove where a pot of water is blowing steam like smoke off a forest fire is Suraya's most promising candidate yet. He's deeply tan with golden brown hair down the middle of his chest and piercing red eyes. Not Miyako eyes, but Amada eyes: the ones with a red color perfectly matching the strings extending from their limbs like spiderwebs. But, of course, this is not the part Suraya is interested in.

Hanging over his broad shoulders like a human-shaped kite, there's a small girl with huge white wings. The wings are batting rapidly, but they make no sound and cause no wind.

A member of The Wings. Under the Sun and the Moon, there are the big eight Divinities and their one "Grouping." The Wings are the Grouping under the Sun. Thousands of them exist, but none have any descendants. Together they have the power of the Divine, but alone they're more like Academy Moguls.

Since The Wings cannot pass abilities, they will occasionally come down to Earth and link themselves to certain people to form a dual-consciousness. In that state, their abilities transcend any other: absorption of superficial attacks, echolocation, omnilingualism, voice mimicry, heightened senses, reality warping in the best case scenarios.

Suraya doesn't want to say she's impressed this newbie has one of The Wings wrapped around his fingers (literally: the red string from his ring finger leads to her like a demented leash), but it's certainly interesting. She can't believe she didn't notice him sooner. In classes so far, she's been so stuck in her head wondering about the M-attacks and the cloaked figure that she hasn't paid attention to any of her classmates. But f or future reference, Suraya would not be disinclined to working with this one . A dual consciousness could simplify a lot for her these days.

The boy picks the exact moment Suraya thinks this to make a fool of himself. The second he touches the knob to adjust the flickering blue flames beneath the pot, the gas stove lights up like fireworks.

Someone shrieks and someone else yanks the nearest fire alarm. All at once water spouts open up across the ceiling and rain down on the small fire and everyone else around it. The light bulbs crackle out and leave the entire kitchen in the dark. Someone shrieks again.

Suraya lifts a hand to retrieve a few sunbeams, but they do not heed her call. She claps, she snaps, she slaps the air, she curses a few times under her breath. Still nothing. The telltale tug in her chest that flares every time she uses her abilities is a tearing sensation now. A sputtering engine.

Mikazi. It has to be.

"Meiling!" she screams into the void against her own will.

"Suri?" Her voice sounds muffled through the shadows.

Suraya pushes off the wall and stalks into the darkness. She strains her eyes trying to focus, but the more she tries, the worse it gets. Zialitos eyes are made for light, after all.

From behind them in the common room areas, a number of voices call out in a panic. Suraya hears the high-pitched voices of Evie, Kai, and the Mogul Tia Rekow in the mix.

"We're okay!" Callum shouts back.

The tips of Suraya's fingers begin to tingle. She capitalizes on it immediately, yanking over a beam of unsteadily sparking light. She throws it forward into the darkest parts of the kitchen in an arc lighting up the whole room.

Everything settles within seconds. Once Suraya's sunlight is there, everyone else finds their way to join her with lamps and flashlights. The Amada boy at the stove straightens his back and puts on a wide smile, acting innocent and unbothered as if he didn't start this mess only moments ago. Suraya bites down on her tongue to keep from shouting at him.

"Where is she?" Suraya asks, shifting her gaze over to Artie and Callum, who are now side by side without little Meiling between them. "Where is Meiling?"

A ball of sunlight spins between her hands. Meiling can't defend herself. What idiot would let her out of their sight?

A bunch of shrugged shoulders and unknowing hums answer her. Suraya spins the ball of sunlight faster. They better start thinking or else she'll chuck this thing at everyone.

Someone shouts, loud and surprised. The member of The Wings hovering over the Amada boy's shoulders copies it perfectly. Suraya is so caught off guard by the girl mimicking the sound that by the time she turns to the source of the original scream, there's nothing to see but

Meiling. She pops up out of the retreating shadows as if she's been spit out from the broken light fixtures. It's a lot like the way Emerson Canmore permeates between objects in a bodiless state.

"Oh. Hi Suraya," she says with a sheepish smile.

"Oh. Hi Suraya," the Wings girl echoes in Meiling's voice.

"Why didn't you come out when I called you?" Suraya asks, dropping the ball of sunlight into thin air.

"Why didn't you come out when I called you?"

"Dao, cut it out now," the boy reprimands.

"Okay, Cyrus," says little miss wings—Dao apparently, though Suraya had been quite certain that members of The Wings don't have names.

Cyrus, she repeats in her head, giving him another once-over. Involving anyone else in her business isn't ideal, but it's looking like she has no other options. With Dao at his beck and call, Cyrus might be her best option. There are many things she can think of trying with their assistance—despite how unsettling his natural individual abilities are with Amada blood. Dao redeems him just enough for it to be worth pushing past.

Cyrus seems to notice her watching and his chest puffs out a little farther. His eyes twinkle as if he's caught someone checking him out; which Suraya must assert is *not* and *never will be* the case. She rolls her eyes as she turns away, summoning a thin sheen of sunlight all around her body in case he gets any funny ideas with those vile red strings of his. His cackling reverberates against the walls as she storms out of the kitchen alone. No one calls after her, not even Meiling.

This might be even harder to tolerate than she thought.

14

Meiling

Surrounded by thick trees and damaged stake lights in the ground, Meiling walks alone in silence down the main trail around the Academy grounds. It's been a few weeks now without her medication and she's realized only one recurring problem: *shadows.*

The shadows follow her everywhere. From her parent's den at home before the exams, to the kitchen at the dorm hall, to her bed alone at night, she can't shake the darkness. Now, well past sunset when there should be darkness everywhere out here, Meiling finds it only clinging to her.

She tries to hang on to reason as she walks along, taking the darkness with her. Her Identification Card has always been clear: *NO PRESENT DIVINE BLOOD.* There's no way the tests could have been wrong; Doctor Sutherland tested her annually to be sure. This must be a terrible coincidence. This and the M-attacks continually inching closer and closer to the Academy now that she's here. Even with Una Zialito's border lockdown order, Meiling knows it isn't safe.

"Terrible, terrible coincidences," Meiling says aloud. Perhaps if she hears the words, she will better believe them.

In the trees overhead, branches shift at the sound of her voice. Meiling slows her pace and tilts her head up, easily spotting four hooded figures. A part of her is relieved to learn the tingle racing up her spine was warranted: she's being stalked.

One of the figures stands at the lowest branch of an oak tree to her right, another crouches in the middle of an oak tree directly beside that, and the other two are balancing terribly on the highest branches of a babylon willow to her left. The babylon willow's branches are so thin and weak that those highest branches have been reduced to nearly ground-level from the weight of the two figures on them.

The Birds of Prey.

Meiling's heart jumps into her throat. Her footsteps falter as she debates between running, screaming, or fighting.

Forcing herself steady, she decides to do none of the above. Instead, she keeps walking ahead, no faster than before. Raised rocks and exposed tree roots line the pathway. Trying to keep an eye on those four birds while stepping over every obstruction beneath her feet is no easy task. Her limbs are heavy and cold, her chest tight and hot, her breathing short and irregular. The darkness swarms her all the while, making it much harder to push on.

Not once has Meiling regretted her decision to come

to the Academy, but many times over the past few days she has allowed herself to believe Suraya was right about her: she's not ready for this, she's not strong enough for this, she's not meant for this at all.

Meiling has half a mind to think her prophecy is not much of a prophecy at all, but rather a curse. Her life's plan lies in the strength she's given herself as an ability-less person in an ability-filled world, but she finds it hard to hold onto this when The Birds of Prey group appear to be stalking her. Because The Birds of Prey would never waste their time following an ability-less nobody.

As if a magnet somewhere within her core is tugging, Meiling follows the faint light of the Moon and stars to take the trail back to the dorm hall. Despite her rapidly increasing pace, the Birds do not seem in any rush to follow. The tree branches rustle as they jump from one to the next to follow her, but there is no urgency in their movements. Even now she is no threat. Whether she fights or flees or falls down flat on her face, no one ever sees her as a threat.

This makes irritation flare hot inside her belly. She knows as much about The Birds of Prey as anyone. If she stopped right now and got a good look at them, she bets she could figure out who they are behind those masks, too. She could make them regret ever thinking so lowly of her.

Someone has sent them, and they have sent them under the assumption Meiling will do nothing, say nothing, *be nothing*.

All she has to do is prove them wrong.

Skidding to a stop, loose plants and rocks get

uprooted and go flying upward around her legs. A long-indented path in the shape of her shoes gets left behind in the dirt.

"What do you want?" Meiling yells, throwing her arms out in annoyance. A tree to her left sways like a massive gust of wind has rocked through it.

The four Birds jerk backward as she finds their eyes one by one. Every last star in the sky has suddenly become its own Sun to light the way for her to find them. She recognizes the Eagle, Raven and Owl from the move-in day attack. The fourth is twice the size of the rest with huge black and white wings built into their cloak and a disturbingly realistic orange face and baby-skin pink gullet. When Meiling meets their gaze, the eyes are perfect red circles with beady black pupils. A Condor.

"Remarkable," he says, voice deep and musical as a bass drum. He swoops to the ground in the near distance in front of her, bringing a slight chill in the air with him. Meiling's heels dig into the dirt as she flinches backward.

"Meiling… *Katz*, is it?"

"What do you want?" she repeats, harsher this time. She tries to be like Suraya: voice hard, chin high, arms crossed. It must succeed to some extent; the Condor's feathers ruffle. The chilled air emanating off of him smells like a musty old jumper.

"There are two ways this can go, my dear: the hard way and the easy way. The choice is yours, of course."

Meiling finds it strange to watch him speak. She knows the voice is his, but the mask over his face does not show it. The curve of his beak remains firmly in place, no visible mouth moving beneath it.

"What will it be?"

The Eagle lands gently by the Condor's side. The Raven floats down to a lower branch in the trees a dozen meters to her right. The Owl remains motionless up ahead. Meiling can feel their beady eyes tracking her every time her chest moves with a breath.

She doesn't want the hard way or the easy way, she wants the answer-my-question-and-let's-be-done way. She steels herself and tells them:

"Answer me or leave me alone."

The Condor laughs. The sound rings and echoes through her eardrums. Without saying a thing, he lunges for Meiling with his arms outstretched. The wings stitched into his cloak curve upward as if he's a real bird taking off in flight.

Meiling flings herself away, running backward until her back smashes painfully against a tree trunk. The leaves above form a thick canopy of shadows. Meiling wraps her arms around the trunk and pretends to be a part of it, hoping the shade will somehow blur enough to keep her safe.

The Condor curses and trips to the ground, staring at his empty arms as if he can't believe them. The Owl scrambles down branches to land with a thud on the ground and shouts, "Where did she go?"

Meiling sucks in a breath and holds it. After being followed by them for this long, all she had to do was hug a tree to shake them off? No more than ten meters ahead, the four of them are huddled in the path where she left them. She watches their gazes flit right over her time and time again, but still they shout that she's disappeared.

The Divinites must be watching over her for once. Meiling prays they continue to for a few minutes longer while she slips back to the dorm hall. If the Birds of Prey are here to kidnap her, she'd rather run away answerless.

The spaces between the trees blur like smoke as Meiling runs through it. Not a bead of sweat breaks out on her hairline as she whips around tree trunks and jumps hurdles over roots. Her feet hardly touch the ground. Aside from her breathing, she is silent.

When the trees lessen and open up to the courtyard, Meiling loses her stride. The Academy is right there on the horizon, but with it comes bright outdoor lights and a lack of tree shade.

"There!"

In a flash, the Eagle flies up beside Meiling and knocks her down. Her bottom hits the ground with a piercing pain. Little rocks dig where little rocks do not belong.

"Truly remarkable," the Condor says somewhere behind her.

Exhaustion hits Meiling all at once. It spreads through her body, a mix between a bone-deep ache and a muscle sprain. It's a lot like when Suraya and her were kids, and they began training with rigorous weight lifting after school "for fun." It left a throbbing pain in Meiling's neck for weeks. *Her neck.*

At the time, Meiling told Suraya, "Feeling pain like this is unnatural."

Suraya only laughed and told her, "Your lack of muscle is unnatural."

Maybe she was right, Meiling thinks. She could surely use some more strength right about now. Even if that strength was solely in her neck. At least then she'd be able to lift her head and look at the Birds head-on.

"She's clueless," the Raven grumbles.

"Yes, it's a complete waste," the Owl adds.

"For now," the Eagle cuts in. "Only for now."

Meiling groans in what she hopes is a very scary and offensive manner.

Whether it is or isn't, it startles the Birds like a shockwave has cut through them. Their fake feathers rumple up and their eyes, though mostly hidden beneath cloth, grow wide. Not all hope is lost if she can still startle them with her sheer persistence.

"Let us try this again." The Condor lifts Meiling's face up by the chin, two glove-covered claws guiding it. "Is the hard way of doing this truly your pick?"

"What is *this*?" Meiling asks, channeling her best Suraya energy yet again.

"Clueless," the Raven says again, five thick rods of metal popping out of their knuckles where fingers should be. "Let's do this the hard way. He's already waited long enough."

Meiling, against her very best efforts, squeaks out loud. Abilities do not often scare her—even when they're objectively scary, because she truly believes every ability is amazing in its own way—but with descendants of Eben, she can't help it. Their modified nonhuman body parts are so unsettling. It makes the threat of them feel more substantial somehow.

The Raven swipes their hand (if she can still call it that) out toward Meiling's skull. With reflexes she had been confident she never had before this very moment, Meiling raises her left arm to stop it. All five rods come down hard on her forearm, but none manage to break skin. The power behind the hit reverberates through her body, spreading across every centimeter of her so as not to make the effect as bad on the place of contact. How she's managed such a feat, she can't say. There are a lot of things she can't seem to explain these days.

It only gets worse from there. The Birds seem to have reached an unspoken agreement to fulfill the *hard way* plan, so they come at her together. Holding off the Raven isn't easy when there is a Condor's beak coming down on her knee, an Eagle flying circles around her head—so quickly her hair is turning into its own little tornado—and an Owl screeching while its talons—yes, actual talons— fight for a solid grip on her shirt.

Meiling screams and musters all of her strength to throw the Raven off. He spins through the air like a frisbee and slams into a tree. She screams again and the Eagle plummets out of the air to land a full meter into the ground. Dragging herself to her feet, Meiling begs the Divinities to give her protection again. Instantly, her whole body feels as if it's being submerged under water. The Owl and the Condor halt their movements. They are mere centimeters away from her, but they stop moving. Straightening out, they look around as if Meiling has gone somewhere else.

"How does she keep doing that?" the Eagle screams, pulling her face from the dirt. Her mask has fallen off so Meiling truly can see her face now. She's rather beautiful with all her sharp, regal features—high cheekbones, pursed lips, dark almond-shaped eyes, and a thick mane of hair popping out of a ponytail. She can't be older than twenty. It's a startling reminder these birds are real people.

"You know who you are, Meiling Katz!" the Condor says, ignoring the Eagle and her lack of proper bird etiquette. "If you can do this, you can figure out the truth. Come on, think about it for a minute. Who are you really?"

Meiling freezes in place. She stares the Condor in the eyes even though he can't see her. Chest heaving, limbs trembling, hands bent at angles that should've broken them long ago, she feels the moment that changes everything. The answer is in her mind before she's fully processed the question.

She's not nobody. She's not nothing. She's… She's…

She needs to throw up. She needs to run inside and lock the doors behind her. She needs to find every last one of her records and see the truth on paper. Yet she can't get her body to move. Even without a human mouth—with nothing more than a large, immobile beak—Meiling knows the Condor is smiling.

"Good," he says, "v ery good."

Meiling doesn't know how he knows. She doesn't

know how *she* knows. But she knows they *all* know and none of them can keep it hidden much longer. That's why she was out on this walk to calm down in the first place, isn't it?

She knows who she is and it's devastating. She wishes she could be someone else.

"It's okay, it's okay, you're okay."

This new voice startles Meiling so much she collapses into a bush. Four heads turn her way and she's back in the light. This voice does not belong to any of them. She's heard them enough by now to know what they sound like. But no one else is around.

The Owl takes a tentative step forward, arms outstretched as if offering peace now. Then he opens his mouth to start talking again.

"You'll be okay, Mei," he says. The voice is not his, but it's so familiar nonetheless. It knocks on something tucked away in the dusty corners of Meiling's memories. "Just lay down. You'll be okay. I'm sorry. I'm so sorry. Just play dead. You'll be okay."

Gripping her knees, Meiling curls over herself and vomits. Whatever it is this Owl is trying to reawaken in her, it hurts. It hurts everywhere. She feels sicker than she's ever felt before; which is just the cherry on top of all of this because she's spent her whole life thinking she's sick.

"You played dead so well you forgot yourself entirely, didn't you Meiling?" It's the Condor asking this now.

She shakes her head vehemently. She hasn't forgotten

herself. If nothing else, her self-identity is the one thing she will not lose. She can't.

"Please stop," she breathes, but it must not come out.

"Come with us quietly," the Owl says in his normal voice. And then, in a distantly familiar voice, he adds, "You'll be okay."

Nothing is okay anymore, Meiling thinks. *Nothing at all.*

And then she accepts who she is—if only for half a second—so she can slip away into the night once more without them seeing. Swallowing her nausea, Meiling races through shadows of her own making up the pathway back to the Academy. No one follows.

When her back is to the slammed-shut door of the First Year Dorm Hall, the clear view of what should be a pitch-black common room stands before her. Meiling slides to the ground and breaks down crying.

Only then does she allow herself to say the word out loud, the word of what she is, and it burns like acid over her tongue:

Miyako.

15
Suraya

Twenty-four hours ago, Suraya thought there could be nothing under Ataru's blazing sun more annoying than Artie Ono and his know-it-all attitude. That was before she officially met Cyrus Chakri and his I've-got-it-all attitude.

Suraya should've known better than to seek out a descendant of Amada in his dorm room late on a Sunday evening. The second the door with his silver nameplate swings open, a plume of cherry blossoms and lavender wafts out. Pink-tinged lights flicker behind the figure of Cyrus Chakri. As his gaze lands on her, his eyebrows raise halfway up his forehead. Then his lips curl into a smirk. It takes every ounce of Suraya's willpower to remain still. For her current plan of action to succeed, she requires someone with abilities like his. Specifically, the dual consciousness he has with Dao. Surviving his conceitedness is part of the job.

The first words out of his mouth make her want to quit the job and leave the world to suffer.

He says, "I thought I caught you staring at me the other day. Drawn to love, are you? I get it. It's alluring."

"Alluring," Dao the Wings echoes over his shoulders, nodding her approval. She has smooth tan skin—the exact same shade as Cyrus's—and a shaved head. Her eyes are stone gray, and her hands are tiny and strangely shaped, like whoever sculpted her body threw them on as an afterthought.

"Touch me and I'll snap your fingers." Suraya glares so hard at the red strings around his limbs that one sparks with the heat of a rogue sunbeam.

Dao puts it out. Cyrus says, "Thank you, my Dao," in a voice so disgustingly saccharine Suraya feels her dinner coming back up her throat.

"I thought Wings didn't have names. Did you name her yourself?" she asks before she can think better of it.

"Course I did," Cyrus answers, twirling the red string around his ring finger absentmindedly. "I caught her with these, you know, and she was rather terrified of settling down, but in the end, she chose to stay with me. For *true* love, obviously. So, it was only fitting. She's my star."

Okay, gross, Suraya thinks. What she says instead is, "Yeah, right, so why not name her *star*?"

Clearly Cyrus is not familiar with the concept of sarcasm, or the use of rhetorical questions as mocking, because he answers her quite seriously. His eyes have a shine to the red of them that makes her stomach uneasy.

"That's what Dao means." He puts a hand over his heart and Dao mimics it, like she does nearly everything. "It's an old language. Generations back in my family.

Before the Divinities interference, if you can imagine. Without her, I'd never have learned it."

"Poetic," Suraya says, eyes rolling up into her skull.

"Thank you," Cyrus answers. Suraya snaps her eyes open to glower at Dao before she can repeat him with the same.

"Stop talking and come with me."

Cyrus props his hip up against the doorway. Running two fingers through his hair, he checks Suraya from head to toe.

"I thought you weren't here to make friends?" he asks.

"I'm not," Suraya says. "What does that have to do with anything?"

"It's after dark, Suraya." He cocks a brow. "Surely you don't expect me to follow some *stranger* without an explanation."

"We aren't strangers, Chakri." Suraya blows out a long breath and steels herself for what she's about to say. "Besides, just because I'm not here to make friends doesn't mean we can't be."

His eyes immediately light up. Suraya swears she can see little red hearts swirling in them. She's already beginning to regret her offer of friendship.

"Listen, the Academy has a history with the Miyako family they're hiding from Malumvia. I want to force the truth to light, but in order to do that, I'll need some backup."

"What?" The stars vanish from Cyrus's eyes. "There's no way!"

"*What?*" Dao repeats. "*There's no way!*"

"It's the truth, Cyrus."

"How do you know?"

"*How do—*"

Suraya interrupts Dao to answer with one name: "Meiling."

Dao closes her mouth silently at the same time Cyrus drops his open. They both bob their heads in understanding.

"Of course," Cyrus says. "So, what's the plan?"

How Meiling has made herself either so reliable or so terrifying that her name alone convinced him, Suraya doesn't want to know. She has bigger things to worry about right now.

"Come with me."

It's surprisingly easy to get Cyrus on board with her plan to secretly question an elder member of the Academy Admin Board when he hardly understands the plan in the first place. Whether this is because he thinks there is something he can get out of her in return (there absolutely is not), or if he simply loves the thrill of rule-breaking (highly likely), Suraya isn't sure. She honestly doesn't care. As long as that big empty head of his is on board so little miss mimic is on board, too, nothing else matters.

Suraya leads the way down dark hallways and stairwells with only a flicker of sunlight in her hand. Cyrus and Dao scurry closely behind, chattering away incessantly all the while. More than once, Cyrus reaches out to try and grab Suraya's free hand.

"I'm scared," he says when Suraya bats him away, adding a little sunlight to her second hand as insurance.

"Get over it."

"Please," he says for his second attempt, "human contact is very important for my ability's effectiveness."

Suraya considers this for half a second. It's probably true, but she'd rather the entire plan fall to pieces than hold Cyrus Chakri's hand. Not when those red strings are blowing back and forth like venomous snakes waiting to snap at her. No way.

"Shove it."

Dao pats Cyrus on the back as if to say *better luck next time*. Then she fiddles with loose strands of his hair until there are so many tight mini-braids around his big braid that his head looks like it's been covered by a rope net.

Suraya leads them along. The Academy campus is organized in such a way that getting to the Admin Building from the First Year Dorm Hall is a maze. After they slip out the front doors—which are heat padlocked, and therefore easily broken through by a Zialitos—they have to take three separate winding pathways. Brick and obsidian, cobblestone and dirt, pavement and gravel. The Second, Third, and Fourth Year Dorm halls form a jagged line behind the First Year's, all of which stand oddly behind the Academy Building itself. Only after winding through all of these, keeping conscious of how bright the sunlight between her hands is, does the Admin Building even come into sight.

The Odaz River runs slowly before them. A kilometer or so to the east, it drops off in a miniature waterfall.

Suraya can't hear the water as it drops, only the quiet flow of it over rocks right here. Mostly absent from fish, it smells clear and faintly salty. Smack dab in the center of the river's placement on the Academy grounds, a wide bridge arcs across. Past this the Admin Building is a massive structure burying the skyline.

"Are you sure this is a good idea?" Cyrus whispers.

"Are you sure this is a good idea?" Dao repeats, her voice even shakier than Cyrus's.

"I only have good ideas, Chakri."

Suraya stomps across the bridge to show them how safe and easy it is. Reluctantly, Cyrus follows. Dao buries her face into his neck the entire way, her wings fluttering restlessly.

The front entrance to the Admin Building is a singular stained mahogany door with a semi-circular window at the top. It's the most average, unassuming entryway for a fifteen-floor building full of Malumvia's finest. Suraya transfers all the sunlight between her two hands into one palm and presses it flat against the padlock.

The hinges rattle loudly enough for Suraya to flinch backward with Cyrus and Dao. Then the doorway settles again and there's only silence. Suraya curses under her breath. Forcing more sunlight into her palm, she tries again. There's only so much sunlight she can muster before it either runs out or alerts someone behind this very door.

"Let me try," Cyrus says after about thirty seconds without success. "We can do this the old-fashioned way with my strings like rope."

A string of red comes out of his wrist as fluidly as blood. Suraya gags and takes a step away. Using the red string, he ensnares the entire doorknob and inches away until it's pulled taut.

"Okay," he says with a strain in his voice, "now kick the door in."

Suraya cocks a brow at him. "Seriously?"

"Kick the door in," Dao repeats.

Feeling like an absolute idiot about to get caught spending her late nights committing crime with an even bigger idiot, Suraya does as she's told. She reels back and rams her foot against the bottom of the mahogany door with enough force to dent the wood itself. At the same time, the knob comes flying off in one piece attached to Cyrus. Dao opens her mouth and makes a high ringing-pitched noise that cancels out any sound from the doorway breaking and creaking open.

"Fine," Suraya says, "not bad."

Cyrus looks far too proud of himself for someone with a doorknob hanging off his wrist like an oversize bracelet.

Inside the building, Suraya recognizes nothing. Growing up, she knew the Academy Admin Building to be a luxurious meeting place made of grand halls, marble floors, and flaming Zialitos insignias painted into the walls. In the dimly lit space before them, all she sees is gray. Dusty bookshelves, ratty couches, scratchy carpeting. Trying to envision the high and mighty Zialitos and Academy staff all cohabitating in a place so dreary is infuriating.

"They live like this?" Cyrus asks, disgust in his voice.

For once, Suraya understands where he's coming from. Of course, he then has to ruin the moment by adding, "Where's the love anyway?"

"Shut up." Suraya breathes deeply in through her nose and out through her mouth three times over.

Despite the difference in aesthetic appearance of the Admin Building from Suraya's memory, the overall layout is the same. The winding staircase is at the edge of the north wing exactly as expected. This leads straight up to the fifth floor where the Board Members live. Suraya takes the stairs up two at a time. Cyrus pants from behind her as he jogs to keep up.

The fifth floor begins with a hall of offices. Each door has a golden name plate with a number and symbol inscribed. The symbols represent the Divine ancestry of whoever works within: suns for Ataru, wind swirls for Irene, saplings for Abungu, and so on. Suraya scratches her nails against each one as they walk by. Cyrus ends up covering Dao's poor little ears from the sound.

Past the offices, the floor turns to carpet beneath their feet and the doorways go from glass to sturdy black cherry wood. The doorknobs are old-fashioned with keyholes in them. The Zialitos Board Member living quarters.

Suraya flashes her eyes to life, quickly scanning every doorway until she finds her man: Turner Zialitos. He's been a part of the Academy for so long he must be ancient now. If there is anyone who knows enough to give her answers, and lacks the strength to fight back, then it's him. Suraya is sort of banking on that.

"This is it," Suraya whispers to Cyrus. "Do it."

Cyrus knocks on the door with a closed fist five times over, loud and aggressive. It shakes the whole doorway.

"Turner," he and Dao say in a perfect imitation of Headmaster Anji's voice, "Turner, wake up. Urgent business."

Suraya presses herself against the wall beside his door, keeping herself out of the line of sight should he throw open the door as planned. Cyrus knocks again, even louder this time. Feet shuffle on the other side.

"Hurry Turner," they say, taking a step back to ready those red strings. "Conflict waits for no one. Not even the best of us!"

Suraya snickers, a full laugh stuck in her throat. Cyrus may be a love-obsessed weirdo, but his Anji impression is impeccable.

Turner, the old geezer, comes barreling out seconds later. His hair—or what's left of his hair after that receding hairline—is frilly and snow white. The lenses of his glasses are thicker than Suraya's wrists and his skin looks like it's three sizes too small for the body it's wrapped around. It stretches like film, veins and bones popping out beneath. He has to be a hundred years old. Suraya certainly hopes he is. It will be easier to confuse some answers out of him if he is.

Before Turner can get a solid grasp on who is *really* standing outside his door, Cyrus latches onto his temples with two thick tendrils of red. Suraya secures her gaze on him and channels the Divinia half of abilities in her veins in order to sense lies, draw out the truth, and keep Turner's happiest thoughts at the forefront of his mind.

Mind manipulation is an ability she's always hated, but this is an extenuating circumstance. As long as her father never hears of it, she'll be safe to pretend it doesn't exist again tomorrow.

"Turner, thank the Divinites you're up," Cyrus and Dao say in Anji's voice.

Turner's hands shake. His century-old brain is going into overdrive. Suraya struggles to drag forward calming memories at the same time Cyrus floods him with the desire to help them. Apparently, those red strings mimic love and every possible emotion tied to it—including, but not limited to, helpfulness and utter stupidity.

"What do you need help with, Headmaster?" Blinking, Turner removes his glasses, wipes the lenses on the loose fabric of his plaid pajama shirt, and puts them right back on again. His head cocks to the side, instinct fighting against Suraya and Cyrus both, but he doesn't have the strength to break away completely.

"Oh, I am so pleased you asked," Cyrus and Dao answer. He winks at Suraya. "It's about the Academy's dark history, if you know what I mean."

"D-dark history?" Turner asks. The red strings at his temples shake as if struggling to stay attached.

Suraya feels uncertainty building in his mind. She wavers trying to push it back. Forcing positive emotions is not her strong suit, even with her own mind, so doing it to his is an extensive exercise. Her lungs constrict as she struggles to breathe.

Think about your stupid great grandchildren or something, you fossil, Suraya silently begs him.

"Yes," Cyrus and Dao confirm. "The dark history we've long since buried."

Turner's lips tremble. "Who found out?"

Suraya senses no sign of lies, but there is a tripling in his nerves. A sweat breaks out on her hairline. She motions urgently at Cyrus to get on with it. He hasn't denied a thing.

"Meiling Katz, sir. I believe she's found out."

Suraya bites down on her tongue hard enough to draw blood. Mentioning Meiling was never part of the script, but if she yells at Cyrus now, it'll ruin everything.

In her brief moment of annoyance, her grip on Turner's mind slackens. It is just enough time for his confusion to take the lead.

"What—Who are you?" His voice is loud in the silence of the Admin Building. He swings his frail chicken-bone arms around like engine propellers. "Let go! Let me go!"

Cyrus's entire body shakes with the effort of keeping his red strings attached to Turner's temples. Suraya watches as they grow thicker and thicker until Turner's eyes glaze over again. She quickly slithers her way back into his mind. It's a mess. Getting to the good stuff and pulling it forward is like unwinding a giant ball of yarn.

"Meiling Katz," Cyrus and Dao say again. This time he is much louder than Dao, making the perfect imitation of Anji into a mediocre echo at best. "She knows about him, sir. The Miyako boy who went here years ago. Do you remember him?"

"I do not…"

Suraya snaps her fingers at Cyrus before Turner can finish the sentence. She senses his lie from a mile away. Cyrus takes the cue and immediately doubles the emotion coursing through those thick red strings. Soon Turner knows of nothing more than his desire to provide them with the truth because he loves them so.

"Do you?" Cyrus asks again.

"Yes."

"Remind me of his name, will you?" Cyrus says. His voice is heavy and uneven now. Dao has turned ashen over his shoulders, drooping so low her wings are brushing the carpet by Cyrus's feet. They will not last much longer.

"Kane Miyako," Turner says in a trance.

Kane Miyako. Kane Miyako. Kane Miyako.

Who under Ataru's sun is Kane Miyako? Suraya wants to slam her head through a brick wall.

Dao slumps completely over Cyrus's shoulders, eyes fluttering shut. His hands instantly fly up to catch her and his red strings fall away from Turner at last. Turner immediately begins to scream shrilly. The sound makes the lightbulbs lining the ceiling spark to life until they shatter. Glass shards rain down on them in a flurry of disjointed light.

Suraya turns tail and runs. She hopes Cyrus has the intelligence to do the same. Turner is screaming louder than any old man with one foot in the grave should be able to, and she can already hear a number of feet shuffling behind doors to find out why. They'll risk far more than her mission if they get caught here like this.

Cyrus crashes onto the staircase behind her at the

same exact time as a number of bedroom doors begin to swing open, tired, but alert, Board Members stumbling out.

"Let's go!" Suraya whisper-shouts, dragging him along by the wrist. She hardly notices his red strings are still out, trailing the ground like limp noodles as he runs.

When they hit the ground of the first floor, they do so running. The lights overhead flicker to life like spotlights, blinding even to a Zialitos like Suraya. She nearly trips over her own feet yanking Cyrus through the broken doorway into the night. Rather than taking the bridge back over the Odaz River, where anyone inside the Admin Building is bound to look, Suraya drags them through the river itself. The water is blisteringly cold, tearing a gasp out of her throat as she swims onward. Thankfully Dao finds the strength to float them back onto land on the other side.

They creep along the pathways back to the First Year Dorm Hall and slip through the front doorway in silence. Thankfully, the lights remain out here, meaning no one is there to be alerted of their return. Suraya drags Cyrus along with her all the way to the far end of the common room where one of the large L-shaped couches falls underneath a low ceiling like a hidden cubby. They collapse there together, dripping wet and freezing, and finally breathe.

Dao knocks out cold in seconds, tiny snores filling the air.

"What just happened?" Cyrus gasps, patting down Dao's wings wrapped protectively around his body.

"Kane Miyako," Suraya says under her breath, ignoring him. Nearly an hour of work and this is all it got her: an unfamiliar first name tacked onto the last name she already knew.

Even from hours scouring Meiling's library-worth of research, Suraya has never heard the name Kane before. How is it possible for a Miyako, of all people, to be so unknown his name rings zero bells? The Miyako family is even more notorious than the Zialitos, and for good reason. Their names are warnings.

What sort of warning is Kane if Suraya has never even heard of him before now?

And more importantly, how can she prove he's the one behind all of this if no one knows who he is?

Cyrus peers over a feather of Dao's wings, watching Suraya curl her fingernails into the cushion beneath her.

"What?" Suraya snaps when he continues staring silently. "Do you have something to say?"

"We *are* friends now, right?"

Suraya pitches forward and screams at the top of her lungs into a throw pillow.

16
Meiling

"Will you help me break into the records room?"

Callum hardly reacts to the question. He blinks once, twice, then a third time, all very slowly and without putting down his spoonful of rice. His twin sister Karina, on the other hand, flies backward into the wall as if the words slapped her. Separating the Kagisos is like pulling teeth, so if Meiling wants Callum by her side, she has to settle for getting Karina with him.

When he finishes chewing, Callum braces his hands on his knees and says, "Come again?"

Meiling breathes out a sigh so loud it feels as if it rocks the entire room around them—which is the smaller of the two dining rooms in the First Year Dorm Hall. Luckily no one else is around to see or hear it. The building has been quiet since last night's break-in at the Admin Building; the entire campus has been locked down for several hours. Headmaster Anji announced it as a disturbance related to the Miyakos. Meiling knew then she couldn't put this off any longer: she needs to know for certain who she is.

"Break into the records room with me. Please."

Callum doesn't look entirely opposed. Meiling's learned a thing or two about her quiet, demure-seeming friend over the past few months, and one of those things is that he's not actually quiet or demure in the slightest. Callum is rarely opposed to the things other people would be, or *should* be. His competitive streak is a mile wide—whether he admits it or not. His craving for success is almost as bad as Suraya's. He simply hides it better.

"All right," he answers after a beat, shrugging his big shoulders.

"No way! Callum, you—" Karina stops short as she sees the clear determination in her brother's eyes. Letting out a long breath, she resigns herself and nods as well, albeit reluctantly.

"Can you tell us what for?" Callum asks.

"I'm a Miyako," Meiling says for the first time out loud. The headache building behind her eyelids from the lights suddenly stops pounding. "Or at least I think I am. I need to get in there and see my records to know for sure."

"You think they'd say?" Callum asks nonchalantly, cocking his head to the side. There isn't a shred of surprise in his voice, almost as if he's been waiting for Meiling to say she isn't actually who she's been saying she is the past five weeks. Meiling would be horrified if he didn't also sound so unbothered by it.

"There's only one way to find out."

Roughly two meters away, Karina murmurs something Meiling can't make out underneath her breath. She looks like a hologram thirty seconds away from exploding. The Kagisos are the strongest lineage of Abungu descent, but they also have the blood of Kaitsja in their veins, too. The Divinities of Nature and Wildlife respectively. This gives them so much Nature Energy that their blood can't hold it all. It's forced to circulate in a nearly invisible sheen around their bodies instead. Karina's energy is currently wavering like she might lose it despite the many layers she keeps around her body to stop this exact tragedy from happening.

"All right," Callum says again, either ignorant or uncaring of his sister's current state of distress. "Let's break into the records room."

For the most prestigious boarding school in the entire world, the Zialitos Academy for Sun-Gifted Children has some of the worst security systems Meiling has ever seen.

Meiling and Callum leave the dining room, pass by a handful of their classmates sprawled around the common room, and waltz right outside alone on a weekend without a word of reprimand.

Despite an emergency lockdown on campus last night after the Admin Building was broken into, oversight remains scarce. After alarm bells rang late into the night, Headmaster Anji swept into the Dorm Halls shouting at students to go to their rooms. Malumvian Officers patrolled the empty hallways for hours, dipping into rooms one-by-one in an attempt to find the culprit.

When they reached Meiling, she was asked a few simple questions about her day and left to her devices. Not long after, the Officers rushed out to respond to a far more important call: Another M-attack. In cases of emergency, there's never enough Officers left to waste time on trivial matters like break-ins.

In the M ain Academy Building, Mr. Arredondo is in his office with the door wide open. A soft breeze flutters the curtains by his window and wafts in the smell of overturned dirt. Callum breathes it in with a soft glint in his eyes. The low murmuring voice of a reporter covering last night's attack trills out of a speaker in the screen across from him.

"Last night around 9:42 PM, a raging wildfire crossed just over the border of Division Two into Division One. The cause of the fire remains undetermined, but sources say the height and rage of the flames was unnatural. Fifteen people have been injured and one pronounced dead on the scene. Here's a survivor, Lucinda Hacienda."

Another voice trills out, much higher, "It was them! The flames were a giant M! I swear to you, a giant M!"

Callum takes Meiling's hand and drags her along down the hallway. Her heart rampages in her chest. Another violent M-attack. They've made it to Division One. All of Malumvia's government strongholds are in Division One, same as the Academy itself.

"Why isn't the records room in the Admin Building if it has such important information?" Karina asks.

Meiling is so shocked to hear her voice that she jumps almost a meter into the air and accidentally slams her shoulder into the wall to her right.

"The Admin Building is for Admins," Meiling says

simply, shaking out her hand as tingles shoot up her fingers to her wrist. "Any information on the students has to be accessible to all faculty at all times. That way, in theory, the teachers and staff alike will know their students inside out even before the classes begin."

Meiling thinks of the nurses and Headmaster Anji whispering about her behind the thin white curtain of the nurse's wing. They certainly knew her. Better than she knows herself, too. For the first time, it hits her how unfair that is. A shadow passes over the hallway and Karina snaps her mouth shut completely.

The door to the records room opens with only a little help from Callum and Karina's invasive plants. Inside, the room is half the size of a dorm and filled with steel and bronze filing cabinets. Each one is clearly labeled with a year, a grade level, and a color class. Rather than heat locks, the drawers are locked behind Nature Energy pads. Only those with precise control over their Nature Energy can hit all the right areas to make them release.

Thankfully, Meiling has two Nature Energy professionals with her today.

Karina stands in the doorway as Callum and Meiling step inside. Meiling credits this partially to Karina's aversion to allowing anyone within arm's reach, but mostly to the fact that she might be hanging out with a rogue Miyako.

It takes no time at all to locate the drawer for Red Class One. Callum places his palm on the Nature Energy pad, squeezes his eyes shut in concentration, and the drawer pops open with a click seconds later. Ten folders of varying thicknesses are lined up inside. Meiling and Callum dig their hands in and push through so aggressively it's a miracle the drawer stays in place. Meiling sees her name and her breathing grows labored. Beside her, Callum's does the same. It sounds almost as if they're fighting to see who can pant more in the span of five seconds. Or who can keep themself from passing out the longest. The sad thing is, Meiling bets Callum would seriously partake in a competition like that.

The folder reading MEILING KATZ is the thickest in the bunch. Across the front there is a black and white copy of her Malumvian Identification Card and a blurred image of her Academy ID card below. Crossing over them both, a bright yellow strip of paper is stapled there with one word: *INACCURATE, see page 18*.

With trembling hands, Meiling pries the file open and flicks to page eighteen. Her Identification Card is once again copied here. Only it doesn't look the way she knows it does in the laminated casing in her bag. There's far too much information here. Meiling scans every word and feels like the file lights itself on fire in her hands.

Descent: MAHINA and VIERA.

Blood parents: KAITO MIYAKO (*deceased*), MAHINA DESCENT, and YUE MIYAKO (*deceased*), VIERA DESCENT.

Blood siblings: KAZUMI MIYAKO (*deceased*), MAHINA and VIERA DESCENT.

Papers scatter everywhere as Meiling drops the file and stumbles away from it. Mahina and Viera descended. Kaito Miyako—the man behind the Lunar Eclipse

Massacre. Yue Miyako, her mother. Kazumi Miyako, her brother. Her *brother*. She never knew she had one. She'll never know him anyway. He's dead. They all are.

"It's okay," Callum reassures, but it isn't clear who he's talking to: Meiling as she gasps for air or Karina as she twitches uncomfortably in the doorway. Vines are popping out from the floorboards at Karina's feet, but they immediately wilt and die again from the strength of Meiling's shadows. The brown remains disintegrate right before their eyes.

Meiling's only ever seen such a thing happen once or twice before when descendants of Perce, Moon Divinity of Destruction, are around exhaling clouds of methane and such. Even then, the process had been much slower and simpler to handle. This is unprecedented power. Power that, right before this very second, was only held in history drawn out by her blood family, the Miyakos.

Oh no, Meiling thinks, drowning in sorrow, *I don't want this power*.

"Miyako or not, you're still you. You can still be you."

Meiling shakes her head vehemently. She can't. Suraya is going to hate her. The whole world is going to hate her.

"Hey, Mei, listen to me. You have a lot of power, okay? That's okay. Right now, you need to focus on controlling it. Do you hear me? Control it. Relax. Control it or it will control you."

Distantly, Meiling hears Karina desperately trying to breathe life back into the hallway and the records room. Thus far, it appears unsuccessful. Plants spring out of the floorboards and through cracks in the walls, but they only survive for a few seconds each. Meiling has bathed the place in darkness so oppressive nothing can live.

Hunching over a filing cabinet, Meiling claws at her throat, then her collarbones, then her chest, feeling jagged rocks lodged within her. Without a lifetime of experience, these abilities can be a killer. Literally.

Meiling digs her fingernails into skin and tugs, trying to set something free from within. She knows that she could very easily lose control and die, taking Callum and Karina with her, if she doesn't tamp down the outburst of her abilities right now. But she has little to no faith in her capability of doing so. If she's never known the truth of her blood before now, how is she meant to control it?

"There was an eleventh nonviolent M-attack at the Abungu Worship Garden in Division Two the other day," Callum says. He grabs Meiling by the shoulders to keep her steady. Meiling tries to shake him off like a wild animal. She does not need to hear this right now.

"Listen to me. Rows and rows of beautiful plants, some hundreds of years old, were burnt to ashes and left in the shape of an M for Miyako."

Even Karina stops panicking in the doorway for long enough to look at Callum as if he has four heads. Meiling clutches at her chest harder, feeling her heartbeat slamming against her ribcage. She knows. She knows all the terrible things the Miyakos have done. That only makes this worse. They may be terrible, but they are her family.

"Were you there?" he asks.

Meiling frowns. Callum raises a brow and shakes her by the shoulders.

"Were you there?" he asks louder.

Meiling shakes her head no.

"Exactly. You are not at fault for the sins of your family. That darkness is a part of you, but it is not all of you. It never has been and it never will be. So prove it. Control it."

Meiling's breath stutters, her gasps become choked sobs. Tears stream down both cheeks and curve around the underside of her jaw together. The room is dark and bitterly cold around them. Based on how Callum's body is straining, but no plants or animals are showing up in response, he can't do anything more than Karina can in the face of it. Meiling opens her mouth and tries to scream. It's up to her. She has to control it.

"Karina," Callum says roughly, reaching for his sister. Meiling knows instantly he is begging for her help.

When Karina steps into the room, Meiling feels the shift in the air. People with lots of Nature Energy like the Kagisos give off strong signals. Their energy is subject to any change in the environment. Changes like Meiling herself with Nature Energy of the Moon—which, unlike theirs, is not gentle and adhering to bounds.

Callum's energy spikes in random directions while Karina's pulses repel Meiling. The mix feels like a thousand bee stings across Meiling's exposed skin.

"Hands," Karina says to her brother, stripping her gloves off.

Meiling feels the shift in the air from this, too. It

instinctively has her summoning more darkness to keep herself from being hurt. "Now, Callum."

Palm to palm, the twins pool their energy together. Meiling shoves herself away, fighting with everything she has not to steal it away to make herself feel better.

With a little burst of light and a mist of warm water, the entire floor of the records room becomes populated with short, dais y-like flowers. They bloom up everywhere all at once, leaning in a dozen different directions. Their centers are bright yellow, their petals smooth white, and their leaves small and feathery.

Meiling collapses to the floor and lets the scent of the flowers steady her. Slowly the ache in her chest subsides and the darkness clinging to the walls slithers away.

"Chamomile?" she asks, her voice wrecked.

Karina nods, breathing shakily. Callum shrugs, staring hard at the flowers. Chamomile. A calming plant.

"Our mother used to use this when we cried as babies," Callum says quietly. "It always helped us calm down."

Apparently, it can also be used to tame a panicking Miyako, Meiling thinks. She plucks one of the flowers from the ground and buries her nose in it. Fresh, herbal sweetness races up her nostrils and into her lungs. She can practically taste on her tongue the sleepytime tea her mom used to make each night. She breathes.

Without her abilities going wild, the records room is once again lukewarm rather than freezing and brightly lamp-lit rather than pitch black. Unfortunately, this warmth and light draws their attention all the more quicker to the figure looming in the doorway.

"If I don't hear an explanation for this within the next thirty seconds, all three of you better pray to the Divinites that expulsion is the least of your worries."

Every chamomile flower within reach sags to the floor, blackened, as shock jolts Meiling's body. Darkness settles over her head like a personal storm cloud.

"Mr. Arredondo," she sniffles. "It's my fault. Everything is my fault."

17

Suraya

Suraya knows what the assembly is about even before Headmaster Anji opens his mouth to announce it: it's about Meiling.

Meiling is up on the stage with him, but Suraya swears she knew before seeing her. It's been roughly a week since her and Cyrus's disaster of an encounter with Turner Zialitos in the Admin Building, but ever since, all signs have continued to point to Meiling Katz. Whatever this assembly means, it has to do with her. Once Suraya figures out why, she'll do her job to stop it once and for all. Clearly, Una Zialito's Division One border lockdown isn't working; a nonviolent attack breached Academy grounds at the Odaz River just a few days ago.

The entire Academy—all four grades of students, every last teacher and administrator, and even the scarce cleaners and cooks—are gathered for this emergency meeting. The assembly hall is like an indoor amphitheater; dozens of red velvet-lined chairs in semi-circular shapes facing the lower stage with spotlights on its center.

Meiling sits in there in the center, her body stiff against a hard metal chair.

Headmaster Anji stands in front of her, a thin headset with a coin-sized microphone over his thinning gray hairs. People are murmuring from every direction, so much so their voices are a loud and constant buzzing. When Headmaster Anji taps the tips of two fingers to the microphone, the room sizzles into uneasy quiet.

"Greetings, members of the Zialitos Academy for Sun-Gifted Children," he says, an emphasis on *sun-gifted* that makes Meiling twitch. "I know it is a shock to be called here so suddenly. It grieves me to hold our first academy-wide assembly under such circumstances."

It would be fantastic to know what those circumstances are already, Suraya thinks, gazing down at Meiling. She truly looks awful these days. The bags under her eyes are black and the natural color in her cheeks and lips are dulled out like an old photograph. If Suraya didn't know any better, she'd think she was an Omni descendant slipping away into the spirit realm—which she knows they can actually do, because Meiling and all her ridiculous research told her years ago.

Recent conversations are starting to make a little more sense now that Suraya is thinking about it. Something's happened to Meiling, there's no doubt about it. All of the first years have taken to theorizing what that could be, acting like hard-pressed official detectives, but everything they've come up with is absurd. While Suraya agrees there's something off, she can't buy into any of her classmates' explanations for why. Especially those from

Cyrus and Dao, who haven't properly left her alone in days. They think they've cracked some sort of code by repeatedly suggesting Meiling is simply in a tough situation of unreciprocated love.

Not that many of the other theories are any better. Evie is convinced Meiling is deathly ill (ill, but not deathly. Or at least as far as Suraya knows); Kai thinks she's suffering late puberty (which, aren't they all, in one way or another?); and Artie's been bumbling about like a chicken with its head cut off, talking nonsense conspiracies such as, "I think Meiling might actually have abilities."

Suraya is still too angry to ask Meiling herself, but she knows her problem can't be any of the above. Meiling is probably still just wallowing in guilt for idolizing a man who likely killed half of Suraya's family. They haven't spoken since then, after all.

Headmaster Anji must have said something else suspenseful, but not at all helpful, in the time Suraya spaced out because no one is gasping or shouting, but the whispers have picked back up. Meiling is scanning the crowd, her eyes fluttering around rapidly as if trying to pinpoint each and every source of the whispering. Then her eyes land on Suraya. The temperature in the auditorium plummets. Suraya can *see* the goosebumps fly up her tanned arms.

She looks away.

"I'm sure by this point in the year, most of you know those in our first year classes," Anji begins. The first years make it quite evident where they are in the crowd by stiffening at this. Suraya jabs both her elbows out the side to knock Kai and Evie in the guts. They jolt, then stiffen again, then finally relax like she wants them to.

"With a heavy heart, I must share that there is one particular student whom none of you have truly known," Headmaster Anji continues. "And I must apologize for my role in making it so."

Meiling flinches. Suraya shifts forward to settle her chin over her interlaced hands. She grips them so tightly together she begins to lose feeling in them.

"It is by a prophecy from Divinia herself that I have kept this secret," he announces.

A number of people gasp. Suraya digs her nails into her skin. *So, this is what Ataru was talking about.*

"But now it is time for the truth to come to light. Miss Meiling Katz here is, at her birth, before her convenient adoption, a Miyako."

More gasps. A couple shouts. A chair rattles as someone flees the room completely.

Suraya feels her skin tear and begin to bleed. Meiling, friendly, nerdy little Meiling: a Miyako? A part of the family that destroyed Suraya's? Is that why she's always idolized Kane Miyako in silence? Has she always known? How could she?

"Calm down now, calm down," Anji says, motioning at the rattled crowd with his bejeweled cane. "I understand your unease. Allow me a moment to explain."

A large board propped up beside Meiling flashes to life. She adjusts herself in her seat to turn toward it, the metal scraping against the floor as she does. The sound is loud and sudden, shocking over half of the amphitheater into chaos once more. Thrown at Meiling are countless curses and threats. At Anji are demands and complaints.

"Order!" Anji booms like a judge in a courtroom. Somehow it works and the theater goes still. "I hear your fears. I hear your concerns. Now you will hear me."

Suraya smothers a scoff with her hands. She stares hard enough at Meiling to accidentally flash her eyes to life and start seeing every split end of her hair and pore on her face. Meiling never looks back.

"If you will, turn your attention to the board."

A map of Malumvia lights up the screen. Jagged lines section off the five Divisions. Division One takes up the most land at the top of the country. Division Two is directly below in the East and Division Three is directly below in the West. Divisions Four and Five are squashed beneath each of them, smaller than some of the towns within the others. Mostly taken over by forests, mountains and caves, Division Five appears nearly nonexistent on the map. Suraya has never taken the time to observe it so plainly before: the divides in their country. It's almost embarrassing to see on screen. If the Zialitos are so strong, why do they need the majority of the land to themselves like this? Suraya can't stand how selfish it makes them seem.

After a second or two, certain roads and landmarks begin to pop to life on the screen, filling the map with life and vibrancy just about everywhere other than Division Five—where it just seems like clutter on top of all else. Dots—mostly red, but sometimes bright blue—populate over these areas sporadically until one is nearly everywhere except the little square labeled the Academy.

"This is a visual documentation of every M-attack in the past six months," Headmaster Anji says smoothly. "Red is violent. Blue is nonviolent—also known as victimless. As you can see, there have been a great deal of them as of recent."

With a flick of his wrist, the screen adjusts once again. Either he has some superhuman ability to control projectors, or someone else is doing it for him, prepared for each step in this performance as if it were choreographed.

The dots now have arrows attached to them. All the arrows point to a chronological list of dates along the far sides of the screen. Each dot is identified in color as either violent or nonviolent, and then each is recorded by the date it occurred.

Suraya snaps her eyes to life at once, despite the strange burn it causes along her waterlines, and absorbs the entirety of it at once. The first date on the violent attack list is from months ago at the Mahina Temple. The most recent is from only two days ago in a forest leading into Division One. As for the nonviolent list, the first date is the move-in day at the Academy when the Mahina Temple exploded. The most recent is from this morning... Also at the Mahina Temple. The already blown-up structure collapsed again, this time in a burst of fire. The ashes left behind were in the shape of an M.

Suraya is not one to defend a Miyako, but even she's

failing to see how any of this could possibly help Meiling's case up there.

"Ever since Meiling arrived here, with each passing day these crimes crawl closer to our home," he says, and yeah, Suraya is truly struggling to see where he's going with this one, "but I have reason to believe this is beneficial."

Now that's a claim.

This time when the murmurs and protests start up again, Suraya is inclined to genuinely agree with them.

"As a Messenger linked to the Divinities themselves, I have firsthand access to their wisdom." He taps his cane on the ground as if to prove his point in gems and gold. "On the day I sought out Divinia about Miss Meiling here, she passed on a prophecy."

People all around the assembly hall hold their breath. A prophecy is a rare, unavoidable matter. If Divinia herself deems it necessary to foretell a human's future, it can only mean one of two things: disaster or salvation. Suraya does not want Meiling's fate attached to either of those things.

"Meiling's existence holds great weight in the future of Malumvia. The first step to stopping these M-attacks is Meiling's acceptance to the Academy. That is what she told me."

One by one, everyone holding their breath releases their breath. Suraya feels a shift in the air as they exhale apprehension and fear. All it takes are the words of a Divinity to change everything for their descendants.

Not for Suraya.

Why would Suraya think, even for a second, that

Divinia knows more about Meiling than she does? Divinia didn't grow up with her. Divinia doesn't know how she sleeps in a tight little ball, and cries when she's overwhelmed, and hides photographs of Kane Miyako in her notebooks. Besides, Meiling's acceptance into the Academy has only increased the M-attacks movement and frequency. Clearly Anji heard her wrong. There's no chance this is a Divine prophecy; it's wrong.

"Allow me to cut in, Headmaster," an elderly woman a few seats down from Mr. Arredondo says. She has vibrant red hair, silver eyes, and wrinkly sun-kissed skin. A distant Zialitos relative on the Academy Board, then.

Headmaster Anji takes a step to the side and introduces her to the room with a short bow: "Mrs. Beatrice Zialitos, everyone."

Though Suraya's family is a bit too large, even now after the Miyakos tried to extinct them, for her to keep track of distant relatives like this, she recognizes the name Beatrice. She's one of the two Government Officials representing Ataru and she's an Advisor to the Academy's Administration Board. Her power rivals the Head of Malumvia.

All attention flies to Beatrice Zialitos as she hops onto the stage and approaches the board with sharp heel clicks. Using coffin-shaped manicured nails Suraya can see the paint on from here, she taps a bunch of dots across the map randomly. It does not seem to do anything.

Then she turns and levels her gaze entirely on Meiling. On Suraya's right, Evie makes a strangled noise of sympathy for her. Suraya glares until she shuts up.

"Meiling Miyako has provided us with a unique opportunity," she says. Meiling's eyes are wide as saucers and blood red like the hands of her family. "With the Miyako family on the move for the first time in over a decade, the chance to finally catch and apprehend what's left of those criminals is finally upon us."

A startled laugh bubbles past Suraya's lips. She gets it now. Meiling is not welcome as a student here at the Zialitos Academy as the Miyako she is, but she is welcome as a pawn to avenge them. Something acidic settles at the base of Suraya's throat. Kai pats her on the back with a palm full of Chae-Won healing energy, seeming to think her laugh was a cough or a sob or something. Electricity races up and down her spine as the energy searches for somewhere to go to no avail. After fifteen seconds, the discomfort is too much and Suraya bites down on her lip until it breaks. There, now there's something to heal.

"Introducing a revised Academy-wide curriculum, we can investigate these scenes, predict their movements, and ultimately capture and charge the Miyakos for their many years of terrorism against our country," Beatrice announces, never once removing her gaze from Meiling, who cowers further and further into her chair. "Though our only hope of success in doing so is to keep Miss Miyako here with us a little while longer. Once we share the truth of heritage with all of Malumvia, her family will surely delay with these scare tactics no longer."

She motions to these so-called scare tactics on the screen: a dozen bright blue dots categorizing an M-attack as nonviolent. First the Mahina Temple in Division Five, then the fire at Essex Orchard in Division Four, then the Inglewood Bridge right down the street from the orchard. On and on until the thirteenth, the Academy's very own Odaz River where a sudden drought stole every last drop of water and left behind only brittle M-shaped bones. Then the nonviolent attacks began all over again at the Mahina Temple this morning.

"A revised Academy-wide curriculum," Anji repeats, stepping back into the spotlight. He nods continually; a walking bobblehead. "My fellow Board Members, there are risks. Miss Meiling poses a great many of them. She also offers us a once in a lifetime chance. Should you see any reason to believe the risk is not worth the potential gain, please speak now or forever hold your opposition."

Suraya watches in stunned silence as a line of people—most of which are elderly distant members of the Zialitos family—stand up at once and bow. Using the prayer to Ataru, they give their approval.

"Then it is settled. We shall announce the news to Malumvia by morning. Students, please return to your dorm halls. Faculty—and Miss Meiling—you may remain to discuss the specifics."

There is a long, weighted silence where no one moves a muscle before Suraya jumps to her feet and attracts the attention of everyone in the auditorium, including Meiling. Her jaw drops open and her eyes blow out wide and pleading. The temperature in the room plummets. Someone a few rows down, much closer to Meiling, screams in response. This jumpstarts everyone else into action. Students file out of their rows and shove their way out of the auditorium in flocks.

Suraya stays put, Evie and Kai standing on either side of her, and stares at Meiling staring at her. There're tears in her eyes. Suraya is torn between the desire to wipe them off or slap them off.

"Miyako?" Suraya asks. She knows Meiling can read her lips without needing to hear the crack of her voice.

Meiling begins to shake her head rapidly.

"No?" Suraya mouths. Please tell me no, she thinks. Please say you didn't know.

Meiling freezes. Her lips shake and a tear falls down her right cheek. Her lips slowly work around two words: "I'm sorry."

Suraya's heart drops. She swallows prickers in her throat and nods once. Then she turns on her heels and leaves without looking back once. She has some other Miyakos to worry about right now.

18

Callum

The thing about being a Kagiso is that you can't trust anyone. Being a Kagiso is the same as being a walking hazard. Because they're the strongest Abungu lineage in history with some added in Kaitsja blood, their Nature Energy is excessive. *Literally*; it floats outside their bodies. Therefore, anyone in desire of some excess Nature Energy of their own need only initiate skin to skin contact with a Kagiso. It's that easy to steal it.

Which is exactly how Callum and Karina's mother died. Once a descendant like them has had their Nature Energy depleted, they go with it. It's a life force. Those Miyakos knew it well enough to take their mother down in thirty seconds flat.

Hardly three years old at the time, Callum doesn't remember anything other than his mother's scream from the backyard as it happened. Before the Lunar Eclipse Massacre, there was a faction of the Miyakos that often hunted Kagiso family members for sport. Even their own property wasn't safe. Back then Callum and Karina hardly left the house.

So, trust is not something a Kagiso should give willingly, much less to a Miyako, and yet here Callum is. His best friend in this whole place is a Miyako, and she's the nicest person he's ever met. Karina is less willing to accept this because she was right by their mom's side while she drained out. That's why she keeps every centimeter of her skin besides her face, and sometimes her hands, covered in thick black fabric. That's why she keeps so quiet. Karina walks around like there's a target on her back, wearing the danger of being a Kagiso like protective gear.

Callum does not.

What's the use? If Callum lives his entire life in fear, is he truly living at all? This is why he's going to stick by Meiling's side no matter who the world says she is. If he, Callum Kagiso, can walk around fighting without burying very real pieces of himself in order to feel protected, then she, Meiling Katz-Miyako, can stick by his side doing the same. The last thing he's ever wanted is to be defined by his family line, because he wants to be better, he wants to be *more*, so the least he can do is give Meiling the same chance.

After all, she's the reason he got into The Academy in the first place. During the physical exam, Callum was certain he was going to fail before she popped out of nowhere and knocked that Perce dude down in one hit. She's been a force to be reckoned with long before the blood in her veins marked her as one.

Beatrice Zialitos' revised Academy-wide curriculum goes into effect the day following the assembly. Rather than in-class coursework and light ability training, their new schedules include field work and special assignments in preparation of "fighting the Miyakos."

Early in the morning, Headmaster Anji gathers all of the First Year students in the Red Class One room to announce the adjustments he and the Administrators solidified after the assembly. Students are packed against one half of the room while Meiling sits alone on the other. Callum can't manage to push through to join her. Artie, trapped between two fawning girls from Yellow Class One, doesn't appear to be faring any better.

"For field work and special assignments, classes will be split. Every First Year class has been split in half. These pairs will be joined by two people from each of the corresponding color classes in years Two and Three, and one from Year Four. Those lucky extra upperclassmen, such as our very own Moguls, get to be sent out in pairs or entirely alone."

"So much for safety and caution," Vale Lochnen whispers under her breath from beside him. Callum grins, glad the storm cloud Vale keeps over her head at all times to keep people out of arm's reach of her—is loud enough to keep anyone else from hearing her comment.

Anyone other than Evie, of course, who has zipped on a rain jacket and climbed through Vale's storm cloud to sit with her anyway.

"As for these special assignments, there will be a number of them given to each group over time," Headmaster Anji says. "These include, but are not limited to, special abilities training, detective units, and surveillance missions. Please defer to your group leaders for such tasks. Good luck."

Callum grits his teeth. Brilliant. In a week, they've become so distrustful of those unlike them, of those with Moon descent, that they're assuming the worst in everyone.

Once Headmaster Anji has left the room, Mr. Arredondo steps up to take his place.

"Headmaster Anji has urged me to remind you all that this is only the beginning of what we assume to be a much larger conflict," he says dryly, reading directly off a script and not trying to hide it one bit. "Be wary of your assignments. Our country is home to many Moon descendants, and who knows how many of them are enemies."

When he sets the script down, he rolls his eyes. They flash through five different colors, shapes and sizes—all different animals—before settling on their natural dirt brown again.

The lights waver along the walls. Callum cuts his gaze to Meiling. She's shivering, gripping her arms like she did in the records room after reading her file. He tries again to push through the crowd her way, but Suraya is on that side, glaring and sparking sunlight at the extremities, so he gives up rather quickly. There is no time to deal with her.

"Any questions?" Mr. Arredondo asks.

Silence.

"Great. Now for the groups. My Red Class One, you have been split into Crimson and Scarlet. When you hear your name, meet with your group and exit into the hallway where the upperclassmen will be waiting for you.

"Crimson Group: Arthur Ono, Callum Kagiso, Jamie Dumas, Vale Lochnen, and Meiling Katz-Miyako. Scarlet Group: Cyrus Chakri, Karina Kagiso, Evie Shineski, Kai Van Alst, and Suraya Zialitos."

Callum feels a stinging tug in his chest from being separated from Karina. Keeping two Kagisos in one place is a bit of a waste if their goal here is to have diverse abilities within each group, but he still wants to protest. That's his baby sister (yeah, yeah, they're twins, but he beat her out of the womb so he's still the older brother here). She's a true Kagiso, coiled up in stress, trusting no one, no one but him. He can't imagine letting her walk out of here alone, but that's exactly what she does.

With a shaking last glance sent his way, she follows Evie and Kai as they go bouncing arm-in-arm out of the room to meet their upperclassmen. The rest of the room parts like the tides as Meiling stands to do the same. Callum and Artie take the opportunity to race up and take either side of her. Her focus is so locked on the floorboards she doesn't seem to realize.

Out in the hallway, a Red Class Fourth Year named Joon Park is waiting for them with the other four upperclassmen. Callum will need Meiling's infinite brain of knowledge to know who they are, though.

"Crimsons, over here," Joon says sharply. "We're on detective duty around the Odaz River. Let's go."

He side-eyes Meiling for half a second before turning around and leading the way down the hall. He breaks into a sprint once they're outside. Callum trips over his feet trying to keep up, whereas Meiling is hot on Joon's heels. As they weave through the pathways around campus toward the river, Joon calls out demands like, "Hurry!" and "Stay vigilant!"

His voice is deep and authoritative, but the more he uses it, the more flowers boom in the ground around and after him. It's hard to stay intimidated with the fresh smell of roses in your nose. Story of an Abungu descendant's life.

"Mei," Callum shouts, breathing out energy to make his presence a breath of fresh air rather than yet another terrifying threat in her life. "Wait up!"

"Callum," Meiling whispers, her steps faltering as she notices him beside her. "You're in this group?"

"About time you noticed," he says, smiling at her softly. He falls into step beside her and they walk together. "Are you okay?"

"I seriously doubt it," comes Artie's voice from the other side of Meiling. He's frowning a bit, looking her over for any visible injuries or signs of distress.

"Yeah," Meiling agrees, "not really."

"Sorry, dumb question. It doesn't matter to me, though; you being a Miyako. I should've made that clearer the other day. This changes nothing. You're still my friend, Mei."

"I feel the same," Artie says in a rush. He tilts his head curiously before adding on, cautiously, "Mei."

Once Meiling's smile starts, it does not stop. Callum can see her struggling to move her mouth around it enough to thank them. Callum waves the thanks away. It is enough that she trusts them.

When the Crimson Group arrives at the Odaz River, it is bone dry. Not bone dry as in extremely dry—although it is—but bone dry as in there are actual bones in the hollowed-out earth where the river water once ran. The news reports have not done this nonviolent M-attack justice.

Joon Park throws both arms out to either side of his body and the entire group behind him halts. Callum does not need to be told in words. Spotting the number of bones in the dirt from afar makes him lightheaded. Meiling wavers at his side, seeming to feel the same. Callum sticks his elbow out wordlessly so she can latch on for support. Her fingers tremble against his skin, energy pulsing, but never fighting, against his own. She clearly does not have control yet, but her instincts are enough for now.

"Let me help, let me help." Artie taps his head with two fingers.

Meiling turns her attention to Artie and allows him to enter her mind. Callum can feel the shift in the air and her posture when Artie successfully dredges up various positive memories and emotions. Callum receives a strange transitive version through her, suddenly calm and content.

The next breath Meiling takes doesn't waver. Neither does Callum's.

Using one hand, Joon pulls a vine up and out of the ground inside the empty river. He only needs to guide it with his fingers to do as he desires. The long green vine functions like a rope and tethers itself very carefully to one of the many bones. Joon lifts it slowly through the air until it hovers ten centimeters from his face. Squinting, he tilts his head side to side, examining every angle.

"Probably not human," he declares.

"Probably not?" One of the Third Year's echoes sourly. "Well that just clarifies everything then. Thank you for the extremely helpful information, Park."

"Who's that?" Artie whispers.

Meiling takes a long look at the girl and supplies a name easily: "Dey Vespetone."

Dey Vespetone is lithe and pale, like many of Divinia's descendants (aside from Artie, clearly), and has pitch-black hair parted down the middle. Paired with her Academy uniform—which she has cuffed at the pants and unbuttoned at the top of her shirt—are platform boots that give her roughly six centimeters extra in height. She's still the shortest one here.

"Most Divinia descendants are known for their emotional control, of course, but Dey Vespetone is on another level," Meiling explains quietly. "Her analytical skills and strength in mind manipulation have already been used in government intel, and she's barely eighteen. I'm near-certain she has the first spot as a Mogul next year."

Callum and Artie hum thoughtfully, watching Dey cross her arms and raise a brow at Joon, who towers over her.

"If you're so smart, why don't you tell us then?" Joon snaps at her, glaring so sharply a few blades of grass begin to wilt around her feet.

Dey shrugs and approaches the bone—still floating precariously by the vine. It hangs over her head because of the difference in height between her and Joon, but he makes no move to lower it. She doesn't seem to care; she simply gets on the tips of her toes to examine it like he did. For a moment, her pupils narrow to slits and her entire body goes rigid. Then she's taking a step back with a self-satisfied grin.

"Those are human, all right," she says.

Behind Callum, Meiling, and Artie, someone sucks in a sharp breath. He turns to find their classmate, Jamie Dumas. When their eyes meet, he flinches. Then, he immediately looks guilty about it. But then Meiling shifts on her feet, and he flinches again.

"I can't do this," Jamie whispers to Vale. "I think I'm going to throw up."

She wraps an arm around his shoulder, steers them around, and disappears back up the trail to the Academy.

"Don't worry about it," Artie tells Meiling gently.

She pulls a face like, *yeah I'll get right on that, thanks.*

"They're human, but they're still dead," Dey says, putting two hands on the ground to lower herself into the river. Her feet make a horrible crunching sound when they land. "It's just a scare tactic. Don't let it actually scare you. Come on. We've got a job to do. The Malumvian Detectives won't be here for a few more minutes."

The first person to follow her in is the boy from her class. Rather than lowering himself in like Dey did, he does a running jump. The crunching sound the running jump makes is a million times worse. It fazes him none as he gathers light in his palms and begins pacing down the dirt, weaving around more piles of bones. He's so calm about it, it's almost unnerving.

"Keegan Zialitos," Meiling says quietly before Callum or Artie can even ask.

That makes sense, then. One of Suraya's relatives. Those Zialitos are basically built for handling any conflict thrown their way. If Callum is being completely honest, he's always found them to be scarier than the Miyakos. Maybe that's just because before Meiling, he's never met one. Their population is the lowest of all Divine lineages, after all.

"We're up," he says, nudging Meiling and Artie forward.

The ground feels unsteady beneath his feet as he walks. He hates this. Abungu and Kaitsja are all about life. H is whole bloodline is about *life* and this is… This is clearly not it.

Jamie hangs back, eyeing Meiling warily as Callum helps her sidestep what appears to be a femur. Vale Lochnen stays with him, completely silent and hardly focused on anything at all. A few meters ahead of them, on the bank of the barren river, Joon Park stands with his arms crossed and his jaw clenched, probably still vexed about Dey. The rest begin their broad search through the canal of bones, not entirely sure what they're actually looking for.

Callum taps his foot lightly on a pile of bones crushed so small they look more like pale ash, and asks, "How'd she know these were human?" He'll admit he doesn't know much about abilities aside from his own.

"Probably took a glimpse into their past." Artie makes a wry face. "Some of us Divinia descendants can do stuff like that."

"Huh," Callum hums. "You?"

"Sometimes," he admits. His eyes are unfocused as he scans the ground at their feet.

Callum can take a hint, so he doesn't ask anything further.

As they continue moving, he follows Joon's example and begins growing plants out of the ground to help them pass with as little bone interference as possible. Watching tall blades of grass sift and sort through ribs and skulls is not how he envisioned his days at the Academy going.

Five minutes later, a caravan of Malumvian Detectives arrives. They file out of their matching sleek cars, in matching satin suits, and hop one-by-one into the river with clipboards and canes and evidence bags. Now the detectives are here, Callum isn't sure why *he* is.

The further they move, the easier it is to lose sight of their goal. How many people must've died to fill this space? How many descendants of Tal must've been here in order to cause this drought in the first place? And how are a group of students expected to solve any of it? These nonviolent attacks should be the least of the country's concern anyway: they're *nonviolent*. And they're repeating now, if that map Headmaster Anji filled the board with yesterday was anything to consider. Surely that can't be very important in the grand scheme of things.

By the time Callum snaps himself out of it, it's too late. Somewhere in the wide-open expanse of an empty river, he's lost sight of Meiling. The Odaz River cuts through the Academy campus before disappearing again into the heavy woods toward Division Two, so he can only assume Meiling wandered over there.

"Artie, where did Meiling go?"

Artie's pale. Very pale.

"Something's wrong," he says. His eyes are lit up. Normally when Artie speaks, it's with so little emotion it's a bit scary. Right now, Callum would kill for it to be that way again because Artie sounds absolutely terrified, which is much scarier. "Callum, something's wrong."

"What—"

A scream cuts through the air and then they're underwater.

19
Meiling

The second the Crimson Group arrives at the Odaz River, Meiling feels something wrong in the air. A strange thumping grows in her chest. It's out of rhythm with her pulse, almost as if she's gained another heartbeat, and the deeper into the woods she follows the path of the river, the harder it pounds on her ribcage. Desperate to figure out why, she separates herself from Callum and Artie.

Under the canopy of thick trees above her head, the bone filled river looks like a cave. The darker it grows, the better her vision. She's nearly fifty meters away from the rest of the group now, but she can still clearly see everyone sifting through bones together.

Mahina, as Divinity of the Moon, fares best in the dark. It stands to reason that her descendants do, too—at least when they aren't being drugged down by high level medication.

Meiling suddenly has X-ray-level vision in the shadowy space before her. She hardly has to move another centimeter to find what has been calling to her.

A few paces away, an M built out of bones lays in the

sand. A singular rock, dark gray and uncomfortably holey, sits horizontally below the letter . About the size of her palm, the rock should be hard to spot amongst the meter-long letter made of femurs, tibias, and fibulas, but her eyes are immediately drawn to it.

Meiling opens her mouth to scream for Joon at the same time something carved into the sand beneath those bones and rock becomes visible. She snaps her mouth shut before anything more than a grunt can escape her.

"What was that?" Joon's voice echoes like the trees are made of metal.

Hearing Joon's footsteps grow closer, Meiling jerks forward to try to block his view of the bones. She can't let him—a Zialitos—see something like this. It will only make things worse.

Underneath the jagged M formed of human bones, there is another letter: the letter K.

The meaning of this couldn't be clearer to Meiling even if the Miyako family popped from the trees and laughed in her face. An M covering a K; a Miyako overtaking a Katz. This is about her. Headmaster Anji was right: Meiling is the cause of everything.

"What is it? What's going on?" Joon asks more urgently, his voice now right behind her.

With no time left to ponder what the right thing to do is, Meiling follows her gut. She snatches the rock, burying it deep into her pocket where it weighs her down like Perce-made cinder, and then she lifts her leg to kick the Miyako's overt display to bits.

Her foot never hits its target.

Instead, she's knocked off both feet and is sent flying backward. A loud whooshing noise fills her ears, and a blisteringly cold weight tugs at her body. She hits the ground, scraping up every bit of exposed skin in the process, and then she's shooting back up again. When she attempts to scream, liquid rushes into her mouth and down her throat.

Panic sets in belatedly. She flails her arms and struggles to break the surface, but the current is more robust than she is. It sends her soaring in every which way with no relief. Water fills her nostrils and floods her eyes. Fighting for her life, Meiling tries to see through the pitch-black water.

If she is from the Miyako bloodline, then she should be able to see clearly no matter what darkness is around her. Stranded within the water now, Meiling wonders why this is happening to her. Has she already lost the ability she only discovered days ago?

With no way of finding her bearings, Meiling is completely lost in the tidal wave suddenly refilling the Odaz River. Her life begins to flash in her eyes.

"Meiling," an unfamiliar voice says, rippling through the waves around her.

Meiling momentarily forgets she's drowning so she opens her mouth to reply. The water is relentless in rushing at her. It tastes like salt and copper—river water and blood.

Then the voice speaks again.

"Meiling." Water pulls itself out of her lungs. For a second, while she listens, she can breathe. "You're smart, my dear; you can figure out what they want. You can be the change we've spent years waiting for."

"What?" she whispers, surprised to hear her voice come out. It echoes in a pocket of air in the water.

"There's something different about you," the voice goes on, melodic. "You can solve this. You're the *only one* who can."

"I don't know what that means," Meiling says, but she is thinking of Divinia's prophecy again: *Meiling's existence holds great weight in the future of Malumvia.*

"Soon you will, darling. Remember yourself."

The rock in her pocket begins to float up, yanking at her pants and dragging her with it. It's no larger than her palm, but it suddenly functions like a full-sized life jacket. Meiling sets her fingers over it and allows herself to be led.

When Meiling's head breaks the surface, she's screaming. Not that it matters. The sound is easily lost within all the others.

Meiling wishes there was a Divinity of time.

If there was, she could pray to them to take her back in time a few hours. Back to before their new curriculum was introduced. Better yet, if a Divinity of time did exist, she could seek them and their descendants out to have herself thrown a couple of *months* into the past. Before she clearly read the word Miyako on her file, before she saw Doctor Sutherland's handwritten note warning against her enrollment, before she learned her medication had never actually been medication, but a tranquilizer so strong it dulls the abilities inside her until they don't exist at all.

But after Meiling found her file, she couldn't keep it

to herself. The reason she brought Callum and Karina along with her to the records room was to make sure she'd stand no chance at hiding the truth—even if she wanted to.

She really wants a Divinity of time. Perhaps if there was one, they could send her far enough back so she could change her mind about nearly everything and everyone. Including herself.

Because if she, Meiling Katz, is truly Meiling Miyako, then her entire life has changed. No one will ever look at her the same, and she will never look at anyone else the same either.

Finally, Meiling drags herself out of the river to see her classmates continuing to fight for their lives. Bleeding limbs, broken bones, blackened eyes. Laying and limping all around her, she seems to be the only one uninjured. A heavy bolt of sadness engulfs her heart as it becomes clear her whole life's plan is destroyed.

She can never be who she wants to be anymore. She can't be the normal girl who changes the world if she's not a normal girl. She can't be the ability-less underdog who brings freedom to both sides if she's actually a descendant of the stronger of them. The worst part of all this: Suraya will never stand by her side if her side is cloaked in darkness.

Lastly, Meiling isn't sure she can go on hating Kaito Miyako.

All her life she's cursed Kaito Miyako's name for causing the Lunar Eclipse Massacre, thinking he in turn caused her sickness, killed her parents, and rocked the country into endless civil war. And yet, this entire time, she's been completely fine and *he*'s been her parent.

With a group full of eyes scowling at her, Meiling understands him. Whether he staged the entire Lunar Eclipse Massacre or not, he is the same as her in at least one way: they never asked to be born with this blood.

"Call the authorities!" someone shrieks. Meiling drags herself over a riverbank and sees it's a Malumvian Detective. There's a large bone sticking out of her arm, dripping blood and river water. Meiling doesn't want to know who that bone truly belongs to.

"Sound the alarm! Call the authorities! It's an M-attack! A violent M-attack!"

Breathing heavily, Meiling looks down at the river, now filled with so much water it's nearly overflowing. There's an oily quality to the top layer, which is only now settling. In that oil, tinged a greenish blue, there is a massive letter M rippling with the current.

Meiling crawls backward on her hands, the rock like a ten-ton weight in her pocket. Scattered screams turn into one relentless, piercing mix of distress. Sobs echo through the forest around them and circle back, rattling in Meiling's eardrums.

Dey Vespetone pops out of the water a dozen paces away, cradling Ruby Devlin's unconscious and battered body. Even amidst all the other noise, Meiling can hear Ceri Melendez's scream clear as day. It pierces straight to her heart where she can feel it stop the beating for a full second.

Detectives and students alike are dragging one

another out of the crime scene all around her. Some of them are knocked unconscious, others are barely breathing, and most have their clothes soaked in more than river water. In the distance Meiling can hear Callum and Artie, so she breathes out a little easier knowing they are okay. Even still, she can't bring herself to stand up and move.

As Keegan Zialitos is transferred past Meiling on a stretcher made of vines from Joon Park's scraped-up hands, the resonant voice from underneath the water returns to her ears.

"The Sun always sets."

Meiling jerks her attention up as if to track down the voice. *The Sun always rises* is the first line in Malumvia's national anthem. Those words are painted onto nearly every government document and landmark, every important household and structure, every legacy of a Zialitos in power. To say the Sun always sets in response is *blasphemous*.

Donned in shadows deep within the trees, Meiling catches a pair of shining golden eyes. Even from a distance, she knows this is not the source of those words she can hear in her head. This is merely someone working for the so-called "Mikazi" that brought tragedy to the Odaz River. Once Meiling locks eyes with this character, one eye winks, and then they are both gone.

It's at this moment Meiling realizes it doesn't matter what she says or does, or even what she intends: these M-attacks are both her fault and her fate to fix.

20

Suraya

Suraya tries not to take offense when her half of Red Class One—oh so cleverly titled the Scarlet Group—is sent to the training rooms for ability sparring while the other half, the Crimson Group containing Meiling, is put on real life detective duty.

She fails. There's nothing inoffensive about a Miyako receiving authoritative duty over a Zialitos.

For the entire walk down to the training room, Suraya stabs her fingernails into her palms, trying and failing to relax. Despite coming from a different Division an hour train ride away, Meiling has always been the person closest to her. When Suraya couldn't rely on her mother to teach her how to control her sunlight, it was Meiling who studied until she could. When Suraya needed to test the limits of her self-healing abilities, it was Meiling who reluctantly took on the role. When Suraya wanted to sit around in silence without feeling so alone—the way she always did when her mother experienced a sudden bout of depression that took her parents away for days at a time— it was Meiling she wanted to sit with her.

The memories are tinted red now that Suraya knows the truth. In all the time she spent trusting and taking care of Meiling, expecting the same in return, Meiling was secretly idolizing a Miyako because she's one, too.

A window nearly shatters overhead. Suraya reins in the sunlight she unwillingly summoned and forces it to dim. Evie, Kai, Cyrus and Dao, who are usually jumpier than frogs raised by the Kagisos, don't say a word to her about it. Suraya blows out a breath in relief.

In the open training room, the Scarlet Group is joined by the Plum Group—a subsection of Violet Class One. Maia Pearson, one of the Academy coaches for assistance in weight, agility, endurance, and skills-related exercises, stands at the front of the room. On the young side at twenty-two years old, she insists on being called by her first name even though she's their coach. Maia has cropped white hair with bangs Suraya can't stand, dark blue eyes, and rosy skin. She's of Divinia descent, and is plenty good at breaking down emotional barriers. Suraya can't stand that about her either.

"Hello Scarlets and Plums," she says as they awkwardly form a semi-circle around her. "Today you'll be honing your abilities via controlled sparring matches. We'll begin by pairing off."

It's immediate pandemonium. Suraya feels three different hands grab her wrist to claim her as a partner. She generates enough heat into her skin to burn them right off again.

"With someone from a different class!" Maia shouts over the noise.

Evie and Kai let out twin sighs of defeat. Then they scurry apart, easily finding new people to cling to. Despite the constant mayhem so far this year at the Academy, the forced cohabitation with other students has made it easy to know everyone. Suraya recognizes every single face in the room, but still she doesn't move. She doesn't want to work with any of these people.

Crossing her arms tightly over her chest, Suraya watches everyone pair off and find open spaces of the room to stand together.

No one is brave enough to approach her until there is no other choice.

"Want to be partners?" Noa Pearson, Maia's younger sister from the Violet Class asks timidly.

Suraya grunts in approval. If nothing else this will be an easy win for her.

"Okay, up first as a warm-up: ability-less sparring. Go!"

In light of recent news, fighting ability-less seems like the dumbest possible activity they could be doing. Suraya considers keeping her skin heated with sunlight anyway out of spite, but she doesn't want to kill the poor Pearson girl. She charges forward with nothing more than her fists instead.

Noa quickly turns on her heels, evading Suraya's fists. She moves with the kind of grace and fluidity you'd expect from a coach's sister. Not bad, but still not good enough.

Suraya takes her out at the knees the second she lets her guard down. Before she gets the chance to regain her bearings, Suraya has her pinned to the ground. Match and point.

They go again. And again. And again. Noa lasts a little longer each time, but she never manages to win. Suraya hardly breaks a sweat.

Suraya rolls her eyes. Thankfully Maia realizes the unfair matchup her sister has been put in and relieves her with a substitute; Jamie Dumas from Suraya's own Red Class One.

"What are you doing here?" Suraya watches his dull blue eyes flash with fear. "I thought you were in Crimson."

"I didn't... No, not anymore."

"Whatever." Suraya drops into a squat. "Ready?"

Noa calls start for them. Suraya takes a second of stillness to see if Jamie will try charging. He doesn't look like the type to try charging, but if there is anything Meiling being revealed as a Miyako has been good for, it's proving to Suraya that looks don't mean a thing.

Jamie does not charge. Instead, he glides backward a couple meters and drops into a squat to match Suraya. Cracking a smile, Suraya charges him herself. She swings with a right hook first, but Jamie drops to the floor like a puddle to dodge it. He's stealthy. As expected of an Omni descendant.

Suraya fixes her pose and attacks again. Jamie does not often fight back, but he dodges perfectly, keeping the match in motion. Half of Suraya is miffed she hasn't been able to finish this already, and the other half of her is thrilled someone can keep up with her for once. Sweat trails down her temples and she's near-giddy about it.

Jamie Dumas, she thinks, watching the pale boy flip backward away from her to avoid a killer uppercut to the jaw, *where have you been hiding?*

Suraya loses track of how long this goes on before Maia's voice finally cuts through the heavy breathing to shout, "Abilities on!"

In the half of a second it takes for those words to process, Jamie has already vanished into thin air. Suraya curses Omni for passing on his abilities, especially to someone like Jamie Dumas who is already well-versed in the art of evasion.

His invisibility in the spirit realm forces Suraya to wrap a protective coating of sunlight around her whole body. Doing this trick is draining in the long term, and it takes way more focus than she wants to give, but it's her only line of defense when she can't see her opponent coming. Shimmering around her limbs like the Nature Energy on the Kagisos, Suraya's sunlight is practically imperceptible, but dangerously exposed nonetheless. Should Jamie touch it, he'll be very sorry.

Jamie is talented, but he can't remain in his spirit state in the spirit realm forever. As his control weakens, he flickers into view like a blinking traffic light. Tracking his movements across the room is a bit like following a trail of mist. He's a full ten meters away and then he's not, body seeming to pop through space and time to appear by her side.

Suraya lashes out at him with her sunlight in bursts, careful to keep it both wrapped around her body and completely separated from the other pairs sparring around them. When it finally catches Jamie, she can feel it like a harsh yank on the ends of her hair.

With most sparring opponents Suraya has faced in her life, one touch of sunlight is enough to knock them off-kilter. Being knocked off kilter leads to dropping powers, which means stumbling physically and giving her a perfect chance to win.

None of this happens now. Jamie Dumas is no usual sparring opponent.

Something about him is most definitely *unusual* right now, though.

Suraya understands the complexity of Omni's abilities well enough (especially in recent days with Evie glued to her side), so she can say with near certainty that Jamie's body should not be doing what it currently is.

Rather than coming in and out of the spirit realm as one full body, he's flickering in pieces: first an arm, then half of a leg, then two floating eyes and a hairline. Suraya drops every ounce of her sunlight, feeling as if she's the one burnt by it for once, but it makes no difference. Within seconds, every section of Jamie's body has appeared one way or another except for his mouth. That stays hidden. I f he calls for help, no one will hear it.

Suraya will never claim to be helpless—because she's absolutely not and never will be—but at this jarring moment in time, with Jamie's fingers popping through the air like one is being tugged around by a string, she's a bit lost on how to actually help.

"Maia!" Noa shouts, the rosy skin of her cheeks now a deep red. "Something's wrong with Jamie!"

Maia comes rushing over, her eyes lit up as if ready to shove her happy-brain powers at someone, but that someone is nowhere to be seen. She halts beside Suraya with a furrow in her brows and asks, "What's going on?"

"Jamie is stuck in a spirit state," Suraya says matter-of-factly, settling her hands on her hips. "And unless the mechanics of Omni abilities have changed in the past twenty-four hours, I'm fairly certain that shouldn't happen. Spirit states are an all or nothing shift."

A jagged section of Jamie's forearm flies by Maia's face inches away from touching. She screeches in surprise and nearly every head in the room turns their direction. Suraya motions at it as if to say, *Told you so.*

"What–"

"Let me out!" Jamie screams, his entire face appearing half a meter away, straining as if pushing against fabric to be set free.

Then he's gone. Again. Suraya tries to feel for his presence around them so the next time he comes into view—however much or little of him that may be—she can reach out and physically drag him back. But she's a Zialitos, and Zialitos are good with light and life, not death or the dark.

No one can ever know, but Suraya feels her chest lighten when Evie shows up by her side. She's damp with sweat at her hairline, ponytail loose and frizzy down her back, and she's breathing heavily, but other than that she's her usual self. Meaning she's more than happy to retie her hair and ask, "How can I help?"

As a descendant of Omni herself, she may be one of

the only ones who *can*. As quickly as possible, Suraya explains the situation. If this is a shock, Evie doesn't show it. If this is a common occurrence, Evie doesn't show that either. She simply nods along quietly, watching body parts materialize around the room as Jamie apparently runs back and forth in the spirit world.

By the end of the explanation, Evie seems to have a plan, even though she doesn't share it. She simply takes Suraya's hands between her own and says, "Got it. Be ready with a lot of sunlight, okay?"

Suraya furrows her brows. "Okay?"

Evie melts into the air, gone with the spirits, before the word is completely out of Suraya's mouth.

The next time Jamie appears, it's almost all of him. Evie has two arms wrapped around him, dragging. He's screaming. Over and over again, he says, "Let me go!" But he's not talking to Evie. He's looking straight ahead at a spirit no one else can see.

Evie continues dragging him. With each step they move, another piece of him turns visible. It's absurd to watch from the outside. To Suraya it looks like nothing more than some ridiculous magic trick; like Evie is pulling Jamie out from behind a fancy curtain or something. She's clearly struggling with the last of him, though. Her skin is red all over as if it's about to burst. When it seems as if she can take no more, she locks eyes with Suraya across the room and shouts, "Now!"

Suraya doesn't hesitate. She wields as much sunlight as she can between her palms and sends it flying in their direction. There are ways for her to make it less harmful so she tries to employ them, but in such short notice, she doubts they matter. The vortex of light collides with both of them and they fly backward ten meters into the wall. Both their forms crumple to the ground, fully visible. Perhaps not fully intact, but fully visible nonetheless.

If Evie looks a minute away from death, Jamie looks mere seconds away from it. His breath is weak and stuttering, his body limp, and his eyes are droopy and red-ringed. Evie takes her arm out from behind him and a chorus of theatrical gasps fly through the room. Arms definitely aren't supposed to bend that way.

"I'm fine," Evie quickly tries to reassure, but her voice shakes with unshed tears. "Jamie needs a nurse first."

Suraya realizes Jamie's not actually conscious. He looks dead. If not for the small puffs of air leaving his cracked lips, she'd truly think he is.

"What happened?" Maia asks, looking desperately back and forth from the Violet class's teacher—who Suraya didn't realize was here at all since she's done absolutely nothing before—and Evie, who is poking at her broken limb with terrified eyes.

"A spirit—a *strong* spirit—wanted him to stay," Evie answers slowly, her gaze finding Suraya's. She looks hesitant to say the rest aloud, but she does anyway. "It was a Miyako. He *really* wants to talk to Meiling."

A Miyako. A dead Miyako. A dead Miyako who wants to chat with Meiling. Yeah, sure. What else could it possibly be at this point, right?

Evie keeps looking directly at Suraya as she adds,

eyebrow ticking up, "His name is Kane. It looked like he had on an Academy uniform."

For the second time in the span of a couple days, Suraya feels the floor give way beneath her feet. First, she was wrong about Meiling, and now she's wrong about the source of this Mikazi character and all these M-attacks, too. She can't be right because her main culprit was the Academy boy from those pictures, Kane Miyako. But how can that be the case if Kane Miyako is dead? Suraya is left with about a million questions, but the one she finds herself stuck on is:

What does the dead Kane Miyako want with Meiling?

A sudden siren shakes the walls around them. Evie shrieks, jostling Jamie nearly a meter off the ground. He still doesn't wake.

By now the sound of sirens and alarm bells shouldn't be shocking. But when a voice pierces through the speakers to announce there has been a violent M-attack right here on the Academy's campus, it's a bit hard not to drop a jaw and shout.

21
Meiling

By the twentieth time the Malumvian detective asks Meiling what the Miyakos want to accomplish with the M-attacks, she's tempted to make something up just so he won't ask again.

After the tsunami at the Odaz River, all of the Crimson Group, aside from Meiling herself, were wheeled off to the nurse's wing. A new set of detectives promptly showed up to take over for the previous—all put out of commission as they, too, got wheeled away on stretchers—and brought Meiling in for questioning. Headmaster Anji had made Meiling's blood status public knowledge after the Academy assembly, so, of course, she's everyone's main target these days.

To her best guess, it's been roughly two hours now. Folded up on a bench in the back of one of their vans, Meiling feels trapped and surrounded. What's worse is the fact she can hear the slow movement of the Odaz River in the near distance. The detectives didn't bother moving the van very far so she has to hear every ripple in the water as it happens.

A ringing earpiece on one of the detectives not actively interrogating Meiling offers a brief reprieve. All heads turn as a tinny voice filters through. Meiling is not close enough to make out any of the actual words, but she can read the expressions on the detectives' faces well enough. She'll be lucky to ever leave this van at this rate.

"Detective Muñoz has been pronounced dead," the detective announces once the earpiece finally quiets. "Keegan Zialitos and Ruby Devlin are in critical condition. No other updates as of yet."

Meiling wants to drop her head into her hands and weep, but she doesn't dare to move. These people have enough against her already.

"You hear that, Miyako?" the burly detective standing before her sneers. "A good man drowned because of you. Innocent children are lying in hospital beds because of you. Are you still going to sit there and say nothing?"

Meiling meets his eyes. Authority figures within Malumvia with Divinia descent are only permitted to use their mind manipulation abilities on willing participants. Meiling gave her explicit permission hours ago—practically the moment they found her at the river, meaning he can easily slip inside her thoughts and read the frustration there.

Meiling is sick of trying to prove the innocence of the innocent. If no one is going to listen to her anyway, she might as well switch up tactics here. She'll be their villain if that's what they want, but she'll never give up on her goals. She'll simply do it a little differently: starting with hunting down those who are actually guilty here.

"Don't be angry with me," the detective says, pulling out of her mind with a scowl.

"I'm angry at all of you," Meiling grumbles. She believes in Divinia's prophecy about her now, and so does everyone else, and that's the problem. A Miyako to take down the Miyakos. It's insane.

"What did you say to me?"

The detective hardly gets the chance to reach out toward her before another steps up to restrain him. A gust of air whooshes past Meiling smelling of salt and metal. Instinct has her clutching down on the rock hidden within her pocket.

"Don't do anything to her we can't rationalize," the detective restraining the other whispers, thinking Meiling can't hear. "We're already toeing the line by ignoring procedure, Lyle."

"That's right," Meiling says aloud, somehow only realizing it two hours in: Malumvian Officials can't interrogate anyone under the age of twenty without a parent or trusted guardian present. "You could lose your licenses *and* your right to public ability usage for this."

Lyle clenches his jaw and shakes himself free.

"I'd be careful what you chose to say, Miyako," he spits. "You're hardly a reliable source."

"*Katz*," Meiling snaps.

"Enough, Lyle." The other detective slaps him upside the head. Then, to Meiling, he says, "You're right. Please forgive us. You're free to go, Miss Katz-Miyako."

Meiling sighs. She tries not to seem too ungrateful as the detective unhooks her from the bench and opens the door for her to leave. Outside the dark detective van, the sun is high up in the sky. The stark contrast burns her eyes, making her trip on the way out.

With a few fresh cuts on her palms and scrapes on her kneecaps, Meiling returns to the First Year Dorm Hall in a blur with nothing but a mysterious rock buzzing inside her pocket as company.

There's another set of interrogators waiting for Meiling inside. Standing outside the door of her dorm room as if guarding something precious inside, three top-ranked Malumvian Authorities have taken position. When Meiling turns the corner to see them, she considers turning right back around. Frustration is a physical lump inside her chest. It's hard to breathe around it.

Unfortunately, she has no choice but to move forward because this time there is a trusted guardian with them—at least on paper. A couple meters down the hallway from the authorities, Headmaster Anji stands reading a newspaper. Meiling doesn't need to read it with him to know it details a recent M-attack.

Approaching cautiously, Meiling grips the rock inside her pocket until it starts to scrape off her skin. Let a Malumvian officer see it and she'll probably be thrown behind bars.

"Miyako."

"It's Katz," she says, exhaling heavily. "Meiling Katz."

Ever since Headmaster Anji announced her true lineage, no one calls her by her name anymore. According to a small print subsection of the Divine Segregation Laws, anyone with Zialitos or Miyako descent must go by that name. Meiling doesn't exactly hate it, but the least everyone could do is call her Meiling Katz-Miyako like that one detective did. Jax and Reena are still her parents, too.

Meiling tries not to think too much about it. It could be worse. For starters, Suraya hardly calls her anything at all; it's been a full day and a half and she hasn't said a single word to Meiling. Not even a curse, which definitely feels worse.

"Miyako," the officer says, doubling down. "We have a couple questions for you."

"Let me guess: you want to know what I know?" Meiling asks, her head throbbing.

She might not have gotten hurt to the extent that anyone else did at the Odaz River earlier, but she still nearly drowned. She can taste salt water in her lungs. She needs to visit the others to see they're safe, and then she needs a nap. A *long* nap.

"I'll save you some time, then: I know nothing."

In a startlingly similar way to five minutes earlier, one officer jerks forward as if to attack her at the same time another hooks two arms around his shoulders to keep him back. Meiling scrubs both hands down her face. Is this her life now that they know she has Mahina blood in her veins? If so, it's no wonder the Miyakos are so angry all the time.

"What is your relation to Kane Miyako?" the third officer asks while those two scuffle amongst themselves.

"I would assume our Miyako blood."

"Funny," he says deadpan. "Would you rather we take this to the Zialitos Headquarters?"

The rock in Meiling's pocket goes ballistic, almost as if responding to the sharp stab of her heart rate. It jerks around in rapid circles that cut holes straight through the fabric of her pants. Meiling has to press down against it until her palm turns white just to keep it from popping out in front of everyone.

The Zialitos Headquarters has the strongest ability users in the country under employment, the strongest ability-suppressing technology in the government, and the strongest security systems in the entire world. Meiling will be dead by the morning if they bring her there.

"No," she says quickly. "Please accept my apologies."

She begins to bow, hand at her heart to pray for Ataru, but a sharp flash of light stops her short. It burns her fingers apart so her hand is no more than a limp open palm. The third officer, apparently a Zialitos, retracts the lasso of sunlight with a harsh grin.

"You've no right to pray to Ataru," he tells her. "Tell me what relation you have to Kane Miyako and we'll leave you to your night."

"I don't know," Meiling says, looking to Headmaster Anji for help and receiving none. He's too focused on that stupid newspaper. Meiling's hand shakes so badly it climbs up her arm and into her torso. The air smells like her own burnt flesh. "I've never heard that name before."

The officers laugh. Meiling keeps her head bowed. If

there's a joke, she missed the punchline. Or she is the punchline herself.

"The Zialitos Headquarters it is."

The hallway gets flooded with sunlight, and it hurts, and Meiling just wants to go to bed and think in silence for a while. Before she can stop it, a scream tears out of her throat. Darkness explodes out of her as if her chest has been cracked open and is bleeding it out. This hurts too.

Meiling drops to her knees on the carpet and screams her throat raw. A dark corner of her brain wishes Doctor Sutherland were around to stick a needle in her neck and take the abilities away for a while. The stronger they are, the more they hurt. The more they hurt, the more the rock in her pocket bounces around as if fighting to be free.

"Hey!"

All at once the shadows fade away. Meiling relaxes on the ground and stares through hazy eyes to watch Suraya stomp up the hallway with Mr. Arredondo at her side. Both of them have their hands poised to strike.

"Trying to start another fight?" Suraya asks, but Meiling doesn't know who she's asking: her or the officers. "Haven't we had enough of that for one day?"

Mr. Arredondo cuts in before the officers can lash back. "Unless you have a warrant for Meiling's arrest, please see yourselves out. This is a dorm hall and it is a school night. As Suraya has so kindly put it, we have all had enough for one day already."

Meiling grabs the wall and pulls herself to her feet.

"We are here by the Headmaster's order, sir."

Mr. Arredondo cuts his gaze down the hallway to

Headmaster Anji, who is now facing them, the newspaper folded beneath his armpit.

"Surely you can leave by his order, too, then?" Mr. Arredondo asks the detectives. He never removes his gaze from the Headmaster.

The detectives murmur amongst themselves with halfhearted nods of agreement. Mr. Arredondo narrows his eyes to snake-like slits.

Headmaster Anji clunks forward on his cane and says, "See yourselves out, officers. Now is not the time."

One by one the officers file out on Headmaster Anji's orders. Each shoots Meiling a sharp look as they go. Headmaster Anji follows after them, pausing beside Meiling only for a moment to say, "I apologize, Miss Meiling, but the elders insisted. It was the condition for not expelling you immediately."

Meiling leans more heavily into the wall, completely drained. Of course, they want her expelled. Her classmates, her *best friends*, are in the hospital because of her relation to the Miyakos.

Mr. Arredondo reaches out a large hand to help her steady herself. "Are you okay?"

Meiling doesn't get the chance to respond before Suraya is cutting in to ask, "What did they want?"

Suraya has ignored her this whole time only to come around and ask her that? Keegan and Ruby are in critical condition, everyone else is injured, and the M-attacks are officially on their campus. Interrogations should be the least of anyone's concern.

Meiling takes three breaths before she answers. "They

wanted to know what I knew about some Miyako named Kane."

Suraya's eyes pop, flashing silver. Meiling rears back. How does Suraya know who Kane is if she doesn't?

"And?" Suraya asks, her voice lower. "What do you know?"

Meiling scrubs a hand over her face before remembering it's been burnt raw. Heat laces up her wrist like poison once more.

"Nothing," she says, shorter than she usually would be with Suraya. "I didn't even know myself as a Miyako until a few days ago. What would I know about some guy named Kane?"

Suraya sneers at her.

"You kept a lot of photographs of someone you *don't know.*"

"What?" Meiling pictures her stolen collection of photographs: a Miyako in an Academy uniform. Images cropped and cut into strange shapes, all hidden in the deep corners of her adoptive parents' closet. *That's* Kane Miayko? Figures she's the last to hear of it.

"I didn't..."

"Stop lying!" Suraya shouts.

Mr. Arredondo reaches out to drop a hand on her shoulder. She flinches, but does not burn him away. Meiling almost envies him. Suraya is looking at her like she'd kill her for breathing the wrong way right now.

"It's been a long day. Let her get some rest and we can all talk about this tomorrow. *Properly.*"

With a scoff, Suraya stalks off down the hallway to

her own dorm room, slamming the door shut behind her. Sparks fly out in every direction.

"Do you need to see the nurse, Meiling?" Mr. Arredondo asks quietly.

Meiling shakes her head no.

"The Academy therapists?"

Meiling shakes her head no again, a bit more aggressively this time.

"Okay," he acquiesces. "Go get some rest then."

Meiling doesn't need to be told twice. Behind the closed door of her dorm room, Meiling soothes her burnt hand around a frozen water bottle and throws the rock from the Odaz River out the window. Five minutes later, her hand is numb and the rock is right back in her pocket, nestling against the fabric in an attempt to get closer to blood pumping through her veins.

22

Suraya

In an ideal world, Jamie would relay the story of his time stuck in the spirit realm with Kane Miyako to Suraya himself. That way Suraya wouldn't have to wake Meiling at midnight to ask her directly what her dead relative wants.

Actually, *scratch that*, Suraya thinks, yanking her shoes on. In an ideal world, no one—dead or alive—would be begging to see Meiling in the first place. She's supposed to be Meiling Katz: a nerdy, ability-less nobody, safe and sound in Division Three reading books and making chai to share with Suraya. For years Suraya has tried to keep it this way, to keep Meiling far away from the danger of a world filled with Miyakos and Zialitos, but Meiling is bull-headed. And, as it turns out, a Miyako herself anyway.

The Academy doesn't seem to have taken many precautions for the latest location of a violent M-attack currently harboring a Miyako. Suraya slips out of her dorm room a few minutes after midnight to silence in the hallways. She flashes her eyes to life in order to see through the darkness and notices nothing more than the usual cameras blinking in one corner of the ceiling. Walking the dozen meters down to Meiling's door is easy. Even those cameras hardly shift to track her movement.

Suraya lifts a closed fist and bangs twice on Meiling's door. It sounds like an explosion in the quiet of the dorm hall. On the other side, she hears Meiling topple out of bed with a squeak. Suraya steps back and waits for her to come out.

The door swings open to Meiling with a head of frizzy hair and crust around her eyes. They're red, and not just the Miyako irises.

"Suri," she breathes. That stupid, cutesy nickname.

"Meiling *Miyako*."

The reaction is instantaneous. Meiling reels back like she's been struck. Her face pales so much the bangs over her forehead look ten shades darker and her freckles stand out like stupid constellations in a cloudless sky.

Then Meiling swallows thickly and asks the last possible thing Suraya expects: "Did you know about me?"

Suraya takes one heavy step closer, just enough for Meiling to feel the heat radiating off her body. She swallows back thorns in her throat.

"Do you think I'd have let you follow me around all these years if I knew?"

"Follow you?" Meiling lets her door close heavily as she steps into the hall completely. "That's not how this is."

"Don't make me laugh. That's how this has always been." Suraya turns around, letting light swirl within her gut like an unsettled ocean under a storm. Meiling follows her down the hallway like a moth to a flame. Half of

Suraya wants to hug her and the other half wants to throw her into the wall. "You're doing it now. Chasing after me like a lost puppy. Or should I say like an enemy stalking its prey? Because that's what you are, aren't you?"

"No !" Meiling insists, jogging up beside Suraya so she can see up close and personal how Meiling's cheeks are flushed an angry red to match her eyes. Her hands wave erratically in front of them. "I'm not your enemy, Suri. I'd never be your enemy."

Suraya laughs. It echoes in the empty stairwell she's currently leading them down to leave the building. If they take the side door exit, there's not even an alarm to set off. So long as Suraya presses the heat lock firmly, they'll be out in the courtyard alone with none the wiser they've left at all.

That's exactly what they do. Meiling chases her the whole way there without a single question asked, her feet and arms bare. In the moonlight, Meiling looks taller and less afraid. Suraya will bet she is, having Mahina blood in her veins. It makes sense now why her hero was a Miyako all this time. Each beat of Suraya's heart stabs through her chest.

"Spill," Suraya says, pulling the light out of her gut and into her hands instead. "Tell me everything you know, starting with why Kane Miyako is holding people hostage in the spirit realm just to get to you and ending with why you're helping Mikazi slaughter people for sport with these M-attacks."

When Meiling's eyes widen in response, she returns to

looking as naive and weak as she's pretended to be her whole life. It grates on Suraya's nerves like a dull blade.

"What are you talking about? That Miyako is... he's dead?"

"Why are you surprised?" Suraya asks, twirling the light between her fingertips and relishing in the way Meiling's eyes track it. "He's a Miyako. You nearly wiped yourselves out with the Lunar Eclipse Massacre, just to take some of us down with you. It's no surprise there aren't many left."

"He wants to see me?" Meiling asks quietly. She doesn't seem to be properly hearing Suraya at all right now. Heat flares in her gut.

"Don't make me ask again. Explain yourself."

"I don't know," Meiling says, back to herself with a deep frown. "I don't know anything. You don't seriously think I would hide this from you, do you? I know nothing!"

Suraya hates to admit it, but Meiling has never *known nothing* a day in her life. She's always fifteen steps ahead with mounds of research and fun facts and hand drawn graphs. For her to truly know nothing, she'd have to be dead. And right now, Suraya is too angry to see any reason why she shouldn't help make that happen.

She lunges.

For someone who "doesn't follow Suraya around," Meiling sure knows how to dodge and fight like a Zialitos-trained warrior. When Suraya swings her right arm around in a circle to pitch her sunlight forward like a baseball, Meiling immediately responds with a thick wall of shadows. The hand motions she uses to call it up are the exact same ones Suraya uses to summon sunlight.

The shadow wall doesn't last long. As soon as it's up, it begins to tremble. Seconds later, it collapses. Meiling stares at the place where it was with wide eyes. Then her mouth twitches into a frown and she stares down at her hands.

Suraya grins. Meiling can copy her all she wants, but a move made for the Zialitos will never benefit a Miyako.

"Wait—"

Suraya charges. This time when Meiling throws her arms up in an attempt to call upon the shadows, nothing comes.

Suraya grabs her around the wrists and yanks. Her fingers dig into raw, burnt skin on one hand and Meiling screams. Using both hands, Suraya tugs Meiling forward to flip her over like a sack of flour. Her back hits the pebbled ground below with a crack. The next scream she lets out gets swallowed by the breath being knocked from her lungs.

Suraya drops down over her, pinning her hands above her head. With her own hands, she weaves the tiniest bit of sunlight. It's not enough to burn or restrain on its own, but it's easily enough to sting. A bead of sweat rolls down Meiling's cheek like a tear.

"You're supposed to be stronger at night," Suraya says.

Meiling scowls and jerks upward in an attempt to shake Suraya off. She shoves Meiling right back down again. Something cracks beneath her.

"Yet you still lose. You wanna try again? Or are you ready to tell me the truth this time?"

Meiling coughs and pants. Her eyes are back to their usual state of wideness, as if she's a little kid staring at the stars. Her body twitches, shadows rolling in like clouds. Suraya pushes her wrists down harder, feeling the resistance of pebbles beneath them. Meiling grits her teeth to cut off a gasp of pain.

"I never once lied to you, Suri."

"Look at me then," Suraya growls, using one hand to grip Meiling by the jaw and tilt her head up, forcing their gazes to meet. "You've always been a terrible liar, Meiling. You always look away when you do, or else everyone will see the way you rapidly blink off tears. You can't fool me."

Meiling sighs heavily. Suraya sits back, knowing she's finally won. Meiling knows something, and she's going to tell her one way or another.

Meiling props herself up on her elbows and makes a conscious effort to look at Suraya as she says, "I don't know much of anything for sure, that's the truth."

She wrings her hands together nervously. They suddenly appear a couple shades darker than the rest of her body, almost as if her shadows are settling permanently into the skin there. Suraya hastily looks back up to Meiling's face, not liking how much she doesn't dislike it.

"I promise you, Suri, I had no idea I was a Miyako before. But now that I do, it's like... It's like all these things keep happening."

"Wow," Suraya breathes, clapping twice for good measure. "*Things*. How very enlightening."

"Listen," Meiling says quickly, Then, even quieter and much higher-pitched, she adds, "Please."

Suraya waves her on. If a little bit of sunlight leaps out from her fingertips in the process, then no one has to know. Tonight stays between them anyway.

"At the Academy entrance exam, I could hardly see. I stopped taking my medicine to prove… It doesn't matter. Point is, I wasn't on my medication and it was messing me up. It was all I could do to take down one guy from the Beams, but I swear he was going to get up before he saw who I was. Then Headmaster Anji smiled at me and I was in. I shouldn't have passed."

Suraya could have told her that.

"Then there was dinner with your parents and the move-in day here and the night at the kitchen downstairs. After that the Birds of Prey sought me out again," Meiling says. "They stalked me through the trees and tried to take me with them, saying *he*, Mikazi, I guess, has been waiting long enough. I barely got away in the end."

Suraya keeps her lips pressed together, letting her speak. If she silently prays to Ataru hard enough, perhaps she'll get to the point.

"Then everyone found out about me. Yesterday at the Odaz River there was a K drawn into the sand with a M of bones built over it. There was a strange holey rock underneath it. I took it right before I started to drown. Underwater I heard someone's voice. I didn't recognize it, but it still seemed so familiar. Have you ever had that?"

Suraya bites down on her lip and narrows her eyes. She has. When Ataru visited her in her dreams, that's exactly how it felt: new, but familiar. But if Mahina is visiting Meiling... *No*, Suraya thinks. She can't afford to entertain an idea that terrible.

Meiling clears her throat when she realizes she isn't going to receive an answer.

"The rock won't leave me alone now. It always finds its way back to me. Just like the shadows, just like the Birds of Prey, just like the violence... It all follows me around now." Her voice cracks. There are tears in her eyes. "It isn't my fault, Suraya. I never asked for any of this."

Suraya swallows the taste of ash in her mouth. On instinct she extends her hand to Meiling, palm up. Before she can snap out of it and snatch it back, Meiling links their fingers the way they used to as kids.

"What do they want from you?" Suraya asks.

"I already told you, I don't know." The shadows circling her hands pulse in and out, larger and smaller. Suraya feels a chill in the veins of her wrist from them.

"Anything I think is a theory. Your guess is as good as mine."

"Then tell me your theory." Suraya grits her teeth. She's never had to ask before.

"Taking into account what you said about Kane, I think they want to be acknowledged," Meiling mumbles, squeezing Suraya's hand tighter. "They want someone like me, someone like *him*, that can offer them a new 'in.' I think the Miyakos just want to be seen and accepted again—despite who they are and what they've done. Because I'm one of them, and I'm one of you, and all I've ever wanted was to be accepted."

Suraya scowls. Where under Ataru's Sun did she get that theory? No sane person who wants to be accepted would choose to do so through terrorism and scare tactics.

"Honestly?" Meiling says, a little stronger now. "I think the Miyakos must want their history back."

"What do you mean by that?" Suraya hisses. The Miyako's have their history and it's all blood; that's the problem.

Meiling retracts her hand from Suraya's to lace her own fingers together. She squeezes until her knuckles go white and another chill sweeps through Suraya. Darkness seeps out of the microscopic cracks between Meiling's skin like smoke off a tea cup. As it rises, it swirls into abstract shapes and shakes as if trying to solidify. One blob looks strangely familiar, like an old relic Suraya saw once on a trip with her parents as a kid. Maybe Meiling recognizes it, too, because she releases a sharp breath that sends it skittering away the second it starts to become too real.

"I'm the only one who can figure it out," Meiling asserts. "That's what the voice told me. That's what the prophecy said about me. If that's true, then there's something special about me, right? And being a Miyako isn't all that special… Not really. But being a Miyako here at the Zialitos Academy—that is. The entire country thinks so because the entire country thinks no one's done it before. Kane's been erased completely."

Suraya lets a long pause permeate the air between them. Meiling's final words ring in her ears like a bunch of tiny knives.

"That's it then?" she asks after a while. "You think all

the Miyakos want is a pat on the back for existing and some changes to a textbook or two?"

"It's a bit more substantial than that," Meiling says, mostly to herself. Then, "Yes, in essence, that's exactly what I think."

"That's ridiculous." Suraya gets to her feet, laughing with no humor. "Stand up. If you won't stop withholding information willingly, I'll have to beat it out of you."

Meiling pushes herself backward across the ground about ten meters in three seconds flat. She leaves behind a path so clear and deep it's like a bulldozer passed through.

"I don't want to fight you," she says miserably, pupils large and shaky. "That's really all I've got."

"Fine," Suraya concedes. "Then at least tell me this: why the mix of attacks and non-attacks? If they want our attention, they've got it. Why bother with all the theatrics?"

"I don't know," Meiling says, but she's thinking about it now. Suraya can see it in her eyes. She can see it in the rigid line of her posture. Meiling's always been a bit of an open book.

"After thirteen, the non-attacks started looping, you know," Suraya points out. "The Odaz River was last, with the drought and bones before the tsunami came and you magically came out unscathed, and then it went right back to the Mahina Temple, starting all over again. Can your place as the *only one who can figure this out* explain that?"

"No," Meiling mumbles, but there's something in her eyes now. Whatever it is, she keeps it to herself.

"That's what I thought."

Suraya takes a menacing step forward. Meiling flinches back. *Good.* Suraya's been raised in a house full of egg shells because of the Miyakos and their bloodshed at the Lunar Eclipse Massacre. She never got to know her mother before her mother did more than cry all day, she never got to see what it was like to walk the streets as the Pride of the Zialitos without also being expected to be the *Savior* of the Zialitos, too, and she's never going to meet all the people in those old photo albums at home who gave her her name and knit her baby blanket and planned on having kids of their own for Suraya to grow up with so she wouldn't be so alone in that mansion of a Zialitos house.

The Miyakos took *everything* from her; she's going to make sure she takes everything from them, too.

"You're going to do what you're here for and lure your family out," she tells Meiling, swallowing thickly. "Once you do, we'll give them their *acknowledgement* and their *history*, and then you'll stay away from me. Understood?"

"Suri—"

"Call me that again and I'll burn your tongue out," she snaps, hands itching. She can't let herself be swayed by the Meiling she thought she knew. It was all a lie. "We're not friends. You're nothing more than a stepping stone to lead me to your family. And once I've gotten my revenge on them, I couldn't care less where you go."

Meiling curls into herself like a turtle retreating to its shell. Her head bobs in a feeble nod, but she says absolutely nothing else.

Well good, Suraya thinks. *That's over then.*

She turns on her heels and leaves.

23
Meiling

As it turns out, some people are not exactly receptive to Meiling's plan to pursue a suicide mission.

Apparently listening to other people suggest she become a pawn was all well and good, but the second she does it, it's some sort of blasphemous crazy-talk.

"You can't possibly be serious," Vale Lochnen says, storm clouds circling her desk lazily, pouring out rain so no one can come within a meter of her. It must be nice to consciously make the choice to keep people away. Meiling repels everyone like the plague these days without even trying.

Meiling is shocked that out of everyone in the first year classes gathered here in Mr. Arredondo's room to listen to her plan, Vale is the first to speak a full sentence in response. Most of the time she's sitting on the outskirts of every group, storm clouds over her head as she reads silently. Meiling's plan must be crazier than she thought if it's gotten Vale to speak up against it.

"I'm serious," she says.

"It's suicide," Vale replies, arching one perfectly sculpted eyebrow up.

"It *might* be, but so what? That's what a Miyako like me is here for, right?" She looks at Suraya, raising a brow, and Suraya looks away. "Divinia's prophecy says these M-attacks end with me. Can't I be willing to stake my life on it?"

A chorus of mixed responses fill the room. Most of the first year students are humming in agreement, thinking exactly what Meiling thought they would: *what does it matter if a Miyako dies?* But others, like her very own Red Class One, are hissing in dissent, wondering why it's necessary to go to such lengths in the first place.

"It's clear now the nonviolent M-attacks are working on some sort of looping pattern," Meiling announces. After Suraya brought that up last night, Meiling understood what she needed to do to prove herself. "Even without knowing why, we can make use of this. If we play our cards right, anyone can be at the right location at the right time to face the Mikazi Group, the Miyakos, head on."

The second time around explaining her plan, people seem more open to it. Meiling chooses her words carefully, enunciates them slowly. If she's to make them believe she is a willing pawn, she has to be sensible about it.

"It makes the most sense for that person to be me. The way I estimate it, we have a little over a week before the nonviolent M-attacks hit Nirnasha's Graveyard in Division Three. That gives us plenty of time to make a solid plan. Then if I give myself up there alone, they're bound to take the bait exactly like Headmaster Anji and Beatrice Zialitos said they would. It could stop everything."

A long pause follows. Meiling tears her gaze away from Suraya and refocuses on the room at large. The first year students are rigid in their chairs. The teachers are lined up against the back wall behind them, suspiciously emotionless.

"It's most likely suicide," Mr. Arredondo breaks the silence to say. As Meiling's teacher, he has the honor of standing up here with her during this mess. The bags beneath his eyes are a dull purple.

Meiling grits her teeth. She wants to snap at the entire room full of lucky Sun-descended people and scream, *fine, whatever, maybe it's suicide, but what do you care?*

"Vale is right," Evie chimes in, cutting Meiling's racing thoughts short. Her usual blinding smile is all but nonexistent. Meiling decides to keep it to herself that she's rather sure Evie would think Vale is right no matter what the context.

"Yeah, Meiling, come on. Isn't that a bit insane?" Kai adds.

"It's reckless," Callum mutters, giving her a harsh look. He's probably upset she didn't tell him first, but can he blame her? Look at how everyone is reacting.

"You could die," Artie says, tactfully as always.

"Die," Dao the Wings echoes over Cyrus's shoulders as he nods along emphatically.

There's a number of other responses from most every

other first year student in the room, but they begin to overlap from there. Meiling knows everyone by now, but she can't pick them out under these circumstances. It's insanely hard to keep track of who's saying what and when.

Well, that is until one voice overpowers the rest to shout: "Oh for the love of Ataru, can you all shut up?"

Suraya of course. Who else?

Mr. Arredondo is pinching the bridge of his nose between two fingers so intensely his abilities are beginning to snap to action. There's a whisker or two popping from his cheeks. Of all the possible animal characteristics he could sprout under stress, whiskers aren't so bad. They make him seem a little more approachable, actually.

"Yes, thank you Suraya," he mumbles. It's unclear if he means that truthfully or sarcastically.

"I'll be fine," Meiling asserts, trying to steer them back on track. If the nonviolent attacks continue to follow the pattern they have thus far—which they better, because that's the basis for this entire plan—then the Nirnasha Graveyard is bound to be dug up and torn to shreds again within ten days tops. This is no time for them to waste arguing. "Listen, there's something else. I did some digging and—"

Mr. Arredondo's loud huff of air cuts her short. He begins to pace the length of the room. Each step he takes has a different sound than the previous one. First it's a quiet tap, then a rumbling slam, then a hollow click, then a scratchy scuffle. He walks funny, too, like his leg keeps giving out, but he doesn't think it will so he hasn't learned to limp through it. Based on the fact his whiskers are now swapping out with tusks and scales every few seconds, Meiling bets his feet are doing something similar. Inside his boots, there's probably rodent paws one second and hooves the next.

"Mr. Arredondo," Meiling says, keeping her feet—perfectly human, last she checked—firmly planted behind the podium. "Are you okay?"

"Am I okay?" he echoes, swiveling on his... *feet*? The corners of his lips are tugging up, but it's a bit manic. He's sweating at his hairline, the dark curls atop his head seeming to wilt. "Are you insane?"

"Uhm." Meiling looks for help from someone else, *anyone* else, but nobody comes to her rescue. Faces are slack and shell-shocked all around.

"Not last I checked sir," she answers, which is funny because she has been checked for something like that before. Doctor Sutherland is a thorough man.

Mr. Arredondo cuts his eyes to her. One is a beaming yellow with a black slit for a pupil and the other is a deep, circular brown all around. He blinks and both return to normal.

For a moment, it feels like no one else is in the room. Just the two of them, staring each other down, no clue where to go from here. Meiling has a plan to finish explaining, but Mr. Arredondo doesn't seem open to hearing it. Meiling almost forgets he isn't the only one she's here to convince.

That is until a girl from Green Class One starts to laugh and the room snaps back into focus.

"It's almost hard to believe you're real," the girl says, settling her chin in the palm of her hand. Meiling isn't one to often feel embarrassed, but she does now. The way this girl looks at her is cruel. By now, she'd hoped to be better about being used to that.

"Do share the rest of your suicide plan, then. Not sure why we're supposed to care either way."

The overhead lights shatter at once, raining down shards of glass. The light within them flickers like a million fireflies swarming above their heads and dying.

Meiling hunches into herself, hugging her stomach, trying to control herself. People are screaming. She didn't even feel that happen. Hardly a couple months with this ability unrestrained and she's already tired of it. She has no control, and no real desire for control, either. What she wants is to be drained of this, even if draining abilities is as dangerous as this mission she's thrown together.

When Meiling's ears stop ringing, it's Mr. Arredondo's voice she hears. He's standing close by, hand hovering, but not touching—because why would anyone touch a Miyako?—and staring at her with his gentlest expression. Which, on him, is not very gentle at all. Meiling still finds herself warming to the sight of it.

He says, "It wasn't you, Meiling."

Raising her head warily, Meiling notes the state of the classroom. Glass shards litter the floor, but no one is hurt. There's a strange mix of dark storm clouds, thick green leaves, makeshift tarps, and a variety of animals that look startled and confused to be in the room all the sudden. The atmosphere is brimming with the lingering residuals of recently used abilities. It's a strange sensation—one Meiling knows well, having spent her life on the outside of it. Everyone, students and teachers alike, reacted quickly. They're all still in a stance to react again, too, should any more lights go out.

Miyakos are those of Mahina descent. Mahina is of the Moon. The Moon is of the darkness. It hits Meiling at once: she couldn't have done this. There's a difference between the absence of light and the creation of darkness. Meiling's descent only allows her one.

Which means the lights shattering in one fell swoop could only be one person.

Half of the room is watching Meiling, not believing Mr. Arredondo's words for a second, and the other half is watching someone else, sitting tense and angry in the front row.

Suraya.

"It's okay, Suri–*Suraya*," Meiling says, watching her shoulders stiffen at her slip-up with the nickname. "She's right. This is all I'm here for."

Before anyone can argue against that, or, more likely, hum in agreement, Meiling rushes to explain the second half of her plan: the lunar rock.

"I found this at the Odaz River," she says, lifting the small gray rock for everyone to see. A few people begin to snicker. "Ever since, I haven't been able to get rid of it. I threw it out my window and it made its way back to me. It buzzes like it's alive when it's near me, and only steadies when I hold it with bare skin."

To demonstrate, Meiling overhand chucks the rock

across the room. Students yelp and duck as the little thing flies over their heads and hits the ground a few meters away with a clink. Everyone watches with bated breath as it vibrates violently on the tiles. Then it inches across dirt and shattered glass right back to Meiling. She crouches down and picks it up between two fingers. The violent vibrations slow down into a soft buzz within seconds.

Pieces of shattered glass crunch underneath people's feet as they shift around uncomfortably. Meiling snickers. She doesn't know anything more about this rock than they do. Everything she thinks she knows is just a theory. But with the looks of awe on their faces right now, she knows she could convince them of anything. There is so little known about those of Moon descent in Malumvia that Meiling could probably tell them this rock has Mahina blood and no one would question it.

"I believe this is a lunar rock. Lunar rocks have innate connections to all Moon descendants, but Mahina's most of all. This thing will go wild around a bunch of Miyakos." She shakes the rock around, watching seventy or so pairs of eyes jerking around to follow it. "Lunar rocks also have strong connections to each other. If we somehow split this one rock into two, we'd have a perfect tracker. I keep one piece, the Academy keeps the other. Then, on the off chance that Mikazi and all the other Miyakos take me at the graveyard before we can apprehend them, you'll have no trouble locating us again, even through the chaos."

Resounding silence. Meiling holds what she seriously hopes is actually a lunar rock between two fingers, continuing to demonstrate the way it moves on its own in her presence. It's a natural compass to hunt down her family, just like they want.

It's also a natural creation of the Moon itself; it could never not be controlled by someone like her. No one seems to realize this.

"Let me get this straight," Mrs. Rees, the teacher for Orange Class One, chimes in. "You wish to—without a singular clue as to how—break a lunar rock in half, and then have us trust you enough to use it as a tracking mechanism toward your family… Only after you hand yourself over hostage to them?"

Meiling cocks a brow and shrugs a shoulder. "More or less."

Much to her surprise, Mrs. Reese doesn't laugh in her face or call her crazy like the rest of them. Instead, a slow smile grows over her face. Her lips are bright red and cracked, reminiscent of the scales on a milk snake. Meiling wonders distantly if Mrs. Rees is actually of Kaitsja descent; she can't remember. For all her knowledge of the Academy, this particular woman is not part of it.

"Brilliant."

Mrs. Rees pushes herself off the wall to strut up the aisle between desks. Her heels click across the tiled floor and crunch over glass. Once she's within arm's reach of Meiling, she gestures at the lunar rock and asks, "May I?"

Meiling hands it over easily. The second it's out of her hand and into Mrs. Rees's, the vibrations become more violent. It jerks between her wrinkly fingers as if fighting to get away—fighting to get back to Meiling.

"Truly brilliant," Mrs. Rees murmurs, twisting the

wiggling thing between her fingers. She settles deep into thought just staring at it. Meiling shifts on her feet to see if the movements of the rock respond to it. They do. No matter how small, they do.

No one dares to speak. Not even Mr. Arredondo, who looks like he has more than a few choice words for her right now.

"Van Alst," Mrs. Rees calls at last, motioning with the rock. Nearly everyone in the room sways away from it like Mahina herself is going to pop on out.

Kai comes forward with a lot less than his usual energy. His neon green glasses keep falling down the bridge of his nose as he scrunches and un-scrunches it rapidly. He's wringing his hands over his chest like he's trying to rip his skin off.

"Won't you do the honors?" she asks. "As our most acclaimed first year Chae-Won descendant, surely you can create two rocks of this one?"

Kai looks at Meiling, imploring. Meiling swallows thickly and looks away. She can feel the change in the air when he gives in and starts trying. It becomes hard to breathe in, almost like the connection she has with the lunar rock goes far beyond what she initially thought. Her head pounds as if someone's hammering at the base of it, trying to split it like a log the same way Kai is trying to split the rock.

It doesn't take long.

Only seconds later, the room is filled with a loud, metallic screech and the overpowering smell of gunpowder.

Meiling nearly topples to the floor, breath punched out of her. Her temples throb and her vision flickers.

Mr. Arredondo steadies her with a cautious hand, not looking too pleased about it.

When Meiling squints her eyes in a way that allows her to actually see, there's a part of her that wishes she couldn't.

Buzzing out of Mrs. Rees's hands toward her, there are two lunar rocks. The final step in her crazy plan.

"That settles it," Mrs. Rees announces. "Headmaster Anji will be most pleased."

Meiling stares at those little chunks of gray, her literal lifelines starting tomorrow, and thinks of how nice life could've been had she been born someone else.

24
Anji

Anji is not a vain man, but he must admit that choosing to allow Meiling Miyako into the Zialitos Academy for Sun-Gifted Children was a stroke of genius.

No other Headmaster—no other human *alive* even—can claim to be directly responsible for a miracle such as this. Tomorrow evening, Meiling is to willingly place herself in both blood and name as a Miyako at the Nirnasha Graveyard in Division Three in order to stop the country-wide conflict plaguing their land. Anji is almost ashamed he held onto her secret for so long. If only Divinia and Viera could have told him *that* the first time around. Perhaps they will be more forthcoming today.

"Divinia of the Prophecy, Viera of Ignor—*Knowledge*, I desire your audience."

With a couple strands of hair from his head and a shining emerald from his cane, the fire lights up with blue-tinted flames. When it settles, only Viera stands to greet him.

"Marion Anji," Viera says in all his dark, shimmering glory, "to what do I owe the pleasure?"

Anji's chest puffs out. He is an honor to a Divinity. *Him*, a Messenger. The stars are starting to align, after all. A wicked grin climbs his lips.

"Have you heard the news about Meiling and the Miyakos?"

"I may have been made aware of the girl's sacrificial plan." Viera smiles, wolfish. His eyes are swirling with darkness. "Mahina is not pleased."

Anji steps as close to the flames as he can. Staring at Viera in the fireplace, he seems tangible. As if Anji could reach in and grasp his long hair, his flowing clothes, his pale hands. In many ways, he looks a lot like a student: young and vibrant, cunning and curious. Ignorance is a dangerous power.

"Mahina?" Anji echoes belatedly. "Mahina knows?"

Viera leans a shoulder against the bricks inside the fireplace. He arches one brow high up his forehead.

"Mahina is her Creator," he says with a strange smile, "of course she knows."

A flicker of panic rises in Anji's gut. If the Miyakos alone are a threat, Mahina herself is certain death for all of them. He can only hope their Divine Laws hold her back from whatever feelings she has against Meiling's decision.

The flames explode outward with a rush of air. Anji trips backward, arms coming up to block his face. When the smoke clears, Divina stands beside Viera. Beautiful as a rainbow over a waterfall, she glares at him with bright narrowed eyes.

"Sir Anji," she greets, monotone as ever. Then her

eyes cut sideways to her Moon brother and a drip of emotion slips into her voice. "Viera."

"Sister dearest." Viera pushes away from the wall to take up more of her space. She squishes herself into a corner to avoid touching him. "Anji here wished to speak to me about Meiling Katz-Miyako again."

Those rainbow eyes turn to Anji once more. Divinia's long white dress blows wildly around her legs as if there's a wind tunnel in the fireplace. Coals pop where her feet should be.

"Is that so, Sir Anji?"

"I only wished to thank you both for sharing Miss Meiling Katz-Miyako's prophecy with me," he says quickly, flicking his gaze between the two of them. "I am most grateful for your counsel in making the decision to accept her to the Academy. It has proven very effective."

Viera laughs. The ground beneath Anji's feet rumbles in time with it.

"I do believe my sister here had nothing to do with such a decision. If I recall correctly, she said—what was it, sis?—*It is my responsibility to urge you to avoid this child?* Some mouthful like that, yes? You can hardly consider such a phrase a prophecy."

Anji jerks away as if the fire has roared to life once more. Viera watches him with a sharp glint in his dark eyes.

"Besides," he says. "It was only I who foresaw Meiling putting a stop to these M-attacks. Thankfully you lowly humans are following the exact course I thought you would."

Divinia's throat bobs with a harsh swallow. Rather than dignifying Viera with a response, she faces Anji and says, "Tell me you will deny her plan. There is still hope to stop this."

"But only this plan to stop those attacks," Viera cuts in.

"I cannot do that, your grace," Anji tells Divinia slowly, his heart in his throat. "Meiling must serve her purpose."

He will never amount to anything if he goes back on his word now. Malumvia is in shambles from this thinly veiled Miyako by the name of Mikazi. Stopping these M-attacks is the first step to stopping and fixing everything. Meiling Katz-Miyako's prophecy, whether the words of Divinia or Viera, must come true. Her willing sacrifice has made it so simple; he can't refuse it.

If only Anji could wipe out the Divine descended in one fell swoop the same way. No one would doubt his strength due to his blood status then.

"Ha!" Viera claps his hands together. The simple movement shakes the room like a flash bomb has been set off. "At last, it is coming."

"What is?" Anji asks.

"Cognizance," he says, watching Divinia squirm. "Competence. *Change*."

"I fear I do not understand."

"Soon you will, lowly human," Viera says, leaning forward so far Anji swears he can feel his hot breath on his face. "And I will rejoice in having led you astray. Ignorance is within you, same as any other. I'm rather thankful you're too proud to have noticed it sooner."

"*Viera*," Divinia snaps. "Do not tell me…"

"Fine, I will not tell you." He grins, those dark eyes flashing like a bolt of lightning across a pitch-black sky. "I will tell Sir Anji."

Viera steps a foot out of the fire. Anji jolts , heat rushing over his body like his hair has been lit aflame. His breath tastes like leather as he heaves it in, trying to calm himself.

"I told you, Mahina is upset," Viera says, scratching his chin as if deep in thought. "Though *upset* is a bit of an understatement at this point. I do believe she's nearly ready to come handle things herself. Which, of course, has agitated Ataru in return. Divine Laws forbid interference, remember?"

Anji nods stiffly. Viera grins.

"Accept the plan, reject the plan, it no longer matters. The result will be the same. Your Sun and Moon are already fighting. Divinia warned you the Miyako girl was a catalyst for great change in your country, but did she ever tell you what kind of change?"

"Viera," Divinia says slowly, reaching for him.

He barks out a laugh. This one is sharper and louder than the previous. The grin stretches across his face like an elastic band being pulled taut.

"Meiling will destroy everything you Malumvians hold dear," he says, mouth falling into a terrifying flat line. "And Mahina herself will have her back. If you think thirteen years ago was bad, you're—"

What both sounds and feels like a thick rolling cloud of thunder fills the room to cut Viera off at once. Anji drops to his knees and cowers. Darkness weighs him down. Fog that smells like spent gunpowder and burnt meat scurries up his nostrils and dives down his throat. The ground quakes beneath him as he gasps for clean air.

Then it is gone, and so is Viera.

The bitter taste of burnt leather fills Anji's mouth. He swallows thickly. The air is dusty and heavy. The darkness has left the room now, but not without taking some of the light away with it permanently.

"Your grace," Anji begins, prying himself off the floor. "Was that…"

"Mahina herself," Divinia confirms darkly.

Now alone in the fireplace, she stands with her body contorted into the corner her brother forced her into. Staring out at Anji, her brow twitches. It causes creases beside her beautiful, wide eyes. The flow of her body, normally smooth and pleasant like trickling water, has turned jagged and rough. Her clothing moves as if it has sharp edges around her limbs.

"Is it true?" he asks. "Is she angry?"

Divinia narrows her eyes.

"You had better pray to Ataru for your lives," she says instead, all in one loud breath. "If you would like a true prophecy, I will give you one now: Meiling Katz-Miyako marks the downfall of Divine abilities as you know them. I trust you know now what to do with her?"

Before Anji gets the chance to open his mouth and respond, Divinia disappears in a puff of light fog. The putrid cloud of dust and burnt leather is washed away by a gust of wind like clean linen.

The downfall of Divine abilities as you know them. Anji grips his cane and laughs.

That's exactly what he wants, and Meiling Katz-Miyako is going to take the fall in causing it for him.

25

Suraya

As if accidentally shattering the lights in the classroom wasn't embarrassing enough, Suraya's parents show up the following week, on the night before Meiling's little suicide plan, on the recommendation of Mr. Arredondo himself. Waiting outside her dorm room where everyone can see, her father says, "Hey, Sunshine, I think we need to talk."

"What are you doing here?" Suraya whisper-shouts, dragging her parents by the wrists into her room and slamming the door behind them. On the other side, she can already hear whispers of gossip forming.

Omar pulls his wrist free first. His hair is a dusty red mess over his head and he's still in his work uniform: dull green scrubs with golden trim around his name, *Dr. Zialitos*. Altogether, it's a rather comical look, but Suraya is in no mood to laugh. Or to smile, even, which is why she immediately lashes out with a bit of heat that forces him to look away. There's no power to his stupid happiness abilities if he can't properly spot his target.

"What is going on with you?" Taru shrieks, bobbed hair bouncing. It's the most Suraya has heard her mother's voice in weeks. Ever since the M-attacks became commonplace, Taru has sequestered herself in the basement of their house like a panic room—the way she always does when she's upset.

Saoirse Zialitos pops into her mind—her mother's cousin that was killed among many in the Lunar Eclipse Massacre. She thinks of bloody hands on the sink and endless crying. She thinks of the Miyakos causing everything and one of them sleeping three doors down the hall.

"Nothing's going on with me," Suraya snaps.

"Evidently not," her mother snaps back, "because we all throw sunlight at our loving families for no reason at all!"

"Come off it. That was hardly anything."

"Is that meant to make it okay, Suraya?"

"It *is* okay! Look at him, Dad's fine. You need to learn to chill out, Mom. What's *your* problem?"

"Who under Ataru's Sun do you think you are? You've been—"

"Enough," Omar interrupts, holding a large, tanned hand under his chin. "That's enough."

Suraya clamps her mouth shut. When her father asks for something without using his Divinia abilities to do it, she listens, especially when he sounds so exhausted. It's her mother's job to be exhausted. She's the one who's always either tired and depressed, or tired and angry. It's what causes so many arguments between the two of them; Suraya is the same way. When the life she's been given is one she has to constantly fight for, there's no other choice but to fight for it even if it drills her into the ground. One day, when Suraya avenges their family and takes over to make Malumvia safer, her mother will change and she will prove this was all worth it.

"Darling, take a breath," Omar tells Taru, reaching out to tap her shoulder lightly. Then to Suraya he says, "You too, Sunshine."

Suraya huffs, but keeps quiet. Her father is full of childish nicknames for her, just like Meiling. As a Zialitos only in name through marriage, Omar is nothing like the rest of their family. He commands respect from his name, but he doesn't care much for it. He's just a doctor and a dad, oddly ordinary.

When their breathing begins to collectively steady, he decides to speak up once more. "Now why don't you tell us what happened to make you shatter those lights the other day."

"Didn't you ask Arredondo already?" Suraya asks, rolling her eyes. "If you already know, then why in Nirnasha's Underworld should I—"

"Suraya Zialitos."

Oh, great, the full name treatment. He's that upset. That's another thing he isn't supposed to be because her mother's already assumed the role. If they're both tired and upset, Suraya will never know another moment of peace—which, frankly, she's had trouble finding recently anyway.

"Fine," Suraya says, taking a breath. She loves her family so much she hates them sometimes. Everything she does, she does for them, and not a single one seems grateful for it. "I shattered a few lights. It was an accident. No one got hurt."

Omar nods, looking her over without meeting her eyes. Suraya is so used to him unleashing his positive thoughts into her mind the second they make eye contact that she's rather adverse to it these days. He's only being respectful by being the one to not look this time.

"Okay. Truthfully, Sunshine, that isn't why we're here anyway," he says, a frown tugging at the corners of his lips. "Can you sit down for a minute?"

Taru drops into the chair at Suraya's desk. Suraya scowls and sits on the edge of her bed a few meters away. Omar continues standing in the center of the dorm room, looking large and out of place on the flaming Zialitos insignia stitched into the rug beneath his feet.

"Your mother thinks," Omar starts, attention drifting to Taru. She clenches her jaw and flutters her eyelids at him, speaking a thousand words Suraya doesn't understand.

"Your mother and I were thinking," he restarts, "perhaps it would be best to unenroll you from the Academy for the foreseeable future."

"What?" Suraya jumps right back off her mattress, the springs bouncing audibly in the aftermath. "Absolutely not!"

"Suraya," Taru says, her lower lip wobbling, "it isn't safe for you here anymore. What if you were at the Odaz River, hmm? They've already killed so many of us, I can't imagine what I would do if—"

The rest of her sentence is lost to a sob. Omar takes

two long strides to stand by her side. She cries into his chest so loudly Suraya feels it rock the floorboards. It gives her motion sickness.

"Mom, I... I'm sorry. I can't leave."

"Suraya, please."

"No, I can't. You know I can't. Trust me, I'm not afraid of a bunch of Miyakos. Besides, Meiling is more than willing to give herself up to them. Come tomorrow, this will all be over one way or another anyway."

Omar watches her for a long moment, the color in his eyes swirling, but no abilities forcing their way into her head. Suraya stands with her chin high and stares back. The only way they're pulling her from the Academy is by dragging out her dead body.

Then, finally, he asks, "Does that upset you; Meiling giving herself up to the Miyakos for this?"

"No," Suraya says quickly, but what she thinks is: *of course, it does.*

"It's all right if it does," he says in that annoyingly soft and consoling tone of his. "Her blood doesn't need to change your past together. I know we should have said something the moment the news broke, but your mother... Never mind. We're sorry to have kept this from you for so long."

"I don't care about—" Suraya cuts herself short so quickly she bites her tongue and draws blood. "Wait. What did you just say? What do you mean *kept it from you?*"

Omar's eyes slightly darken at the edges. They rarely

ever come out of that obnoxious sparkly state so Suraya knows she's somehow struck a nerve.

"The Katz are my best friends, Sunshine," he says tightly. "Of course, I knew. Meiling's adoption and true birth was a tightly guarded secret between them and a scarce few Zialitos elders within the government, but, of course, they told us, too. I've known Jax and Reena since I was four years old."

"And you're okay with this?" Suraya asks her mother.

Taru bites down on her bottom lip and looks away. Her eyes are red-rimmed.

Suraya swipes a hand toward her mother as if to say, *See?*

Omar frowns and Suraya drops her hand once more. When it comes to making points about Miyakos or friendship, Taru Zialitos is hardly a glowing endorsement for either. She hates the Miyakos more than anyone Suraya's ever met—which is a feat in Malumvia—and her only friends are the Katz, who are, of course, Omar's friends first.

"She's a Miyako and you never told me," Suraya says, getting back to the pressing issue here. "You let me sleep over at her house and share beds and go for walks together at night. How could you do that? Have you forgotten what they've done to us?"

Taru twitches uncomfortably.

"Enough," Omar says. "She's a child, Suraya. It has taken us both a long time, but we don't blame her. Right, Taru?"

Suraya's stomach plummets through the floorboards

when her mother only nods curtly in response. She doesn't look up from her hands.

"Seriously?" Suraya asks. After all the mental breakdowns and nights spent in the hospital because of them, her mother suddenly decides to stop hating the Miyakos on principle? "Why wouldn't you tell me?"

Omar grimaces. He looks to Taru for help, but she doesn't offer any. She never does.

"She's your best friend, Sunshine. For many years, she was your *only* friend. I didn't—*we* didn't—want any prejudices to ruin that. She's still the same Meiling you love. Don't shut her out."

Suraya sucks in a ragged breath. She feels like there are thorns blooming in her lungs. Based on the blood Taru has drawn out of her palms with her fingernails, she doesn't feel quite as open and forgiving as Omar says she does either.

"Jax is your best friend and you still never let me be in the room alone with him because he's of Moon descent," Suraya says. "Who are you to lecture me on who I love and how?"

Omar flinches as if he's been struck. "I'm sorry, Sunshine."

Taru finally lifts her head. Though her eyes are bloodshot and teary, she glares with as much strength as ever.

"We aren't here to talk about the Miyakos," she snaps, "we're here to talk about *you*."

"I'm fine," Suraya says. "I'm not leaving the Academy, Mom."

Taru stands, shoving the chair back until it hits the desk and rattles everything on top. There's sunlight popping out of her palms in sporadic bursts. Suraya takes a step back. Her mother rarely uses sunlight; she isn't very good at it.

Suraya waits for an outburst that never comes. Taru opens and closes her mouth a number of times, hands weakly forming the sunlight into beams, but she never says or does anything. She simply grabs Omar, swings open the door, and storms right out.

"Taru, wait, hold on—I'll call you later, Suraya!"

In the hallway, a bunch of first years are lingering with their ears pressed to the walls. They watch Taru drag Omar down the hallway and out of sight in silence. Then, they slowly turn back to Suraya.

"Show's over," she snaps, slamming the door.

There's hardly enough time for Suraya to properly calm herself down before more nuisances come barreling into her dorm room uninvited.

"Hiya Suri," Kai says, waltzing through her door and beelining for her bed. He dives onto it like he's done it a thousand times before. Let the record show he has *not*.

"Don't call me that."

"Hi Suraya!"

Evie is next. With a big grin, she chases after Kai to jump onto the bed as well. Together the two of them curl up on her neatly folded comforter, wrinkling the whole thing.

"Get out."

Suraya yanks the comforter out from under them. Rather than toppling over onto the floor, they roll into each other and re-steady themselves on her sheets. Suraya takes hold of a pillow and smacks them both over the head with it. This does nothing to deter them.

"What do you want?"

Kai and Evie share a silent conversation with their eyes. Suraya's chest aches with the heat splitting it open.

Before she can demand an answer, her door opens to another pair of unwanted guests. Cyrus and Dao. Dao is hanging over Cyrus's shoulders with droopy eyes, and Cyrus is smirking as he pats her head. As he meanders into the room, he grabs Suraya by the back of the neck, tugs her near, and plants a sloppy kiss on the side of her head.

"How are you feeling, love?"

Suraya throws a fist without looking to see where it'll land. Based on the groan Cyrus lets out, and the way he then situates himself in the farthest corner of the room, legs crossed, the hit landed right where she wanted it to.

"That'll teach you to kiss someone without their permission," Suraya grumbles, wiping the slobber from her hair. Cyrus frowns like he genuinely doesn't understand what he did wrong. Suraya nearly feels bad for the love-obsessed weirdo.

Artie, Callum and Karina are next. Artie leads the pack, entering Suraya's room and examining her intricately placed belongings as if he owns the place. Callum stands at the door with Karina glued to his side.

"Okay, what is going on?" Suraya asks. Her eye twitches. She still can't close her door. The influx of Red Class One students who live to irritate her hasn't stopped yet.

There's still Vale and Jamie. Jamie still looks rather out of it from the concussion he got during training a week back. Suraya has hardly seen him since. Suraya sweeps past him to look into the hallway, verifying Meiling isn't following. Then she slams the door shut and stares at her over-packed room.

"I don't know when I gave the impression any of you were welcome to my bedroom, but let's make one thing clear: you're not. So, you can all explain what you want and leave or I can light the entire place up. Your call."

"Hold on," Evie says, sitting upright. She has bedhead now. "This is important. We need your help, Suri."

"I've told you not to call me that," she snaps, sick and tired of hearing that nickname, sick and tired of any reminder of Meiling. It all hurts.

"Why not?"

Suraya whips her head to the source of that question. Her neck cracks in a way that leaves the back of her head numb. Artie stares back at her. His black hair is a frizzy mess tied half-up at the crown of his head and his hazel-brown eyes are still hazel-brown—meaning he hasn't activated those Divinia abilities of his. *Yet.*

"What does it matter?"

Hazel is replaced by gold in a split second. Suraya hates to admit it, but in all her years as a Zialitos heir meeting all the most powerful ability-users in Malumvia, she's never met a descendant of Divinia as quick as Artie. He switches into power like he has a light switch for it in that big hollow head of his.

"It seems to matter."

Suraya squeezes her eyes shut. *Get out of my head*, she thinks, but all she says aloud is, "Get out of my room."

"Come on guys," Kai cuts in, scooching until he's sitting at the edge of the bed. "Let's not fight. We're all in this together."

"In what together?" Suraya hopes her voice doesn't sound as sincere as it feels leaving her mouth. For whatever reason, Kai has that effect on her. She gets sincere and borderline soft when he's around. She's never known Chae-Won descendants to possess this sort of ability, but she hasn't ruled it out either.

"Everything," Evie answers, smiling wide.

"Right," Suraya mutters, "because that's helpful."

"All right listen," Vale says, arms crossed over her chest. There's a little rain cloud hanging above her and Jamie's heads, but neither of them are getting very wet. Maybe a little misty at most. Jamie actually seems to appreciate that, as if he's been waiting this whole year for Vale to invite him under the storm she carries everywhere. "No one wants to fight, much less me, but we have to. Meiling's plan is suicide. We all know that."

Suraya opens her mouth, ready to argue she doesn't care about Meiling or her stupid plan, but Vale cuts her off before a single word can make it past her lips.

"I honestly couldn't care less about what your deal with her is right now, Zialitos, because it doesn't matter.

Evie's right."—Evie lights up like Suraya's accidentally engulfed her in a sunbeam at this— "We're in everything together now. So, you join us and help, or we walk back out that door and you're on your own from now on. The choice is yours."

Suraya feels her jaw falling open and snaps it shut. Luckily, everyone else seems to be reacting about the same way. Vale Lochnen is a stickler for the rules, and notoriously quiet, but that right there was a speech.

Suraya squares her shoulders and grins sharply. "Sure, I'll help. Want to tell me what I'm helping with?"

"I'll explain," Callum says.

Vale sighs and falls against the wall as if her energy has been depleted. Her dark blue hair splays out across the plaster like a static rain cloud.

"Evie and Jamie went back into the spirit realm right after Meiling announced her plan. They tracked down a few M-attack casualties to question them."

Suraya scowls. How did she not think of that? How did the *detectives* not think of that? Or, if they did, how come they haven't said anything?

"From what they told us, we don't think the people leading these attacks are Miyakos. At least not all of them."

Suraya curses. The reality settles over her at the same time Callum says it aloud: "So even if Meiling gives herself up to them, there's no guarantee it will solve any of this."

Resigning herself to the greater good, as awful as it may be, Suraya says, "Okay, so what's our plan?"

"We don't let Meiling go to Nirnasha's Graveyard alone."

Headmaster Anji will want Meiling to do this herself with the lunar rock pieces split between the two of them, but that can't be an option. Because if Meiling goes alone, then she's getting taken hostage, and allowing Meiling to be taken hostage is no longer an option. Not when it won't guarantee the end of these M-attacks.

Suraya curses again.

"Fine. We'll trail her."

26
Meiling

It could be worse. That's what Meiling continues to remind herself as she walks alone through a graveyard to her potential death: it could be worse.

For example, she could be walking alone through a graveyard to her potential death empty-handed. But she's not! She's got herself a nice little lunar rock for company. Every cloud has its silver lining, right?

Nonetheless, this isn't exactly a desirable way to spend the afternoon. Meiling is beginning to regret suggesting this plan at all. Headmaster Anji loved it, though, and after Mrs. Rees told him about it, there was no going back.

Hiding within a plethora of trees somewhere behind her, Headmaster Anji has the other half of the lunar rock. Making use of Kai's Chae-Won abilities once more, a special bracelet was made for it. The rock is encased in a ball of glass attached to a band around his wrist, bobbling around like a mini snow globe. Meiling, on the other hand, has only her own two hands to hold onto her rock with. Based on experimentation, that's more than enough.

Ataru forbid she drops it, it'll only crawl back to her anyway.

The sacred Nirnasha Graveyard in Division Three—which took hours to get to from the Academy by train service—is in ruins. Since the last nonviolent M-attack here, nothing has changed. Fear has kept anyone from restoring it. Fear and perhaps a bit of hatred. In the eyes of Malumvia, Nirnasha is no better than Mahina herself. Maybe even worse. Nirnasha, Divinity of Death and the Underworld, is thought to breed negativity. No one likes death. No one but Nirnasha themself, who has no other choice.

All around Meiling, gravesites are overturned with mounds of loose dirt forming the letter M beside them. Caskets are visible in the open holes of the ground, some rusted with age, others shiny as if new. Thankfully none of those are tainted. Nor are any of the many headstones. Meiling has an uneasy feeling deep in her gut that this may change tonight.

For a long while, pacing the paths formed between these grave sites is all Meiling can do. She reads headstones and swipes dirt from their corners; she prays over the desecrated sites and pushes dirt back into holes to cover caskets; she plays with shadows in her hands and then a strange version of tag with the lunar rock by dropping it every few paces. It always comes back to the palm of her hand, sometimes with a nip of force so strong it feels alive against her skin.

Her only form of communication with Headmaster Anji comes from the lunar rock, as well. It can't pass words between them, of course, but by the pattern of its vibrations when she holds it, she can tell where he is and if he's moved. He's moved about ten times now. Not by much each time, but it's clear what he's doing: he's stalking through the trees to stake out the perimeter. Since the graveyard is the shape of a capital N for Nirnasha, trees form a square around the outside while tall grass and flower beds take up the other spaces in between.

Meiling assumes Headmaster Anji hasn't found anything since she's still kicking rocks and blowing air through her teeth. No threats to her life are here yet.

Night falls and Meiling is still standing in a long row of the graveyard. At this point, the only threat to her life is immense boredom. She's already done everything there is to do in Nirnasha's Graveyard while waiting for a bunch of criminals to come take her hostage. All that's left is their arrival.

Right when Meiling has become nearly certain there's been a mistake of some sort—a mix-up in the pattern, or the day, or maybe some leak making this even more of a trap than it already is—a familiar energy pulses through the air.

The lunar rock bounces in her hand before pushing itself so hard against her that part of it breaks skin and embeds itself underneath. Meiling clamps her teeth down hard, biting back a scream. In the distance, someone else screams for her.

At the same time, a spark like a firecracker going off illuminates the far edge of the woods where Headmaster Anji began the afternoon. A whooshing sound like a hundred kilometer per hour wind blowing through bushes overtakes the entire graveyard. Meiling ducks for cover with her hands cradling her face—even with the rock digging into one palm, blood beginning to bead out.

All at once there's light everywhere, heat everywhere, crackling noises everywhere. Meiling has to shield her eyes in order to raise them and meet the cause of this disruption.

Flames. Flames all over; bursting out of the ground around grave sites, swirling up trees without burning, zigzagging around the woods in maze-like patterns. Rings of blue-red fire surround Meiling, keeping her right where she is, right out in the open, alone.

The familiar energy she felt for a moment earlier is gone now. It's been replaced by the popping of flames and the distant sound of shouting. Meiling may not know what's going on here, but she knows the one voice overpowering the rest. She'll never *not* know that voice.

"Suraya?" she yells as loud as possible, knowing her voice has a ninety-nine percent chance of being drowned out before it ever reaches its target.

"It isn't worth it, Meiling Miyako."

Ice fills Meiling's veins. She knows this voice, but she also does not. It reverberates through her entire body and scratches at her skull, but still there is no name, no face, no solid memory, in which she can pin it to. Only a vague sense of panic.

She knows she's heard that previous sentence correctly—*it isn't worth it Meiling Miyako*—but all she can get out of it is, *you're okay, it's okay, you're okay.*

Her vision blurs before it settles. When it does, the Owl from the Birds of Prey is right there in front of her. A thick tan cloak billows around his body. A pinched white owl mask with empty sockets for eyes stares her down.

"Not you again."

The resulting laughter coming from the Owl's beak—unmoving—is his own. Meiling almost rejoices in it. Anything, even this loud and croaky noise echoing from out of the Owl with no clear point of origin, is better than that strangely familiar voice. At least this one doesn't echo through her skull and rattle her brain.

"Me again," he confirms, gesturing out with those talon-hands Meiling has vivid memories of being poked by. "You didn't think our last visit would be the end of it, did you?"

A beat of silence passes between them. A flame roars to her right. Suraya's voice can no longer be heard.

"No," she admits at last, because there's not much else she can do right now. There's nowhere to go; the fires are not dying down any time soon. And the lunar rock is still lodged inside her palm, making no move. At the very least this tells her there's no other Miyakos around.

Wait. *No other Miyakos around?* Meiling startles briefly, casting her eyes around. Through the flames and the shadows alike, she can make out multiple figures—waiting in trees, standing behind bushes, leaning up against headstones. She's surrounded on all ends by the Mikazi Group responsible for the M-attacks. But if none of them are Miyakos, then who are these people?

"Good," the Owl says, drawing back Meiling's

attention. "Now come quietly, Meiling. Don't make this harder than it needs to be."

He shifts, his owl get-up moving gracelessly along with him. Suddenly it looks a lot less foreboding than before, like a kid hiding under a cheap costume.

"Take it off," Meiling says.

"What?"

"The mask, the robe, your uniform. Take it off."

"Why would I ever do that?"

"I'll come with you."

"You're coming with me anyway," he snaps, but his hands have trailed up to the clasp of his robes at his neck. With one quick motion, it falls to the ground in a heap. He then cups the mask over his face in one hand and releases it.

What's underneath is a thin-framed body with a deep tan and lots of freckles. His blue eyes are soft. His hair is a fluffy white, like an actual owl's feathers.

He's just a kid. Thirteen years old at the most.

"What's your name?" Meiling asks softly, shocked by the pang in her chest at seeing him. She never expected a kid.

"Hugo." He meets her gaze with big eyes. "Hugo Wilks, of the strongest Eben descendants there ever were. Now let's go."

"Hugo—"

"*It's okay, you'll be okay.*"

Meiling instinctively clutches at her head, pushing both palms against her ears in an attempt to drown out the voice—the voice coming out of his mouth, but not belonging to him; the voice that churns something in Meiling's stomach the same way the shadows do; the voice that she wants to listen to anyway.

Voice mimicry. Of course, Hugo is a member of the Wilks family. Who else could so easily accomplish such a thing? Such a vile, impressive thing.

Her feet move before her brain catches up. She walks right up to him, then after him, following the path he's cutting through flames to lead her away.

When Meiling imagined being taken hostage, she always envisioned herself putting up a bit more of a fight.

Turns out she hands herself over willingly.

From the center of the graveyard, they cut a path through the tall grass and flower beds to reach the treeline. The flames open up like a doorway for them to pass through with each step. Walls of flames pulse upward everywhere else—a warning to Headmaster Anji and Suraya and whoever else decided to come along to stay away.

Outside the N of the graveyard, the Mikazi Group has reconvened as one. Front and center are the other Birds of Prey Meiling met before: the Condor, the Raven, and the Eagle. Various others flank them, from hawks to falcons to birds Meiling's never even seen before. Behind them, dozens of others stand, each adorned in black jackets and cloaks, golden gems in the shape of the letter M at their necks. Unlike the Birds of Prey, no masks cover their faces.

There are adults, but there are also many more children. There are people with clawed hands and hardened skin, and people with pitless eyes and fanged teeth, but more than that, there are people who are only that: people. People whose blood resembles Meiling's own, people who are desperate.

The lunar rock settles under her skin, no more jittering. Surrounded by those of Moon descent who are not Miyakos, it settles. Meiling's heart rate, against her will, does the same. She knows she is not entirely safe here, but she feels it anyway. That's the problem with feelings; they cannot be explained away by research, they cannot be discredited by common sense. They are because they are, and for nothing else. Feelings are innate, just the same as her love for the stars, for her connection to the dark, for her distant relation via the Moon to these people standing before her.

A small boy, perhaps a year younger than Meiling herself, snaps his fingers and the flames disperse, retreating back to the pads of his fingers. Watching it is like watching a million flashlights turn to one precise spot before abruptly going out. Despite how utterly amazing this is, no one seems fazed, much less the boy himself. He rolls his shoulders afterward like it was nothing, then returns his gaze to the ground by his feet.

"Thank you, Hugo, Jasper."

At the same time Meiling jerks her head up to meet the heavily-masked face the muffled voice came out of, the lunar rock rips itself out of her skin and begins gyrating in the air above it. The man takes a step back , as if feeling the vibrations of it, and Meiling knows at once she's found a member of her blood family. Her hand throbs with pain, but that's nothing compared to the ache in her head, the pull in her gut, and the rough pattering in her heart.

Roughly twenty meters in the distance, he stands behind the others with all but his eyes concealed—those are dark red and sharp. With both hands in the pockets of his dark jeans and a dull yellow cardigan over his bare torso, a hundred scars in various stages of healing are visible across his chest. They crawl all the way up to his neck until the excessive fabric covering his mouth buries them.

On uneasy legs, Meiling takes a step closer. The lunar rock stops shaking as her feet move, only to vibrate violently again when she stops. She takes another step to feel it happen again. Then another, and another, and another. The crowd parts for her as she moves, nearly in a sprint, toward her bloody family member. Her breaths come fast and hard.

All the while, the man simply waits. His red eyes the same as Meiling's own shine in her direction as if glaring stop lights that she completely ignores.

The moment she comes within arm's reach of him, reaching out to what—*hug him?*—someone screams.

"Mikazi!"

Jasper, the boy with the fire, is the one who calls the name. The Miyako standing before Meiling is the one who reacts to it. He stumbles back as if he's been stabbed. Meiling squints at him as he shifts into the darkness, claps, and disappears completely. Even as a Miyako herself, she can't locate him again.

Mikazi Miyako? Another unfamiliar name. An alias,

maybe? If he's the only Miyako behind these attacks, what chance does Meiling stand at stopping them as a bargaining chip? That ruins everything. Especially if he can slip away from her that easily.

Meiling's chest aches. The lunar rock reacts to her stress, or maybe she's reacting to the lunar rock, but both tremble violently. It's much worse than when she first saw Mikazi. It's as if he's everywhere and the rock can't decide where to go now.

"They're here!" someone shouts, then curses. "Go! Grab her and go!"

Meiling makes it easy on them: she offers her wrists and allows herself to be tugged away. Her best chance at answers still remains with these so-called criminals.

The Birds of Prey close in around her and escort her through the graveyard toward the dark tree line. Through the sudden violence and screaming, everything turns to white noise. Fire returns to the graveyard and the ground wavers beneath her feet.

In the distance, Suraya's angry voice echoes through the air. Meiling straightens up and swings around to find her through the flames. In a blur, she sees not only Suraya, but the rest of her class in the midst of fighting the Mikazi Group. The Mikazi Group, on the other hand, seem a bit preoccupied fighting someone else.

"What's going on?" Meiling chokes out to the person behind her.

It turns out to be the Raven.

"Miyakos," they say gruffly. Their fingers tighten

around Meiling's waist, but no metal rods pop out to impale her.

"What?" Meiling squeezes the lunar rock between her palm. It starts to tear apart her skin in an attempt to get away.

"Miyakos," they repeat. "I told him—Ugh. Never mind. Mahina's sake, why now?"

To their left, a figure comes flying out of the trees as if materializing out of thin air. The lunar rock spins rapidly in the tear it's opened in Meiling's skin. The Raven swears and shoves Meiling forward with so much force her feet come off the ground. The Condor catches her with claw-like hands before she can hit the ground. Then they're flying. Meiling's stomach plummets.

From high up in the sky, Meiling surveys the entire graveyard. Jasper has set fire to nearly every square meter of ground, including the gravesites themselves and the tall grass separating them between each carefully treaded path. Flowers laid beside headstones are burning. Caskets are popping open, their hinges falling apart. Meiling does not let her eyes linger on those; she's nauseous enough already.

In the center of the N-shaped graveyard, her classmates are fighting. Suraya has lassos of sunlight jumping out in every direction, ensnaring enemies attempting to hide in the dark. Callum and Karina are yanking roots and vines out of the ground, tripping people into the flames with them where Artie waits to steal their fighting spirits with his mind manipulation abilities. Cyrus and Dao are spinning in circles with red strings encircling them like some strange sort of love lure. Kai is generating weapons out of his arms and stomach at record speed, tossing them out to whoever passes by in need. Jamie and Evie both are popping in and out of spirit states. Evie is using open caskets to her advantage by reappearing beside them to scare people. Vale follows her around, ready to launch storm clouds at anyone who tries to fight her back for it.

Which they inevitably do; these are Miyakos. *Actual* Miyakos. Meiling can tell them apart from the Mikazi Group easily. Enshrouded in dark clouds, her eyes are immediately drawn to them. None of their eyes are drawn back to her.

Did she miscalculate? She's already being taken away in order to stop all this fighting, but they don't seem to care. The fighting only grows worse the farther away she gets.

From the top corner of the graveyard, Meiling notices a shadow twice as dark as the others. It snakes through the path of the N to the center where everyone is congregated and fighting. Meiling's hands get torn to shreds as she grips the lunar rock and watches, helpless to do anything. In seconds, the shadow has crossed the length of the graveyard and reassembled itself as a solid, looming figure behind Artie.

"*ARTIE!*"

The Condor makes a swift nosedive at the same time Meiling screams, smothering the sound into nothing. Even then, Meiling knows it would have been too late anyway. The darkness seems to cut right through Artie and he collapses to the ground in a heap. Meiling's stomach turns over itself. He doesn't get back up.

"Wait," she says helplessly to the Condor, "please. I have to go back and help him first."

The Condor flies on without a word. Soon the graveyard and everyone in it turns to a blip of smoke in the distance. Meiling chokes on her tears until she can hardly breathe. Then the world tilts into complete blackness.

27

Suraya

Suraya does not realize she's on fire until the flames begin licking up her pant leg and scorching her bare skin.

As a Zialitos, her skin is made to withstand intense heat, but even these flames are cutting through to her. Suraya opens her mouth to curse, in frustration and in irritation and in response to the sharp, stinging pain from the flames tearing open her skin, but the sound is punched out of her before it can even begin. Or, tackled out of her, to be more accurate.

"Suraya!"

Evie's weight crashes into Suraya and takes the two of them to the ground. Suraya's head bounces off the dirt with a high-pitched ringing in her ears. Evie sits up and wraps her bare hands around the fire at Suraya's ankles in a failed attempt to put it out.

As the flames burn her instead, Evie howls and flings herself backward.

"Are you stupid?" Suraya shouts, thumping her legs against the dirt in a much better attempt to put the flames out.

"Ow, ow, ow, ow" is Evie's only response.

Great, Suraya thinks, *this is just great.*

Not only is Meiling gone, but everything here is in shambles. Scanning the graveyard, she can't find Anji anywhere. A ll she sees is Artie in a heap on the ground with Jamie and Callum hovering over his unconscious body, screaming, and the rest of Red Class One in varying states of dishevelment. Evie and her both have third-degree burns bubbling across their skin, Kai has a wide gash across his forehead dripping blood into the lenses of his glasses, and Karina is missing her usual black gloves and mask, exposing far more skin than usual.

Thank Ataru for Vale Lochnen. Looking unimpressed, she kneels down in front of Suraya and Evie—so close the fire turns her brown eyes to burnt orange—and claps her palms together to weave a cloud between them as she slowly spreads them apart again. The cloud raises over her and Evie's heads and empties out until the fire is smoke. The rain hammers down on Suraya's burnt skin like daggers.

Once she's thoroughly covered in cold rainwater, Vale blows out a soft breath and the cloud disperses. A tiny rainbow fills the place where it once was. Evie loves rainbows.

With the fires put out, the uncomfortable heat is gone. Unfortunately, the pain is not. Nor is Evie's wailing from beside her.

Suraya turns her head slowly, feeling the shift in her neck like a machine cranking, and levels a glare on her. It takes both eyebrows raised and a warning, "*Shineski*" before Evie responds.

"I took a calculated risk," she says.

The palms of Evie's hands are bubbly red, practically radiating heat. They steam like asphalt in the summer after a thunderstorm. Kai rushes over, shoving Vale out of the way to kneel by Evie's side. He gently takes hold of her hands, one at a time, to heal her like the personal aloe plant he is. Now a yard away, Vale forms more mini rainbows in the resulting steam.

"That was calculated?" Suraya asks.

One side of Evie's face scrunches up as Kai presses into a particularly bad section of her raw burnt skin with his thumb.

"I never said I was good at math."

Suraya's resulting curses are swallowed up by the sound of another wall of flames roaring to life to their left. Evie screams, loud and high-pitched. When she starts screaming, Kai starts screaming with her. Vale works double time to crank out rainbows to distract them both.

The boy who caused the flames steps directly through them, entirely unaffected by their heat. Fire lifts the dark brown curls atop his head and shifts the color of his matching irises, making the young kid look like a walking ember. Outstretching his hands, as if surrendering, he curls his mouth into a hesitant smile.

As Red Class One jerks back in shock at the sight of him here, Suraya rolls her shoulders back and glares. There's an old myth about Nirnasha, Divinity of Death, stating that at the time the Divinities collectively came into creation, Nirnasha vanished. While the other Divinities resumed their rightful places on the Sun or Moon, Nirnasha disappeared for dozens of years. They appeared only in brief glimpses during tragedies to collect fallen spirits from the spirit realm. To amass great power, they dragged those spirits to the U nderworld—an underworld they created and buried layers deep into the Earth's core directly beneath Malumvia.

As no more than an amalgamation of death themself, each spirit fallen strengthened Nirnasha's abilities. In time, Nirnasha became a Moon Divinity rivaling Mahina herself. It's said that had they remained in their underworld any longer, there soon would have been nothing else.

The way the myth ends never sat right with Suraya. After all that collecting, Nirnasha simply hung over the sky in full form—eyes and hair aflame, skin dusty like ash itself, eyes swirling with those of the millions of spirits they consumed—and submitted to their fate. They stayed there in the sky long enough to frighten all of humanity, and then they took place on the Moon beneath Mahina never to be seen again. Underworld and all its power abandoned.

The only Divinity with less known descendants than Mahina is Nirnasha. Rarity raises vigilance. Nirnasha's story is a cautionary tale told in grade school to warn against those of their blood, and those who think they can amount to more than their Creators in the first place.

That's why this boy, with all his flames and gentle smiles, raises every last one of Suraya's shackles. He looks exactly the same as Nirnasha was described in that very tale. Only a lot younger, with baby fat in his cheeks rather than harsh lines.

"Oops, sorry!" he says, his voice squeaky. The flames go down, crackling out against the dirt. "We didn't expect so many people tonight."

Suraya steps ahead of the rest of her class, glaring harder.

He cowers, but only the slightest bit. *Not bad*, Suraya thinks.

"Oh, uhm, hi," he says. "I'm Jasper. Jasper Kapoor. Descendant of Nirnasha, as you probably figured out already."

Suraya raises a brow at the kid. Who is this Mikazi guy, Jasper's ringleader, if Jasper is so careless with his name and friendly with his enemies?

Jasper scratches the curls at the nape of his neck. Ashes flutter out and to the ground.

"Listen, we saw y'all fighting the Miyakos with us. Thanks for that, by the way. We didn't—"

Callum screaming for Artie once more interrupts this little pow wow of theirs. As everyone turns around to help, Suraya takes a long moment to stare at Jasper. From the wrinkles across his forehead and the singed black cloak over his thin shoulders to the hunch of his shoulders and the rigid line of his posture, he does not seem like much of a threat. Besides... What was that about fighting the Miyakos? If the Mikazi Group he's with is against the Miyakos while at the same time staging these M-attacks,

Suraya has a lot more work cut out for her than she initially thought.

Behind her, Callum lifts Artie off the ground in a bridal-style carry. Cyrus must love that. Artie's eyes are open, but unseeing, the usual hazel now a murky greenish and the pupils void of light. His pale skin is flushed red. Even in Callum's arms—which is quite the sight given the size of Artie—his head lolls to the side and his body sags. If not for the breaths punching out of his mouth every second, harsh and uneven, Artie could pass for a corpse.

"Something's wrong with his spirit," Jamie announces, looking to Evie, his fellow Omni descendant, for help. She's quick to bat away Kai's hands and Vale's rainbows so she can.

Once Artie is laying down in a new patch of dirt between them, Evie places both injured hands over his chest to hold him down. Jamie keeps two fingers pressed to his temples at the same time.

"It's off center?" Evie says to Jamie. He nods and shrugs at the same time in response. They both look grim.

Jasper stumbles back a number of feet at once, his face ashen. The veins around his eyes pop out as if trying to escape him—similar to how Suraya has seen her mother's when stressing use of her sight abilities. What this means for a Nirnasha descendant, though, Suraya doesn't know. Begrudgingly, she wishes Meiling were around to do her little nerd-thing and explain it. Without her, she's forced to twirl a few sunbeams between her tired, overheated fingertips and simply assume the worst.

"What's that mean?" Callum asks. He has a vice grip

on Artie's hand, unconsciously sprouting moss beneath it to serve as a strange sort of padding. "What's off center?"

"His spirit," Evie says.

"What does that *mean?*"

"It means it's off center," Jamie says, at the same time Evie says, "Well you know how our spirits are housed in our bodies?"

Everyone nods. Jamie sighs, as if everything coming next should be obvious.

"Right, well, there's a specific spot for it in all of us. Our spirits have extremely particular needs so they have special containers within us that they fill out perfectly. We call it the spirit core." More nods follow this. Spirit cores are another grade school topic. "And, uh, you see, Artie's is off its center. Like someone took a cookie cutter to his core and tried to yank some out. As in: some of his spirit is spilling over the lines."

"*What?*"

Artie's body arches upward suddenly as a gargling scream tears its way out of his throat. Jamie flies out of reach and into a spirit state, disappearing just before Artie can knock him with his head. Evie shrieks, lifting her hands in surrender as she scooches backward. Callum refuses to let go until Karina comes flying by and physically pries him off.

As quickly as Artie's fit begins, it stops. He collapses into the dirt once again, this time without any heavy breaths. His eyes are shut now, too. The graveyard is so still Suraya can only hear the crumbling of ash left over from the fires.

"Is he… Is he dead?" Cyrus asks, clutching the fabric of his shirt over his chest. Red strings from out of his knuckles are floating up to wrap around Dao and support her weight as she slings across Cyrus's shoulders like a deflated balloon.

"No." It's Jasper who answers. Nine pairs of eyes turn to him at once. His confidence wavers as he acknowledges all the Academy students before him and he lets out a weak breath. "I would, uhm, I would've felt that."

"Jasper," snaps a new voice. The Eagle from the Birds of Prey comes into view as she floats over an uprooted grave and lands by his side. "Enough of this. Rami succeeded."

Jasper's eyebrows fly up. A smile dances across his lips.

"Yes, really," she says tiredly before he can ask. "But the Miyakos are hot on his trail, so who's to say for how long. Come on, we have to go."

Her feet have hardly left the ground, Jasper's wrist in her hands to drag him along with her, before Callum is shouting at them to wait. For whatever reason, they listen immediately.

"How would you have felt it?" Callum asks, looking between the two of them and Artie, who is whimpering a bit now as Evie and Jamie return to grabbing his chest and temples; presumably trying to right his spirit core.

Jasper frowns a bit. "Nirnasha abilities, man. I can sense the dead—I mean spirits."

It's Callum's turn to frown. Suraya keeps her grip on the sunlight nice and firm. The Eagle looks about three seconds away from attacking someone unprovoked. If they are underneath this Mikazi character, she wouldn't put it past them. Miyakos or not, they're still murderers.

Evie grunts as her hands light up blue and Jamie shouts "Move!" She goes flying backward the same time Artie wakes with a gasp. Cyrus catches her with a bunch of red strings before she can hit the ground. Dao pouts about it.

"It's back on center," Jamie says, rather unhelpfully.

"Where is she?" Artie asks, his voice broken by continuous wheezing. He's clutching his chest with a grimace and darting his eyes—obnoxiously golden again—around the graveyard. The color drains for a split second at the sight of Jasper, as if he knows something the rest of them don't.

"Where's who?" Callum asks.

"Meiling!"

The actual goal of tonight's fighting comes back to hit them all at once. Meiling was taken. And here they are standing around making measly conversation with members of the team who took her.

The Eagle takes to the air with Jasper so quickly they leave behind a mini sandstorm. No one can move fast enough to catch them again. Jasper's shouts of disapproval echo long after they disappear into the trees beyond the graveyard.

28
Meiling

Suraya's fingers burning. Callum tangled in his own vines. Cyrus and Dao torn apart. Evie head-first in a grave. Jamie disappeared. Vale struck by lightning. Karina swarmed by bees. Kai stabbed in the gut. Headmaster Anji nowhere in sight. Artie grabbed. Artie shouting. Artie down. Artie….

"Why'd they have to get the message *now*? I mean, seriously, we've been going at it for months and they pick this one night to use their brains?"

"Shut up," another voice hushes, waving air lukewarm toward Meiling's face.

"Y'know, this kid sleeps real awfully for a Moon descendant."

Fingers prod at Meiling's temples. Light trickles into the corners of her eyes. It stings beneath her eyelids.

"What does that have to do with anything?"

Her eyelashes flutter as the fingers pull away. *Is this real?* There's an oversize bird sitting to one side of her and a small, tan girl with tiny antlers poking out of her dark braided hair to the other. Meiling tries to awaken her consciousness all the way, but it feels like there's lead in her blood. No part of her body will respond to her mind's directions. *Where is Red Class One?*

"Well, the Moon coming out means it's bedtime, right? So, if we're connected to the Moon, shouldn't we be innately good at sleeping?"

"It doesn't work like that."

Better yet, where am I? Meiling wonders, trying to follow along with the conversation ringing around her ears.

"Think about it: if the Moon equals sleep, then Moon descendants must have good sleep."

"That makes literally no sense."

"No but listen—"

"Temi, if you don't shut up, I'll rip your antlers straight out of your head."

"Don't! I just grew these!"

"Hey," Meiling gurgles as she sits up suddenly, vision swimming. It swims so hard she drowns in it, hallucinations taking their place. Either that or the girl who poked her temples does have antlers cupped protectively under her tiny palms, and the oversize bird is actually the Condor from the Birds of Prey, and she's trapped alone with the two of them in a dark cave.

"Up for real this time, moonshine?" the girl—*Temi?*—says, cocking her head to the side so they're face to face.

Meiling reaches out to tap her on the nose. It scrunches. Then her brows knit together and her line-like pupils enlarge. One hand comes off the antlers to grab Meiling's. Hard and cold. She's real, all right.

"Who are you?"

"Temi of Hala."

Meiling tugs her hand back and rubs at her eyes. Then over the bridge of her nose. The name Temi still rings zero bells. Hala, though, that's the Moon Divinity of Hunting . In traditional lineages from years back in history, last names were dropped in favor of naming their Creator. Meiling didn't think anyone still did that.

"Where are we?"

Temi looks around the tunnel of darkness surrounding them and back to Meiling with one raised eyebrow. Deadpan, she says, "A cave."

"Why?"

"Full of questions, aren't you?" Temi sighs, rubbing one antler in the same way Dao runs her fingers through Cyrus's hair.

Thinking of them makes Meiling's heart ache. She has no idea if they, or any of the rest of the class, are okay. Her last memory before blacking out—all the fighting, the screaming, and Artie going down—doesn't necessarily suggest good things. Neither did those overly vivid dreams of hers.

Meiling groans, wanting to turn back time. She looks down at her left palm. The lunar rock is sitting still atop torn, bloody skin. The sight jumpstarts her heartbeat to rage in her chest. Tonight was supposed to be a cut and dry capture to get her to her *family*. These people are nothing of the sort.

"Who are you?" she asks again, scrambling backward on her hands in the dirt. "You aren't Miyakos. Why were you at the Graveyard? There was supposed to be an M-attack there tonight."

"Duh, that's why we were there," Temi says, squinting. "It's all Mikazi's plan."

"And you're with Mikazi?" Meiling whispers, turning over the rock in her hand. It reacted to Mikazi, if no one else. "My family?"

Continuing to stare with furrowed brows, Temi nods. Meiling still has about a million questions about the situation, but none of them seem to matter anymore. Mikazi is who she came out here for, and if they work for him, she's right where she needs to be.

"I want to see him."

The Condor barks out a laugh. Temi throws her head back against the wall of the cave with a sigh. The sound echoes in both directions.

"Don't we all?"

"When can I see him? Why is he doing this?"

"We will lay low here until the coast is clear," he says, slowly peeling the mask from his face in pieces. Without the layers, his voice is slightly accented in a way Meiling isn't familiar with. "Then you can ask Mikazi anything you want for yourself."

Meiling bites her tongue on all of her remaining questions. She'll get her answers in time. All it'll take is waiting this out in a cave with some criminals before being transported to another criminal, all while hoping and praying Red Class One is safe and won't come to find her before Mikazi takes his mask off to answer her real questions. Simple.

There isn't much to do while waiting "for the coast to clear." Especially when Meiling is keeping her mouth shut from the hundreds of questions burning in her brain. Temi chatters on and on about absolutely nothing of substance, staring at the gravel her feet are kicking out of the wall as if it'll respond, and the Condor, who's actually a young man that looks quite a lot like the Owl, Hugo Wilks, is folding and unfolding the cloth aspect of his mask with nimble fingers repeatedly. Meiling returns to staring at the lunar rock in her palm, which could be just another part in that pile of rubble for how motionless it is right now. This is both good and bad. Good, because it means the overly violent Miyakos who showed up earlier haven't tracked them, and bad, because it means Mikazi is nowhere near either.

If Mikazi is the only actual Miyako behind the M-attacks, then he's the only person she wants to speak to. At least for now.

After a long while, without so much as blinking, Meiling's head starts to throb. The lunar rock sits like a log in her hand, jagged edges continuing to push through her damaged skin. Impatient with all the waiting, and irritated at everyone for ruining her perfect plan to unite with Mikazi and learn what she needs to, Meiling hurls the rock out of sight. Temi jolts in surprise, but the Condor's fingers don't miss a beat in their folding cycle.

With a scratch along the ground like the grinding metal noise Meiling sometimes hears Perce descendants make when contracted to forge large-scale projects or buildings for the government, the rock makes its way back to her. The stupid thing always comes back to her. Meiling snatches it up between two fingers at the same time Temi snaps her head to the opening of the cave and shouts, "Someone's here."

Having no grip on her own abilities is getting old. Every single time something startles her, they kick in and mess something up. This time Meiling accidentally blankets everything in shadows so thick no one can see through them. Except for her, of course, but she's not exactly paying much attention to the problem at hand. S he's fighting to reign her abilities back in the place beneath her ribcage, because that's where it feels like they stem from most of the time, while a number of voices shout and swear.

"It's okay!" someone yells through the darkness.

Recently, Meiling's felt conditioned into becoming nauseous and distinctly *not okay* every time she hears that phrase, thanks to the Owl, Hugo, who keeps using it in someone else's voice. But this time it works like a nice muscle relaxant. Or more like a suppressor, sort of like her old mediation, because her control over the shadows seeps away at once. Moonlight filters in through the opening of the cave before little fires spring up along the walls, lining the space between them and the new arrivals.

With the sudden light, Meiling has to shade her eyes and squint in order to see. The Condor and Temi must not have that problem; they stand up and approach the two figures in the entryway with no malice whatsoever. Meiling figures it must be more Mikazi Group allies.

Straining to focus, Meiling feels a sudden barrage of

anxiety hit her. She collapses backward into the wall with the force of the thoughts beginning to race through her mind. Screaming, in someone else's voice, are the words: *It can't be, it can't be, it can't be.* Meiling clutches her head between her two hands, feeling the lunar rock wriggle against her temple, and the strange thoughts continue: *If it is, it's over. And it's all my fault. It's over. We're over.*

There's a throbbing deep beneath her eyes when Meiling manages to push the feelings away. Standing a few feet away, dusting off their cloaks and pant bottoms, are the Eagle and the small Nirnasha boy—Jasper, as Mikazi called him—who lit half the graveyard on fire earlier. The Eagle is panting and gesturing with her hands to the Condor while Jasper stares across the cave, smiling gently at Meiling. There's an irregular twitch to his left eyebrow.

Time fast forwards from there. The Eagle and Jasper are hardly able to regain their breath before Temi's eyes go wide—her instincts are insane, like a sixth sense for danger lies underneath her skin—and there's panic again. Meiling stumbles to her feet at the same time the Condor's talons pop out and Temi swears loudly, warning them they have to run, *right now.*

"Grab the girl," the Eagle shouts, throwing Jasper toward her with a swing of her arm. It looks like wind formed beneath wings even though she doesn't have real wings and generating wind is more of an Irene or Tal descendant thing. Jasper lands by Meiling's feet. He stands quickly, but doesn't reach out to restrain her. Meiling isn't positive he can; he's even smaller than she is. She offers her wrists to him the same way she had to Hugo earlier.

"How many?" the Condor asks.

"At least eight," Temi says.

"Miyakos?"

"I can't tell."

But Meiling can. The lunar rock is unmoving in her palm. Whoever's coming, they're not Miyakos. And if there's at least eight of them? It must be her class. Why can't they give up?

More cursing follows. The Eagle stands at the edge of the cave, which appears to drop off like a cliff, and spreads her arms out.

"Wait, there's more than eight now," Temi shouts. "Way more. Zialitos. It's Zialitos. We have to go!"

"Jasper, come on!" the Condor says, urging him to grab Meiling and get moving.

Jasper links his fingers through Meiling's to hold her hand rather than yank her around by the wrists. Meiling grins and squeezes back. Together they dash out the opening of the cave, chasing after the Birds as they half-run, half-fly down the jagged pathway ahead. Out of the cave, there are only rocks and cliffs leading to more caves. The outskirts of Division Four, and most of the interior of Division Five, are unlivable for the average person in this way.

The Birds lead the way. Meiling holds Jasper's hand in a vice grip with one hand and the lunar rock like a tracker with the other. The farther they cut through the darkness ahead, the more the rock begins to come alive again. *Mikazi.*

The Condor and Temi come to a skidding halt a couple meters in front of Meiling and Jasper. They kick up rocks and dirt as they stumble to a stop. The Condor throws his arms out to either side of himself to catch the rest of them before they do the same. Meiling rams into his elbow. All the air in her lungs comes flying out with a gasp.

"Sorry," he says, breathing heavily. "It's the South Cliff's edge. We're almost to Mikazi now."

He motions with a long bony finger across the large expanse of still water sitting at the bottom of the cliff. It stretches out for almost a full kilometer before reaching land again. Within the thick plethora of trees over there, Meiling can swear she sees a figure standing alone waiting for them.

"Can you fly?" the Condor asks.

The Eagle nods, but there isn't much enthusiasm there.

"Can you carry one of them while you do?"

This time the Eagle doesn't bother putting on a tough front. Her lips wobble and she turns her attention down to the water. She shakes her head once.

The Condor curses sharply. He motions Jasper forward and picks him up with one arm. Then he motions at Meiling to come over and do the same.

Meiling remains still. "Will you be okay?"

"I won't know until I try," he grits through his teeth. Scattered shouts echo from the cave where they once were.

Meiling hears Suraya's voice mixed in there. "Come on. We don't have time to waste."

Meiling steps forward and lets him loop his arm around her waist. She only comes a few inches off the ground before he wobbles and they all go down again. The shouts grow nearer. Meiling can hear the rustling of loose tree branches and the sharp skittering of kicked rocks.

"Again."

The Condor jumps to his feet, tugs Jasper into his arms once more, and grabs Meiling to do the same. The Eagle does her best to support Meiling's weight from the side, but her hands are shaking too badly. It's clear to Meiling this will never work. The lunar rock wriggles underneath her skin. Mikazi is so close. They've gotten this far only to be stopped short by a long body of water?

"Wait." Meiling pushes the Condor back to stand steadily on her own two feet again. She shifts until her shoes peak out over the cliff's edge and stares down at the murky dark blue water below. "I can swim."

"*MEILING!*"

The sound of Suraya's voice nearly tips Meiling over the edge. Luckily, the Eagle has enough strength left to grab her by the back of the shirt and pull her to safety again. Meiling lands on her butt in the gravel, her heart racing.

Jasper slams his palms against the Condor's chest so he'll be let go of as well. He drops unceremoniously to the ground and swings around with hair all in his face to see Suraya leading a group of Academy students and Malumvia Authorities directly to them. He doesn't waste a second. With a single snap, a thick wall of fire breaks the path between them.

Suraya is fast enough to not let him get a second. Her sunlight whizzes directly through the wall of fire and wraps around Jasper's fingers. She slams his hands into the ground and holds him there, unable to do a thing. The wall of fire quickly dies out until it is no more than steaming kindling.

For the first time in her life, Meiling willingly summons a thick cloud of darkness in order to fight back. It swirls around in an uncertain blob before her, tugging those hidden nerves in her gut. The air is thick as she tries to breathe through it.

"Go," she says to the Eagle. "Tell Mikazi I'll catch up."

The Eagle hesitates for only a second before she jumps off the cliff. A number of people in the crowd coming for them gasp. Then the Eagle pops back up, soaring through the sky across the water, and the gasps turn into grunts and curses instead.

Meiling motions with her head for the Condor to do the same. Putting all her focus into her shadows, she sends a thick burst of it toward Jasper to free his hands. A rush of adrenaline spikes through her body when the shadows easily snuff out Suraya's sunlight.

Suraya stares at her like she's never seen her before in her life. The angle of her eyes is cruel, the scowl on her face unforgiving. Meiling knows she just did something she'll never be able to take back, something she'll never earn forgiveness for.

Then she sees the line of Malumvian Authorities carrying ability-suppressing handcuffs and mouth gags behind Suraya and thinks it doesn't matter because right now Suraya has done the same.

Her whole cloud of shadows is thrust toward Suraya in the next second. Clearly surprised Meiling has come for her so quickly, Suraya is caught off guard. She trips backward, coughing in the thick darkness. Meiling presses forward harder.

For a moment, it almost seems like she will succeed. The crowd is held at bay, the Eagle, the Condor and Jasper are flying away free, and Meiling is only centimeters away from the cliff's edge to jump over and swim to Mikazi.

Then Suraya comes alive again, sunlight bursting out in every direction. The heat lights Meiling's chest down to her toes. She drops to her knees on the ground, throat too dry to scream.

Suraya stomps forward, pushing authorities to the side so she can face Meiling first. Kneeling in front of her, Suraya grabs Meiling around the chin and forces her to look up. Her face is blurry through the tears in Meiling's eyes. The heat hurts.

"You're a liar," Suraya says.

Meiling swallows thickly. She bats Suraya's hand off and scooches away . A little further and she'll topple right over the edge. No one will be stupid enough to follow her into the water.

"Oh no you don't." Suraya pulls Meiling into her in what could almost be called a hug, if not for the sunlight circling her fingertips and the Malumvian Officer standing at the ready with ability-suppressing cuffs to hook around her wrists.

"Meiling Katz-Miyako, you are under arrest for aiding and abetting the terrorist group under the name of Mikazi."

29
Suraya

Once the cuffs click into place around Meiling's wrists, the shadows overhead seep away to reveal a sky full of stars. Dotted across the skyline, they look a lot like the splattering of freckles on Meiling's face—which are currently being covered by black cloth as the officers gag her.

Suraya shoots a thick beam of sunlight upward to momentarily blur the sight of the stars. She's had enough of anything to do with Meiling. As restricted as Meiling is, she still flinches in response. The heat seems to carve scars down the exposed skin of Meiling's arms.

The officers yank her to her feet, four sets of arms blocking her in on every side. She keeps her head hanging down, lolling, almost as if she's passed out. Suraya digs her feet into the dirt to keep still.

"Stop that," Artie says, pushing forward. His steps are wobbly and his voice is hoarse. They should have left him laying down flat in the dirt of the graveyard. "Stop that, you're going to hurt her."

Five sets of sharp Zialitos eyes cut toward him. A

spark of sunlight zips out from someone's hand latched around Meiling. Her whole body jolts, but still her head hangs low.

"Stop that!" Artie shouts.

"Artie," Callum warns, holding him back. It seems the Kagiso has finally come to his senses. There's fear in those stupidly pink eyes of his.

Artie freezes in place. Unlike Callum, he doesn't seem afraid. Only confused and angry. Suraya almost appreciates that look on his face. He's usually so blank. But when he's only showing that much emotion for someone like Meiling Katz-Miyako—who just attacked them; the people trying to save her—it's hard to appreciate anything.

A sharp static noise hisses out of a tiny device hooked over one of the detective's belts. He presses down on the little red button lining the top of it and says, "Come in, Officer Oso."

"Reporting. Mikazi has been restrained at Nirnasha's Graveyard. Return back immediately. Orders to abandon the other culprits."

"Noted." The officer clicks off the device, turns to his team, and announces, "We keep the girl in cuffs."

They nod along dutifully and escort Meiling forward through the very same rocky trail she just ran through in an attempt to escape them.

Suraya is the first in Red Class One to follow. It only takes one snap of her fingers to have Evie and Kai chasing after her. The rest fall into place after. Taking up the rear, Artie limps along, grumbling all the while. Callum and Karina serve as both his crutches and his emotional support. As many times as Artie says, "Mei isn't a criminal," or "They're gonna hurt her," Callum and Karina reply back, "I know," and "It'll be okay." Suraya wishes she had ear plugs to drown them out.

It's a long trek back. Without the adrenaline of chasing Meiling and the Birds of Prey she was escaping with, the uneven ground beneath their feet and the steepness of the cliff edge they have to hike down are terribly inconvenient. Air rattles in Suraya's lungs from the effort. Pain laces up her calves and exhaustion spreads an ache across her chest. It's a wonder the whole lot of them make it back to Nirnasha's Graveyard at all.

There are hardly half a dozen people there waiting for them. Headmaster Anji, a couple low ranking detectives, a couple emergency doctors, and a man in black cloaks tirelessly shoveling dirt into gravesites are the only ones in sight. The M's that had been formed out of piles of dirt are now gone, rounded out into normal mounds or used to re-cover caskets in the ground. Nearly all the damage from the fight earlier is gone as well, smoothed over as if wiped away with a giant cloth.

"Mikazi?" Meiling whispers. If the officers hear it as clearly as Suraya does, they don't show it. No one responds to her.

The lunar rock Meiling used to have is now pressed between the fingers of an officer beside her. Suraya watches as Meiling's gaze snaps from that to the man in the cloaks and back again. The rock is subtly twitching. Meiling's face drops as she shakes her head.

"It's not him," she says. Still, no one answers her.

"Officer Oso," the officer leading them calls across the graveyard. A slim man with messy brown hair pops up at the sound of his voice. He jogs over, eyes huge at the sight of Meiling.

"What…"

"The Miyako girl. She attacked us."

"She wouldn't have if—"

The rest of Artie's sentence is smothered beneath Callum's hand. Apparently the lack of oxygen is too much for him. His knees buckle and he drops into a heap on the ground for what's probably the fiftieth time today.

Headmaster Anji finally decides to grace them with his presence then. With the lunar rock bracelet dangling on his wrist and his dark facial hair perfectly sculpted around his jaw, he looks young and rejuvenated beside the rest of them. Suraya scowls at him. His signature cane is missing half of its gems at the top.

"What happened to Arthur?" he asks, eyes skittering right over Meiling in handcuffs with her mouth covered.

"His spirit was off-center earlier," Evie responds. "One of the Miyakos tried to… It seemed like they were trying to steal it."

There's a short beat of silence before Headmaster Anji begins to laugh. It's a deep, guttural sound. Meiling's entire body stiffens at it. For this Suraya can't blame her. The old man has never laughed in front of them before. Honestly, Suraya wasn't sure he knew how to.

"Don't be silly," he tells her, shifting so he can lean his weight entirely over his cane. "Spirits cannot be stolen."

"What about Reapers?" Cyrus asks suddenly. It must

be a touchy subject of some sort because Dao doesn't bother repeating him. Instead, she buries her face into his neck and shivers.

The Zialitos officers are half listening, half jerking Meiling around as they murmur amongst themselves. Suraya feels her head split as she tries to keep up with both conversations at once. Is Meiling going to jail? Is she being set free? Is that seriously Mikazi cleaning up gravesites alone over there?

"Ah, interesting question, Cyrus. Tell me, what do you know of The Reapers?"

Cyrus blanches. He looks around for backup and his eyes land on Suraya. She shoots him a look she hopes he understands as: *Leave me out of this.*

"Well, uh, they're the Moon counterparts of The Wings."

"Yes, and?"

"Rather than guiding lives by connecting with people, they guide spirits by collecting them to amass power. They have no descendants, no partnerships, no desires with us at all aside from, well, aside from stealing our spirits. They're rather loveless."

The Wings and The Reapers are Divine Groupings that get little to no conversation in school, but because Meiling has always been attracted to the unordinary, she figured out everything there is to know and told Suraya anyway. The Reapers are exactly as Cyrus said: spirit collectors who want nothing else to do with humans.

"Precisely; they desire nothing to do with us." Headmaster Anji smiles. "They guide fallen spirits, students. *Fallen.* No Reaper wishes for any contact with us before or beyond our deaths."

"Oh," Cyrus says, nodding along. "Right."

"Then what—"

Evie's voice is cut off by Artie groaning awake again. His eyes pop open and he flies up into a seated position.

"Arthur," Headmaster Anji says, "I trust your spirit has been realigned?"

"Yes sir," he says automatically, holding a hand to his chest. He's blinking around the graveyard in confusion.

"Good. Spirit wounds are not to be taken lightly; do get rest." He paces a few feet. "In fact, all of you children should. While we surely appreciate your initiative here tonight, this is out of your hands now. Mr. Arredondo will be here soon to retrieve you."

Without thinking much of it, Suraya's eyes trail from the class to the man shoveling dirt into a nearby grave. Something on his arm reflects the moonlight with every movement. Suraya squeezes her eyes shut hard once before opening them again, forcing any remaining bits of her strength to go into bettering her eyesight. With improved focus, it becomes clear the sparkling spot on his arm is a mass of gems from Headmaster Anji's cane. So, this is the man they've claimed as Mikazi.

Suraya doesn't know much about the Headmaster, nor does she understand much about Messenger types like him to begin with, but from countless bouts of babbling by Meiling, she knows they can call down Divinities at their will by combining any of their DNA with something of value. Normally these meetings are done in enclosed spaces, safe places, where the Divinities are shrunk and confined. If Headmaster Anji attached the necessary pieces to this man, out here in the open, then this is the most impressive form of threatening Suraya's ever seen. She only wonders how someone so powerless managed to do it.

"That's Mikazi?" Suraya asks.

Headmaster Anji taps his cane against the ground once. The gems attached to Mikazi glint. He drops the shovel and swivels around to face them. The lower half of his face is covered by a mask, leaving only two wide blue eyes visible. Meiling sucks in a breath. Suraya does the same.

Blue eyes? That isn't a Miyako.

"That is Mikazi," Anji confirms. "He turned himself over rather willingly in the end."

While her posse of officers are distracted, Meiling swings her whole head around like a deranged spirit until the cloth tied around her head falls to free her mouth. Immediately, she says, "No it isn't."

Anji acknowledges Meiling at last. He surveys her quickly, from the spit-covered cloth now hanging at her neck to the cuffs digging needles into her wrists behind her back, and smiles slowly.

"Miss Katz-Miyako. Have you double crossed us?"

"No," Meiling growls. "Why would I tell you this if I wanted to double cross you? That isn't Mikazi."

The officers apologize and trip over each other in an attempt to re-cover Meiling's mouth. She screams as she fights back, shoving and kicking. She's like a rabid animal.

"I know you aren't Mikazi!" she shouts at the man in

the black cloak. She motions wildly at the lunar rock, still barely moving in the officer's fingers. "You can't be; Mikazi is a Miyako like me! So, who are you and what do you want?"

"Meiling," Callum cuts in weakly. From a meter away holding Artie on the ground, he can't do much more.

"Who are you?" she demands, attempting to break away from the Zialitos and charge him.

'Mikazi' digs his shovel into the ground at his feet and leans against it. The crinkles by his eyes never disappear.

"Mikazi," he tells her. His voice echoes against headstones.

Like the slippery snake she apparently is, Meiling breaks free of the officers holding her and runs. She screams the whole way. When she makes it to 'Mikazi,' she throws a shoulder into his chest and knocks him to the ground. The headstone behind him shifts, crooked over the casket he's just recovered. Suraya lights up her burnt fingertips with sunlight despite the prickling pain it shoots up her arm.

"You're a liar!" Meiling shouts. Suraya twitches. That's exactly what she said to Meiling earlier. "You're a liar! You aren't Mikazi. He was a Miyako, he was my family, he…"

When the officers grab her again, she cuts herself short. She's crying. Suraya takes a step closer, sunlight twisting between her fingertips. Meiling wanted to be with Mikazi and his group of flying rodents. She fought Suraya over it. So why go this far to argue against him now? There's something they're missing here. No one seems to care as cuffs get snapped onto Mikazi, him and Meiling both being dragged away together this time.

"Liar," Meiling whispers once more. She sounds unsure now.

Suraya is sick of being the only intelligent one around here. "Meiling."

The tension bleeds out of Meiling's shoulders at the sound of Suraya's voice. Suraya feels as if it all enters right into her instead.

"I believe you," she says. It might be the first time she's ever said that to her.

A fresh wave of tears pour out of Meiling's eyes. Evie and Kai start to murmur from either side of Suraya, wondering why she believes Meiling with the way she's acting.

As Mikazi and Meiling are shackled side-by-side into the back of an officer's van, neither one of them fights back. Mikazi appears to be smirking behind his mask and Meiling is too busy staring at Suraya.

Even as the van begins to pull away with them and Mr. Arredondo pops out of a bus to round up Red Class One, Suraya and Meiling can only look at each other.

30
Evie

Call her crazy, but Evie assumed detaining Mikazi would put an immediate stop to the M-attacks. Turns out it doesn't.

The day following Mikazi's arrest, while Mr. Arredondo is going in on the class for breaking curfew, rules, trust, and about a hundred other colorful nouns, news breaks across Malumvia that another attack has taken place. The announcement rings through every classroom, every hallway, every household. After the fifth or sixth violent M-attack months back, they stopped broadcasting them as breaking or urgent because they weren't anymore. They were commonplace.

Until now.

When the location of the attack is stated as the Zialitos Mansion, a huge residence where many of the elders within that family live out their final years, waited on hand and foot, Evie gets a bad feeling Meiling might be right: There's the Mikazi the officers brought in to await trial, and then there's the real Mikazi—a full-blooded Miyako who runs without other Miyakos. Unheard of, certainly, but not entirely unrealistic.

Shortly after, when the number of casualties is stated as a confirmed twelve so far, the most of any singular M-attack this year, Evie prays Meiling is wrong so this will end.

Either way, another violent M-attack while their criminal is suppressed by three sets of cuffs in a cell underground doesn't bode well for anyone.

Least of all Suraya, who was the last to want to save Meiling, but the first to speak in her favor afterward. *I believe you*, she had said. If Suraya believes Meiling, Evie has no reason to feel otherwise. Suraya is smarter than she is, stronger than she is, braver than she is. Besides, Evie isn't exactly keen on turning against Meiling to begin with: she's always been just as smart, strong, and brave as Suraya—if only in a much quieter, calmer manner. Aside from her outburst in the graveyard, Evie has never questioned Meiling even once.

The news of the M-attack earns them an early dismissal from classes. The Zialitos Mansion is in Division One, same as the Academy, and there's no telling when they'll be a target again. The Odaz River was bad enough, and only one Zialitos detective on duty died there. The students can't be risked.

"Go directly to your dorm hall and stay in your rooms or the common areas until the threat has been neutralized," Mr. Arredondo says, scanning the class with a scowl. His trust in them is nonexistent after the graveyard debacle. "Stick together; no one should be left alone right now. And please, for the love of Ataru, no more meddling."

Everyone packs up quickly to heed his command. Or at least pretend to heed his command. Evie spares one last glance at Meiling's empty chair and follows Suraya into the hallway, knowing she's not getting anywhere without her.

Case in point: she hardly makes it one foot out the door before Suraya's hand is latching onto her shoulder to steer her around.

"With me, Shineski," Suraya says to Evie.

As the rest of Red Class One file down the staircase to leave the building and head toward their dorms, Suraya and Evie turn the other way. The hallway lights flare until they sputter out, bathing them in darkness. Suraya begins to laugh.

Evie doesn't know if it's fair to say someone is lucky they're scary, but she's going to say it anyway: Suraya is so lucky she's scary. Otherwise, there's no chance she'd follow her all the way through the dark hallway, chuckling like a maniac, until they reach an empty classroom.

Once the door clicks shut behind them, Suraya flicks on a sun-powered lamp with the back of her hand and says, "I need you to go into the spirit realm and find someone who was just killed at the Zialitos Mansion."

Evie's jaw drops open. "No way."

The closer the spirits are to their lives—as in, the more recent a person's death—the more likely it is that something will go wrong with anyone trying to interfere. People go through stages once they die, like the five stages of grief, but from the other side—for those who have been lost rather than those who have been left behind. For the most part, the stages are the same. Denial comes first. Then anger. Then bargaining. It's steps four and five where they begin to differ. Instead of passing through depression to reach acceptance, most spirits backtrack to anger again. It's a volatile adrenaline rush that makes them a hundred times stronger than they ever were alive.

That's exactly why Nirnasha collected these spirits from the spirit realm hundreds of years ago. If an angry spirit sees any chance of clawing their way out of the spirit realm to return to their life, they'll go for it. No matter what it takes.

"Why not?" Suraya asks sharply.

Evie forces her jaw up with her hand. Suraya raises a brow. Oh, she's serious.

"It isn't exactly the safest place for a living person to put themself," Evie says slowly. "I mean, look, hanging out in the spirit realm for too long is dangerous to begin with. It's not fit for the living; it can suck you away into nothingness."

Just like Evie's grandpa. He used to spend nearly every day in the spirit realm, doing research and making friends. Then, one night, he simply never came back out. His body was ash on the tiles of their shared house. Evie doesn't remember much about that day herself, but her parents definitely do. It's why they pretend to be ability-less these days.

Evie forces the memories down and continues, "But with twelve deaths in the past twelve hours within a twelve kilometer radius? That's practically signing my own death warrant."

"I know," Suraya says, "but I won't let anything happen to you."

Evie swallows. She believes that, but it's still no guarantee. Kai isn't here to tether her down and heal her physical body. She'll be in a full spirit state, entirely alone. Suraya told her once that Kai is a bright green wrench in any plan to be discreet. Evie can't exactly argue with that, but right now she wants to anyway. Kai may be a bright green wrench subtlety, but he's her emotional support bright green wrench. Without him, the room Suraya's dragged them into feels hot and airless. Evie can already smell the stale dust of the spirit realm, the sharp tang of fresh blood.

"Did you believe her?" Suraya asks.

"Meiling?" Evie asks, though she knows Suraya could be asking about no one else. Suraya nods once. "I dunno. I don't *not* believe her."

Suraya cocks another brow. She props herself up against the desk at the front of the room and folds her arms over her chest, feigning nonchalance. Muscles pop out of her arms. She may seem lithe at first glance, but she's built like a professional athlete.

"I mean, why was everyone fighting with those Miyakos at the graveyard if the attacks have always been that one guy and his group?" Evie asks. "And why are people still dying if we have that guy cuffed in a holding cell? And why would Mikazi let *Headmaster Anji* capture him so easily in the first place?"

"Not to mention, there's still nothing linking this so-called Mikazi and his group to Kane Miyako," Suraya adds.

"Exactly!" Evie snaps, more and more sure of herself. "I'm not saying Meiling's right about everything, or that the authorities are wrong about Mikazi, either, but it's fishy, isn't it?"

Suraya smirks, her hands and shoulders relaxing. "It sure is."

"So, you really do believe her?"

"I believe the Mikazi in custody isn't the Mikazi behind everything."

Close enough, Evie thinks. She plops down onto the tiles and laces her hands together. If she has no tether, she needs to tether herself. Squeezing her nails into the backs of her hands might do the trick. Anything to remind herself she has a body to return to.

"Okay. I'll try."

Suraya's lips twitch as she nods.

Pressing her eyes shut tight, Evie switches into a spirit state and immediately hits a wall. Figuratively, of course. The reason she's sitting is to make sure that doesn't happen literally.

"Uhm. Suraya?"

"What?"

Evie cracks her eyes open to a room in limbo between worlds. In her peripheral vision, Suraya is there, but in front of her, there is nothing but a film-like blob of gray. It wavers as if mist, but pushes back against her like a rock wall. The spirit realm has always had a wispy, muted-color quality to it, but not like this. It's never tried to keep her out.

"Something's wrong."

Understatement of the year, but Suraya doesn't care for long winded explanations and Evie isn't sure how to explain this one briefly.

"Elaborate."

Evie curses. Of course, she'd say that. Spots fly over her vision as she presses forward some more, only to be pushed back twice as hard.

"I can't get in."

A tremble starts up in her fingertips. As much as Evie loves her abilities, and spirits, and everything that comes along with them, the drawbacks terrify her. Resistance from spirits isn't common, but she's experienced it once or twice growing up. Before now she's never pushed back. Her father raised her not to. In fact, he raised her not to use her abilities at all. After losing his own father to the spirits, he'd do just about anything to keep Evie from that fate.

Including secluding her from schools and training until she felt the spirits were the only friends she had.

Which is why she worked relentlessly to get accepted to the Academy in the first place, and why she's not gonna stop working even now that she's here. Especially when there's someone as impressive as Suraya Zialitos relying on her. To have someone this Divinely gifted relying on *her*? She can't let her down.

Warmth floods her shoulders. It takes a second for her to realize this is due to Suraya's hands on them.

"What are you—"

"It's easier with a tether, isn't it?" she grits through her teeth.

Evie smiles. Already her skin feels less tight around her bones. "Yes, thank you."

Suraya nods without meeting her eyes. With Suraya's hands holding her here, Evie takes a deep breath and tries again.

"Please," someone says, sounding so close it's like headphones are over both her ears. "Don't. It's not what you think."

"Saoirse?" she asks, straining.

"Not again," the voice replies—the deep, croaky, distinctly-not-Saoirse voice.

The gray blob before her eyes is darker now, nearly pitch black, but something glints gold in the center of it. Sparing one fleeting glance down at her own uniform, Evie understands.

"Kane?"

"Not again," he repeats more forcefully. "Not again. Please don't let them do it again."

"Do what again?" There's lenience when she pushes this time. Her body gets a submerged-under-water feeling that comes from passing completely into the spirit realm. "Kane, what are you doing? Let me go."

She jerks backward, trying to fall back into Suraya and ground herself, but it's like Kane has invisible hands holding her hostage. She can't see, she can't move, she can't do anything.

The panic Jamie expressed in the training room all

those weeks ago makes a whole lot more sense now that Evie's experiencing it first-hand. Trapped at the edge of the spirit realm, entirely alone, there's only one feeling Evie can grasp, and it's death. This feels a lot like dying.

"Evie, fall back!" Suraya screams, her voice muffled and distant even though Evie knows she's right there, holding on to her.

"...please... keep... safe..., can't... not again." Kane's murky voice cuts off as Evie yanks her abilities back inside and off all at once. It's like tugging a breath you've already exhaled back into your lungs and then shutting off the airway entirely. Evie collapses into Suraya, gasping.

She's never done something like that before. She should've kept it that way.

Any ability, no matter what Divinity passed it on, is not meant to be flicked on and off with no forethought. Abilities take time to heat up and cool down, so to speak. Evie just allowed hers to boil and then get dunked under a bucket of ice within the same five minutes. If one tiny movement had been different, she could've trapped herself in the spirit realm, or blown up the blood coursing through her veins, or somehow dragged a spirit to earth, or, or, or...

Evie sees Suraya's mouth moving, but she can't hear a word she says. Kane's words replay in her head over and over again. Ringing fills her ears. Together they form what sounds to Evie like a jumbled, off-key slam poetry session. The thought makes Evie laugh, which in turn makes her gasp as she feels a stabbing pain in her chest. She attempts to suck in a large breath of air and feels a wall like Kane

Miyako blocking her entrance to the spirit realm.

Her pulse spikes. Tingles race down her arms and bleed into her chest. Sometimes when she spends too long in the spirit realm, her whole body starts to vibrate like this—as if she's been shocked by a bolt of lightning.

Suraya's mouth moves faster and she reaches out to tap Evie on both cheeks. Her palms are hot. Evie gasps back to reality. Staring into bright silverish blue eyes, her whole body relaxes. She's not in the spirit realm, she's in an empty classroom with Suraya Zialitos.

That almost makes her feel worse. Evie swallows prickers in her throat. Suraya pulls her hands away, damp, and Evie realizes she's crying.

"I'm sorry," she wheezes. "I couldn't do anything."

Suraya nods once in acceptance. Her brows are furrowed in displeasure, but she's biting down on her bottom lip as it twitches and she will no longer meet Evie's eyes. She hasn't pulled away to put a meter of distance between them the way she usually would.

Evie smiles. Maybe she isn't half bad at picking friends after all.

With one cautious hand, Suraya awkwardly pats her on the back. Through blurred vision, Evie can see her mouth screwed up in a way showing she's severely uncomfortable with this situation. Evie chokes out a sob meant to be a laugh and Suraya scrunches her nose in disgust.

"There, there," she grumbles haltingly, as if she's never been around a sad person in her life. There's a rigid line to her shoulders and her gaze is steadfast on the floor.

Evie sniffles. Suraya trusted her and she couldn't do anything.

Suraya pats her on the back again, now only touching with the tips of her fingers—like crying is some sort of contagious illness.

Evie covers her mouth with both hands, and at last she manages to actually laugh without feeling any pain.

The corner of Suraya's mouth twitches, and then she's laughing too. It's the first time Evie's ever seen that, too.

They learn nothing about the M-attack at the Zialitos Mansion, or Mikazi, or the Miyakos in general, but Evie thinks it's safe to say they learn a thing or two about each other, and that's enough for her.

Not that she'll get herself bullied by saying that out loud to Suraya "keep-your-feelings-to-yourself" Zialitos.

31
Meiling

Meiling spends two days and two nights in a dimly-lit cell alone before her first visitor is permitted through. Rather than her parents, who she hasn't spoken to since the truth of her blood came out, it is Mr. Arredondo who stands on the other side of the thick Chae-Won enhanced glass keeping her contained.

"How long are they going to keep me here?" Meiling's voice is so scratchy it hurts.

Mr. Arredondo drops to a knee on the hardened floor and bows his head to her. His eyes are flickering through shapes and colors—yellow and slanked, brown and circular, orange and beady.

"I don't know, Meiling," he says quietly. "Are they treating you well?"

Meiling slowly looks down at herself. Dressed in the same exact outfit she was wearing that night in Nirnasha's Graveyard, she's coated in dirt, sweat and grime. Her shoes are damp, her hair tangled, and her hands are sporting nasty infections from where the lunar rock cut them open.

"No," she says honestly. "Can I see him?"

Mr. Arredondo snaps his gaze up to meet hers. His eyes are normal again, dirt-brown and surrounded by bags.

"You know I can't answer that."

"He isn't Mikazi." Meiling knows it. She can prove it. All it will take is a little time outside of this Divinity-forsaken cell they've cuffed her in. And perhaps a bit of time without those ability-suppressing needles jammed into her veins because of the cuffs.

"How do you know?" he asks. He's rubbing circles into his temples now.

"When I saw Mikazi—the real Mikazi—at the graveyard, the lunar rock went ballistic. He's a Miyako like me. But this guy they brought in? He's not. There was nothing. It isn't him."

Meiling drags herself to the end of the cell, metal clanking around her ankles. Mr. Arredondo flinches every time a step rattles the chains she's stuck to. Much closer now, she can smell musky pine. Even through the ridiculously thick Chae-Won enhanced glass separating them, Meiling can sense him as if nothing is there. She begins to slowly scan the length of the enclosure. There's always a flaw in the system.

Mr. Arredondo drops into a seated position across from her. "How do you know the one you saw first is the real Mikazi?"

"I just know it."

Sighing heavily, Mr. Arredondo runs a fingertip across the glass and says, "Conjecture."

"What?"

"That's what they'll write your argument off as: conjecture. You understand this, don't you?"

"Of course, I do," Meiling snaps. They'll write off anything she says, anything she does, one way or another. She's a Miyako. That will be her whole life now. "But if you let me see him, I can prove it."

"Meiling," Mr. Arredondo says, frowning deeply, "How am I meant to help you do that? It was difficult enough getting in here to see you at all. I'm only a teacher."

"But you haven't always been," Meiling says. There's a lot she doesn't know about the true history within their country, but there's a lot she does know, too. "For seven and half years after graduating from the Academy, you worked as an undercover detective for the Zialitos Authorities."

Mr. Arredondo's entire body shudders. One eye turns black with a yellow slit pupil before resettling. His glare is harsher than ever.

"How do you know that?"

"There's a lot I know."

She crosses her arms, trying her best to come off as tough and intimidating like Suraya so Mr. Arredondo won't see how terrified she is. It falls a bit short when her cuffs clank against one another, forcing the needles into her skin a little farther. She bites back a groan. The needles suppressing her abilities are a thousand times worse than the medication she used to take for the same thing. Sometimes it feels like they're draining her blood completely.

"When you spend your whole life being forced to the sidelines, you get good at watching the game."

Mr. Arredondo's resulting sigh is both exasperated and fond. Meiling only has to say, "Let me see him," one last time before he caves.

"I'll do what I can."

Down the cement corridor to where fake-Mikazi is being held, Meiling is reminded somewhere around a thousand times of how Mr. Arredondo pulled a lot of personal strings to get her here, and if there's any trouble—any at all—it could be the last trouble she ever causes.

"Uh huh, yup, I get it, yeah for sure." Words string out of Meiling's mouth in response with no thought, simply agreeing the way everyone always wants her to. It's like people suspect she'll lay down and die if they so desire. And while that's not entirely untrue, she'd like to remember she doesn't *have* to.

"Meiling," Mr. Arredondo says when they arrive at the barred door fake-Mikazi is chained up behind. Mr. Arredondo looks hardly more well-rested now than he did when he visited her yesterday.

Meiling stops, looking between him, the door, and the officer escorting them—who has Suraya's eyes and thick silver hair down to her hip bones. She's silent now that they've made it, seeming to trust Mr. Arredondo with the final warnings.

The barred door has the tiniest sliver of window at the top. Meiling isn't tall enough to see anything through it, but Mr. Arredondo is. His gaze flits there and stays for one second, two seconds, three seconds, before he addresses her again. "Keep a steady head in there."

He turns and walks off in the direction they came, feet clinking and clunking against the hard floors in uneven strides. The lights down here are minimal, leaving Meiling to see nothing but his shadow after only a few moments. She tries tugging some darkness inward but it's no use. They may have swapped out her cuffs to let her walk here, but they're still ability-suppressing. With Mr. Arredondo gone, it's only her, Officer Zialitos (one of a bunch with this name), and the man on the other side of the door.

"Listen kid," Officer Zialitos says with clear disdain, "you're only here out of a courtesy to Jay. I don't know what you think you're doing, but it's a mistake. I can already tell you that. Make one more and I won't hesitate to implicate you right alongside Mikazi. Understood?"

Embarrassment and fury both lace up her spine with unpleasant heat. Rolling her shoulders weakly in an attempt to keep it all hidden, Meiling tells her, "Understood."

She nods stiffly. Then she unlocks the door with both a blast of heat to a heat lock pad and a large golden key off a thick ring containing a dozen. Upon the first step inside the room, Meiling sees nothing. No one. She stops, scanning the high cement walls and floors, and the sun windows a dozen meters overhead.

Officer Zialitos must sense her confusion because she starts to chuckle.

"Did you think we'd let you in the same room as him?

This is an interrogation room outside of his cell. You stay here with me the entire time, Miyako."

She stomps on a button on the floor and a thick panel of glass much like the one Meiling's been staring at for three days pops out from behind the far wall. The room behind it is half the size of the one Meiling is in now, like a broom closet, and it is flooded with twice as much light. Fluorescent whites beam down on fake Mikazi from every direction. Chained up in four different sets of cuffs, he sits in the center of the floor with a smile.

Without the protective cloth that covered his face the other day, Meiling can make out his every feature. From the piercing blue eyes to the dry white skin to the shaggy light brown hair, he's everything the real Mikazi is not.

The man tugs himself to his feet using the cuffs latched around his wrists. Similar ones wrap around his ankles, calves, and thighs, keeping him from taking even a single step forward.

"Go on," Officer Zialitos says, scraping a stiff wooden chair over for Meiling to sit in. "Say whatever was so urgent you had to threaten an Academy teacher for it."

Meiling scowls. The man masquerading as Mikazi laughs.

"You threatened an Academy teacher for me?" he asks. Meiling drops into the wooden chair, feeling wooden herself. "That's sweet."

"Shut up. You aren't the real Mikazi."

"No?" the man asks. His voice is light, impassive. "I put my spirit on the line that I am."

Though Officer Zialitos does not seem surprised at

this, Meiling nearly tips the chair over backward in shock. Historically, putting one's spirit on the line was a torture method for breaking trust. With time it became a vow used in courtrooms and trials to solidify pleas. What it means is to offer your spirit up for forceful drainage from its core should your words prove weightless or untruthful. With abilities from Divinia and Amada, or even Viera and Zilla, it's a guarantee the truth will be discovered one way or another. It's not a claim to be taken lightly.

"You're lying," Meiling says anyway. "If you were the real Mikazi, why didn't the attacks stop right away?"

News of the last violent M-attack, right down the street at the Zialitos Mansion, reached Meiling's ears only hours after it occurred. Officers came parading into her cell screaming, demanding she tell them what she knows and why she did it. Meiling kept silent the whole time, only gathering what tidbits of information she could. Twelve dead, a subsection of the Zialitos family wiped out, a couple spirits drained—like this man's could be, should he be caught in this lie he's woven.

"This is exactly what should be happening," he says. There's a glint in his eyes making the blue stand out more strongly. This isn't a Miyako.

"You planned this then?" Meiling asks. "All on your own? *Mikazi?*"

With an irritating smirk trapped on his face, he only nods.

"Are you sure about that?" Meiling presses, hoping to crack him somehow. His trial is slated to begin tomorrow.

If she can't get something out of him before then, she never will. He'll condemn them both to certain death.

He chooses then to go silent. Meiling stands and slams both fists against the glass. The metal cuffs around her wrists bang against it with a splintering crack. A few more times and she could probably break through. It's worth a shot. She slams again.

"Hey!" Officer Zialitos grabs her chains and yanks her back like a disobedient dog on a leash. Meiling chokes as she falls back into her chair, spitting out expletives. "Behave or you'll add another charge to your list. Is that what you want?"

Meiling glares.

"He isn't a Miyako. Mikazi is a Miyako. That's what everyone said from the start, right? Only a Miyako could be behind this sort of terrorism?"

Officer Zialitos crosses her arms and looks away, refusing to answer. Meiling feels a stirring in her gut, the kind that comes with an explosion of her abilities. The cuffs tighten around her wrists in response. She wants to shatter them to pieces and smother the room in shadows.

"You aren't Mikazi," Meiling says, turning to the man in the cell again. "You can't be. He's a Miyako."

"No?" he asks again, never blinking. His bangs fall loosely over his eyes as he cocks his head to the side. "Is he?"

"Why are you doing this?"

"I put my spirit on the line."

"Why? What are you getting out of this?"

A slow smile climbs his lips again. "My spirit is on the line."

"Are you stupid?" Meiling shouts, watching the lights inside his room flicker. Shadows appear to be wiggling their way through the cracks in the walls between them. "That's not a good thing!"

His smile only widens in response.

"Answer me!"

"That's quite enough," Officer Zialtios announces. With a snap of her fingers the lights in his room flare to the strongest level. Those shadows Meiling thought she saw are gone at once.

"What's wrong with him?" Meiling growls.

The officer laughs, a surprising guffaw out of such a thin, sharp mouth. "Look in the mirror and find out. He's a terrorist just like you are, Miyako, what did you expect?"

The officer taps the side of her head roughly. Meiling swallows. She gets dragged from the room in more chains than she entered it in.

32

Suraya

The entirety of Malumvia and a good portion of the surrounding countries show up for the public trial of "Mikazi."

As home to the majority of Divinity-descended people in the world, Malumvia is always a spectacle to behold to other countries. Especially to those surrounding where there are areas with little or no people of Divine blood at all. I t's not much of a surprise that the turnout is this intense today. Luckily Suraya has a seat secured for herself in the front row beside her parents. By the time the courtroom overflows with people, she's settled in comfortably so she can watch the uproar as a comedy.

The issue is, just as much as she watches, she's watched back. Zialitos stick out like sore thumbs no matter where they go. From the sharp bluish-silver eyes to the vibrant hair to the heat they apparently radiate, there's no hiding. Suraya feels like a caged animal in a Kaitsja visiting enclosure with the way people eye her. Everyone is here to witness the same thing, the same person, yet half the crowd ogles her as they enter the room like she's the criminal. Fear of those with abilities runs deep outside of Malumvia where they originated.

"Don't stare," Taru whispers in her ear, eyes glued ahead. None of the officials, witnesses, or Mikazi himself are here yet so there's only open empty space before them. She must be staring at a spot on the wall.

"They're the ones staring at me," Suraya grumbles.

Her father pats her on the knee. Suraya only narrowly avoids lashing out at him with sunlight. She still hasn't forgiven her parents for keeping the truth about Meiling from her for so long.

A hush falls over the room when the large oak door bangs open and the judge strides through. She wears a long cape-like jacket and so much jewelry she rattles with every movement. Each step sounds like the wind chimes in the Katz's backyard when Meiling was a kid. Like most judges for Division One cases (those of high-level crimes), she's a person of no Descent, but special blood nevertheless: a Messenger.

Which is senseless, honestly, because it's illegal to call upon the Divinities themselves for Divine intervention in trial. Why bring someone of her caliber here if she can't be of use?

"Order," she says softly, approaching her chair and perching on it slowly.

More silence. Even when the doors open once again and numerous officers escort Mikazi in, bound by cuffs at his neck, torso, hands, knees, and ankles, no one speaks. He clacks almost as much as the judge.

"Today's trial will be to determine the sentencing of

defendant 'Mikazi,'" the judge says, surveying the room. "Charges include forty-eight counts of trespassing, twenty-nine counts of vandalism, one hundred and eighteen counts of assault and sixty-six homicides, attempted kidnapping, terrorism, and conspiracy to overthrow the Malumvian government.

"Given his cooperation in being arrested and his oath to put his spirit on the line, the defendant seeks leniency in the form of life in prison rather than a death sentence. We will begin with hearing from him."

She motions to the stand beside her. Two officers lead Mikazi to that spot. He nods at the judge cordially as he takes the seat. The collar around his neck is turning his skin red all around it.

A public lawyer of some sort, wearing a worn-down gray suit and an off-center tie, stands across from him. He places a stack of papers before the judge and turns his bright eyes to Mikazi. The judge quickly reads the papers before stacking them to the side.

She then announces, "Let it be known that lawyer Aldric Monague, a descendant of Divinia of Prophecy, will enable the ability to make the defendant speak the truth while on the stand."

Mikazi smiles, his laser-blue eyes locking onto the lawyer. Shouldn't he be more concerned that his lies will be revealed? Suraya halfheartedly springs her own mind manipulation abilities to life. She only trusts herself, but she hates invasions of privacy like this.

"State your legal name for the record," the lawyer says.

"Simon Saunders."

"Simon Saunders, do you go by the name Mikazi?"

"Yes."

Suraya finds no trace of dishonesty in his words. She digs harder than she ever has before, but still comes up empty.

"And are you of Mahina descent?"

"Yes."

Gasps fill the room. Suraya unconsciously seeks out Meiling, wondering how much of a hissy-fit she's throwing after all her assertions that this man can't possibly be the real Mikazi because he isn't even a Miyako. But she can't find her anywhere. Ever since she got taken away in cuffs at Nirnasha's Graveyard, she's been nonexistent. Whatever Simon's fate is, hers will likely follow suit.

Despite not finding Meiling, Suraya does find her parents. Standing together rigidly at the back of the courtroom, Jax and Reena Katz hide beneath dark hoods concealing half their faces. Suraya turns away from them, angrier than before. She's seen enough of Meiling scowling down at her message-less cell phone over the past few weeks to know they haven't been around much since everything came out.

"Do you take full responsibility for the terrorist attacks against Malumvia within the past twelve months?" the lawyer asks Simon.

"Yes."

The lawyer nods, turning to the crowd to show them his eyes swirling with color and light—a telltale sign his abilities have been in use this whole time. More gasps follow. Suraya huffs out a laugh in disbelief, and her mother's elbow ends up in her ribs.

"That will be all."

As Aldric Monague steps away to take a seat, Suraya catches Mikazi's gaze. Or more like Mikazi catches hers, seeing as his pupils flit in her direction without missing a beat, almost as if seeking her out. Once again he smiles. He has a wide, slow-moving smile made of straight white teeth that makes Suraya's skin crawl. With her Divinia abilities still in use, she can sense that this smile is not genuine. It's hard to tell for sure since she often makes a point of *not* using her Divinia abilities, but it feels like resentment fueling his expression. It's too bad she can only narrow her eyes before his attention is torn away by the judge declaring it's time for victim testimonies.

For hours on end the stifled courtroom hears sob stories of anyone who's been even the slightest bit affected by this past year's M-attacks. Rather than sticking with the few impactful testimonies, like those who lost family or those severely injured because of them, it's a free-for-all. Anyone afraid of the Miyako family takes this chance to bumble on about it.

If Suraya has to hear one more privileged person from Division One cry about the deaths of people they hardly knew from violence in Division Five, she's going to lose it. Light fixtures be damned. Don't they know there are Zialitos here, like her mother, who lost half their family because of the Miyako family?

As if Ataru has heard her and is answering her silent prayers, it all comes to halt when the oak door bangs open again to show Meiling flanked by four officers. People holler and boo as soon as she squares her shoulders and steps into the room. There are dark bags under her eyes. She hasn't changed her clothes since the graveyard, leaving them wrinkled and dirty. Her hair is greasy and visibly split at the ends. There are bruises on her arms that weren't there before. She makes Simon Saunders, the real criminal, look like he's been living in luxury.

Someone gasps from the back of the courtroom as another stifles a sob. Omar swings around, sucks in a sharp breath, and jumps out of his seat to go to them. The Katz.

Offering up her hand to her mother, who is crying now from the many testimonies about how awful the Miyakos are, Suraya drops the Divinia abilities in her eyes. She does not want to know what's spinning around in Meiling's head right now. Her mother takes her hand and together they collect sunlight to calm themselves. It swarms up through their veins and is pressed flat between their palms. The overhead lights in the courtroom dim.

"If she may," one of the officers leading Meiling inside says, "Miss Katz-Miyako would like to speak in defense of both herself and Simon Saunders."

The judge pauses only briefly before saying, "Approved."

The hissing disapproval and threats thrown Meiling's way only increase as she takes a stand behind the podium opposite Simon Saunders.

"You idiot," Suraya grumbles, her voice lost to the noise of the courtroom. "What are you doing?"

"Allowing this man to take the fall for Mikazi, and in

turn all of this year's M-attacks, would be a disservice to Malumvia. He is not the one you want."

Suraya squeezes her mother's hand tighter. She told Meiling she believed her about this Mikazi—Simon—being the wrong arrest, but what she meant was that he's wrong to arrest alone. Mikazi or not, Miyako or not, he's a criminal. He deserves to be put away for life. But allowing him to take the fall alone will only open the door for the rest of the Miyakos to do worse.

If only Suraya could figure out what Meiling wants from this.

"Think about it!" Meiling raises her voice over the rowdy crowd. She doesn't sound right. She doesn't look right either. Her skin is pale and red-tinted, sunken and dry. Suraya feels as if the floor has dropped out from beneath her. "There have been, what, thirty-two violent M-attacks? Nineteen or twenty nonviolent? Isn't it too easy to let one man take the fall for every last one of them?"

"Too easy?" someone explodes from two rows down. "Sixty-six lives lost is easy to you?"

"That's not—"

"She's a Miyako!" another chimes in. "Obviously , she'd try to protect him!"

No, Suraya thinks, *she isn't trying to protect him; she's trying to sentence the rest of them to death at his side. But why?*

"How could he possibly be lying with Mr. Monague's abilities on him the entire time?" yet another person shouts.

The judge calls order, slamming a gavel down on the tabletop.

"That is enough! Miss Miyako, do you have any last words for consideration?"

"All of Red Class One was there that night at the graveyard," Meiling says. "They know as well as I do Mikazi isn't working alone. We know there's some sort of fighting between his group and the Miyakos. That alone should be enough to keep this case open." She gives a shuddering exhale. "That is all."

"We will take your testimony into account. Thank you, Miss Miyako."

"Katz," Meiling snaps, turning her attention to the back of the courtroom for the first time, almost as if she could feel the presence of her parents long before seeing them. "My name is Meiling Katz."

Some people snicker. Others hold their breath. Most look around uncomfortably, embarrassed for her. Suraya feels an itch deep in the back of her throat as she avoids turning around to see her father with Jax and Reena. Meiling is of Mahina descent, but those two blubbering idiots back there are still her parents.

"It's true, I was there that night," Suraya says before she's aware she will say anything. The sudden influx of heat in her palm from her mother burns as the unspoken warning it is.

All attention cuts her way.

"I was there that night," she repeats. "At the graveyard. No doubt Simon Saunders is a criminal, but he's not a mastermind. He let himself get caught, didn't he? These attacks were no solo act."

Meiling's jaw drops open silently. Suraya avoids her eyes. This isn't for her. It's for Suraya's own peace of mind, for the safety of their country, for the truth, for justice, for all the rest of his lackeys that are out free right now when they don't deserve to be.

"I never claimed to work alone," Simon cuts in, his voice cutting through the room like a knife. "I simply assume sole responsibility."

Suraya barks out a laugh. Taru's hand is so tight in hers it's cutting off circulation.

"The rest of you are fine with that?" Suraya shouts, gesturing wildly around the room with her free hand. "He's not the only terrorist, but we'll take him and charge him like a catch all, anyway? That's fine with you?"

Her skin feels red hot and pulled too tight over her bones. She wants to peel it back and crawl out of it. No, she just needs to get out of this room. There's too much heat, too many windows, too much light. There's no way her current mood can withstand it. Ataru's begging to make an appearance.

All at once the feeling dies out. It feels like she's been submerged underwater. Drenched in a cold sweat, Suraya opens her eyes, not knowing when she shut them, and sees Meiling. Her hands are outstretched and her brows furrowed as she stares at them, shadows like plumes of smoke curling around her fingertips. The cuffs at her wrists are cracked open.

"She attacked her!" someone cries.

People from border countries push and shove their way out of the room, screaming bloody murder. Meiling trips backward into the stand Mikazi sits behind and he reaches out at once to tug on her hair. When she screams in response, that's the last straw.

"Contain the Miyako!" an officer calls out.

Reena's distinct voice screams out, "No!" at the same time Meiling is tackled to the ground.

In seconds she's cuffed with new suppressors, no better than Mikazi who's on trial for more than Suraya can keep track of. In utter silence, Meiling is dragged out of sight while Omar drags Jax and Reena Katz out of the courtroom in the other direction, his eyes flooded with light as he tries to calm them down.

Nothing follows. Nothing more than two sentences from the quiet judge who's remained unmoved this whole time.

Simon Saunders-Miyako is charged with every last crime and the case is closed. Due to his "spirit on the line" oath he somehow never broke by being found to be lying, he receives life in confinement rather than death. Intercrossing both hands over his chest and turning his chin to the ceiling, he smiles.

He's still smiling when he gets dragged away the same as Meiling.

Suraya maintains her dignity by walking out with her mother all on her own.

33

Meiling

As it turns out, Simon Saunders's guilty verdict spells Meiling's freedom. Once he's locked up on every charge related to the M-attacks, Meiling's record is swept clean. Even her scuffle with the officers on the South Cliff and her loss of control that somehow broke grade-A ability-suppressing cuffs in the courtroom are overlooked.

Headmaster Anji speaks in her favor to the Zialitos Academy Board and the Malumvian Authorities. He pulls up proof of her poor treatment in the cell for those four days, her lack of ability control due to Doctor Sutherland's medication—Zialitos-mandated, as it seems—and even five months of security footage proving she hardly ever stepped out of her classrooms. This serves to be enough to keep her out of jail and in the Academy.

Headmaster Anji is the first person she sees once she's a free woman again. He hands her the folder on her case, all of it retracted or overruled to guarantee her freedom.

"Thank you," Meiling tells him, "but why'd you do all that for me?"

"I told you already," Headmaster Anji says. "I expect great things from you, Miss Meiling Katz-Miyako."

When he steps away, leaving her at the oversize gate into the Academy campus, her parents are there waiting. Meiling stares into the soft eyes of Jax and Reena Katz and all the anger that's been building up toward them for months seeps away in seconds. After being held in a prison cell and put on trial for no real reason other than her Mahina blood, the grudge she's held over her parents for not telling her the truth about it sooner seems insignificant. Meiling rubs the swollen red marks around her wrists from the ability suppressing cuffs and feels tears well up in her eyes.

"Meiling…"

Meiling takes two long strides forward and throws her arms around their shoulders.

"I'm so sorry," Reena whispers into her hair.

Meiling swallows acid in her throat. She still isn't ready yet to say it's okay. They lied to her for thirteen years, left her messages unanswered for months after she learned the truth, and only showed up to apologize *after* the damage was done. They have so much explaining to do, and Meiling isn't sure where to start. She just needs a hug right now.

"We'll tell you everything, I promise," Jax says as if reading her mind, even though Meiling knows he wouldn't in a moment like this. "Right now, we're just happy you're okay."

He pries her off to cradle her cheeks and swipe tears away with his thumbs. Meiling chokes on a sob and Reena pulls her back in. Meiling squeezes her eyes shut. Her mother's head is buried in her hair and she can feel the breath on her neck. Everything about this hug is familiar, but the feeling of a thick sheet of cardstock separating them highlights the divide between them. This may be her mother, but this is not the same mother she left before the academy.

Meiling slowly removes herself from her touch completely.

"I've been cleared to return to classes as usual, at least for the remainder of this year."

"Meiling, honey," Reena whispers.

"I want to finish," she says quickly. She needs time before she can handle listening to their side of the story without screaming or crying. "We can talk about everything when you come to pick me up in a couple weeks. Okay?"

"Okay," Jax whispers. "Anything you want."

Meiling nods sharply. Her father's gentle voice used to make her feel safe, but now it only grates on her ears like the ringing of sirens. Her mother's small smile used to make her feel warm, but now her skin only ever feels cold. Until she figures out why and how they could have done this to her, nothing stands a chance at returning to the way it was.

"I don't want to talk to you until then," Meiling says, pinching her bottom lip between two fingers to keep it from wobbling.

"Okay," Reena says, breathing out shakily. "We'll see you then. We love you, Meiling."

Meiling crosses through the bronze gate onto the Academy's campus, eyes on the building ahead, and closes her mouth into a thin line in response.

Meiling returns to classes the next day.

Everything falls from chaos to normalcy in the blink of an eye. Crime rates plummet as time goes on. Suraya refuses to look at or speak to her, and Artie and Callum hardly leave her side. Everyone accepts that peace has once again reigned, and Meiling tastes blood on her tongue biting back the fact she knows it has not.

After the one outlying violent M-attack the day following Simon Saunders's arrest, nothing more happens. With him heavily guarded and subdued behind bars in a prison cell underground, all the torment stops. This is all the proof anyone needs to put their faith in the judge's ruling. Headlines read that Simon is Mikazi, Mikazi is a Miyako, and the Miyakos are the source of every last M plastered around the country within the past twelve months. It's so easy how they frame it. Too easy.

Each time a paper shows up, Meiling wants to tear out the wrong parts and piece them together until they form something right. Though she doesn't know all of that. She does know that Mikazi is a Miyako, but he's definitely not Simon. Or at least not *only* Simon. There must be a group.

In the spare time Meiling gets alone in her dorm room, after all her homework is done and friends are shooed away, she buries herself in notes and deep-dives into history textbooks, piecing together what little she can in her case to prove otherwise.

The working theory Meiling has come up with is that Mikazi is the head of a Miyako imitation group (even though he's a Miyako himself) and they have staged every last one of these M-attacks to some end. She just can't figure out what that end may be. To invoke the Miyakos hiding out somewhere across the globe? To cause fear to the Sun-gifted around Malumvla? None of it is sufficient for what they've lost with Simon caught. Worse than that, she can't even begin to imagine their purpose for allowing Simon to be caught and charged before any of those reasons could come to a head in the first place.

And where does *she* fit into all of this?

Spiraling down the rabbit hole of these endless questions leads Meiling to the end of her first year at the Zialitos Academy for Sun-Gifted Children. The final day wraps up in an anticlimactic flurry of pointless fieldwork and monotone lectures from Mr. Arredondo, who assures them that while this year was challenging, it'll have nothing on what's waiting for them in their more advanced courses next year.

Meiling's fairly sure that isn't true, given the course of these past few months, but she's also fairly certain she won't get to find out anyway. Since her stunt at the trial, protests have popped up over her admission into the Academy. Not only because she's a Miyako and the Miyakos bear the blame for most conflicts around the country (from the Lunar Eclipse Massacre to all of the M-attacks), but because she's Moon-descended in general.

Technically her being here breaks laws. Multiple. Nearly every last Descent Segregation Law, in fact. Those laws maintain distance in schools, houses, and places of business based on descent unless specially authorized otherwise—which Meiling is not. Now that it's been aired to the world she has Mahina's blood and is a student, the pushback has come. Headmaster Anji has bore it well until now, but with the term coming to a close, it's hard to imagine he'll continue to.

"They can't just kick you out," Artie says around a spoonful of soup. He eats a lot of soup these days—something about how it warms his spirit core and soothes the ache left from nearly having it torn out. He's technically fully recovered from that by now, but the nurses say he'll probably feel phantom yanks and stabs for the rest of his life. So, soup.

"Stop that," Meiling says, shaking her head around.

She's sitting in one of the dorm hall dining rooms with him and Callum (and Karina, who's sitting silently a few seats away because she tends to keep her brother within eyesight without ever talking to anyone herself), and sharing what she suspects will be her final dinner here at the Academy. Except she's not having soup; she's having steamed vegetables and ginger tea because that's what her parents always made her when she was upset as a little kid and despite her lingering irritation with them for all the lies, she misses them right now like a little kid.

"This won't be your last dinner here, Mei," Artie mumbles.

"I said stop that!" Her fork rattles against her plate as

she drops it to wave her arms around. "I've told you not to do that, Artie. Stick to your own thoughts."

Somehow, Artie's strength in Divinia abilities has doubled over one singular school year. Rather than simply seeing through lies or making someone speak the truth, he's become quite adept at legitimately reading thoughts. In this final stretch of the term, he's worked on it religiously every day, sitting there with his golden eyes trained on Meiling to read what's on her mind. His absurdly fast growth is great and all, but it's no excuse not to mind his own business.

"Wait, so that was right?" he asks, eyes settling to their normal hazel. Another heaping spoonful of soup goes into his mouth. "I read your mind?"

"For the hundredth time, Arthur," Callum cuts in, using *Arthur* sometimes like a scolding parent, "yes, you can read our minds now."

Seeing how much he's grown in such a short period of time only solidifies Meiling's belief that she doesn't belong here. If anything, she's regressed. Coming off her medication and finding out the truth of her blood has made everything worse. Even her regular course grades like history and mathematics have dropped, never mind her ability course grades. Not to mention Suraya has never been farther out of reach and Meiling misses her like a vital organ cut straight out of her.

Speaking of Suraya, she steps through the doorway then. Kai is to her left and Evie is to her right. The two of them are laughing, practically hanging off Suraya's arms; they're so close. A stab goes through Meiling's chest, and

Artie flinches. She flicks her eyes to him and sees he's already looking back, gold swirling in his irises yet again. That should teach him.

"Get out," Suraya says, looking at the four of them together at the table.

Kai's mouth twists into a frown. Evie chokes out a laugh, seeming to think Suraya might be joking. Meiling knows she isn't so she scratches her chair back to stand and clear her plate.

"Mei," Callum says, reaching for her.

"It's fine." She takes his plate and Artie's bowl. "We should go."

"What'd she ever do to you?" Artie hisses at Suraya on the way out.

Meiling pushes through the doorway out of the dining room before she can hear Suraya's response. There's too many answers Suraya could give and too many ways each and every one of them can hurt her.

Somewhere along the path from the dining room to dorms, Karina disappears without a word of goodbye, leaving Callum, Artie, and Meiling alone for the first time in days. Instead of taking the quiet moment to discuss anything that has happened recently, the boys complain about Suraya's attitude instead.

"I don't understand her at all," Artie mumbles, scuffing his feet along the rug.

"Does anyone understand Suraya?" Callum scoffs and

looks at Artie's face, all pinched eyebrows, "But what makes you so agitated with her right now?"

"Sensing lies with Divinia abilities isn't like you can see what the actual truth is, you know?" Artie says. "Even if you can truly read minds, it's hard to know what exactly is being covered up. We can only feel a flickering sense of alarm for any dishonesty."

Meiling nods, keeping her eyes peeled ahead. Her dorm room is about a dozen meters away, but they're ambling so it might take another minute to get there. Although Meiling knows all of this about Divinia abilities already, Callum does not. His nose scrunches up and his mouth drops open. When it comes to any ability that is not his own, understanding how they work is far beyond him—not that he'll ever admit it.

"I constantly sense dishonesty in Suraya," Artie continues, head cocking to the side. "Even if what she's saying can't be the truth or a lie, the alarm is always going off."

"What does that mean?" Callum asks, coming to a full stop in the narrow hallway. "Is she just a deceitful person or something?"

"No," Meiling cuts in, loud and defensive. Many things can be said of Suraya Zialitos, but deceitful is not one of them.

Callum throws his hands up apologetically despite the steely glare in his pink eyes. Meiling blows out a long breath, shakes her head, and turns around to keep walking to her room. After a short amount of whispering back and forth, Callum and Artie follow. This time no one says anything.

Until her door comes into view and they see the huge, jagged letter M carved into it.

"Oh fu—"

Artie wraps one arm around the back of Callum's head and slaps a hand over his mouth. Meiling does the same to herself, keeping her sharp gasp trapped inside.

Wood shavings are piled on the floor from where the message was scraped out of her door, the doorknob is hanging on by a single loose screw, and the door itself is cracked open just enough for Meiling to see the glare from her window inside.

"Mei, shadows" Artie whispers, releasing Callum only enough so he can tug brown roots from underneath the carpet. "I need you to make some shadows."

"*What?*" she hisses back. What is he thinking? When have Mahina's abilities ever made a situation better?

"Please do it," he says, dragging all three of them until their backs hit the wall.

Meiling shakily pulls together a thick wall of shadows as requested. They serve as a barrier between them and the doorway only she can see through. Callum pushes his roots ahead all the same, cutting a path for their feet to follow as they shuffle ahead.

When Meiling's shadows hit the edge of the doorway, they freeze. Artie looks her dead in the eyes, helping her to stay calm, and says, "Send them in."

Using all her energy, Meiling launches the darkness from inside her to the place through the crack of the door.

The force of them all rushing in at once snap the door open the rest of the way and send leaves from the roots flying in every direction.

The breath knocks out of Meiling's lungs.

And absolutely nothing else happens.

After a beat of silence, Artie murmurs, "I don't sense anyone?"

M is for Miyako, and it's for Mikazi, and at this point it's probably for Meiling herself. She can't escape this—whatever the truth may be. It follows her around like a shadow she never asked to have; because she has plenty of those.

I t's only fair she steps through that door alone. While Callum and Artie are hesitating, confused, she rushes forward into her room before her mind can catch up to her and demand she stop. She's fully prepared to be immediately struck down or kidnapped again.

Inside there's nothing there waiting for her. Well, not nothing. No one, but not nothing.

"Mei!" Artie whisper-shouts, barreling in after her. "What are you… What is this?"

The window is open, screen torn out, drapes waving with gusts of wind coming in from outside. On the ground in front of it, a line of papers rustle. Moonlight cuts in to illuminate them.

"I don't…" Meiling stops mid-sentence.

There are thirteen papers laid out across her carpet, every one of them composed of a photograph and a line or two of blood-red handwriting. The photographs all have the letter M in them at least once—smeared in blood on the wall, built out of rubble, formed by a landslide off a mountain. Thirteen. Lined up starting from the Mahina Temple that began this whole mess. Numerous Zialitos Officers were slaughtered during a routine patrol there, leaving the M that resulted in all the rest. It only became a nonviolent attack location months later when the structure caved in, forming an M out of the building itself.

"Wait, are these…"

"The nonviolent M-attacks." Callum takes the words straight from Meiling's mouth.

These photos are clearly from the looping nonviolent attacks, and each line of writing beneath is the location where it happened. They're in order from oldest to most recent, some with so many Ms it's hard to make out anything else.

A Mahina Temple in Division Five. Essex Orchard, Inglewood Bridge and Lilith Road in Division Four. Irene's Statue, a sacred Nirnasha graveyard, Gardner Street and the Mystic War Memorial in Division Three. Ingrid House, Yorkshire Mountains, and an Abungu worship garden in Division Two. The Kaitsja Sanctuary in Division One. The Odaz River in Division One.

Using the tips of her fingers, Meiling shifts the papers around. Nothing pops out, no alarms blare, no meaning to any of this filters into her brain. It's just a line of warnings no one heeded; photographic evidence that there are ends untied.

Artie crouches down and takes the thirteenth page between his fingers. The thirteenth, the final, the Odaz River: where someone drained the river and left bones everywhere, even a few in the shape of an M for Meiling to find right before the location turned violent with a tsunami.

"I thought this was only a violent location," he says, leaving fingerprints across the image as he wipes at it. "Where was the M from the drought?"

Meiling snags the photograph from him. "I found it."

She thinks of how she found it, what she was feeling when she did, and why she never told anyone afterward. When Artie's gaze turns to her, she allows him to enter her thoughts and read it all for himself. His features go soft and he asks nothing more.

"Look at this," Callum says through a deep breath.

What neither Meiling nor Artie noticed when he picked up the Odaz River picture was that there was another beneath it. Callum has his hands hovering over it, shaking terribly. As he stares down at the words written, his pink eyes go nearly red and his jaw falls open.

One of Meiling's pictures of Kane Miyako is back. They've been missing all year, long before she learned his name, but now one of many is back. It's back and there's one line of words in all capitals scrawled right across his chest, covering the Z of his Academy uniform:

THEY KILLED HIM, AND THEY WILL KILL YOU TOO.

"Who's they?" Artie asks shakily.

"Put that back down," Callum demands, motioning at the Odaz River picture Meiling is clinging to with a vice grip.

Sometimes being around Artie and Callum is like

having one toddler who never knows what's going on and another who always wants to be in charge of what's going on. Meiling almost can't believe she has enough brain power left to see what she does in the display while they go back and forth asking questions and making demands. But somehow she does. The second she listens to Callum and sets the final location on the floor again, it's almost too obvious.

Mahina Temple.
Essex Orchard.
Inglewood Bridge.
Lilith Road.
Irene's Statue.
Nirnasha Graveyard.
Gardner Street.
Mystic War Memorial.
Ingrid House.
Yorkshire Mountains.
Abungu Worship Garden.
Kaitsja Sanctuary.
Odaz River.

This whole time, Mikazi, or whoever it is, hasn't been wreaking havoc as a scare tactic with these nonviolent M-attacks; they've been communicating a code. A message.

A person.

Meiling Miyako.

34
Suraya

Even in her sleep Suraya can't find any peace these days.

"My child, I fear the time has come."

Ataru has visited her in her dreams every night for weeks now, saying the same cryptic nonsense each time, making them more akin to nightmares after a while. His appearances began at almost the exact same time Suraya cut off all contact with Meiling, so it's become quite clear to her that no matter what she does, someone is going to be driving her out of her mind for it.

"I beg of you, put a stop to this senselessness."

Suraya opens her eyes to the bluish-white realm of space that greets her when Ataru infiltrates her rest. Hovering together in nothingness, Suraya faces Ataru and Ataru faces her. *Again.* The first few times he came to her it was an honor, but by the twelfth and thirteenth times, Suraya just wanted her sleep schedule back.

"I know you can hear me." He cocks a brow and puts his dry hands on his swim trunk-clad hips. His stringy blond hair is loose this time, hanging down his shoulders and over his chest in knots—which is revealed through the unbuttoned front of his white collared shirt. It's embarrassing.

"Unfortunately," Suraya grumbles. Turns out even Divinites lose their appeal in time.

Not because he continuously calls her "my child," or because he wants her to do things, but will never say exactly what those things are for reason of "you must learn for yourself," but because he invades her privacy with these nightly visits so often, Ataru has become like the third parent Suraya never asked for. Nothing like a little parenting to take away the prestige of a literal higher entity.

"So, what is it you want but won't elaborate on this time?" Suraya asks.

Ataru's lips, chapped almost as bad as his hands are dry—this guy seriously needs to invest in lotion or something—tick up into the slightest smile. Not fueled by happiness, but rather by bemusement.

"My child," he begins, because that's how he always begins these things, "circumstances are dire. As such, this very well may be our last visit."

"Thank..." Suraya trails off. Saying 'thank Ataru' doesn't exactly suit the moment. Besides, she'll be glad to be rid of him and these confusing visits, but not without explanation. So, she simply asks, "What circumstances?"

No M-attacks have taken place for weeks now. Simon Saunders is heavily guarded in a jail cell, serving his life sentence without problem. Suraya isn't naive enough to be lulled into a sense of security by either of these things, but most everyone else is. Aside from the Descent Segregation

Laws being called into question by a few Academy student's families because of Meiling, things are fine across Malumvia. Not great, but fine. Far from dire, especially in comparison to where they were six months ago.

"I cannot say," Ataru sighs, eyes flashing an even brighter silver than usual. "It's not a Divinity's place to meddle in human affairs."

"Because that's stopped you before." Suraya rolls her head around her shoulders, easing the tension out. Days without proper sleep are adding up.

"Suraya Zialitos."

She blinks her eyes open slowly, eyeing him with impatience. Each night it's, "you are smart, my child," and "you must solve this, my child," and "you are the only hope, my child," but never once has it been, "you've done enough already, my child." And that's the only sentence Suraya wants to hear right about now. She's tired of trying to do a Divinity's work. It's hard enough to do her own work; to pass her courses and control her growing abilities and swallow down every last emotion that gets in the way of those. Either way, she knows this isn't the end of the Miyakos, or of the name Mikazi, or of the conflict.

"What?"

"I will be gone for a long while," he says. Normally he sounds so flippant, but right now his voice echoes in a grave tone. "In that time, my trust, my power, my leadership, it will be placed in your hands. Do you understand?"

"Obviously." Though she's not sure she does.

He smiles sincerely now, as if he knows this. "I am counting on you, my child."

"Right, great." Suraya's heart thunders in her chest, but she refuses to show Ataru. What if he rescinds the offer? "Can I go to sleep now?"

"One last thing," he says, stepping in close. He's so warm Suraya shuts her eyes and flinches back. Being close to him is worse than being lit on fire—which she now knows the feeling of, thank you Jasper of the Mikazi group.

"About Kane Miyako, the former Academy student you tried to contact: Don't. I already warned you away from him once, my child. I do not want to do it again."

"Why?" Suraya snaps. The more he warns her away from Kane, the more she wants to know about him. If it wasn't important, Ataru wouldn't care.

"Don't. This is your first and only warning. Knowing any more of him than you already do would be detrimental to your cause."

"My cause?" Suraya asks, barking out a laugh. "And what might that cause be, Ataru?"

An unsettling tremor goes through the air.

"You show up here every night and tell me nothing. Do you think I appreciate it? You think I'll bow down to you as my Creator for gracing me with your presence? Because I won't. I never will. These abilities are *mine* and I owe you nothing for being the initial source of them. You get that? My cause is *my cause* and it has absolutely nothing to do with you."

"Yes," he murmurs, seemingly to himself, "yes, it must be you."

"*What?*"

"So long as you leave Kane Miyako out of it, that's quite all right. Do as you will, Suraya Zialitos."

With one hand he reaches out and taps his fist over her chest. It burns from the spot he touches and out in intervals, heat racing down her belly and then across her arms and lastly up into her head. Her vision whites out for a full minute from the pain. Over the years, Suraya has lost her grip on her abilities many times, as anyone with as much power as she does would, and that's what this feels like, except much worse. Her body pops and creaks like it cannot hold all the blood inside of her. She feels seconds away from bursting.

She wants to ask what he's doing, or what any of these visits meant, or why her, but her mouth will not move. It's snapped shut, biting down so hard she can taste blood as it floods her mouth.

"Ataru will be with you," he says with one final pat in the space between her collar bones.

Suraya wakes up coughing blood and running a fever.

Suraya spends eight days in the intensive care unit at the hospital her father works at. For each of them, she is tended to night and day by him and about a dozen others, all poking and prodding at her, flooding her mind with happy thoughts, pricking her skin to draw blood, and generally being intrusive.

This is what Ataru has given Suraya. At the very end of her first term at the Academy, too. Not only does she miss move-out day, forcing her father to pack her things and bring them home—which he always does wrong—but Suraya misses the chance to complete any of her research, any of her plans, any of her communication with classmates that aren't entirely horrible. It all leaves her with the least fulfillment possible.

Not to mention the absolute most pain she's ever felt in her entire life flaring through her body. It goes through every cell inside of her, pulsing red hot through her bloodstream and beating erratically in her chest. It's the feeling before passing out, it's the feeling when a bone snaps, it's the feeling of burning alive, it's the feeling of a couple thousand bricks to the face. Suraya fights to breathe, and then she physically fights everyone who tries to help her breathe, and it only gets harder. It's an awful cycle.

Nirvana forbid Ataru ever visits her again. Dream or not, Divinity or not, she's strangling him for this.

"Sunshine?" her father's voice filters through the buzzing in her head. "Are you all right? Meiling's here to see you."

"No," Suraya snaps, her voice garbled like she's holding a bunch of liquid in her cheeks.

"Suraya—"

"It's okay, Mr. Zialitos," comes Meiling's voice, soft, but firm. "It's enough to know she's okay."

Suraya struggles to sit up so she can see Meiling's face. After Meiling's Divine descent became public knowledge, she changed. She seems to think she's invincible now, never backing down to anyone or anything. She even gave herself up at the Nirnasha Graveyard like it meant nothing. Heat floods into Suraya's chest. She tried *everything* to keep Meiling out of things like this just for her to turn around and proudly be the ringleader of the chaos.

"Why…" Suraya's voice is too rough to finish the sentence. She closes her dry lips together in relief. She isn't sure where it was going anyway.

In the doorway, Omar is whispering to Meiling with a weak grin on his face. Meiling nods along stoically. She doesn't spare a single glance behind him to Suraya. Suraya swallows thickly and takes the moment to stare.

Meiling stands with her back straight and her shoulders rolled back. Her eyes are a brighter, sharper red, larger and more hooded than the last time Suraya looked into them. The skin of her face has paled, swallowing up the freckles splattered over the bridge of her nose and cheeks. Wearing a thin black turtleneck instead of the Academy uniform, she could pass for just another member of Mikazi's Group.

Suraya looks away. She doesn't want to see Meiling like that; she wants to see her the way she always has: kind and innocent, ability-less and safe.

The air shakes as Meiling's Moon Nature Energy leaks through the walls and scratches at Suraya's exposed skin. Feeling the Energy of others has never bothered her much before, but right now it closes over her like ice water. The shock steals Suraya's breath. She unintentionally lashes out with sunlight that lights the room up in a blinding white. Omar shouts a curse.

By the time the light settles, Meiling is gone and the room is filled with ash. The curtain to her right, the bedsheets at her ankles, and the wall across the room are all crackling, burnt as if a bomb has struck the room.

"Oh dear," a doctor says from the doorway, hugging a clipboard to her chest and smiling nervously about the room.

Suraya glares down at her hands. Strength has always been a part of her, but controlling that strength has always been a part of her, too. This? It's not right. Suraya has no idea what just happened. She's never done so much at once accidentally and stayed awake afterward to see the result.

"Oh Divinities. How…" The doctor clears her throat nervously and gestures to a page secured against her clipboard. "The concentration of Ataru abilities appears to have doubled in your daughter's bloodstream, Dr. Zialitos. They currently sit well above levels we've ever witnessed in history. She's broken her own record. It's a miracle she's alive at all."

"Can she live with that?" he asks, eyes blown out wide.

"Of course, I can," Suraya cuts in. *I will be gone for a long while. It must be you. Ataru is with you. Ataru is with you. Ataru is with you.* "This is Divine intervention. Ataru's chosen me."

Suraya is a living legend. Not once in the entire history of humankind has someone with her potency of abilities from any Divinity—much less Ataru himself—existed to tell the tale. Yet here she stands. Word spreads like wildfire once she's discharged from the hospital to share the news. In no time she's being proclaimed Malumvia's hope, Malumvia's future leader, Malumvia's everything. *Ataru Reborn*. As often as there are arguments about the Miyakos and against Meiling, there are praises sung for Suraya and trust placed in the Zialitos.

Fulfilling all these roles and more, it's clear what Suraya must do from here on out: lead the people. With so many eyes on her, so much riding on her back, there are things she must let go of. Namely Kane Miyako. Not because Ataru told her to, but because if it's true that a Miyako attended the Academy long before Meiling, it's best to keep it buried. For the sake of everything she knows already, and more importantly, everything she's still searching for the answers to.

Suraya is a mortal with the will of a Divinity. She's a descendant that's been chosen above all others.

And she knows exactly what she's been chosen for because it's exactly what she's wanted from the start: *Revenge*.

35
Meiling

Dropping out of the Academy was never a thought that passed Meiling's mind—even with the backlash her attendance has brought about within recent days—but it's nice of Headmaster Anji to assure her she doesn't need to do so anyway.

"We have no intention of losing you as our student here at the Zialitos Academy for Sun-Gifted Children, regardless of your descent or the country's current civil conflicts," he explains. "Workarounds are often made for promising individuals. Una Zialitos has agreed you are one. The Descent Segregation Laws will not apply in this case."

Meiling nods dumbly. It's been well over a week since the term wrapped up and she found that display in her dorm room spelling out Meiling Miyako, so returning to speak with the headmaster "to discuss her future" was the last thing she suspected to go her way. Honestly, she expected only to get her feet through his office doorway before being expelled. Even after everything he did to keep her here after Simon's trial.

"With a Divine prophecy in your name and the Head of Malumvia on your side, your place here is safe for the full length of your schooling," Headmaster Anji reassures her. He keeps repeating the same thing in different words, as if Meiling hasn't understood them yet. "Miss Katz-Miyako?"

"Yes, thank you." She folds her hands tightly over her chest to help keep the jitters away. Placing them over her chest helps calm down the abilities within her that jump at the slightest provocation.

"That being said, I need the two of us to be on a team."

"Right," Meiling mumbles, not entirely sure of where he's going with this. She doesn't *want* to be on a team with him, she wants to go find her blood family and learn the truth about them.

Headmaster Anji smiles wryly. His dark facial hair is overgrown, and the perfect shape around his jawline is temporarily lost. He's more scraggly than she's ever seen him, though his posture is still strong and his suit jacket has no wrinkles. Behind where he sits at his desk, the fireplace is splattered with ash and covered in gems. A single candle sits in the center, flame wavering. Haloed by the scarce light of it, he looks nothing like the leader of this Academy who welcomed her at the exam by saying, "I expect great things from you, Meiling."

"What I mean to say is that you have no contact with your blood family; no connections to the Miyakos aside from the name given to you at your birth. Yes?"

"Yes." *Meiling Miyako. They killed him, and they will*

kill you too. Meiling Miyako. Meiling Miyako. Meiling Miyako. "I have no contact with them."

"Meiling." He levels a look at her and her mouth snaps shut. He hasn't called her by only her first name since her descent was revealed. Not many people outside of Red Class One have. "The criminal has been caught, thanks to you. I understand you had a tough time coming to terms with Simon Saunders's role as Mikazi, but surely you know better now. With him locked up, you have nothing to worry about. The Miyakos should be deterred from further action based on this. We're safe, are we not?"

As opposed to all of Headmaster Anji's previous questions, this one feels genuine. *We're safe, are we not?* Meiling knows this is a test of some sort, but she's not sure what the right answer is. With context clues and gut instinct, she's normally great at narrowing down to the proper response, but this time she draws blank after blank. Are they safe? She doesn't know. Maybe, but probably not. Someone is out there that still wants her; someone that's probably the real Mikazi. And she has no idea what lengths he's willing to go in order to succeed this time around.

Still, Meiling nods feebly.

"Good. It's settled then." Headmaster Anji claps. Clamped tightly around his wrist, the lunar rock bracelet jiggles around with a soft tapping noise as it reacts to Meiling's presence. "It's time we restructure the mold, don't you think?"

"Well, uh, yes, of course. That's why I applied here in the first place," Meiling admits, trying to find any trace of doubt in his eyes. There is none; they're clear and calculating as ever. "But about Mikazi—"

"Do not trouble yourself with thoughts of that criminal," he says. "It's a closed case."

"Yes, sir." Meiling resigns herself to the fact she won't be getting help from anyone else in the case of the real Mikazi.

"Beautiful. I'm ever so grateful we could clear that up." He flashes her another wry smile. "As I'm certain you already know, our Suraya made quite the splash in the news these past few days."

Meiling nods. The last thing she wants to do is to talk about Suraya, or *Ataru Reborn*, or whatever Headmaster Anji or anyone else in Malumvia is going to address her as now that she's ever stronger than all of the other Zialitos. To Meiling, she'll only ever be Suraya, her childhood best friend.

"Brilliant child." Shifting in his chair, his eyes go to the candle perched on the fireplace's ledge. The single flame dances. "Truly brilliant. Yet still a child, yes?"

I am, too, Meiling thinks, yet all she can do is nod once again.

"Put out the flame," he says suddenly. "Put it out without moving a muscle."

It's startling how little thought Meiling has to put in for this action to be carried out. The command hardly finishes leaving his mouth before shadows are barreling out from within her and smothering the light. As opposed to the harsh fire of Nirnasha descendants like Jasper Kapoor, little flames like this are almost effortlessly easy to hide within her darkness. All it takes is the slightest will for her to do so. She doesn't move, doesn't blink, hardly even breathes, as shadows slither around the column of the now-dark fireplace before falling to the floor and creeping back toward her. She sucks them in like a dry sponge in water, absorbing every last drop.

In the aftermath, the entire room feels cold, eerie, and foreboding. None of it feels as bad as Meiling herself. If this guilt-riddled prickle that breaks out across her skin is the same for every other Mahina descendant after using their abilities, she doesn't know why anyone bothers at all. It's nauseating.

"As I suspected," he murmurs, "you're quite brilliant yourself."

Meiling takes a moment to ponder why receiving his praise doesn't fill her with pride like his comment back during the physical exam did. She's been waiting her whole life to prove herself, but now that she's being complimented—for the abilities she only recently learned of and still has no solid grasp over—it's like a bamboo shoot grown quickly through her stomach at the hands of Kaitsja herself. She doesn't want to be brilliant because she's a Miyako. She doesn't want to be the antithesis of Suraya. Her entire life, her whole dream, her very being; it's all meant to have her and Suraya together, bettering Malumvia side by side.

"Have a restful break, Miss Katz-Miyako," Headmaster Anji says, still watching the fireplace even though there's nothing left to see there.

"Yes, sir." She makes a fist with her left hand, covers it

with her right, bows her head, and then lifts it simultaneously as she extends her fingers to the sky. She uses gestures of respect like this more than ever these days, even to those who are not Zialitos or legitimate government officials, because everyone acts like she owes it to them and she doesn't have the energy to fight over it.

With each slow, heavy step she takes toward the door to leave, another sliver of light returns to the room behind her. She carries darkness everywhere she goes now. So much of it that she feels her entire being has been clouded. It gets hard to think. Everything is so weighted, dark, and out of her control. Headmaster Anji may have secured her spot here at the Academy, and he may genuinely believe she's brilliant, but he doesn't trust her. No more than any other Malumvian does.

Hand wrapping around the doorknob, chilling it over instantly like water exposed to below-freezing temperatures, Meiling understands them. She hardly trusts herself anymore. If this is who she is, and she knows nothing of it, how can she promise anyone she's not a danger? The only ones who can help her are her blood family.

"Miss Katz-Miyako," Headmaster Anji calls.

She stills, but doesn't turn to face him.

"Is there something you wish to ask me before you go?"

There are plenty of things she wishes to ask him, but only one thing pops into her mind: Kane Miyako. She swings around and sees Headmaster Anji unmoved at his desk chair.

Swallowing thickly, she asks, "Who's Kane Miyako?" *Who killed him? Why did they kill him? Will they kill me, too?*

For a moment, he looks surprised by this question, as if he had expected something entirely different. Then his face falls flat and the corner of his lip twitches, almost as if fighting another one of those strange smiles.

"Kane Miyako. Why, I haven't heard that name in ages." He rubs his thumbs together. The lunar rock continues to jangle on his wrist. There's a dull pang in Meiling's palm in sync with its movements. "That would be your blood uncle, of course."

Uncle. Yeah, of course.

Meiling nods sharply, twists the doorknob, and steps out without another word.

36
Callum

By the third time Callum screams and flails around in response to a perfect line of ants crawling up his bare leg, he works out the fact that Karina is somewhere nearby. She may seem like a great and protective sister and all, but when it's just the two of them, she's a bit of a jerk. With her affinity for Abungu's abilities over Kaitsja's abilities, rather than being a sweet humanitarian and sending pretty flowers his way, she takes every chance she gets to make bugs—which he's terrified of—crawl all across his body.

"Come out already," he shouts across their backyard training grounds, voice bouncing and echoing off the surrounding trees.

As many high Sun lineages do, the Kagisos live in a mansion among a village of relatives. Meaning their backyard is a vast open space meant for training, encircled by a plethora of wild and rare plants and scattered animal habitats, and their home itself is one of many in a line that looks the very same. When Callum speaks, his voice carries like a wolf's howl; the whole Kagiso village probably hears him.

This is the first indication that Karina is purposefully ignoring him. The second is how the ants scatter and disappear like wildfire into various mounds of dirt around his feet. They go in every direction, stumbling like people in a large crowd, and burrow beneath the ground carelessly. When influenced by descendants of Kaitsja without full focus, animals of all kinds lose their finesse in varying levels. Ants, as it turns out, lose their sense of colony and flee as every ant for themself.

Callum shivers, the ghost sensation of their tiny creepy legs itching at his skin long after they're gone. Slapping at his legs does nothing to stop it. Neither does standing up and violently shaking around like one of the koi fish he's accidentally dragged out of the house's moat about a hundred times.

Karina's laughter gives her away. It's quiet, as always, but not quiet enough. She tends to choke on her laughter, making it fall out in coughing bursts. So much as she tries, she's never been good at hiding from Callum—especially when all her devious actions and reactions are aimed at him anyway.

"You're the worst," Callum says, crossing his sweaty arms over his bare chest.

It's the peak of summer, late in July, and he's been at it out here for so long his clothing has slowly started to come off, becoming too much underneath the high sun and stifling heat. Even still he feels muggy and constricted. His Nature Energy vibrates with use, but in an unpleasant way that rattles every bone beneath his skin. *Overuse*, his father would say. He and Karina both take everything too seriously, too cautiously.

"Take a break," Karina replies.

Exhibit A.

"No," Callum says, flicking a wrist to draw a mass of leaves from off the trees to his right and then swarming Karina with them. He's better with animals than plants, but when fighting his sister, who's the opposite, he always goes for plants anyway. Winning feels better that way.

She emerges from the leaves kicking and punching, swaths of insects buzzing around her body. Callum cringes at the distant hum of their wings in the air. Karina notices, and the mask covering her mouth tilts as she smiles beneath it. Kagisos play dirty.

Karina entertains him for far longer than he expects her to. Back and forth, they launch piles of leaves and clouds of flies, sharp blades of grass and stinging bees, thick clumps of dirt, and colonies of beetles. Callum's skin is alight with energy, sizzling like third-degree burns from Zialitos' sunlight. His muscles are similarly pained, each flexing a sharp stab and every contraction a punch to the gut. Despite everything, he wants to spar with Karina until she's worse. Anything to gain a win right now. With Malumvians protesting on every street corner of every Division, and Meiling ignoring his calls ever since they found that display in her dorm room, and Artie unable to provide any advice better than "give it time, I'm sure it'll work out fine," Callum is itching for a fight. Preferably, it's one where he'll come out the other side victorious.

Which, he'll be honest, is not looking likely right

about now. In contrast to his frizzy curls, sweat-coated face, and rash-flushed dark skin, Karina is in perfect shape. Her long pink hair is tied into a clean knot over her head; her sharp green eyes—the only place in her face in which Callum doesn't see himself when he looks at her—are clear and wide; and her usual coverings—long sleeves, turtleneck, face mask, high socks, long pants, heavy boots—seem to weigh on her none. She's wearing approximately ten times more than he is (which is approximately five times more than their usual difference), and yet she's unfazed by it.

"Oh, come on," Callum says, wrapping moss around himself so he at least has some sort of barrier between his body and the horde of bugs Karina is setting on him. Ladybugs, gnats, dragonflies, fire ants, wasps, a couple of spiders. If one more gets thrown into the mix he's going to explode. Potentially for real. His abilities are overextended and unstable as is.

"Take a break," Karina repeats. Her voice is soft and level, same as always.

Callum is so frustrated. Karina knows it, and she knows exactly why, too. It drives him mad. It's not Meiling's fault she's a Miyako and Miyakos are thought to kill. No more than it's his, or hers, or their mother's, that they're Kagisos and that makes them easy for anyone else *to kill*. He can't stand any of it sometimes: Karina's overbearing and excessive fear, Meiling's silence and self-sacrificial nature, Artie's endless patience and optimism, this entire country itself.

He'll take a break only when he's earned himself at

least one singular triumph. Or when he's dead. Whatever comes first at this point.

When his mouth parts to say no once again, something immediately lodges itself inside. It pries his lips open and gets stuck against his inner right cheek. In shock, he bites down with enough force to lock his jaw. Thankfully, whatever it is Karina has forced upon him is pliant. No teeth shatter, and no blood spews. Tangy sweetness floods his taste buds instead. Then he's chewing, savoring the fruit like a Divinity-send.

And Karina is laughing again.

"Shuddup," he grumbles, collapsing to the ground and trying to enjoy his plum in peace. It's perfectly fresh and ripe, probably pulled right from the branch. They have a handful of plum trees, nestled away, along the far-right side of the house beside his great aunt and uncle's place next door, but he never remembers to grab them in his attempts to stay as far away from his great aunt and uncle as possible. Once they start talking, they don't stop.

"You first," Karina says. As she plops down crisscross in the space beside him, she strips the mask from her face so he can see the taunting smile playing over her purple-stained lips.

Callum can't help it; he laughs.

It feels good, even when it tugs on his stress-lined cheeks and pulls at the little air left in his breath-torn lungs. It feels so good. With the way everything's been recently, Callum had nearly forgotten. Leave it to his twin—his other, better half, though he'll never admit that out loud—to remind him.

Belatedly, plum still filling his mouth, he tells her thank you.

"You owe me," she says in response.

"I do," he confirms, nudging their shoulders together. She only jolts away from him after the contact has already been made. Callum makes a point of never reacting to her Nature Energy, even if he can feel it through her clothes. Still, Karina makes a point of always transferring some of that very Energy to him before she inevitably does react herself. Both things are instinct: one inherent and one learned. Callum isn't sure anymore which one bothers him the most. He's a Kagiso, too; he doesn't need her energy.

"Listen, Callum," she begins, staring at her hands as she fiddles with the sleek gloves over them. "You need to take a break."

I am right now, he thinks, but Karina shoots him a glare before he can say it out loud, already knowing.

"A real break," she tacks on. "You're overworking yourself for no reason. Stop worrying about everyone and everything else; start worrying about yourself instead. The Miyakos—"

"No," he says sharply. They are not doing this right now. She can nag at him to rest all she wants, and he'll give in—at least a little every time—but he won't listen to her drone about the Miyakos being dangerous like everybody else. Of course, they're dangerous, but no more so than any other lineage is. At least not until they got marked otherwise and everyone began placing them on a rotten pedestal. That's what Callum believes.

"You owe me," she repeats sagely.

"Not that," Callum mumbles, wiping the juice of the plum from his chin. "Anything else, 'rina, but not that."

The childhood nickname softens her, but only a little. When Karina decides something isn't safe, it's game over. She'll never let it go, at least not completely. This means even if she does like Meiling—which Callum knows she does—her own self-preservation, and more than that, her preservation for her family, will always come first. Karina will always be terrified of Meiling because of her birth and Callum will always be stuck somewhere in the middle of them.

"I'm just saying," Karina begins, meeting his gaze. Steady green eyes, just like their mom. Suddenly Callum feels nauseous, the acidity of the fruit fighting to come back up his throat. "Don't you find it a little strange? Something's been off this entire year. I think something still is."

"But Mikazi's been caught," Callum argues weakly, even as his thoughts scream over and over *Meiling Miyako*, and flashes of images begin to burn behind his eyelids: charred orchards, defaced statues, bent guardrails, overturned graves, a man who looks a lot like Meiling in an Academy uniform. *They killed him, and they will kill you too*, the writing had said.

Callum knows Karina is right. Something's still off. He simply doesn't want to face it. If he faces it, he's not sure if he'll ever be able to turn around and stop facing it. And he's not ready to lose faith altogether.

Malumvia, clearly, feels otherwise.

A steady wailing sound blares through the air,

followed by an even louder rising and falling tone repeating over in intervals of three. Together, the noises vibrate everything so loudly it's impossible to place their origin. Not that it's necessary to know where they're coming from when everyone knows what they mean anyway. These are the overlapping sounds of their country's warning sirens. The endless wailing is a civil emergency warning, and the on-and-off beeping is a national security threat.

The first is mostly for extreme weather or something of the sort, so the proper descendants know the government needs their help. The second is exactly as it sounds: threats to the country as a whole. Callum remembers learning to memorize them both back in grade school, but he never suspected he'd have to hear either of them in real life, much less at the same time.

For a full thirty seconds, he isn't sure if any of it is real or not. Karina is frozen, as if she's stopped breathing entirely, and the sound—though loud—is distant, as if belonging to some other reality.

Then the automated voice starts.

"Attention: Malumvia officials have issued a nationwide lockdown in response to a high-security prison breach. Attention: Malumvia officials have issued a nationwide lockdown in response to a high-security prison breach. Attention..."

It repeats over and over, echoing around their bright, open yard, and across the Kagiso village, and all over the rest of the country. There's so much noise it's hard to tell that some of it is coming from his own mouth. With

Karina suddenly trapped between his arms, cradled as she trembles in absolute panic, Callum knows for a fact this reality is their own.

"It's okay, it's okay, it's okay," he tells her, over and over so much as the alarms and alerts themselves. "We have to go inside, okay? Where it's safe. I'm gonna pick you up, okay?"

Karina is rigid, deadweight as he lifts her and clambers to his feet. He breaks into a run across the yard, scrambling to get through the back door together as the warning sirens crescendo.

Their father is already waiting on the other side to take Karina from him and lock them both inside. The lights are all off, and the shades are drawn. The room is covered by thick layers of plants and guarded by animals.

"Dad?" Callum asks, being dragged deeper into the house, the protections, the darkness.

"It's not safe here," he replies. Callum can barely make out the twitch of his mustache, which always comes when he's nervous. It's unclear what he means by *here*, if it's safe anywhere.

The sirens cut off first, leaving a ringing silence in their wake. The automated voice repeats twice over again, "Attention: Malumvia officials have issued a nationwide lockdown in response to a high-security prison breach. Attention: Malumvia officials have issued a nationwide lockdown in response to a high-security prison breach," and then they, too, stop entirely.

His dad breathes heavily. Karina cries. Callum's pounding heart hammers inside his ribcage. It's a loud, loaded quiet. Callum should probably be concerned for himself, or his blood family right here with him, but all he can think about are his friends. Specifically, Meiling.

One final alert comes through only moments later. The words are said only a single time, and they come in a real voice—that of Una Zialitos, the current Head of Malumvia. It only takes these two sentences to turn his stomach over on itself.

"Terrorist Simon Saunders-Miyako's spirit has been drained. The Miyakos move."

37

Meiling

When the Malumvian warning sirens blare out through each of the Five Divisions, Meiling is in the middle of writing a note to Mikazi—a man wanted in every last one of them.

Over the past couple of weeks since the Academy year ended, Meiling has had nothing but time to think. Back home in Division Three with her adoptive parents, she locks herself in her bedroom and refuses to see anyone. After learning Kane Miyako was her uncle, she hasn't been able to think straight.

They killed him, and they will kill you too.

Those words taunt her. Scrawled across her Uncle's body, young and adorned in Academy uniforms, the ink has sunk through to ruin the picture. Irritated, Meiling runs her cold fingertips over all the curves of every letter. Despite reading the warning a thousand times, she can't figure it out.

"Meiling, please open up, there's a security breach!" Reena says, banging on her locked bedroom door.

Despite their promise to talk about everything once

the academic year closed, Meiling hasn't said more than three words to her parents since returning home. Not for their lack of trying, but for her own unease. Until her loose ends with the Miyakos are tied, she's unsure she can handle hearing whatever they need to say to her.

"I heard," Meiling says, plopping into her desk chair to flatten the photograph of her Uncle Kane. The waning sunlight catches his faded smile and the cruel words painted in red below it.

Whether by coincidence or out of spite, Meiling has rearranged her childhood bedroom to look nearly identical to the Academy dorm. Her door is reinforced wood, the floor has a new Zialitos insignia rug in the center, the walls have been painted a muted cream, the window lacks her old blackout curtains, and her desk sits directly below it with a clear view of the Sun and Moon as the days pass.

"Come on out," Jax tries this time, wriggling the doorknob. "We should lock down in the cellar together for a while."

Meiling flips over the photograph, uncaps a thick silver marker from the cup on her desk, and finishes the message she's been trying to write for ten minutes: *Who is they?*

Opening her window, allowing in the harsh blare of the sirens, Meiling summons every bit of strength within her and ricochets the photograph into the rapidly approaching night. With any luck, the right people will find it and answer her.

She watches the photograph until it disappears in the

wind atop a strip of her shadows into a cluster of trees. The sirens cut out, leaving a ringing silence.

"Meiling?" Reena calls timidly.

"Okay," Meiling answers, exasperated. "Give me a minute."

She takes another moment to breathe. Someone wants to kill her. Without reaching out to those who run around killing just about everyone else, someone probably *will* kill her. Right now, she only knows one person who won't. And that person is Mikazi.

As Meiling stands from her desk to pull her window shut once more, the Head of Malumvia's voice ripples through the country.

"Terrorist Simon Saunders-Miyako's spirit has been drained. The Miyakos move."

Meiling locks her window with a wry smile. Whether it be the worst decision she's ever made or not, it doesn't matter: she's placing her trust in a criminal.

Suraya and Meiling's story will continue in
THE CURSE OF ALDEBARAN
Coming soon...

Character Guide

SURAYA ZIALITOS

Descent: Ataru, Divinity of the Sun, and Divinia, Sun Divinity of Prophecy

Abilities: Strong sunlight manipulation, self-healing and enhanced eyesight from Ataru blood; short glimpses into the future and weak mind manipulation (ability to sense lies, draw out truth, shift the mind to positive thoughts or emotions) from Divinia blood.

Background: Born with three times the average Blood Divinity Count—a number unrecorded in a living person—Suraya is coined the Pride of the Zialitos. Three years old at the time of the Lunar Eclipse Massacre which wiped out a large chunk of her extended blood family, Suraya's view of the Zialitos is limited to her mother and the surviving Malumvian Authorities and Academy Board Members. She does not want to be like any of them.

MEILING KATZ-MIYAKO

Descent: Mahina, Divinity of the Moon, and Viera, Moon Divinity of Ignorance

Abilities: Shadow manipulation, durability, and increased stamina and strength from Mahina blood; mind manipulation (ability to read minds, draw out negative emotions and memories, and tamper with memories by changing, removing, or rearranging them) from Viera blood.

Background: Adopted by Jax and Reena Katz at three years old, Meiling grew up on ability suppressants unaware of her Divine status. After learning the truth and coming off the suppressants, Meiling experiences shaky control over her abilities. Three years old at the time of the Lunar Eclipse Massacre staged by her blood family, Meiling only has a few blurry memories of her brother and parents who died. She seeks to avenge their deaths by abolishing the Zialitos-controlled government and Divine Segregation Laws.

EVIE SHINESKI — red class student

Descent: Omni, Sun Divinity of Order

Abilities: Sensing spirits and darkness, communication with spirits, and shifting into a bodiless spirit state.

ARTHUR (ARTIE) ONO — red class student

Descent: Divinia, Sun Divinia of Prophecy

Abilities: Strong mind manipulation (ability to sense lies, draw out truth, shift the mind to positive thoughts or emotions) and weak glimpses into the future and past.

KAI VAN ALST — red class student

Descent: Chae-Won, Sun Divinity of Creation

Abilities: Strong healing, relatively weak creation.

CALLUM KAGISO — red class student

Descent: Abungu, Sun Divinity of Nature and Kaitsja, Sun Divinity of Wildlife

Abilities: Average control over and creation of plants from Abungu blood; strong communication and manipulation of animals from Kaitsja blood.

KARINA KAGISO — red class student

Descent: Abungu, Sun Divinity of Nature and Kaitsja, Sun Divinity of Wildlife

Abilities: Strong control over and creation of plants from Abungu blood; average communication and manipulation of animals from Kaitsja blood.

VALE LOCHNEN — red class student

Descent: Irene, Sun Divinity of Weather

Abilities: Creation and manipulation of rain, clouds, winds and general heat, and ability to walk on water.

JAMIE DUMAS — red class student

Descent: Omni, Sun Divinity of Order

Abilities: Sensing spirits and darkness, communication with spirits, and strong handle on shifting into a bodiless spirit state.

CYRUS CHAKRI — red class student

Descent: Amada, Sun Divinity of Love

Abilities: Red strings—manipulable extensions of his body that can mimic love and the many emotions linked to it. Paired with Dao of The Wings to form dual consciousness capable of echolocation, invulnerability, and omnilingualism.

TARU ZIALITOS — suraya's mother
Descent: Ataru, Divinity of the Sun
Abilities: Very weak sunlight manipulation, weak durability, very strong enhanced eyesight.

OMAR ZIALITOS — suraya's father
Descent: Divinia, Sun Divinity of Prophecy
Abilities: Strong mind manipulation for targeting positive emotions, weak glimpses into the future and sensing of lies.

REENA KATZ — meiling's adoptive mother
Descent: Irene, Sun Divinity of Weather
Abilities: Weak creation and manipulation of rain, clouds, winds and general heat.

JAX KATZ — meiling's adoptive father
Descent: Viera, Moon Divinity of Ignorance
Abilities: Extremely weak mind manipulation (sensing of general moods and lies)

YUE MIYAKO — meiling's birth mother
Descent: Viera, Moon Divinity of Ignorance
Abilities: Average mind manipulation (ability to read minds, draw out negative emotions and memories,

and tamper with memories by changing, removing, or rearranging them)

KAITO MIYAKO — meiling's birth father

Descent: Mahina, Divinity of the Moon

Abilities: Average shadow manipulation, durability, and increased stamina and strength.

KAZUMI MIYAKO — meiling's blood brother

Descent: Mahina, Divinity of the Moon, and Viera, Moon Divinity of Ignorance

Abilities: Shadow manipulation, mind manipulation, and blood manipulation. *Full list of abilities unknown.*

KANE MIYAKO

Descent: Mahina, Divinity of the Moon

Abilities: Above average shadow manipulation, durability, and increased stamina and strength.

JAY ARREDONDO — red class teacher

Descent: Kaitsja, Sun Divinity of Wildlife and Chae-Won, Sun Divinity of Creation

Abilities: Healing (stronger on animals than humans), transformation into animals, and control and manipulation over animals and descendants of animal-sensitive Divinities (Kaitsja, Sun Divinity of Wildlife, Eben, Moon Divinity of Battle, and Hala, Moon Divinity of Hunting); all accredited to unique blend of Kaitsja and Chae-Won blood.

JAY ANJI — headmaster of the academy
Descent: None; Messenger-type human
Abilities: Can call Divinities down to Earth for brief meetings. Must be done with an offering and a piece of his own DNA, such as a strand of hair.

UNA ZIALIOS — head of malumvia
Descent: Ataru, Divinity of the Sun
Abilities: Average sunlight manipulation, and enhanced eyesight, below average self-healing.

LIAM SUTHERLAND — meiling's childhood doctor
Descent: Chae-Won, Sun Divinity of Creation
Abilities: Strong healing abilities, average creation abilities.

SIMON SAUNDERS — 'mikazi'
Descent: Mahina, Divinity of the Moon, others unknown.
Abilities: Average shadow manipulation. Others Unknown.

EMERSON CANMORE — fourth year academy mogul
Descent: Omni, Sun Divinity of Order
Abilities: Strong sense of spirits and darkness, strong communication with spirits, and strong shifting into a bodiless spirit state.

TIA REKOW — fourth year academy mogul
Descent: Chae-Won, Sun Divinity of Creation
Abilities: Strong healing, extremely strong creation. Rules of creation are limited to items created to help others, but Tia can bend the rules to be anything of use to herself.

CONNAH MELENDEZ — fourth year academy mogul
Descent: Amada, Sun Divinity of Love
Abilities: Strong emotional manipulation (love, admiration, hope, patience), strong manipulation of red strings.

SAOIRSE ZIALITOS — Taru's Cousin
Descent: Ataru, Divinity of the Sun
Abilities: Average sun manipulation and slightly enhanced eyesight

TURNER ZIALITOS — Zialitos Elder, Academy Admin Board Member
Descent: Ataru, Divinity of the Sun
Abilities: Weak sunlight manipulation and self-healing, nearly nonexistent enhanced eyesight.

BEATRICE ZIALITOS — Government Official Representing Ataru, Academy Admin Board Advisor
Descent: Ataru, Divinity of the Sun

Abilities: Average enhanced eyesight, weak sunlight manipulation and self-healing.

RAMI WILKS — The Birds of Prey Condor, Mikazi Group Member

Descent: Eben, Moon Divinity of Battle

Abilities: Condor alter-ego living inside of him, allowing him to turn into the bird of prey and use any abilities the bird has on its own. Extremely strong battle instincts and reflexes.

HADLEY MOLINA — The Birds of Prey Eagle, Mikazi Group Member

Descent: Eben, Moon Divinity of Battle

Abilities: Strong battle instincts and reflexes, flight, and special attunement to changes in the weather or seasons.

HUGO WILKS — The Birds of Prey Owl, Mikazi Group Member

Descent: Eben, Moon Divinity of Battle

Abilities: Strong battle instincts and reflexes, weak flight, incomplete owl ego that gives him talons, and voice mimicry.

JASPER KAPOOR — Mikazi Group Member

Descent: Nirnasha, Moon Divinity of Death and the Underworld

Abilities: Creation and manipulation of flames, photographic memory, connection to spirits and the dead (can feel when people are dying/dead and can grasp spirits (weakly)).

TEMI OF HALA — Mikazi Group Member
Descent: Hala, Moon Divinity of Hunting
Abilities: Rare modified body of a deer giving her antlers and small stature (rare in that it is not from a predator animal). Immunity to mind and emotional manipulation. Strong instincts.

KEEGAN ZIALITOS — Fourth Year Academy Mogul
Descent: Ataru, Divinity of the Sun
Abilities: Above average sun manipulation, enhanced eyesight, self-healing

DEY VESPETONE — Fourth Year Academy Mogul
Descent: Divinia, Sun Divinity of Prophecy
Abilities: Above average glimpses into the future and mind manipulation abilities

Acknowledgements

This book would be tremendously different, and much worse, and, likely, unpublished, without the immense help of the following:

Everyone at Dreamsphere Books, of course: Craig Gibb, Cali Kitsu, John Robin, Margaret Larson, and all the rest of the team.

All the early beta and sensitivity readers who took the time to read this book in its early stages.

My street/ARC team. Each one of you is an invaluable part of the publication process, and I thank you deeply for being a part of mine.

My professors and classmates at Southern New Hampshire University, where I received my MFA in 2023. I only shared bits and pieces of this book when it was a work-in-progress in classes, but I still received feedback and suggestions I think of to this day. Thank you.

My friends and family. The support and faith you all have in me is immeasurable. It means the world to me to have such loving people at my side. A special shout out to: my husband, Paxton Lippert, who has spent many hours listening to me rant about *The Construction of Shadows*; my best friend, Jae Wells, who may or may not have inspired a few characters and their traits; my brother-in-law, Brandon, who was the first to listen to the (rough) synopsis of this series; and my siblings, Kerra Hogan and Jay Jackson, for showing me what a good family should look like so I always know how *not* to write it.

About the Author

Dakota Jackson is the award-winning, Kirkus-recommended author of *The Other Side of the Looking-Glass*. She published a short story in the Penmen Review in 2023 and was twice shortlisted in the Six Word Wonders contest.

Dakota writes fantasy and contemporary young adult fiction that will always feature queer characters, complex families, and a whole lot of angst before the hopeful ending. Her mission is to shine light upon queer identities like her own and show readers that fear, confronted head-on, can give way to hope.

Dakota has an MFA in Creative Writing from Southern New Hampshire University and a Bachelor of Arts in English with a minor in Film Studies from the University of Connecticut.

When she isn't reading or writing (or pretending to do one of the two), Dakota loves Zumba, kickboxing, rearranging her bookshelf, and binging a good anime.

Connect with her online at dakotajacksonbooks.wordpress.com.

More From Dreamsphere Books

Pillars of Cloud
Connor Irving

In the celestial high courts, the Seraphic Council has spoken: It's time for a new era.

The Arcadian Laws have been decreed, a cryptic code of control clamping down on the Alium—the clandestine community of the supernatural.

Lilith, the formidable Queen of Hell, shrouded in demonic legacy, amasses a mighty army. She is led by her four dangerous children: Astaroth, the ruthless, Estrie, the cunning, Loukas, the darkly charming, and Mania, the unpredictable.

As the shadow of war looms, Lilith takes arms to rebel against the celestial shackles imposed upon her and her people. Ancient entities grapple with contemporary chaos, and layers of secrets peel away with every tick of time.

The world shakes with the violence of battle, and one question remains: Would you sell your soul to save your people?

More From Dreamsphere Books

Realms of Valeron
Alison Cybe

When Roka joined the Realms of Valeron, he was a fledgling elven cleric with only a minor healing spell and a dingy brown robe to his name. But that was just fine, since it was the hottest fantasy MMORPG, with over a million players, and Roka could not resist the allure of this rich, bright fantasy world, eccentric NPCs, and ravenous monsters.

And best of all, he met his friends—a wild and eccentric band of misfits who would change his life forever!

Join Roka and his newfound guild as they face devastating Razor-Squirrels, confront the Labyrinths of Ancient Storylines, and rush to max level in order to take part in end-game content (while probably not reading any of the quest text as they go!). But the real treasure that they find isn't the Bejewelled Anklets of Monster-Commanding or even the mythical Pointy Stick—it's the friendship they make along the way.

Enter the Realms of Valeron, a tale of high humor and eager adventuring like nothing before!

www.ingramcontent.com/pod-product-compliance
Lightning Source LLC
Chambersburg PA
CBHW031157310726
48969CB00001B/125